Time for Hope

by

Suzie Peters

GWL
PUBLISHING

First Published in 2020
by GWL Publishing
an imprint of Great War Literature Publishing LLP

Produced in United Kingdom

ISBN 978-1-910603-76-5 Paperback Edition

GWL Publishing
2 Little Breach
Chichester
PO19 5TX

www.gwlpublishing.co.uk

Also by Suzie Peters:

Escaping the Past Series
Finding Matt
Finding Luke
Finding Will
Finding Todd

Wishes and Chances Series
Words and Wisdom
Lattes and Lies
Rebels and Rules

Recipes for Romance Series
Stay Here With Me
Play Games With Me
Come Home With Me

Believe in Fairy Tales Series
Believe in Us
Believe in Me
Believe in You

Never Say Sorry

Time for Hope

Dedication

For S.

Chapter One

Hope

I suppose, when you're born in the countryside, like I was, you tend to go one of two ways; either sticking with the life you've always known, or fighting against it in a desperate need to escape. Without a doubt, I fall into the former category. I love the familiar sanctuary of my life, and I dread the uncertainty of anything new, especially anything that might disrupt the calm, safe haven of my home.

Even if that wasn't the case… even if I hadn't been born with an inbred suspicion of the unfamiliar, my fears – be they justified, or otherwise – have grown much greater over the last eighteen months or so. Still, I suppose I've got a good reason for that, and maybe that's a part of the reason why I love living in Portlynn so much.

It's well off the beaten track and is certainly small, even as villages go, with no more than a couple of dozen houses, a village shop, a church, and a local pub. It's also the sort of village where you need to have lived for at least a couple of generations before you'll be considered anything other than an 'incomer'. That's never been a problem for me, because while I grew up not far from Truro, in a very similar village, which is over half an hour's drive away, and where my parents still live, I had the good fortune to visit Portlynn regularly, being as my grandparents lived here, in the house where Granny's mother had been born, and her mother before her, I believe. My mother also lived here for the first twenty years of her life, until she married my father and moved away, and between them, my ancestors give me the pedigree I need to fit in. It was on those childhood visits that I learned to truly love this little village and the surrounding countryside, the dense woods, the long cliff path that overlooks the sea, the narrow country lanes and quiet walks. That love has never died, not even for one second. I love all of it. And I love it even more now that my view of it is fading…

Coming out of the woods and onto the main road – if the road that leads through the village can be called 'main', being as probably no more than a handful of cars and two buses pass along it each day – I sigh deeply and pat the outside of my thigh, silently bringing Archie to heel. He's a very well behaved and extremely loveable border collie, who sits beside me obediently. He's not trained as a guide dog – and I'm not in the position of needing one yet – but he seems to know, with that innate sixth sense that dogs have, that I need his eyes a little more than I used to, and he pauses before nudging into my leg, which also seems to have become his signal that it's safe for us to cross.

"Good boy." I lean down to pat his head, before we cross the road and enter the wide gateway that leads into Orchard House, although I'm not sure why it's called that, because in the whole of my twenty-nine years, even when my grandparents used to live here and I came to visit as a child, I've never been aware of an orchard on the property, or even a single apple tree, for that matter. Anywhere.

There's the beautiful, thatched double-fronted house where I've lived for the last seven years, its chimney belching smoke, its casement windows letting in the meagre light on this dull mid-January morning. There's a garden to the side, and also to the rear, both big enough for my needs, but not on a grand enough scale to feature an 'orchard', although there is a very lovely climbing rose, of which granny was always very proud, which works its abundant way around the arch that leads from the terrace to the lawn. Its flowers are a beautiful creamy white and, looking at it through the living room window in the height of summer, always brings a smile to my face.

I let us in through the pale blue painted front door, glancing over my shoulder to 'Orchard Cottage', the small, one bedroomed holiday let which, when I inherited the property from my grandmother – my grandfather having died when I was sixteen – was a ramshackle barn, of sorts, until I had it converted. There's no-one staying at the moment and I let out another sigh, because I know that if there were, I'd at least have something to look forward to. Today being Friday, I'd be getting the linen ready, preparing the provisions, and checking on the cleaning equipment, ready for the changeover tomorrow. I take my time these days, finding that a slow and steady routine makes things easier. But as it is, until Valentine's week, when my first couple are booked in, I've got nothing to look forward to. Nothing whatsoever.

While I take off my coat and hang it up on the peg behind the door, put my keys on the hook, then remove my gloves and hat, and deposit them, along with Archie's lead and my phone, on the small hall table, my beloved dog runs straight into the kitchen and sits patiently, his tail sweeping across the quarry tiled floor, until I join him and set about preparing his food. His eyes don't leave my hands and, as I pick up the bowl, his excitement mounts to fever pitch, even though we go through this same routine every single day.

Stroking his head as he ducks down to eat, I leave him be, and put the kettle on to make myself a cup of tea, then drop some bread into the toaster, my own appetite awakened by our brisk walk.

Archie is finished before my tea has brewed and, after a quick drink of water, goes to his basket by the radiator just inside the kitchen door and, after twisting and turning a few times, as though this is a new spot for him and he needs to check which way will be the most comfortable for him to sit, he settles down, yawns and then closes his eyes, seemingly satisfied. If only life could be that simple for the rest of us.

Sitting at the table, with my back to the wide range cooker, I butter my toast and pour my tea, and while I eat, I contemplate my laptop, nestling over on the work surface, and wonder whether I should spend my morning taking a look at my accounts. The problem is that I can't raise the enthusiasm. I rarely can for anything mathematical, and instead, once I've finished my breakfast and put my crockery in the sink, I go back into the hall, pocket my keys again, grab my coat from the peg, and head straight back out of the door, pulling it closed behind me.

The lane is still quiet and I turn right, sticking close to the wall for safety. I pass Sonia Anderson's very neat little house, and then George Wenlock's, which isn't quite so neat, although it is equally little. George and Sonia are both in their sixties, both widowed, and both life-long residents of Portlynn, and Sonia, who is sweetness personified, is responsible, along with Joss Kilbride, who lives further down the road, nearer the other end of the village, for providing me with most of the soft fruits I need for my jams. There is a rumour, which has been circulating for at least the last two years, that the gate which Mr Wenlock had put in the back fence between their two properties, sees frequent use… especially late at night. But I say, why not? They're both adults. And why shouldn't they enjoy each other's company, if that's what they want?

Wiping the slight smile from my face, I bypass the village pub – The Rising Sun – the main source of local gossip, and finally I reach my destination: the village shop, which provides us with just about all of our earthly needs, from milk to matches, wine to wine gums, and is the home of my best friend Amy, and her husband, Nick.

I push on the door and step inside, to be greeted by the smell of fresh bread, which is delivered from a bakery in St Austell and always kept on a rack close to the door.

"Hello, Hope," Amy says warmly, and I turn in her direction, so I can see her properly as she looks up from the counter to my right. "How are you?"

"I'm fine," I reply and she frowns, her dark eyebrows furrowing over her deep brown eyes.

"I believe you, thousands wouldn't," she says, stepping down from the stool she's been sitting on and coming around the counter to hug me. She's wearing skin tight stonewashed jeans and a thick navy blue jumper, with a check scarf pulled up around her neck – but then it can get chilly in here during the winter, with the door opening and closing every few minutes. Despite the heels on her black boots, Amy is still a couple of inches shorter than me, and a dress size or two slimmer, but neither of those things have ever bothered me – or her – and as she stands back, looking up at me, I can see the doubt in her eyes. "Want to tell me what's wrong?" she asks.

"Who says anything's wrong?"

"I do. You look like you've got the weight of the world on your shoulders. Has something changed?" She stares directly into my eyes, looking from one to the other, as though she expects to find the answer to her question hidden there. "Have you noticed something different?"

I want to tell her that my life doesn't revolve around my failing sight; that there's more to life than spending it waiting for the next symptom to appear. But I let out a slow sigh instead, because I love her dearly and I know she's just concerned. I'm about to explain what's really wrong, when the door behind the counter opens, and Nick steps through, ducking his head to allow for the low doorframe. He's just about six feet tall, but that particular doorframe is very low indeed. I'm five foot nine and even I have to duck, just to be on the safe side.

"Hello, gorgeous," he says, when he sees me, a broad smile forming on his lips.

"Hello yourself," I reply as he comes over, giving me a quick hug, before he leans down and kisses Amy softly on the lips.

"How did it go?" she asks him, looking up into his pale brown eyes.

"I told them not to bother supplying us again." He pushes his fingers back through his sandy coloured hair and sighs.

"Oh." Amy's shoulders drop and Nick grasps them and twists her around to face him.

"It's the third week in a row they've messed up the order," he explains gently. "I know they're friends of your parents, but we're running a business and their mistakes are costing us money, as well as annoying our regular customers. We can't afford to keep them on… I'm sorry, sweetheart."

"I know," she replies, "and I do understand."

"I'll explain it to your mum and dad, when they get back from their holiday."

She leans into him, resting her head on his chest and Nick looks over her shoulder at me, rolling his eyes just fractionally. I smile back at him, just as Amy straightens and turns to me. "Sorry about that," she says, taking a deep breath. "It's all a bit of a mess."

"I gathered that."

She manages a smile. "Some very old friends of Mum and Dad, Fran and Ian, decided to go into cheese making when Ian took early retirement last summer. God knows why. It was an incredibly random decision…"

"I think they'd seen something on television about it," Nick supplies.

"Yes, I think you're right," Amy says. "Anyway, my dad suggested to them that we might be able to stock their produce, so Fran came to see us at the beginning of December and we talked it through. She left us with some samples, we tried them, and they were very good, so we agreed."

"But they keep messing up the orders?" I guess.

"That's putting it mildly," Nick responds, putting his arm around Amy's shoulder. "The first week was fine, and quite a few of our regular customers liked the cheese so much, they placed orders, but since then, it's been cock-up after cock-up, and excuse after excuse."

"I think they saw it as a hobby to start with," Amy continues, "and then realised they might be able to make some money."

"Only they didn't think about the logistics of it." Nick finishes Amy's sentence, which is something they're prone to do, after over ten years together, and which always makes me smile.

"Anyway," Amy says, squaring her shoulders, "you didn't come here to listen to our problems. You'll be alright if Hope and I go through the back for a while, won't you?" she calls to Nick over her shoulder, even though she's already taken my hand and is guiding me towards the counter, and the door behind it, not really giving him much choice in the matter.

"I'll be just fine," he says. "You take all the time you need."

"You do know how lucky you got with him, don't you?" I whisper, once she's closed the door, pulling my hand from hers at the same time. I know she means well, and that she thinks she's helping me by guiding me around, but I can find my own way. And even if I couldn't, I have to learn. There won't always be someone to hold my hand.

"I count my blessings every single day," she replies, giggling, and then she turns and starts down the short corridor, past the storage room. I follow, keeping my eyes fixed on the back of her head, which is my first mistake, because my blurred peripheral vision means that I miss the box that's been left outside the storage room, and I trip over it, grabbing for the doorframe to prevent myself falling.

"Hope!" Amy turns and reaches for me.

"I'm fine," I reassure her.

"I should have got Nick to move that," she mutters, taking my hand again and guiding me around the box, even though I'm now more than aware of it.

"Why? You didn't know I was going to come around here and fall over it, did you?"

She turns her head and smiles at me. "No, but..." She doesn't finish her sentence, leading me instead into the cosy living space at the rear of the shop. It is, essentially, a large kitchen, with a table and chairs in the centre and a two-seater sofa off to one side, and provides somewhere quiet and comfortable for them to relax when the shop isn't busy.

She and Nick moved here just over five years ago, taking over the shop when the previous owner, Mrs Middleton, retired. They're both originally from St Austell, which is about a ten minute drive away, and both of their families still live there, but not long after they married, the opportunity to buy the shop came up, and they decided to go for it, and they haven't looked back since. They made lots of improvements, including stocking a much wider range of produce from local farms and suppliers, as well as changing the layout and modernising the flat upstairs. Amy and I became friends straight away. She was a newcomer in the village, which might have caused a problem, at least until the locals realised that she and Nick only had the village's best interests at heart, and they were promptly accepted by everyone around here. In those first few months though, I think she welcomed a friendly face; and I was certainly glad of someone my own age to talk to.

"So, are you going to tell me what's wrong, or do I have to deprive you of chocolate chip cookies until you eventually surrender and reveal all?"

As she's talking, she picks up the biscuit tin, clutching it to her chest, as though it were her most prized possession, which if it's full of chocolate chip cookies, it may well be.

"Is it even socially acceptable to be eating chocolate chip cookies at…" I check my watch, bringing it close to my face, so I can see the dial clearly. "… At eight-thirty-five in the morning?"

"It's socially acceptable to eat chocolate chip cookies at any time of day," she replies.

"In that case, I'll talk." I hold up my hands in surrender, and she releases the tin, putting it on the table and taking off the lid, as I pull out a chair, and remove my coat, laying it over the back, before I sit down and help myself to a cookie. "If you must know, I'm lonely," I whisper, almost to myself, taking a bite of the gooey, sweet, chocolatey biscuit.

"Oh, Hope…" Amy comes and sits beside me, twisting in her chair, so she's facing me.

"Don't be nice to me," I say quickly, tears brimming in my eyes.

"Okay," she replies, gently punching my arm with her clenched fist. "Pull yourself together, woman, and stop feeling sorry for yourself." She stops talking and I turn to look at her. She's biting her bottom lip. "Was that mean enough?" she asks.

"I think so."

"Good. Now can I be nice?"

"No, I'll only cry."

"Well, I've got boxes and boxes of tissues in the store room, and crying never hurt anyone," she reasons, and I blink, letting the first tear fall. "Come here." She puts her arm around my shoulder and we lean into each other. The tears fall, not hard or fast, but they fall, nonetheless, until I do indeed manage to pull myself together and sit back, taking a deep breath.

"Sorry about that," I murmur.

"Oh, be quiet." Amy gets up, fetching me a few tissues from the box on the work surface, and then comes back to sit beside me, handing them over at the same time. "Don't shoot me down in flames, but do you think you might be bored, as much as anything? You've been pretty cooped up in the house, since your diagnosis, and this is a really difficult time of year…" Her voice fades, and while I'm not about to disagree with her on either count, I know that's not the whole problem.

I shrug my shoulders. "It feels like more than that," I reason. "I agree that my life has changed dramatically in the last couple of years, but over the last few weeks, it's really struck me how alone I am."

"You've got me and Nick… and your mum and dad."

I gaze at her, smiling. "And I love you all."

"But it's not the same?" she guesses and I nod my head. "Is it because the anniversary is coming up?" she says softly. "I couldn't help but notice you'd taken your wedding ring off when you came round on Christmas Eve."

"It seemed like the right time," I murmur.

"That's good," she says, trying to sound encouraging. "It shows you're moving on. But don't expect too much. It's only been two years, Hope, and I know some people might say that's a long time, but grief affects people differently."

"I know it does."

She places her hand over mine. "Your husband died. You're going to feel lonely. It's part of the process."

I look directly at her and am about to reply when the door opens and Nick comes striding in. "Are you making coffee?" he asks.

"I was…" Amy smiles at me, going to get up.

"Stay where you are, beautiful," Nick says. "I'll do it."

He boils the kettle, and sets about putting a few scoops of coffee into the cafetière. "Everything alright?" he asks, without turning around.

"Everything's fine," I say, before Amy can reply.

"Good." He reaches into the cupboard for the cups, gets the milk from the fridge and pours the coffee, then brings two cups over, putting them in front of us, giving Amy a quick kiss.

"You couldn't move that box in the corridor, could you?" she asks, looking up at him. "Hope fell over it."

"Of course," he replies, looking at me a bit sheepishly, and then he leaves us to ourselves again, his own cup clasped in his hand as he makes his way back out to the shop, closing the door behind him.

"He's like a whirlwind sometimes," Amy sighs, smiling. "I get tired just watching him."

I do my best to smile back and take sip of hot coffee to try and disguise the fact that I'm not in the mood for smiling.

"I'd really like to have someone special in my life," I murmur quietly, not wanting to make eye contact with her while I bare my soul.

"You mean I'm not 'special' enough for you?" I can hear the smile in her voice and force myself to look up. Her lips are twitched upwards, but her eyes give away her kind concern.

"You know you are."

"But I know what you mean," she says. "It's not like having someone there who understands you like no-one else does… someone who won't laugh at you for being scared of spiders, or who'll buy you chocolate cake because your period's due and only chocolate cake will do… someone you can cuddle up to the sofa in leggings and a baggy t-shit, and they won't judge you because your hair's a mess and you're not wearing any make-up." She sighs. "Actually, someone who'll love you so much, they'll tell you they prefer you without any make-up… and you'll love them so much, you'll believe them."

I blink back more tears, knowing I can't tell her that I've got no idea how that feels… not first-hand, anyway. I've seen it in other people's relationships, like hers with Nick, or in my parents' marriage. But as for myself? No. Greg and I may have been married for three years, and together for nearly ten, but we were never that close. Never. He lived for his work, not for me. And what little spare time he did have was devoted to golf and watching sport, or drinking with his friends at the pub. I was just someone who he happened to find in the kitchen, or the living room, or the bedroom, when he came home. He didn't cheat. At least, I don't think he did. But probably only because he couldn't find the time. I'd love to be able to tell Amy the truth; what it was really like living with Greg and how lonely I was, even then, but I can't. It'd be like speaking ill of the dead.

"It'll happen," Amy says softly, interrupting my train of thought. "There'll be another Greg out there for you, somewhere."

God, I hope not.

I smile at her and nod my head, helping myself to another cookie.

"Not in the village, there won't," I mutter, using a lack of availability as an excuse, rather than mentioning my real fear… my long-held dread that no man is going to want me now. Not when he finds out that I may well be legally blind by the time I'm forty – just over ten short years from now. After all, who wants that as their future?

"No," she says, pensively. "I can't think of a single eligible bachelor who lives here."

"Not under the age of sixty-five."

"I said 'eligible'," she replies, shaking her head and smiling. "Have you thought about trying an online dating site?"

"Not yet," I reply honestly, because it has crossed my mind to give it a go, at roughly the same time as I wondered whether it would be ethical not to mention in my profile that I was diagnosed with Retinitis Pigmentosa, just over fifteen months ago. I don't say anything about that to Amy though, and instead I just add, "Although if I keep eating these cookies, I'm going to have to use an old photograph of myself, because I'll have put on too much weight."

"You know perfectly well that all snacks served in this kitchen are calorie free," Amy quips, judiciously putting the lid back on the biscuit tin. "And anyway, you look perfect, just as you are."

I smile at her, and I don't disagree, although I do think 'perfect' may be overstating it. That said, I'm not unhappy with how I look. I am who I am. I'm curvy, not slim like she is, and I'm okay with that.

"Any man would be glad to have you," Amy adds, leaning back in her seat and appraising me.

"I just need to find this elusive man, I suppose," I muse and she giggles, getting up and putting the biscuit tin back on the work surface, well out of reach.

"Who knows? Maybe he'll find you…"

"In Portlynn? You must be joking."

Logan

My coffee is boiling hot, but I take a quick sip anyway and sit down at the end of the sofa in the staff room. I call it a 'staff room', but really it's a converted bedroom in the upstairs part of the veterinary practice where I work. It contains a couple of armchairs, slightly worn, but perfectly serviceable for all that, and a comfortable sofa, together with a small kitchen area in the corner, consisting of a sink and a couple of cupboards, on top of which there's just enough space for a microwave and the kettle. It's basic and functional, but it gives us somewhere to put our feet up, when we have a few minutes to spare. The room itself is on the first floor landing, sandwiched between the staff toilets and the senior partner's office, where I've just spent the last fifteen minutes of my half hour break, between my first appointment of the day, namely Mrs Gerald's spoiled and over-fed Maine Coon, and my eight forty-five – Miss Hayward's snappy Jack Russell – asking if it would be even remotely possible for me to take the next two weeks off, starting tonight. Zoe – my boss – had been typing furiously on her laptop at the time, but stopped abruptly and stared at me, over the top of her glasses.

"You are kidding me, Logan…"

"No."

Her expression changed, from disbelief to confusion. "Let me get this right," she said, leaning back in her seat, removing her glasses and placing them on top of her blonde head, her pale blue eyes drilling icily into mine. "You expect me to let you have two weeks off, with no notice whatsoever?"

I was tempted to point out that I haven't taken a holiday – apart from the odd long weekend – in the last eighteen months, and that I've worked here for five years, without asking for any favours whatsoever, but I didn't. Instead, I just said, "Yes."

Her frown deepened. "Have you forgotten that you've already got a fortnight booked, starting at the end of the month? For your honeymoon, in case it's slipped your mind."

It hadn't slipped my mind in the slightest. In a way, I wish it had.

"The honeymoon's off," I said bluntly, just to get it out of the way. "And so's the wedding, before you ask."

Her eyes widened. "Off?" she whispered.

"Yes."

"Oh my God... what's happened?"

She was concerned, not gossiping, and as such, I didn't mind telling her. I owed her that much, considering the favour I was asking of her.

"I went home early last night," I began, leaning forward in my seat, opposite hers, and resting my elbows on my knees, my gaze fixed on the back of her laptop to avoid making eye contact, for the moment at least.

"I remember," she replied. "Your last two appointments cancelled, didn't they?"

I nodded my head. "They did. So I thought I'd head off early, and I went back to Brianna's place."

"Is yours still being decorated then?" she asked.

"Yes." I took a deep breath. "Unfortunately, Brianna clearly wasn't expecting me to come home that early, because when I got there, she was in bed... with another man." I wasn't willing to elaborate any further. As far as I'm concerned, what happened subsequent to that discovery is too personal to share, and if I'm being honest, I'm still feeling too shocked about it all. But I didn't need to worry. Zoe got up from her desk and came around to my side, fiddling with her wedding ring at the same time, which struck me a slightly ironic in the circumstances.

"Are you okay?" she asked, leaning on the desk in front of me as I shifted back in my seat again.

"No." I knew I was being blunt, but at least my answer was truthful.

"Is there anything I can do?" I made eye contact with her and tilted my head to one side. "Other than give you two weeks off," she added, as an afterthought.

"No, but thanks for offering."

She nodded and stood up straight, smoothing out her black skirt as she did so. Zoe had taken a back seat in the practice a few years ago, when her twin daughters left home for university and she'd decided she wanted to spend more time with her husband, John. From then on she'd taken to coming in early every morning, most often within a few minutes of our eight o'clock opening time, spending a couple of hours checking the post, looking over the accounts, and making sure that Ethan, Liza and myself – the three vets she employed on a full-time basis – weren't ruining her business, before leaving again, usually in time for a late morning coffee with John. It was a nice lifestyle, built on over twenty-five years of bloody hard work.

"I'll cover for you," she said, returning to her seat. "Your appointment book is far too busy for us to reschedule."

"Really? You'll cover for me?" I was so stunned I ignored her second statement completely and my surprise must have shown, as she turned a smiling face on me.

"I know it's been a while, but I'm sure I'll manage for a fortnight."

"I didn't mean it like that."

"I know you didn't. Although I'm sure I'll be a bit rusty to start with."

"I doubt that, Zoe... it's a bit like riding a bike." I tried to sound reassuring in the face of her uncharacteristic moment of self-doubt.

"Don't tell our clients that." She shook her head, smiling, and replaced her glasses on the end of her nose, tapping a few keys on her laptop, then she stared at the screen for a second or two. "Okay... I've moved your holiday, so it'll start tonight..." She frowned again. "But do you think you'll be able to cover the following two weekends, after you get back?"

"Sure. I don't see why not." It wasn't like I was going to have anything else to do. Not anymore.

"It's just I've got plans for this Saturday, and next, and being as John isn't likely to be overjoyed when I tell him I'm going to be working full time for the next two weeks, I daren't change our weekend plans as well, so I'm going to have to ask Ethan and Liza to cover... but then it doesn't seem fair to get them to work the following two weekends as well, especially as I think Liza's got a family christening to attend."

"It's absolutely fine, Zoe. I really don't have a problem with it. I'm just grateful you're giving me the time off... and tell John I'm grateful too, will you?"

She nodded her head. "I'm sure, when I explain the circumstances, he'll understand." She looked up from her screen, glancing at the photograph of her husband on the corner of her desk, before removing her glasses again. "What do you want me to tell everyone here?" she asked. "I'm going to have to tell them something. They're going to notice you're not here for one thing. But I don't want to make things difficult for you…" Her voice faded and she coughed, as though embarrassed.

"You can tell them the truth," I replied. I didn't see the point in trying to hide behind a falsehood. Everyone would find out soon enough.

"Well, I won't make a big announcement," she said and I struggled not to show my relief at that. "I'll just speak quietly to Ethan and Liza between patients, and then I'll tell everyone else before I go."

"Thanks, Zoe."

In all honesty, I'd never been more grateful to anyone, for anything, in my life, and a mere 'thanks' felt wholly inadequate…

"What are you up to, sitting all by yourself in here?" Ruth's voice breaks into my thoughts, and I glance over to see her pick up the kettle, jiggling it to check there's enough water inside and flicking the switch, before leaning back on the work surface and staring across the room at me. Probably in her early sixties, so about ten years older than Zoe, Ruth is everyone's idea of an archetypal grandmother. She wears a permanent smile, accentuating her rosy, rounded cheeks, and half moon spectacles sit on the end of her nose at all times. She has grey, curly hair and fills out her 'uniform' of a plain black skirt and white blouse, with ample ease.

"Not much."

Ruth and Betty – our other receptionist – are like mother hens, which is great when it comes to appeasing worried clients, but not so good when you're trying to keep yourself to yourself, and while I know she would sympathise and make all the right noises about my current predicament, I've done enough sharing for one day. It'll be a lot easier to just let Zoe tell everyone what's happened, so I don't have to actually see the expressions on their faces at the time.

I don't want to be antisocial, and I really do like Ruth, but I'm not in the mood for conversation, so I make a point of staring at my phone, opening up a browser and typing into the search engine the words 'private secluded self catering cottage'. I don't want to stay in a hotel, because the thought of being around other people at the moment makes me shudder, but I wonder if I should put in a destination. I ponder for a moment about where I'd like to go, but I can't think of anywhere, so I leave it blank and press the 'enter' key.

"Can I get you another coffee?" Ruth offers.

"No, I'm fine, thanks," I reply. "I don't have long before my next patient's due in."

The screen of my phone fills with a list of properties and I feel a little overwhelmed. I click on the first one, to discover it's on an island off the north coast of Scotland, and while it's definitely secluded and private, I'm not sure I want to travel quite that far. The second one on the list is actually not secluded at all. It's one of a group of three cottages, all of which seem to be identical, and featureless, from what I can see, and I let out a sigh, before clicking on the third... Orchard Cottage.

The website is essentially purple. It's a very pale purple, but it's purple nonetheless, but I try not to be put off by that, and read the home page, picking up my coffee and taking another long sip. Although it soon becomes clear that Orchard Cottage is situated on the owner's property – which is a bit of an issue for me – I quickly find myself reading words such as 'remote', 'countryside', 'cliff-top walks', and 'privacy guaranteed', and sit forward slightly, my interest piqued, despite the ever-present purple, as I continue to navigate my way through the website. There's a gallery of photographs and I click on that, waiting for the images to load and then I settle back again, while I scroll through some very artistic, evocative pictures, showing a beautiful living room, with a large pale cream coloured sofa, a roaring fireplace and an antique writing desk, followed by photographs of a kitchen, that seems to feature every modern convenience you could want, all in a delightful farmhouse style setting, with a pine table and chairs in the centre. There appears to be an ensuite bathroom, which looks very modern and sleek, and finally, a bedroom, with a super-king sized bed, made up with white bedding and a grey fleecy-looking throw laid on the end. My one criticism would be that it looks a bit romantic, which is – frankly – the last thing I need, but I can't help remembering that it's also 'remote', and that privacy is 'guaranteed', and I check the 'contact' page, finally wondering where on earth this idyll might be.

"Portlynn," I mutter to myself, none the wiser.

"What was that?" Ruth says.

I'd forgotten she was still in here. "Nothing," I reply. "I'm just talking to myself."

"First sign of madness, so they say," she retorts, grinning, and picks up the two cups of coffee she's just made, one for herself, and the other presumably for Betty, before she leaves the room.

I scroll further down the page, where there's a map, showing the position of the cottage, which reveals it's in on the southern coast of Cornwall, just a few miles from St Austell. I've never been to Cornwall before and I quickly do another search to find out how long it's going to take me to drive there. When the result comes back as 'four and a half hours', I smile to myself and decide that's extremely do-able.

There's a 'book now' button at the top of the page, so I click on it, reading the instructions printed in bold at the top of the screen, which state that all fees are payable in advance and the 'changeover' day is Saturday, which is fine with me. It also says that anyone wishing to book a holiday within two weeks of their proposed departure date, is advised to telephone the owner of the property, prior to booking. Well, being as I'd like to go tomorrow, I think that probably includes me, so I make a note of the number and, checking my watch, which shows that I have just a couple of minutes before Miss Hayward is due to arrive, I make the call.

The phone rings four times, and then I hear a voice, a very pleasant, female voice, with a soft lilting accent.

"Hello, you've reached Hope Nelson. I'm sorry I'm not available to take your call, but if you want to leave a message, I'll call you back as soon as I can. Thank you."

"Hi," I reply. "This is Logan Quinn. I'm enquiring about Orchard Cottage, and I wondered if it would be possible to come and stay there for a couple of weeks… starting tomorrow. I know it's really last-minute, but you'd be doing me a huge favour, if you said 'yes'." My request is out of the ordinary and can feel myself starting to fumble over my words, only just remembering to give my phone number, before hanging up, feeling a bit of an idiot in the end.

I quickly finish my coffee and get up, putting my phone in my back pocket, then I go over to the sink to rinse my cup.

I may have just left a garbled message on the answerphone of a complete stranger, but I still feel as though I've done the right thing. It seems to me that, if I don't get away, my whole life is going to come crashing down around me, and I don't think I want to be here when it does.

Chapter Two

Hope

Archie raises his head rather nonchalantly as I enter the house and I roll my eyes at him.

"I remember when you used to come and greet me," I tell him and he lowers his head again, as though it's all just a bit too much at the moment. "Well, thanks for that… traitor." His ears prick up, but he doesn't move a muscle.

I shake my head and remove my coat, hanging it up on the peg and then place the keys on the hook, before I turn round and glance down, realising that I went to Amy's without my phone, because it's still sitting on the hall table, where I left it earlier. It's most unlike me to go anywhere without it, especially since my diagnosis, which just goes to show how messed up I'm feeling at the moment and, although I doubt anyone will have called in my absence – it's too early in the day for my parents, and too early in the season for holidaymakers – I pick it up and unlock the screen, surprised to find I've actually got a missed call, from a number I don't recognise, and they seem to have left a message. Expecting a sales call, I hold the phone to my ear and let it play while I go through to the kitchen to put the kettle on, stopping in my tracks, when I hear what the man has to say. He wants to rent Orchard Cottage for a fortnight… starting tomorrow? Is he insane? I've heard of last-minute bookings, but this is taking things to the extreme, and while I play the recording for a second time, just to make sure I haven't misunderstood, I contemplate how confused the man sounds himself.

I mean, he sounds nice too, with a deep, well-spoken voice, but his words are muddled, as though he's not used to talking on answerphones very often, which I find hard to believe in this day and age.

I save the message, just to be on the safe side, and putting my phone down on the table, I lean back against it, wondering how feasible it's going to be for me to say 'yes' to this man's request. He sounded rather desperate in his message, but I'm not prepared to agree unless I know I can offer the cottage at its usual standard. It only takes one bad review to ruin everything. And while I'm aware I'd be doing him a favour if I said 'yes', I'm also very aware that he'd probably be the first to forget that if he found something at fault.

I think back to my last guests, John and Vicky Hammond, who came to spend New Year here, just over two weeks ago. They explained on their arrival, that they'd shipped their young children off to spend the New Year with her parents, who were more than enthusiastic at the prospect, and they themselves were both looking forward to a week of 'peace and quiet', as they put it. I huff out a half-chuckle, shaking my head and recalling that their idea of peace and quiet didn't exactly coincide with my own, being as I could hear their drunken celebrations, which overflowed into the garden, not long after midnight, even with my bedroom windows closed. They didn't limit themselves to saluting the New Year, either. No, they'd clearly decided to make the most of having a week to themselves, and it seemed to me that, every time I went outside, whether it was to empty the bin, fetch wood for the fire, or go to the shop, all I could hear were the screams and groans of their unsubdued passion. When they left on the Saturday morning, after the New Year break, they'd looked longingly at the cottage, and then at each other, through what appeared to me to be bleary, and rather exhausted eyes.

That's often the way with Orchard Cottage – although it's much worse in the summer, when the windows are open and absolutely nothing is left to the imagination – and I suppose I shouldn't be surprised, being as I made a point of decorating and furnishing the place with romance in mind – possibly to make up for the total lack of anything even remotely romantic in my own life…

I shake my head and concentrate on the matter at hand, trying to remember how thoroughly I cleaned the house after the Hammonds' departure. I obviously had to take down the Christmas tree – an artificial one, unlike the pine scented fir that graced my own living room for the duration of the holidays – and I had to pack all the decorations away in the box room of my own house, because my dad would be more than a little cross if he thought I'd climbed up into the attic. Then I know I changed the sheets, which is always the worst and most tiring job, being as it's a six foot wide bed, and I also remember giving the kitchen and the bathroom a thorough clean, so the most onerous and time-consuming jobs are done, in which case, there's nothing I won't be able to get ready this afternoon, and tomorrow morning.

With that in mind, I pick up my phone again and redial Mr Quinn's number, because while his request might be unusual and last-minute, there's no need to look a gift horse in the mouth, is there?

My call goes straight to voicemail and I listen, once again, to the deep tones of Logan Quinn, telling me to leave a message, if I want to. He sounds a lot less flustered now, but then I suppose that's not surprising. Like most people, he probably either practised this message a dozen times, or re-recorded it, until he felt happy with how he sounded. I know I did.

"Hello, Mr Quinn. It's Hope here… Hope Nelson. You phoned earlier about Orchard Cottage. I'm sorry to have missed you. The cottage is available for the next fortnight, so if you're still interested, perhaps you can call me back when you have a chance, and we can discuss the details? Thanks."

I make sure the volume is turned up on my phone, put it in my back pocket and then, taking the keys to the cottage with me, I leave the house.

Half way across the wide gravel driveway, I stop for a moment and look to my left, into the section of garden to the side of my house, which I share with any guests who happen to be staying here, because it only seems fair to me, being as the cottage has no outdoor space of its own, and I notice how bare the whole place looks. I much prefer it in the spring and summer, when the flowers are budding and blooming, and there's more colour to be had, and for a moment I wonder why on earth Mr Quinn and his partner are so keen to come here at this desolate time of year. As I continue down the short pathway that leads to the front door of the cottage, however, I ponder the fact that they probably won't even notice that there's barely a green shoot to be seen, or that the rose trellis that grows around the cottage door is more 'trellis' than 'rose' at the moment, or that the pale sun doesn't even reach the far side of the garden at any time of day during the cold winter months… because they'll be too busy, with each other.

"Stop it," I mutter to myself, pushing aside my unusual outburst of jealously, as I unlock the cottage, feeling the warmth envelop me. I keep the heating on in here all the time in the winter, just on a low setting, in case I should happen to get a last-minute booking, like Mr Quinn's. It's never happened before, but I feel vindicated now in that decision.

Closing the door behind me to keep the heat in, I move directly into the kitchen to my right, turning on the light as I enter and feel pleased that I did, indeed, give it a really good clean at New Year. Even I can see that the work surfaces are spotless, the appliances are gleaming, and other than putting out fresh tea-towels and topping up the supplies, everything looks perfect in here. Going back through the tiny lobby area, I move into the living room, which looks clean and tidy, requiring just a quick run-through with the vacuum cleaner, over the thick-pile mushroom coloured carpet, and for me to make up the fire and get in a supply of logs to fill the basket. The bedroom is through the door on the far wall, and as I walk in, I can't help but lean against the doorframe, letting out a sigh. This room is simply perfect. It has 'romance' written all over it, without being overly feminine, because I never forget that men stay here too, and hearts and flowers are not always their thing. Even so, the furnishings are soft, the bedding crisp, white and fresh, and there are tea light holders dotted around on the bedside tables, the tops of the chests of drawers and the small bookcase. The love seat in the corner of the room has a blanket lying across it, perfect for curling up together, and the lighting is subdued and flattering. I made sure of that. Because while I may be quite happy with myself, and quite comfortable in my own skin, I know that isn't a universal feeling; it wasn't always like this for me either. I can still vividly recall the self-doubt that pervaded almost all of my time with Greg, right from the very moment when he asked me out, until the day he died.

For a moment I think back to my earlier conversation with Amy, wondering to myself why it is that I've never told her how distant my relationship with Greg really was. I suppose my diagnosis coming just a few months after his death didn't help matters. It certainly gave me something else to focus on – if 'focus' is the right word. But that only accounts for the last two years. What about before that? While he was still alive? Why didn't I spill the beans then? Greg and I discussed it between ourselves, although I honestly think he believed that what we had was perfectly normal. I know whenever I brought the subject up, maybe by asking why we didn't spend more time doing things like curling up on love seats in each other's arms, or spending lazy Sunday mornings in bed together, he told me everything was 'fine', and always asked what I was 'going on about', and I suppose from his point of view, his answers made sense. After all, he got to do whatever he wanted, whenever he wanted. There was no way he was going to make any changes, just to accommodate me, even though I think he must have known, deep down, that I wasn't happy. I think he thought I was expecting too much of our relationship, or of him... that I was being too demanding. If I pushed him, if I actually asked him outright, he'd tell me he loved me, in a roundabout fashion, but he never volunteered that information, or said it with any conviction, and about a year into our marriage, I stopped asking. It was too humiliating.

I never told my parents how it really was either, despite being close to them, because my dad and Greg had never hit it off. And anyway, at the beginning, I'd been adamant he was the man for me, in part because I'd lost my virginity to him quite early in our relationship – on our third date, to be precise, blown away by the situation and his exceptional good looks – and didn't want to admit I'd been wrong about doing that... or about everything else that followed. There's something about the stubbornness of a seventeen year-old that no amount of common sense will overcome. Still, even if I couldn't speak to Mum and Dad, and Greg wasn't willing to listen, Amy's my best friend so, you'd have thought, of all the people I could have shared my secret with, it would have been her. And yet I never have. I've never told anyone. Perhaps, now Greg's gone, it has got something to do with not wanting to speak badly of him. But before? I think that maybe I was just too embarrassed to admit out loud that, while I could create the perfect romantic retreat for other couples to enjoy, my own marriage was a complete failure.

I sigh deeply and push myself off the door frame, focusing my efforts on the job at hand, as I glance around the room, going over to the far side, into the darkest corner and checking carefully for cobwebs and spiders, being as this part of the house is right next to the boundary hedge, and does seem prone to unwelcome visitors. I don't find any. Not that I'd mind if I did, because unlike Amy, spiders hold no fear for me… moths, on the other hand, are a completely different matter.

In the bathroom, I check the cupboard under the sink, counting the number of spare toilet rolls, of which there are six, and making sure the supplies of bleach and cleaner are topped up. I don't expect my guests to do any cleaning while they're here, but I do leave supplies in the house, just in case they should need them.

I go back through the bedroom and into the living room, resolving that the work needed in here can be accomplished this afternoon, without any trouble at all, and I'm just about to leave, when I remember I haven't checked the spare pillows in the top of the wardrobe. It's been known for me to forget to re-cover them – because I often make the assumption that they won't be used – and then I have to dash over at the last minute, prior to the arrival of the next guests, just to make sure.

Going back into the bedroom, I open the wardrobe door, and I'm about to retrieve the pillows, when my phone rings loudly, making me jump. Feeling certain this is probably Mr Quinn again, I pull out my phone, answering it quickly before the voicemail kicks in and we miss each other once more.

"Hope Nelson," I say, a little breathlessly.

Logan

Buddy the Jack Russell had an eye infection, which I could diagnose without getting too close to him, being as he hates vets – or at least me – with a passion, and growls the whole time he's here, making every effort to try and remove at least one of my fingers during each consultation. Fortunately, and I was able to give Miss Hayward some eyedrops and, despite her advancing years, she seemed confident he'd let her administer them. If it was me, I think I'd need surgery, but she went away with a smile and, after a few minutes' pause, during which I clean down the examining table and update Buddy's records, I call for my next patient, Mrs Willis, who's carrying a small basket in one hand, while the other is being clutched by her young daughter, Ellie, who grins up at me.

"Who have we here?" I say, managing to smile back at her, even though I know perfectly well that the basket contains their three month old kitten, Sykes, who's come for his booster vaccination.

"It's Sykes," she says, with a very slight lisp, which warms even my recently frozen core.

"And how is Sykes?" I ask, playing along with my own ignorance, while Mrs Willis puts the basket down on the examining table.

"He's nervous," Ellie replies.

"Is he? How do you know? Did he tell you?"

She giggles, and even I can appreciate the beauty of that sound. "No. Sykes can't speak. He's a cat. But he pee'd in the basket while Mummy was driving us here," she replies.

Her mother frowns down at her and then turns to me. "I did put an old towel in there, so it should be okay," she says apologetically.

"Don't worry about it." I'm talking to her now and not Ellie. "It's an occupational hazard."

She smiles and I turn away, going over to the bench at the side of the room to prepare the vaccination. "How is Sykes doing?" I ask over my shoulder. "Is he eating well?"

"He's very greedy," Ellie replies and I smile, turning back to her, with the syringe lying in a kidney dish, clasped in my hand.

"Well, he's a kitten," I tell her, unfastening the basket and smiling down at her, "he's allowed to be greedy. He probably spends most of his time running around."

"He certainly does," she says. "He went up the curtains in my room the other day and clung on for ages with his claws."

"Didn't he just." Mrs Willis rolls her eyes. "I don't know how you persuaded your father to buy you a kitten for your birthday, but next time you put in any secret requests, I'm going to make sure he checks with me first."

Ellie leans into her mother, looking up into her face endearingly. "You know you love Sykes too, Mummy," she says sweetly. "He purrs more for you than he does for anyone else."

"Hmm… only because I'm the one who feeds him," Mrs Willis allows, although I can see she's trying not to smile.

"And he loves it when you rub behind his ears, far more than when Daddy or I do it," Ellie continues, her persuasive powers ramped up to full power.

"Oh stop it, child." Mrs Willis shakes her head, grinning wildly. "You're incorrigible and the sooner you go back to school, the better."

"It's not my fault I've had a cold," Ellis says, sniffing loudly, for effect more than anything, I think.

"Well, you're going back next week," Mrs Willis says, just as I open the basket and the most gorgeous furry ball of orange and white fluff pokes its head out, looking around nosily.

I know better than to be deceived by all that cuteness though and, before Sykes can make good his escape, I grab hold of him, pin him down, and quickly administer the vaccination. I've learned over the years, that it pays to work fast.

"Good boy," I coo, picking him up and holding him in my arms, before he's even realised what's happened. He nuzzles into me, and licks my cheek, despite the fact that I'm the man who just stuck a needle into the scruff of his neck. He'll learn.

"Is he okay?" Ellie asks.

"Yes, he's fine. It's all done," I tell her and she stares at me, wide-eyed.

"Really?"

"Yep… really."

I hand the kitten over to her and she cradles him like a baby, playing with his paws while he lies in her arms, until her mother says it's time to leave and she places him carefully back in the basket. Sykes takes a look around my consulting room, seemingly reluctant to leave, and then with a 'goodbye', a 'thank you, Doctor Quinn', and a wave, they're gone.

I have about ten minutes before my next patient is due, so I take the opportunity to check my phone, which I always keep turned off during consultations. While it's coming back to life, I clean down the examining table and then check the screen, to see I've missed a call, and that I have a message. I've got my fingers crossed that it's from Hope Nelson, and I replay the message, with the speaker on.

"Hello, Mr Quinn. It's Hope here… Hope Nelson. You phoned earlier about Orchard Cottage. I'm sorry to have missed you. The cottage is available for the next fortnight, so if you're still interested, perhaps you can call me back when you have a chance, and we can discuss the details? Thanks."

She sounds very efficient, with a definite West Country accent, and while I know I should probably wait until I have more time before calling her back, I don't want to. I want to get this sorted. Now. So, I re-dial her number straight away. It rings three times and I'm about to swear at the prospect of getting her voicemail yet again, when I hear a slightly breathless voice on the other end of the line say, "Hope Nelson."

"Hi," I manage to reply, a little surprised that she actually answered, and that her voice sounds a lot softer than it did on the answerphone. "It's Logan Quinn. I'm really sorry I missed your call. I had to see a Jack Russell with an eye infection and then vaccinate a cat."

There's a moment's pause, before she replies, "Well, that's either some kind of mysterious code for something I don't want to know about, or I'm going to hazard a guess that you're a vet."

"I'm a vet," I say, although I can't help smiling. It's a real smile too, not one of the fake ones I've been plastering on my face for most of the day.

"Oh, that's a relief." I can hear it in her voice too, along with what sounds like a natural good humour. "So, you got my message?"

"Yes. I understand your cottage is free?"

"Well, no. I'm afraid it's not free," she says slowly and I feel the hairs on the back of my neck stand up. Can someone else have booked it already?

"Am I too late?" I ask.

"No," she says. "What I mean is, I'm going to have to charge you for staying here."

We both laugh at the same time. It's something I didn't think I'd be doing for a long time yet, not considering what happened last night, but here I am, laughing down the phone with a complete stranger, who's just made the corniest of corny jokes. And that isn't even the best bit. Because while I might have thought that Ellie Willis had a beautiful giggle, the sound of Hope Nelson's laughter is like the sun filtering through dark rainclouds. It's like a ray of hope… which I suppose is quite appropriate really.

"Okay," I say, when I finally remember that I ought to speak again. "How much?"

"It's five hundred and sixty-five pounds per week," she replies, almost like she's embarrassed to be asking me for money, although to be honest, I'd have paid twice that, just to get away to somewhere quiet and secluded for the next two weeks.

"Do you take cards?" I ask, being practical and remembering the rule on her website which stated that fees have to be paid in advance.

"I do."

I reach into my back pocket and retrieve my wallet, pulling out my credit card and giving her the details. She goes quiet for a moment or two, and then says, "That's fine. It's all gone through."

"Great."

"I can text you with directions to the cottage, unless you'd prefer an e-mail?" she says, sounding very efficient. Again.

"A text is fine," I reply.

"The cottage will be ready for you any time from three o'clock tomorrow," she adds, "but if there's anything you need to know, just call… or maybe text me, being as we're not great at catching each other."

I smile. "I'm sure it'll be fine. And thank you for this. I really do appreciate it."

I do. More than I can possibly tell her.

Chapter Three

Hope

I set my alarm for six o'clock, instead of six-thirty today, although Archie doesn't seem to have noticed the slightly earlier start and is waiting for me at the bottom of the stairs as usual when I come down after my quick shower. I suppose he's used to it, being as this is quite normal for a Saturday when we have guests at the cottage. Of course, he's not aware that, until yesterday morning, we didn't have any guests coming to stay. And now we do. And that means there's work to be done.

Once I'm wrapped up in my thick coat, scarf, hat and gloves, we head off for a cliff-path walk, because it's a shorter route than the one through the woods.

Today is, if anything, even colder than yesterday; the kind of cold that seeps through to your bones and makes a home there, breath hovering, wraith-like in front of your face. There may be a low fence between the path and the edge of the cliff, but I've kept Archie on his lead. I'm not taking any risks with him. Even so, because of the bitter cold, I switch hands every few minutes, taking the lead and burying the alternate hand in my deep pockets, trying to ward off the growing numbness that has started at my fingertips and seems to be working relentlessly towards my knuckles, in spite of my bright red woollen gloves.

The path is frost-hard, crunchy underfoot, the grassy knoll to my right bejewelled with icy crystals, and as Archie stops briefly to sniff around one of the fence posts, I shiver, pulling my scarf up around my face a little higher, taking in the wonder of my surroundings. Before my diagnosis, I probably wouldn't have noticed something so everyday and insignificant as a frosty patch of grass, but now I notice everything, and I'm grateful for the beauty of it all.

After twenty minutes, we turn back and, for once, Archie doesn't seem to object. It's even too cold for him, and we make our way home quickly, looking forward to a hot cup of tea for me, and a warm bed for him.

After breakfast, for both of us, Archie settles gratefully into his basket while I get dressed up again, making sure I've put on my hat and gloves, because it's too cold to go out without them, even for a quick trip to the village shop. I grab my shopping bags and, double checking that I've got my phone this time, I step outside, shivering as I close the door.

Inside the shop, Amy is sitting behind the counter, her scarf wrapped tight around her neck, her fingerless gloves clutching a cup of something hot, as she chats to George Wenlock, who is taking his time over buying his morning newspaper, while Nick – clearly not so affected by the cold – is standing to one side, looking at his laptop, wearing just a thick shirt over his heavy corduroy trousers. More fool him.

I take a basket and start to fill it with milk, butter, bread, tea, coffee, vegetables, chocolates, some dried fruit, and some self-raising flour, because I'm fairly sure I've run low. I know my way around the shop well enough to cope by myself, and I know exactly what I need to buy. And, in any case, it's not like I can't still see sufficiently to find my way – not at the moment – but sometimes, when I was first diagnosed, Amy would come and 'help' me. That was, until Nick pointed out – in the way that only a husband can – that she wasn't really helping by doing everything for me. I had to learn to cope for myself. He knew that, and so did I, and no amount of sympathetic assistance was going to make it any easier. It was something I'd desperately wanted to tell her myself, but it sounded so much better coming from him. Bless him.

Going to the counter, I wait for Mrs Moorcroft to finish making her purchases, the topic of conversation – not surprisingly – being the icy weather, before I step up and give Amy one of my best smiles.

"You're looking more cheerful today," she says, putting down her cup.

I'm not sure that 'cheerful' is the best word to describe how I feel, but I'm busy – or I will be when I get home – and that's the next best thing, as far as I'm concerned. Well, it's the best I can hope for at the moment, anyway.

"I've got a hectic day ahead of me," I explain.

"Oh?" She starts taking the items from my basket and then looks up at me. "You've got someone coming to stay at the cottage?" she asks, recognising some familiar things amongst my shopping.

"Yes. I got a phone call yesterday morning while I was here. Stupidly, I'd left my phone at home, but we managed to touch base eventually, and the man asked if he could rent the cottage, starting today."

"That's very last minute," Nick chimes in, even though he's still engrossed in his computer.

"I know… but it's not as though I had anything better to do with my time, and who am I to turn down over a thousand pounds?"

"A thousand?" Amy queries.

"It's a fortnight's booking… so yes, over a thousand."

"Don't these people realise how cold it is down here at the moment?" Nick asks, looking up from his laptop at last.

I manage a half-laugh. "If they're anything like my usual guests, they won't care."

Nick laughs properly and shakes his head. "No, they probably won't. And who can blame them?" He sidles closer to Amy, his arm snaking around her waist. "Imagine… a whole fortnight. Just you, me, and a roaring fire."

Amy leans back into him, letting out a long sigh. "Sounds perfect," she says softly and I pack up my shopping to avoid looking at them, and reminding myself of how lonely I am. Being busy is one thing, but it's not the same as being wanted; and I know which I'd rather be.

"Can you put this on my account?" I say, not wanting to interrupt them, but wanting to, all the same.

"Naturally." Amy smiles at me as Nick moves away again and she makes a note in the book she keeps under the counter, knowing that I'll settle up with her at the end of the month, just like I always do. "At least this will give you something to do," she says, lowering her voice.

I smile my agreement, unwilling to admit that, while I appreciate having something to focus on, other than my loneliness, I'd rather it wasn't the prospect of getting my 'romantic getaway' cottage ready for a couple of lovers to enjoy.

"Any idea why your new guests are in such a hurry to get down here?" Amy asks, helping me pack up my last few items.

"No. But the man sounded kind of desperate."

She chuckles. "Maybe he'd forgotten their wedding anniversary and needs to say sorry."

"A fortnight's holiday is one hell of an apology," I remark. "Most men would buy flowers, wouldn't they?"

"Flowers?" she scoffs. "I'd expect a lot more than flowers if Nick ever forgot ours." She glances at him, and although he seems to be busy on his computer, he looks over at her, grinning.

"As if I'd ever forget," he whispers, blowing her a kiss.

She smiles and returns the gesture

"I'd better get on." I pick up my shopping bags. "Or I won't have everything ready in time."

I say goodbye and let myself out, sighing my relief that they didn't ask about mine and Greg's wedding anniversaries, so I wasn't forced to admit that, out of the three years Greg and I were married, he only remembered one of ours. The first. And that was because I booked us a long weekend in North Devon, just for the occasion, so he could hardly forget, could he? He moaned the whole time we were driving there though, that he was missing out on playing golf 'for this', as though 'this' was nothing special, which I guess it wasn't for him. His mood improved somewhat, when he discovered that I'd inadvertently booked us into a hotel just a couple of miles from the local golf club, and after dining with me in the hotel restaurant and then falling into bed, half drunk and half exhausted, he took himself off to the clubhouse the very next morning, paid his green fees, and spent the ensuing three days making new friends. While I was wandering around the hotel's expansive gardens, by myself, I vowed that I wouldn't bother going to so much effort again. But when I handed him a card the following year and he was forced to admit he'd forgotten, and that he'd already made plans for that evening, to go out with his friends, he did so while maintaining that anniversaries weren't 'important'. I got the message that I wasn't important either and our third anniversary passed without any recognition whatsoever. From either of us.

Back in my kitchen, I put the oven on a medium heat and, while Archie continues to snooze in his basket, I set about making a cake. This is something I do for all of my guests, as a 'welcome' gift, and ordinarily, I would make a madeira, or if I'm feeling particularly adventurous and have the time, a Victoria sponge. But because it's so cold, I've decided on a fruit cake. It feels more appropriate somehow. It's also really quick and easy to prepare and just involves putting all of the ingredients into my trusty food mixer and setting it running for five minutes, which gives me time to prepare the tin and make myself a cup of coffee.

Once the cake is in the oven, I let out a sigh, knowing my first job of the day is well in hand, and that I've got a couple of hours until it's ready. Then, before I can get too carried away with my own efficiency, I go to the tall cupboard in the corner of the kitchen, pulling out my 'cottage box', as I call it. It's one of those large, lidded plastic storage boxes, big enough to hold everything I need, with carry handles that make it easy for me to lift, even when it's full.

Setting it down on the table, I take off the lid and check inside. There are some rubber gloves, cleaning cloths and dusters, along with the herbal soaps, shampoos, shower gel and hand lotion that I have delivered every couple of months by a local artisan manufacturer. I add a couple of jars of homemade jam – blackcurrant and strawberry – and some wine, the bread, milk, chocolates, tea, coffee, and vegetables I just bought at the shop, and some dishwasher tablets from the stock I keep in my cupboard. Once I'm sure I've got everything, I go upstairs to the airing cupboard on the landing and pull out four, fresh fluffy white towels and two bath robes, all soft and neatly folded, then carry them downstairs and place them on top of the box. All of that makes it very heavy to carry, but luckily I don't have far to go and, grabbing my phone and keys, I head out of the front door, laden down with my box of tricks.

I let myself into the cottage and, after depositing the box on the kitchen table, I firstly stock up the fridge with milk, butter, bread, potatoes, carrots, parsnips and beans, and the two jars of homemade jam. It's a sort of starter pack, which I leave for all of my guests. Then I leave the kitchen for the time being and fetch the log basket from beside the fire in the living room, going straight back out into the chill morning air to fill it from the store at the side of my house. Guests have free use of the logs, but I like to leave their first supply, ready and waiting. After that, I make up the fire, leaving it all set up to light later on. I'll do that at about two-thirty this afternoon, so the house is warm and toasty for my guests' arrival.

Once all of that messy stuff is done, I get the vacuum cleaner from the large 'utilities' cupboard, as I call it. In here, as well as the washer/dryer, which takes up more than half the floor space, there's an ironing board and iron, a broom, and dustpan and brush, and a mop and bucket, just in case any of them should be required.

It doesn't take more than twenty minutes to vacuum the cottage, because it's so small, but I make sure there are no cobwebs in the corners, especially in the bedroom.

Sticking to my usual routine, because I have to, I put the cleaner away and, taking the towels and bathrobes, I go into the ensuite. The towels are placed on the heated rail, while I unfold the bathrobes and hook them up behind the door.

Back in the kitchen, I collect the toiletries and the chocolates and return to the bedroom once more, placing the soap and hand lotion on the vanity unit in the bathroom, and the shower gel and shampoo on the small shelf in the walk-in shower cubicle, and then carefully put the wrapped chocolates on the pillows of the bed, before plumping up the cushions that rest against them. I take a last look around, feeling satisfied with the overall impression, which is calming and romantic.

Finally, I top up the dishwasher tablets that are kept in the tin by the sink in the kitchen, making sure there is enough washing up liquid, and placing clean tea towels and a pair of oven gloves on the draining board. Then, I put fresh tea, coffee and sugar in the relevant caddies on the tray beside the teapot and the cafetière, before placing two bottles of wine on the table – one red and one white – alongside the little printed card I've had made up, which has my mobile number, and instructions for what to do with recycling and household wasté, and where the fresh logs can be found, as well as the name and address of the local doctor and dentist, in case of emergencies.

Taking a deep breath and replacing the lid on my box, I take one last look around. I still need to bring the cake over later on, once it's finished cooking and has cooled down, but other than that, everything appears to be in order, so I make my way outside, closing and locking the door behind me, and go back to my own kitchen, where I'm greeted by the smell of fruit cake, and Archie, who looks up upon my entrance, yawning widely.

"Hello, boy," I say, putting the box on the table and going over to him, crouching down and giving his chin a rub. "I bet you didn't even notice I'd gone out, did you?"

He nuzzles into my leg and I try to focus on his deep brown eyes, set into his black fur, his white snout resting against me. I try to think about the bond we've shared in the last two years, and how much joy he brings me – especially now – rather than the fact that Orchard Cottage is soon going to be filled with the sounds of love and happiness, while my own life has been bereft of either of those things – at least in human form – for far too long.

"Did I have my chance?" I ask Archie, even though I know he can't answer me. "Has it passed me by?" He pulls his head back slightly and licks my hand, and although I have no idea what that means, I find it rather comforting.

Logan

I worked late last night, just to avoid the decorators really, then went home, picking up a take-away en route, which I ate surrounded by dust sheets and pots of paint, sitting on my sofa with my feet up on the coffee table. I had to uncover the furniture first, including the television, on which I watched an hour or so of one of the *Star Trek* movies, before I cleared away, and adjourned to the bedroom, where I found my holdall in the bottom of the mirrored wardrobe, and packed it full of warm clothes and books.

I've got every intention of spending the next two weeks in splendid isolation, reading and walking and not talking to anyone, if I can help it. Hopefully by the end of it, I'll have put the last few days – no, the last few months – behind me. And I can start thinking about the future. A future that doesn't involve a cheating fiancée, but which might – just maybe – give me some much needed time to start planning the opening of my own practice. It's a long-held dream… one which I've been putting off for far too long

This morning, after a disturbed night, probably due to the paint fumes that are permeating my flat, and also my head, I woke at just after half past five and, knowing I wouldn't get back to sleep again, I got up, made myself a black coffee – because there's no milk in the fridge – took a shower, and after checking I'd re-covered all the furniture and left the place as I found it, ready for the decorators to start work again on Monday, I loaded my holdall into my car, and set off for Cornwall.

I've been driving for nearly forty-five minutes, my desperation to escape still more acute than anything else, when my stomach starts to grumble, just as I pass a sign for a service station. It's like cause and effect, I suppose and I indicate left, exiting the dual carriageway. The car park is quiet, but that's not surprising. After all, it's only just gone seven o'clock in the morning, and it's absolutely freezing out here. It's the sort of Saturday morning in January that most sensible people would spend cuddled up in bed, wrapped in a warm duvet, and the arms of someone they love… always assuming that the someone they love isn't lying in the arms of another man, that is.

I shake my head and climb out of my car. I need to stop thinking like that. It's not going to help. And that's not why I'm here. I'm not here to look back and feel bitter and twisted about what's been done to me. I've booked this holiday so I can get my life back on track; so I can forget about Brianna and what she did. I'm not saying it's going to happen today… or even tomorrow. But it will happen. I've decided. I decided that almost straight away. I think possibly before I'd even left her flat on Thursday night. And once I put my mind to something, I usually find a way of making it happen.

Breakfast is a full English. Well, I'm on holiday, so why not? That said, it's a service station full English, so it's all a bit manufactured, but it hits the spot. The large pot of tea is even more welcome and, after forty-five minutes, I'm back on the road, heading south-west.

I by-pass Stonehenge, by which I mean I sit in a traffic jam for nearly forty minutes until the Neolithic stones are behind me, and then, before long, I start to see familiar West Country towns on the road signs. Taunton and Exeter drift past and it doesn't take me long to realise that, if I keep going at this rate, I'm going to reach my destination well in advance of the three o'clock admittance time. I stop for a coffee, and then lunch, eking out the time as much as possible, and take the final leg of my journey at a snail's pace, arriving at Portlynn at literally one minute after three.

I drive through the village, as instructed in Hope Nelson's text message, and just when it looks as though there are no more houses, I turn into a wide driveway, with a sign on one pillar which says 'Orchard House', pulling up onto a gravelled drive.

Despite the icy cold, I can't help the smile that forms on my lips as I climb slowly from my car, stretch my arms above my head, and look across at the most picture postcard perfect house I think I've ever seen. Stone-built, like most of the properties I've noticed in the village and beyond, it's double-fronted, with a sky blue painted front door and window frames, and a thatched roof. Although most of the flowers in the garden – which wraps around the side and possibly the back of the house, beyond a high hedge – are little more than twigs, it's easy to imagine that in the summer, it would be an abundance of climbing roses and flowering shrubs, and I take a long slow breath, simply to absorb it all, before turning around and closing the car door, only to be faced with another house, very similar in style to the one I've just been admiring, but on a smaller scale. The painted sign on the pale lemon yellow door says 'Orchard Cottage' and relief washes over me. This will do very nicely indeed.

I'm just admiring the neatness of the property, the twin planters either side of the door, and the pathway that leads to them, when I'm startled by the sound of a voice behind me.

"Hello?"

I spin around and, quite literally, lose the capacity to draw breath. The woman pulling the blue painted door closed behind her and walking towards me, is without a doubt, the most beautiful creature I've ever seen in my life and I take a moment just to drink her in, noticing firstly that she's tall, but not too tall, and that her jeans and chunky sweater fit her curvy figure like a glove. My eyes wander upwards to her thick, curly, honey coloured hair that falls in luscious ringlets over her shoulders, and settle finally on an absolutely perfect smile that lights up her whole face. And with that, I'm smitten. Truly smitten.

"Mr Quinn?" she says, coming to a stop in front of me, holding out her hand. "I'm Hope Nelson."

I'd liked her name when I first heard it, but hearing her say it, seeing the words form on her lips, in that delightful, lilting accent… I can't help thinking how appropriate it is that I should have come here. Just when my life had seemed so devoid of hope, there she is, utterly perfect, utterly right, and standing here before me.

She's staring now, her hand still outstretched, and I make a concerted effort to pull myself together, taking her hand in mine. "I'm Logan Quinn," I manage to say, and she smiles again, presumably because I've just stated the blindingly obvious.

She leans down slightly, glancing into my car. "You… You're alone?" she queries, sounding surprised.

"Yes." I'm not in the mood for elaborating. I'm not in the mood for doing anything, except staring at Hope Nelson for the next two weeks… or much, much longer, if she'll let me.

She nods, recovering from her evident surprise, then takes a step towards Orchard Cottage. "Would you like to come inside out of the cold? I can show you around, if you'd like?" she offers.

"Yes, please."

I feel like a puppy, being offered a treat, but I follow gladly in her wake, as she continues, "The cottage is small, so to be honest, there's not much for me to show you, which means this won't take long, and then I'll leave you in peace…"

I honestly don't mind if it takes her the whole two weeks – or the rest of my life – to show me around, but I can't really say that, and instead I stand to one side while she opens the door and then wait while she enters, closing the door behind us, switching on the lights, and then moving into the kitchen, which is to our right. The photographs were atmospheric and beautiful, but they didn't do the room justice. It's larger than I'd expected, the two longer walls being filled with farmhouse style cupboards, painted in duck-egg blue, covered by a beech wood work surface. On top of one there's a microwave and toaster, together with one of those retro blenders, while the other is empty, save for a knife block and a couple of wooden chopping boards. Beneath the window, overlooking the front, there's a white ceramic sink and drainer, on top of which are stacked some clean, folded tea towels and oven gloves, with a large double cupboard beyond, and in the alcove on the opposite side, which I presume used to house a fireplace, there's a built-in cooker, with just enough space surrounding it for a few bottles of oil. The pine table in the middle of the room has four chairs surrounding it, and in the centre, are two bottles of wine; one red and one white, and what appears to be a fruit cake, sitting on a pretty earthenware plate.

"Are those for me?" I ask, nodding towards the table.

"Yes," she replies and I notice a couple of spots of red highlighting her soft cheeks as she blushes slightly.

"Thank you."

"There are some other bits and pieces in the fridge, but I'll let you find those for yourself later," she adds, moving further into the room. "The dishwasher is here." She indicates the cupboard beneath the draining board, which has a handle at the top. "And the washer/dryer is over here." She crosses the room and opens the tall double cupboard beyond the sink, revealing the machine concealed inside. "There are dishwasher tablets in the tin by the sink, and I've left some non-biological capsules here…" She points up to a carton on the shelf above the machine. "There are user manuals for all the appliances in the top drawer, although everything is fairly self explanatory."

I try to take in what she's saying… dishwasher tablets… washing capsules… user manuals. But it's hard, because I'm distracted by the way her deep blue eyes keep focusing on mine, the shimmer of her hair in the soft down lighters, and the way her full lips form around her words.

"Shall we go through to the living room?" she suggests, making me realise I've been silent since I thanked her for the cake, and the wine.

"Yes… after you."

I stand aside and let her pass back through the small lobby area, into the living room, which is every bit as lovely as the photographs on the internet. And to make it even better, there's a roaring fire, which is most welcoming after the freezing temperatures outside.

"This is beautiful," I murmur under my breath, but she must have heard me because she smiles and, as her eyes sparkle, I struggle not to sigh audibly, turning my attention instead to the walls behind me, which are lined with books, on either side of the picture window. Hope clearly notices the direction of my gaze and informs me as we pass through behind the long, cream coloured sofa, that faces the fireplace, that I'm to feel free to read anything I want to while I'm staying here.

I already feel at home and wish I could kick off my shoes, put my feet up on that couch, and have a cup of tea, and a slice of that very appetising fruit cake… and that maybe Hope might like to join me, and stay here with me, cocooned in the warmth of this perfect haven, and my arms… forever.

I stop myself. And by that I mean, I actually stop walking. I even scratch my head. What on earth is wrong with me? I need to pull myself together. I'm here to forget about a woman, not fall for someone else straight away…

Dear God. Is that what I'm doing?

I may be smitten – or physically attracted, if you want me to be more precise – but 'forever'? Where did that come from? I mean… can I actually be falling for her? Really and truly falling for her? After just a few minutes' acquaintance?

"Is everything alright?" Hope's voice permeates my thoughts and I glance up to see her waiting for me, by the doorway that's directly ahead of us.

"Yes. Sorry."

I give myself a mental slapping as I move towards her. Okay, so I've got a reputation for being impetuous. It's well deserved. Very well deserved. But to fall for someone within five minutes of meeting them, two days after walking out on my cheating fiancée… that would be impulsive in the extreme, even by my standards.

"This is the bedroom," Hope announces, standing aside to let me enter, and I get that same breathless feeling again.

This is very probably the most romantic room I've ever been in. The carpet is just like the one in the living room, rich and thick, and sort of mushroom coloured. There's an enormous bed, at least as big as my own, made up with crisp white sheets, and that grey throw that I remember from the picture on the website, lies across the bottom third of the bed, although it's much more luxurious than I'd imagined it would be. On the far side, by the window, there's a fawn coloured love seat, with a grey and cream check blanket draped over the back, and on each of the two chests of drawers are three tea light holders, all made of cut glass, with ornate metal rims, seemingly scattered at random, but I'm sure arranged judiciously. Placed on each of the pillows are two chocolates, and in front of them, are grey covered cushions, with the words 'love' embroidered in cream thread.

A lot of thought has gone into this room. It's been designed with love in mind… love and romance. And I've never felt more out of place in my life. I don't belong somewhere like this. Well, not at the moment, anyway. Not when my brain is in such a confused state. It's still recovering from the sights that met my eyes on Thursday evening, and the discovery that the woman I thought I was in love with is, in reality, the worst possible kind of cheat. I came here to remove her from my memory, to settle any lingering doubts and confusions, and to start again. What I hadn't intended was that I'd happen upon the woman of my dreams. Especially as I didn't even know I'd dreamt her up. I also hadn't anticipated that she'd literally steal the breath from my body. That's never happened to me before. In fact, I've never felt anything even vaguely close to this. Nothing so instant, or intense. But I feel fairly confident that if I told Hope that I'd quite like to share her romantic hideaway with her, she'd kick my sorry backside off of her property, and send me packing. And quite rightly so.

"The bathroom is through that door over there," Hope says, as though she can sense my discomfort.

I nod my head and, after just a couple of seconds, she turns and makes her way back through to the living room, talking as she goes. "I'll leave you with the key," she says, putting it on the windowsill as she passes, en route to the front door. "But if you need anything at all, I'm only over the way. Just knock, and if I'm not there, you can either pop a note through the letterbox, or if it's urgent, you can call my mobile."

We're back at the front door now and I finally manage to come to my senses. "Thank you," I say, looking down into her sapphire eyes. "This is amazing. It really is."

"Well, I hope you enjoy your stay, Mr Quinn."

"Call me Logan, please."

She smiles and opens the door, stepping outside into the dusk. "Goodnight," she says.

"Goodnight… and thanks again."

She walks a couple of steps away, then turns and smiles once more, before going back to her own house. I don't close the door until she's inside, although when I do, I'm struck by the fact that, while she may not be here anymore, her scent and the echo of her voice still linger.

Chapter Four

Hope

Well, I hadn't expected that.

I hadn't expected to still be smiling over half an hour after I returned to the house. I hadn't expected to be floating on air and humming a tune while I made myself a cup of tea and started preparing a batch of bolognese sauce. Archie, who's still tired after his lunchtime walk, keeps looking at me as I move about the kitchen, tilting his head, as though he thinks there's something wrong with me. And maybe he's right… maybe there is.

You see the thing is, I hadn't expected that.

Not only is Logan Quinn down here on his own, but he's utterly and completely gorgeous. He's the original tall, dark and handsome and, the moment I stepped outside the house and caught sight of him standing by his car… the moment he turned around, it was as though someone had sucked all the air from my body. I managed to talk, to hold a conversation, to go through my welcoming routine, but only because I've done it so many times before, it's like second nature to me now. What I actually wanted to do was to invite him into the house – my house – to sit on the sofa with him for maybe forever… to gaze into those rich chocolate brown eyes, run my fingers through his short dark hair and across his stubbled beard, while sharing a glass or two of wine and talking about absolutely nothing.

"I must be mad," I mutter to myself, as I chop up some mushrooms, and Archie barks, just once, as though in agreement, which makes me chuckle.

Once I've put the lid on my flame red cast iron pan, I settle down at the kitchen table with my tea and Archie pads over, clearly disturbed by my unusual cheerfulness.

He rests his chin on my leg and gazes at me, as only a loving dog can, and I scratch behind his ears, just because he likes it.

My thoughts naturally drift back to Logan Quinn and the way I felt his eyes drifting to mine as I showed him around the cottage. I'd like to say it was gratifying, but thinking about it, he seemed distracted, rather than interested, and I suppose the thing is, that I don't know why he's here. After all, this is not the kind of place people usually come to by themselves. Not when it's billed as a romantic getaway cottage for couples. It's very strange. And I did notice that his eyes darkened and his face sort of tightened when we went into the bedroom. But then I suppose that doesn't necessarily mean anything, does it?

I'm just about to pick up my cup, when the doorbell rings. Archie jumps, but I point to his basket and he obediently saunters over, turning around once and settling down.

"Good boy," I mutter, as I go out into the hallway, closing the kitchen door behind me.

I always make a point of shutting Archie into the kitchen when someone calls. He has a tendency to be over-friendly and I'm well aware that dogs aren't everyone's cup of tea.

The light is already on out here, because I find it easier to keep the lighting at a similar level in each room, so I open the door, to find Logan Quinn standing on my doorstep, a half eaten slice of fruit cake in one hand. Although I'm standing inside the house, and he's on the step below me, I still have to look up to see into those deliciously molten eyes. Butterflies flutter around in my stomach at the sight of him, in his dark blue jeans and pale grey, chunky knitted sweater, but luckily I'm not required to speak, because he's chewing and holds up his free hand until he's swallowed.

"Sorry about that," he says.

"No problem." His eyes sparkle in the bright outside lights that have come on, because it's getting dark out here now.

"And I'm really sorry to disturb you, being as I've only been here for half an hour," he adds, smiling, "but I've just realised that, in my haste to get away this morning, I forgot to bring any food with me."

I purse my lips to stop myself from smiling at his expense. "You forgot food?" I question.

"Yes." He nods his head. "I mean, I've noticed that you've provided me with milk and bread… and vegetables… and all manner of things. And I can't thank you enough for that. But can you suggest somewhere that I can buy some dinner?"

"Well, there's a pub in the village," I suggest, leaning out of the front door and pointing towards the gate and to the right.

"I think I passed that on the way in," he says.

"Yes, you would have done."

He shakes his head slowly. "The thing is, I wanted to buy something I can cook, rather than going out to eat. I—I'm not really in the mood for company."

I think it must be the fact that I've just been contemplating inviting him into my living room to share a glass of wine and some pointless conversation that makes me feel so unaccountably hurt by his comment, because I can see no other reason why my stomach suddenly feels like it's full of lead, instead of butterflies.

"Sorry," he says out of the blue. "I didn't mean it like that. I'm just not in the mood for lots of people, that's all."

"It's fine." God, am I really that transparent? I guess I must be for him to have back-tracked so quickly. I know my cheeks are as flame red as my casserole dish, and I wish we could just get this conversation over with as quickly as possible, so I can crawl back inside.

"Is there a supermarket?" he prompts, when I don't say anything else.

"There are two… at St Austell." He nods. "Or we've got a village store, a few doors down, just the other side of the pub. You'll probably find something in there for tonight, and then you can always go to St Austell tomorrow."

"That sounds perfect," he replies, grinning.

"If you're going to walk down there, make sure you stay close to the side of the road. The village may be quiet, but people do tend to hack down the country lanes… and maybe take a torch with you. Have you got one on your phone?"

"Yes."

I nod. "Okay. But if you ever need one, there's an old fashioned battery operated one in the top drawer in the kitchen. We do occasionally get power cuts."

"Would that be the top drawer where the user manuals are kept?" he asks, smiling.

"So you were paying attention…"

"Of course I was paying attention. I was fascinated."

My tongue dries in my mouth. "Fascinated? By my welcome speech?" I manage to say.

"Not necessarily," he replies, and the butterflies return to my stomach, just as he seems to shake his head and frown, momentarily. It's a fleeting gesture, but I'm sure it happened. "I'd better be going. I'm sorry again… for disturbing you."

"You didn't," I say, as he turns away.

I watch him step onto the driveway and am about to close the door, unsure whether to feel happy or sad at that altercation, when he turns again, although he's still walking backwards, away from me.

"Hope?" he calls.

"Yes?" I smile broadly. I don't remember saying he could call me 'Hope', and I don't care. My name sounds hypnotic when it's on his lips.

"Great cake, by the way…"

I chuckle, putting my hand over my mouth as he raises the cake to his and takes another bite, before turning away properly this time.

I close the door and lean back against it, letting out the longest sigh.

I'd love to know what happened to him… why he's so contrary. Why it is that he says he's fascinated one minute, but then shuts down on me the next, only to open up again seconds later. I'd love to know why he arranged this holiday – by himself – at the last minute, and why he seems so keen to avoid being with people. I'd love to know why he sometimes has a tortured look in his eyes, and why being near him makes me smile like I've never smiled before, and my stomach fill with hordes of fluttering butterflies.

Logan

What on earth am I doing?

Well, I know what I *was* doing. I was flirting. With a woman I've known for about ten minutes… maybe not even that. And when I say 'known', what I really mean is, she spent those ten minutes showing me around the cottage I'm going to be staying in for the next two weeks. It was barely even a conversation… and half an hour later, I stared into her eyes and told her I'd been fascinated… by her. At least that was what I was implying, even if I didn't actually say it out loud. And I think she knew it too.

I know I was trying to make up for my earlier foul-up, when I'd said I didn't want to be around people at the moment, but it needed making up for. I could tell, just from the look on her face that she'd felt hurt by that. And why wouldn't she? It was as though I was saying I didn't want to be with her. And yet I do. I really do. I want to be with her more than I've ever wanted anything in my life. That's why I had to try and explain. Even so, I have to ask myself whether any of that gave me the right to flirt with her. I mean, I don't know anything about her, do I? Well, I do. I know that she's beautiful and graceful, and charming, and that her laugh makes my skin tingle, and as for her eyes… It's odd, but when she's off guard, when she doesn't think you're looking, there's something achingly sad about her eyes, as though she's been hurt. Badly. So, apart from the fact that her eyes are such a deep, dark blue that I just want to dive in and drown in them, I also want to know what's behind them… and why they're so sad. And what I can do to make them happy again.

"What on earth am I doing?" I say out loud, picking up the keys to the cottage and putting them in my pocket.

For heaven's sake… It's only two days since I caught Brianna in a very compromising position. I should be taking some time to process that, before moving on with my life. What I shouldn't be doing is thinking about getting involved with someone else, even if she is a ray of hope… quite literally; even if I do think I'm already falling for her… really hard, after just a few minutes of knowing her.

This is ludicrous. And I know I should stop it. Somehow. But how? How do you stop yourself from falling in love?

I let myself out of the cottage, glancing over at Hope's house. The window to the right is lit up, although there's no sign of her, while curtains shroud the opposite window, shielding the interior from the chill night air, dim lights glowing behind, and I wonder where she is and what she's doing. I regret shutting her down now. I know I tried my best to rectify the situation, but she looked so hurt by my thoughtless response, and I don't like the idea of Hope being hurt, especially not by me. It had crossed my mind, you see, even as we were standing there, that I shouldn't be flirting with her, or falling for her, not when I know nothing about her, or so soon after what happened with Brianna. But if the alternative is to see that look in her eyes, then I have to say, I think I'll take my chances… because I don't ever want to see that look again.

As I bow my head against the wind, contemplating whether I should have put on a jacket, even for the short walk to the store, another thought occurs to me: why on earth did I waste more than five minutes on Brianna, when there was someone like Hope out there all along?

Although there are street lights along the road, they're fairly intermittent and I can see why Hope suggested a torch might be useful, especially as there's no footpath and the road surface is a bit uneven. Still, I manage without, and arrive at the store just as a man is leaving. He nods a greeting and holds the door open for me, and I thank him as I enter.

It's warm in here, away from the biting wind, and the first thing that greets me is the smell of freshly baked bread. There are a couple of loaves lying on a rack just inside the door, but I don't need bread. Not today. Not considering that Hope was kind enough to leave me with a really nice looking artisan style loaf in the fridge, together with some butter, jam and vegetables… and a pint of milk. I smile to myself, still pondering over her bright, sparkling eyes, as I wander off to my left, passing the bread, and a display of fresh fruit and vegetables, in the direction of the refrigeration units, where I think I'm most likely to find what I'm looking for.

The shop itself is well-stocked, with two rows of shelving running down the centre, from left to right, stacked with various boxes, tins, jars and packets. The wall along the back is filled with wine, beers and soft drinks. The fridge contains milk, cheese, yogurts and – most importantly, from my point of view – a selection of meat, which judging from the labels, seems to have come from a local farm. I select a rather nice looking sirloin steak, and move back to the vegetables, picking up a small punnet of button mushrooms and a bulb of garlic.

Earlier on, while I was nosing around the kitchen at the cottage and helping myself to Hope's delicious fruit cake – while trying hard not to think about the beautiful woman who baked it – I couldn't help noticing that the cupboard above the microwave is stocked with herbs, spices, salt and pepper, mustard and vinegar, so I don't need to worry about any of that. Instead, I make my way to the other end of the shop, where the counter is situated, thinking that I'll probably be able to give the supermarket a miss, being as between this place and Hope's thoughtful provisions within the cottage itself, my needs seem to be pretty well catered for.

Behind the counter, there's a very attractive young woman, with short dark hair and a scarf pulled up around her elfin face. She jumps down from her stool as I approach, revealing her diminutive size, and greets me with a smile.

"Good evening," she says, as I place my purchases on the counter, and right at that moment, the light green painted door behind her opens and a man steps through, ducking his head as he does so, before closing it again.

He turns and places his hands on the woman's waist, and I notice, as she covers his with hers, that they're wearing matching wedding bands. Then he bends and kisses her neck, and asks if she wants him to take over so she can put her feet up. She leans back into him, smiling, and says, "No, I'm perfectly alright… but thanks for offering." The man doesn't move, his chin resting gently on the top of her head, as the woman rings up my few items, then offers me the chip and pin machine, when I pull my credit card from my wallet.

I can't help the slight smile that forms on my lips, seeing the interaction between the two of them. It's kind of heartwarming to realise that it is possible to be happily married. It's not a state that I'm familiar with. My parents are hardly shining examples, and of course, I didn't even make it to my own wedding myself, but then I suppose I should count myself lucky. How much worse might it have been if I'd only discovered Brianna's true nature, after we'd tied the knot?

The woman hands me my receipt, with a polite, "Thank you," which I return, just as it dawns on me that, if I'm going to try and avoid the supermarket, I'll need to do some more shopping tomorrow.

"Are you open on Sundays?" I ask, picking up my items from the counter.

"We are," the woman replies, "but only until twelve."

"Okay," I say, taking a step backwards. "I'll come back in the morning."

The man frowns, just slightly. "Are you staying here then?" he asks.

"Yes. I'm at Orchard Cottage for the next two weeks."

As I say those words, a funny thing happens. Their expressions are mirrored. Their eyes widen, their mouths drop open and they both tilt their heads, just fractionally, to the right.

I'm almost tempted to laugh, but I don't. Instead, I say, "I just arrived today," feeling that an explanation might be helpful. "Only in my haste to leave London, I forgot to bring anything useful… like food. And while Hope may have given me a whole stash of things… I'm afraid I can't live without meat."

I nod towards the steak I'm holding, and the man in front of me laughs.

"A man after my own heart," he says, stepping out from behind his wife and stretching his hand across the counter to me. "I'm Nick Griffin… and this is my wife, Amy. We've known Hope for years."

I put the steak, garlic and mushrooms into my left hand and use the other to grasp his in a firm handshake.

"Logan Quinn," I reply.

"Welcome to Portlynn," Nick adds.

"I have to say, I've never been to such a hospitable place in my life." I smile at the two of them, as Amy nestles into him, her arm tucked around his waist, while she purses her lips, as though she's trying not to smile herself, which seems odd.

"That's Hope for you," Nick replies, and a wave of disappointment washes over me. For some reason – probably my uncontrollable attraction to her – I'd started to feel as though Hope had baked the cake, left the provisions, and created the perfect atmosphere, just for me… but it occurs to me, standing here in front of her friends, that she does this for everyone who comes to stay at her cottage, and that I'm nothing special at all. Not to her, anyway.

"Well, I'll be back in the morning," I repeat.

"See you then," Nick replies, and I make my way out of the shop, the freezing air hitting me directly in the lungs. At least I think that's what the sudden discomfort in my chest is all about.

The exterior of the house and cottage are lit up by outside lights – lots of them – on the gate posts, above the main doors and also in the garden, placed strategically on the driveway and along the paths, so it's easy to find my way back, and once I've deposited my provisions in the fridge, I come back out to retrieve my holdall from the boot of the car. I'm just about to close it again, when I turn and catch sight of Hope, standing in the right hand window of her house, her hair haloed by the light coming from behind her. She looks up at that moment and our eyes meet, and then she smiles and I realise that, because I'm lit up by the lamp that's literally right beside me, she must be smiling at me. So

I smile back, my stomach lurching at the same time, and that earlier pain, the one I felt when I came out of the shop, is a thing of the past, despite the icy easterly that's whipping around the enclosed space.

The seconds stretch, as we continue to stare at each other, her lips just slightly parted. And it's as though nothing else exists – which, for me, it doesn't. It's like I'm lost in her. Completely.

Then suddenly, she turns her head, as though distracted, and with a blush and a final, fleeting nod of her head, she moves away from the window.

I let out a long slow sigh as I quietly shut the boot of my car and wander into the cottage, glancing back to check that she hasn't returned to the window. She hasn't, and I close the door behind me.

Well, that was odd. Odd in a good way though.

There may have been roughly twenty or so feet between Hope and I, not to mention a closed window, but I've never felt anything quite so intense in my life.

I dump my bag in the bedroom, beside the bed, then sit on the edge, before lying back and staring at the ceiling, trying to work things out in my head, although all I can see is a perfect smile and a pair of sparkling blue eyes, which is quite distracting, and it takes me a moment to focus.

I know the timing may be unusual, and this whole situation may be unorthodox, to put it mildly. I know there are all kinds of people – most especially my family, and probably Hope herself – who'd tell me I'm insane. I also know, beyond a shadow of a doubt, that I'm definitely not falling for her. You might ask how I know this, and the answer to that is simple. I know, because I've already fallen.

I'm in love with Hope Nelson.

And there's not a damned thing I can do about it.

And what's more… I don't want to.

Chapter Five

Hope

How embarrassing was that?

I was just washing up a couple of plastic containers, so I can use them to freeze the left-over bolognese sauce, when I happened to notice Logan coming back from the shop. I stood and watched him go into the cottage, but being as he left the door open, I knew he'd be coming out again and I'll admit it, I lingered, taking a lot more time over rinsing the soap suds off of the containers than was strictly necessary.

I didn't have to wait long though, because he reappeared within moments and walked over to his car, his stride long and purposeful. Because the outside of the property is so well lit, I could see him quite clearly and it was hard not to admire the way his jeans fitted him perfectly, or the way his broad shoulders flexed when he reached into the boot of his car. I wanted to kick myself for being so superficial, and reasoned that perhaps I was admiring him simply because I'd been starved of male company for so long. But then, as he pulled out his holdall, I realised that wasn't the case at all. Logan Quinn is genuinely, hands-down, the most beautiful man I've ever seen.

The outside lights gave me a good view of his face, which seemed thoughtful, and as I continued to stare, I wondered what was going through his mind, and – yet again – why he'd decided to come down here so suddenly. And alone.

When he glanced up and our eyes met, I was tempted to look away, out of sheer self-consciousness, if nothing else. After all, he had just caught me gazing at him. And yet, I found I couldn't. I couldn't drag my eyes away from him. And what's more, I didn't want to. And it seemed neither could he, because for the next few seconds – or was it minutes? – we just stood and stared at each other.

I don't remember breathing, or blinking, and for that brief time, it was as though nothing else existed.

It was the sound of my phone ringing that broke the spell, making me jump and I turned to look at it, lying there on the work surface, just beyond the draining board. If you were to ask me why I bothered to look, I'd have to say, I have no idea. After all, my phone rings on a fairly frequent basis without me feeling the need to pay it too much attention. Perhaps it was because it'd had the temerity to interrupt that perfect moment, or maybe it was just to make sure it really was ringing.

In any case, whatever I've been sharing with Logan, is over, and now, when I take a breath and look back up at him, I feel myself blush, awash with humiliation that I've just been staring at him, for a considerable length of time, and for no good reason, other than that I wanted to. I nod my head, just briefly, because I can't think what else to do, and to simply turn away and take the call would be rude.

Just before my voicemail kicks in, I grab the phone and, walking away from the window and through to the living room, I hold it to my ear.

"Hello?"

"Hello yourself." It's Amy and she's sounding very pleased with herself.

I sit down on the sofa and lean back into the cushions, putting my feet out towards the fire, which is burning away in the hearth. Archie follows me in, climbs up beside me and plonks himself down, his chin on my lap, and I tickle behind his ears.

"How are you?" I ask, trying to sound sociable, although I'm very confused about what just happened, and a part of me would still like to be standing by my kitchen sink, staring through the window at the perfect view beyond.

"I'm absolutely fine," she says, sounding dreamy. "We've just closed up for the evening – thank God, because I really need to put my feet up – and I thought I'd give you a call to enquire about your latest guest."

"My latest… guest?" I reply, my breath catching in my throat.

"Yes. You know… that utterly gorgeous man who's staying in your cottage." I can hear the smile twinkling in her voice.

"Might I ask where your husband is?" I enquire, smiling myself now.

"He's in the kitchen, preparing dinner."

I picture the two of them in their open plan living space, Amy probably lying out on their corner sofa, facing Nick, who I imagine will be standing in the kitchen, behind the island unit, creating something wonderful, since he's an amazing cook.

"So he can hear every word you're saying?"

"Yes," she says playfully.

"And he doesn't mind you admiring other men, or referring to them as… what was it now… 'utterly gorgeous'?"

"No. Because he knows I've only got eyes for him."

There's a moment's pause and I hear Nick whisper, "And that's entirely mutual," loud enough to know that he must have wandered over and probably leant down to kiss her, or murmur in her ear at least… and that he won't have been at all embarrassed by me having heard his declaration either.

"Now, stop changing the subject," Amy says, her voice becoming more serious. "Your new guest is edible, and even you can see him well enough to know it."

I chuckle, and she joins in, as I relish one of the best parts of our friendship, because while Amy can sometimes be overprotective and a little prone to forget that I'm still me, she's also the only person I know who ever makes jokes about my sight – apart from me, that is – and I love her for the normality of that.

"I wasn't going to deny it," I reply. I'd be stupid to do so. It's what I've been thinking ever since he arrived, after all.

"I couldn't help noticing that Logan only bought one steak," Amy adds, like she's digging for information, with about as much subtlety as a pneumatic drill.

"Logan?" I remark, picking up on that. "You're on first name terms, are you?"

"Yes. He and Nick ended up introducing themselves over said steak... it's a man thing."

"I suppose it must be."

"So..." she says, continuing her mining expedition. "Is there a reason why the luscious Logan was only buying for one?"

'Luscious Logan'? God, that sounds cheesy. Accurate, but cheesy.

"Because he's staying here by himself," I reply.

"I knew it," she crows, even though my words have barely left my lips. "I just knew it. Nick didn't believe me, but I knew I was right."

"Right about what? What on earth are you talking about?" I stop tickling Archie's ears for a moment, intrigued by her outburst. He glances up at me, and then seems to roll his eyes, before lowering his head again.

"After Logan had left, I said to Nick that I thought he was staying at Orchard Cottage by himself, not just because he'd only bought one steak, but because he'd also referred to himself as 'I' and not 'we', when he talked about coming down from London and forgetting to bring any food with him. Nick maintained that men often do that, but I knew I was right..."

Her voice fades, and I let my mind drift back to my time with Greg, when I'd sometimes overhear him making arrangements with his parents, or one of his two brothers, for birthdays or at Christmas, and how he'd often refer to us in the first person, saying things like, "I'll be there for lunch," or "I can't make Saturday, but Sunday will be okay," as though I didn't exist, as though I didn't form half of the couple that we were supposed to be.

"So there's no Mrs Logan, then?" I hear Amy ask, coming back to reality.

"I have no idea," I respond, that leaden feeling returning to my stomach once more as the thought takes root. "We... we didn't get around to talking about it." No, we just talked about stupid things like washer/dryers and user manuals, and cake, and then gazed at each other across the driveway for much longer than could ever be considered remotely normal. Why did I do that? The man could have a wife, and maybe even children, at home in London. What's wrong with me?

"Well, does he wear a wedding ring?" she asks, interrupting my thoughts again. "I mean, I didn't have time to notice myself, and I know not all married men do, but it would be big clue, wouldn't it?" Why are we looking for clues all of a sudden, I wonder.

Instead of picking up on that, I just say, "You must be slacking, if you didn't have a chance to notice," and she giggles.

"I had less than five minutes," she reasons. "Give me a break."

I think about the way my eyes met with Logan's just now, and my heart sinks at the thought that he could be married... and that he'd be prepared to stare at another woman like that. He just stared at me. Nothing more. Does that make him a cheat? In my fading eyes, it goes a long way towards it. But surely, that can't be right. He doesn't seem the type. Although I wonder if a few minutes' acquaintance is sufficient for me to make that judgement. *Probably not...*

"He's the first solo guest you've ever had, isn't he?" Amy asks.

"Yes. And like all the others, he's entitled to his privacy. And I intend to respect that." Even as I'm saying the words, I realise that they're true. I need to stop staring out of the window at him, and to stop drooling every time I see him. He came here for a relaxing break, and regardless of his personal circumstances, it's only fair that I should let him do that.

"Do you now?" Amy replies and I can hear the humorous doubt in her voice.

I don't comment, because I know I can't hide anything from her and I'm afraid I'll give away the fact that, in reality, even if there can't be anything between Logan and myself, I really would like there to be. I can't hide the fact that, ever since he climbed out of his car earlier this afternoon, I haven't been able to stop thinking about what it would be like to feel his arms around me, or his lips on mine, or...

"Nick's gesticulating at me." Amy's words slice through my daydreams.

I smile to myself. "Is this something I want to know about?"

"I think our dinner's nearly ready," she says. "We'll talk tomorrow."

"Why? I mean, don't get me wrong, I love hearing from you, but why are you so keen to talk tomorrow?"

"Because hopefully by then one or other of us will have worked out whether Logan is married, and if he isn't, then we can plan a strategy."

"A strategy for what?"

"Making him fall in love with you… or at the very least giving him a jolly good shove into your bed."

"You can't make someone fall in love, Amy. And I'm not the sort of woman who has casual sex. You know that."

She chuckles. "And you wouldn't make an exception? Not even for Logan Quinn?"

I ponder that question to myself, even if it is pure hypothesis. I wouldn't consider it if he was married. I wouldn't consider it if he was even remotely attached to someone. But if he was single? Would I? Well, he is gorgeous, and it's been so, so long… and just the thought of…

"Your pause tells me everything I need to know." Amy giggles in my ear and I can feel myself blushing.

See? I told you I couldn't hide anything from her.

Logan

The steak last night was really good – juicy and tender and, if I say so myself, cooked to perfection, with sautéed mushrooms and potatoes. I opened the bottle of red wine that Hope had left, which was a very fine Burgundy, and drank a couple of glasses while I ate.

It felt odd eating by myself though. Other than my Chinese take-away on Friday night, it's not something I've done for the last few months, and it's surprising how quickly you get into habits and routines, when you think you're in love, when you're planning on building a life with someone. I didn't eat at all on Thursday. Obviously.

After discovering my fiancée in such a compromised state, food was the last thing on my mind. Prior to that, I'd shared most evening meals with her, either at her place, or mine, before it was being decorated. Brianna could never be called a great cook, so she used to watch and occasionally chop things up, while I did all the cooking, and we'd talk about our days at work. Actually, looking back, that's not strictly true. She would talk about her day at work, as a marketing assistant for a publisher in Central London, and I would listen to her complaining about schedules, deadlines and mainly office politics, but when it came to my turn to unload, she would invariably announce that she had a phone call to make, or that she just wanted to grab a quick shower… or she'd come over and place her hand in a strategically distracting place, and I'd forget all about Mr Sharp's Dachshund that had bitten my thumb, or Winston… the fourteen year old cat belonging to Mrs Harper, who'd finally succumbed to the cancerous tumour we'd been trying to treat.

Brianna was always a bit selfish that way… or maybe I was just too easily distracted.

Anyway, after I'd finished my steak, cleared away and loaded everything into the dishwasher, I went through to the bedroom and unpacked my holdall, and then decided I was too tired to sit up. So, I had a quick shower and, with the chocolates safely stored on the bedside table, and the 'love' cushions placed more appropriately on the love seat by the window, I settled down to read in the very comfortable bed, and promptly fell asleep.

Considering everything that's happened over the last few days, and the fact that I was in a strange bed, in a strange house, I probably should have had a disturbed night. But I didn't. I slept like a log, and woke early this morning, feeling refreshed and with a smile on my face, caused by the fact that my dreams hadn't been haunted by Brianna, but had been filled with Hope instead.

After another shower, I dress in jeans, a t-shirt and thick jumper, and make myself tea and toast, smothering the latter thickly with blackcurrant jam. The label on the jar is handwritten, printed in capital letters, leading me to assume this must be homemade, presumably by my host, and I start to wonder if there's an end to Hope's talents.

I wonder if I'll see her today, or if I can engineer a meeting between us, without it being too obvious that I'm desperate to see her. Of course, I suppose she might be busy. It is Sunday after all, and she might have family commitments. I pause with my second slice of toast half way to my mouth.

Family?

The toast drops to the plate, landing half on, half off, and I let my head fall into my hands. I was only thinking to myself yesterday evening that I don't know anything about Hope… and one of the many things I don't know, in spite of the fact that I've fallen in love with her, is whether she's even available. She could be married, or engaged, or in a relationship with someone. She could have kids for all I know.

I rub my hands down my face at that sobering thought, just as my phone beeps, letting me know I've got a text message and, without thinking I pick it up and glance at the screen, feeling my blood chill as I see that it's from Brianna.

— Logan, baby. I've given you a couple of days to cool off, but enough is enough. You know you didn't mean what you said on Thursday, about calling off the wedding. That's not what either of us wants. And giving me the silent treatment is really childish. It would be much more sensible for us to get together, so we can talk this out, and get back on track again. I'm happy to come to your place this afternoon. The decorators won't be there and we can spend some time together, talking, making up, and doing what we do best. I'll see you later. Love you. Brianna xxx

'Love you'? Is she kidding? She rarely said those words to me when we were together – a fact which is only just dawning on me – but she chooses to utter them *now*? By text?

I re-read her message, just to make sure I haven't misunderstood it. No, I haven't. She actually thinks I want to 'get back on track' with her? After what she did? *And* she's making the assumption I'll simply say yes to this arrangement, and go along with everything she's suggesting, rather than asking me to text her back and confirm… she's just telling me she'll be there.

I tap out a response, holding my breath as I type and trying to keep it as polite as I can.

— Don't bother. I'm not at my flat. I've gone away for a couple of weeks, and I'm not telling you where. I'm not interested in talking to you, Brianna. We're over. I meant every word I said on Thursday night. And I'm not going to change my mind. Not now. Not Ever. Do us both a favour and GET THE MESSAGE.

Okay, so it's not that polite, but it's to the point.

I put my phone down, letting out the breath I'd been holding, just as another thought occurs to me, and I pick it up again, going to my contacts, looking up Rachel and connecting a call to her. My sister won't thank me for phoning her this early on a Sunday. She's never been one of life's larks, but I need to ask her to do something for me, even though the last time we spoke, on Thursday evening, we argued. Badly. After I'd caught Brianna in the act, as it were, I went straight round to Rachel's. I needed to talk to someone, and although it's usually the other way around between Rachel and me, with me being her guide and counsellor, I had to tell someone what had happened, if only because I thought that saying it out loud might help me to make sense of it. I was wrong. On so many levels. I knew I'd be placing Rachel in a tough position by going to her, being as she and Brianna are friends and they work for the same publishing company – albeit in different departments – and also because it was Rachel who actually introduced us, at her thirtieth birthday party, but I didn't really have much choice. At the time, it didn't feel like I had anyone else I could turn to. After she'd sat me down and asked why I looked so pale and shocked, I explained what had happened – that's to say, I told her that I'd just come from Brianna's place, and that I'd caught her in bed with another man. Before I got the chance to say anything else, my sister wanted to know what I'd done. What *I'd* done? I felt a bit affronted that she'd assumed it had to be my fault, but she then clarified her question, explaining that she'd actually meant what had I done after I'd made my discovery. I told her I hadn't really done anything… well, nothing other than decide to call off the wedding, of course. It was a decision I'd taken while sitting in my car, staring at the lit-up window of Brianna's bedroom, where I had no doubt she and her lover were still wrapped up in each other – being as they'd remained blissfully unaware of my presence.

And that was when Rachel looked at me as though I'd just grown a second head.

"Why on earth have you done that?" she said, putting her hands on her narrow hips and glaring at me.

I stared at her. "Why do you think? I've just found my fiancée shagging—"

She waved her hand in my face. "I get that," she interrupted. "What I mean is, why do you have to always be so rash?"

"Rash?" I was starting to wonder if I'd entered a parallel universe. Was I the only one who thought it was perfectly reasonable – even recommended, actually – to break off your engagement when you discovered that your fiancée was cheating?

Rachel let out an exasperated sigh at that point, and then pushed her fingers back through her shoulder length, mahogany coloured hair. "Bloody hell, Logan. You rushed into getting engaged; don't you think perhaps you should at least take your time before rushing out of it?" She sounded so supercilious I couldn't think of a polite response, and after a moment she just said, "God, you're so fucking impetuous. You always have been."

"Well at least I'm being consistent," I yelled, and before either of us could say something we'd really regret, I stormed out of her flat.

With our argument still fresh in my mind, I'm not sure I want to talk to her now, but I have to, because I've just remembered that Brianna still has a key to my flat, and the last thing I need when I get home is to find that she's taken up residence. I wouldn't put it past her.

"Logan?" Rachel's voice is bleary on the other end of the line, telling me, in no uncertain terms, that I've woken her.

"Yes."

"What time is it?"

"Eight."

"On a fucking Sunday? Are you mad?"

"Very probably. Sorry."

"Christ almighty." She yawns. "I'm assuming you've got a good reason for waking me up at this ungodly hour of the morning?"

"Of course."

"It's not just to apologise then?" she says.

"Apologise?" I reply, feeling my anger rising all over again. "What for?"

"For the fact that your fiancée has roped me into helping her with cancelling your fucking wedding... *and* for the fact that she keeps phoning me, crying and wittering on about how perfect you are, and how great you are in bed... which isn't something I needed to know, by the way. I'm not kidding, Logan. I've heard things about your sexual prowess no sister should ever have to hear about her own brother. It's unnerving."

"Well, I'm sorry about that, but can I just remind you that she's not my fiancée. Not anymore. And she is your friend."

"Hmm. Well, friend or no friend, she's like a dog with a fucking bone. So why don't you just arrange to meet up with her, which is all she's asking for at the end of the day, and then you guys might be able to sort out your differences, and we might be able to call this 'cancellation' a 'postponement' – which would make everyone's lives a great deal simpler, I can tell you – and I might get ten minutes to myself?" she suggests.

"For two exceptionally good reasons. One, I don't want to; and two, I'm not there."

"You're not here? Where are you then?"

"I've rented a little cottage for a couple of weeks, and I'm not saying where it is. That way you can't feel pressured or obligated to tell your friend."

"Well, you could have talked to her first, before you decided to do a disappearing act," she says, sounding less angry now and more dejected.

"I did talk to her," I explain. "I went back to see her on Thursday night, about an hour after I left you. I took back all her things from my flat, told her we were over for good, that I'd pay my share of any fees that the wedding organisers, caterers, venue, and anyone else involved wanted to charge, and gave her the honeymoon tickets. And then I left."

"Oh. I didn't realise. She said you just broke off the engagement, leaving it all to her, and walked out, without even talking about it."

"Well, I did leave it all to her – because she's the one who cheated, and I'm damned if I can see why I should have to spend my time dealing with the fallout of her actions. And I didn't hang around for a heart-to-heart because, let's face it, when you find your fiancée shagging someone else's brains out, polite conversation isn't really uppermost in your thoughts."

"You didn't want to hang around and punch the guy, then?" she asks.

"In this instance, no. Look, the upshot is, I don't want to know her anymore and the quicker she gets that message, the better for everyone."

"And you don't think you'll change your mind?"

"No. Never." Why would I?

"Even though we both know you've always been the kind of guy who acts first and thinks later? I mean, I love Brianna to bits, but you know we all thought you were crazy getting engaged so quickly, even if you did seem really happy…"

"I was," I interrupt. "At least I thought I was, until Brianna decided the grass was greener elsewhere."

"Are you sure you're being fair about this?" she asks, and I try to stay calm, even though I think she's about as far out of line as she can get.

"How do you mean?"

"Well, you played the field, didn't you?"

"Yes. Before I started seeing Brianna. But I never cheated. There's a difference between playing the field and playing around. How would you feel if you discovered Lucas in bed with another woman? Would you want to sit down quietly to discuss your options, or would you be calling off your wedding too?" I think quickly about Rachel's plans for her own lavish ceremony, which is due to take place in May.

"That's different," she says, sounding defensive. "Lucas and I have been together for five years. You and Brianna were together for somewhere approaching five minutes."

"Which makes absolutely no difference whatsoever," I counter, wondering how I let her get us into all this, when all I wanted was to ask a favour of her. "We were two weeks away from taking our vows, from committing ourselves to each other, for life… supposedly. Rightly or wrongly, as it transpires, I was willing to do that, but she clearly wasn't."

Rachel sighs. "Okay, okay. But you need to know that Brianna's really upset about the whole thing."

"And why exactly do I need to know that? I think you're mistaking me for someone who gives a damn."

"Don't be such a hard-nosed bastard, Logan. It doesn't suit you," she snaps.

"For Christ's sake, Rachel…" I finally lose it. "I called to ask a favour, not to get a lecture on the rights and wrongs of my relationship choices. I need you to do something for me, as my sister. Is that too much to ask?"

I'm breathing faster now, angered by her attitude, not just her words.

"Of course it's not," she whispers. "What do you need me to do?"

I take a deep breath, letting it out slowly, then sip my lukewarm tea. "Can you get the locks changed at my flat?" I ask, calming quickly. "I'm obviously not going to be there for the next couple of weeks, and I don't want Brianna letting herself in, in my absence. I stupidly forgot to get my key back from her on Thursday and you're the only other person who has one, apart from the decorators, and I'd rather leave this in the hands of someone I can trust… so, can I trust you?"

"You know you can." She sounds hurt now, and I wonder if I've gone too far.

"Sorry. I didn't mean that."

"It's okay," she says quietly. "Look, I've got tomorrow off. I'm going for a dress fitting in the afternoon. But I can deal with your locks in the morning… unless you want to pay for an emergency call out on a Sunday?"

"No, tomorrow's fine. Brianna sent me a text message just now, telling me she was going to go round to the flat this afternoon to see me, so we could talk things through. But I've sent her one back, explaining that I've gone away… and I'm not interested in talking. While I know she's not great at taking 'no' for an answer, I doubt she'll let herself in, knowing I'm not even going to be there for two weeks."

"You don't think so?" Rachel queries.

"No. I'm sure she's got better things to do with her time. And anyway, what would she do? Camp out there waiting for me, while the decorators work around her? I doubt she'd be able to stand the humiliation." I let out a sigh. "If she's going to do anything, it'll be when I get home. But at least she won't be able to just let herself in… if you can get the locks changed, that is."

"I'll deal with it," she replies.

"Thanks, sis."

"Don't call me 'sis'."

"You know I only do it because it annoys you."

"Yes. And you know I only let you because I love you."

I'm stunned into silence. I'm not sure Rachel's ever said that to me before, or that I've ever said it to her, but I suppose there's a first time for everything.

"I love you too," I reply. "Let me know how much the locksmith charges and I'll transfer the money to your account."

"Will do."

"And thanks again."

"Can I go back to sleep now?" she asks.

"Be my guest."

I hang up, and am about to put my phone back down when it beeps with another message from Brianna.

— You know you don't mean that. We're meant to be together, Logan, and you know it. What we have is too good to walk away from. I'll give you your two weeks to get your head together, and I'll be waiting for you when you get home.

I don't care what you say, we're NOT over. And I'm not giving up. I love you. B xxx

I'm fuming, but I don't bother to reply. That might give her the impression I'm interested in having a conversation with her, and that's the very last thing I want. I block her number instead and then, getting up from the table, I go into the bedroom to put on my shoes and coat, trying hard not to think about the arrogance of Brianna's messages.

Once I'm dressed, I come back into the living room, pick up the house keys, check I've got my wallet, and head out of the front door, slamming it closed behind me.

Then I remember, it's not my door to slam.

Chapter Six

∞

Hope

The weather seems slightly less grim today.

It's still cloudy and overcast, but at least it's not so dull, or maybe it just seems that way because I slept so well. I did. I slept really well. And when I woke this morning and stretched my sleep-laden arms above my head, I couldn't help smiling, because the first thought that entered my head was that, with any luck, I might see Logan today. That probably makes me the adult equivalent of a giddy schoolgirl, but I really don't care.

I got up and showered, to be met at the bottom of the stairs by Archie, keen as ever for his morning constitutional, walking in tight circles, then stopping every so often to gaze longingly up at his lead, which hangs from one of the coat hooks on the back of the door.

I never dare to keep him waiting too long, in case he starts barking, so I dressed quickly in my shoes, coat, hat and scarf, grabbed my gloves and hooked the lead to his collar, and we set off at a pace.

Outside, there wasn't the overriding damp chill that's accompanied our recent walks, but as I say, maybe that's because I was feeling distracted; my eyes naturally drawn to the cottage, my thoughts to the man inside.

The curtains were still closed, and I crept out of the gate, aware in the still morning silence of the crunch of my footsteps on the gravel, not wishing to wake him, because as much as I'd have liked to see him again, he is here on holiday, and I doubted he'd appreciate being woken at seven o'clock in the morning, especially not on his first day.

I took Archie up into the woods for a nice long walk, which he seemed to appreciate, although the breakfast I fed him when we got back seemed just as welcome. I know I'd worked up an appetite myself, but that didn't stop me stealing a wistful look out of the window as I filled the kettle. There was a light on in the kitchen over the way, and I leant against the sink, daydreaming, imagining Logan preparing his breakfast, or making himself a cup of tea or coffee, perhaps in a bathrobe, his hair tousled from a night's sleep... until the kettle overflowed and I came to my senses, turning off the tap and silently chastising myself for being so juvenile.

After I've eaten my two slices of toast, and drunk two cups of strong tea, I pop upstairs to make the bed and fetch some washing. In reality, I'm putting off doing my accounts. I'm aware I'm procrastinating, but that doesn't stop me. I'm a master procrastinator when it comes to my accounts. Besides, if I don't wash some clothes soon, I'm in danger of running out of underwear, so what better reason is there for taking my time over sorting through my laundry... oh, and re-folding the blanket that I always leave on the window seat... while glancing out at the cottage at the same time?

I'm just replacing the blanket in its usual place, when I notice Logan leaving, slamming the door behind him with such force that it makes me jump and I stand still, hoping he won't notice me. I wonder what can have happened to inspire such anger in him, because even though it isn't any of my business, it is my door. He walks towards the gate, his stride even longer than usual, his head bowed low, so I can't see his expression, and his hands plunged in his pockets, which means I have no way of seeing whether or not he's wearing a ring. Not that I'd be able to see from this distance, but I suppose a wedding band might glint in the morning light...

"Seriously, Hope?" I mutter under my breath, even though there's no-one here to hear me.

There's obviously something wrong with Logan, something which has upset him greatly and all I can think about is whether or not he's married. As if that matters.

He turns right out of the gate and I imagine he's taken himself off for a walk. I know, if I'm upset, that's what I like to do…

I stare at the gate post, at the space he's just vacated, and wonder about going after him to ask if he's okay, if there's anything I can do to help… but then, as I've already said, it's none of my business. And in any case, I suppose there might be nothing wrong at all. Maybe he's just not a morning person. Or perhaps he's just generally morose.

I shake my head. No… no, he's not morose. There may occasionally be something dark and tortured in his eyes, but behind them, I can see something else… something bright and good natured.

Downstairs, I load up the washing machine and then realise I've really got no more excuses. The time has come, and I can't put it off any longer. I haven't done anything with my accounts since before Christmas, and there's a pile of receipts in the drawer of the sideboard that need entering up, so I pick up my laptop from the work surface, and place it at the end of the table, opening the lid and turning it on. While it powers up, I go through to the living room, where I open the drawer and pull out the receipts. It might sound disorganised to keep them in here, but they're all in date order, and at least when they're stashed away, I don't have to look at them all the time and be reminded of how slack I am when it comes to my own book-keeping.

As much as I despise this aspect of my business, I know the time will come when I can no longer see well enough to do it, when reading the fine print of receipts will be too much for me, even with a magnifier, and I'll be forced to hire someone to help me. And for that reason alone, even though I hate it, and despite the fact that I could afford to pay someone else to do it for me, I continue to do it myself. Just because I still can.

Back in the kitchen, the receipts piled beside my laptop, I refill the kettle, and then open the cupboard above the microwave.

"Oh, no." I utter the words out loud, in abject despair, because the space where I normally keep my emergency stash of cookies is staring back at me – empty.

There's no way I can even consider looking at figures if I don't have cookies. Not a chance.

"Stay here, Archie," I say over my shoulder as I go into the hall and slip on my shoes, pulling on my coat, as I grab my keys from the hook. "I won't be long."

He doesn't even raise his head and I roll my eyes at his nonchalance, closing the door behind me.

It genuinely does feel slightly warmer out here. It's only a degree or two, but when it's been bone-numbingly cold, like it has been for the last few days, a degree or two makes all the difference, and while the sky is still grey, it's not that dark, threatening, gunmetal colour, but more of a dirty white, which feels a little more promising.

Inside the store, I head straight for the biscuit section, finding my favourite chocolate chip cookies – the ones with a slightly squidgy centre – and as I'm about to make my way to the counter, I remember that I've run out of eggs. I used four in Logan's fruit cake, and I decided while on this morning's walk that I feel like a mushroom omelette for lunch, in which case... I'm going to need mushrooms, as well as eggs. I shake my head and sigh. What's the matter with me? I'm not normally this forgetful.

Clutching my cookies, I move back to the door for a basket, being as it seems I'm going to be buying more than a few items, and after I've picked one up and put my box of cookies inside, just as I turn back around, I walk straight into something very hard, and very tall.

"Sorry," I mutter.

I look up, a smile already settling on my lips as I find myself gazing up into the deep, espresso eyes of Logan Quinn. He's smiling back at me, and in the bright lighting of the shop, I notice for the first time that, while his hair is a really, really dark brown, his beard is just very lightly flecked with grey. It's only one or two strands, here and there, but I hadn't spotted that before, although I suppose that's understandable, being as I've never been this close to him, until now. After all, we are standing almost close enough to touch... close enough to kiss...

"My fault entirely," he replies and I snap out of my trance, taking a step back, before I make a complete fool of myself by actually leaning in.

I can feel my cheeks heating, the blush creeping up them, not only because of the thoughts that were just wandering through my brain, but also because this is the first time we've met since we stared at each other for a ludicrously long time last night. I wonder if I should say anything about that, or whether he will.

"I didn't hurt you, did I?"

"Sorry?" How could him staring at me across the driveway have hurt me?

"Just now… walking into you… I didn't hurt you?"

I realise my mistake and shake my head, then reply, "No… I'm fine," realising that I'm making too much of something insignificant. Gazing at him in the dusky evening light might have meant something to me, but I'm sure he's got much more important things going on in his life. He frowns, just briefly, although I don't know why, and I'm reminded of the manner in which he left the cottage this morning. He seemed angry, or upset, but looking at him now, now that his brief frown has gone and he's smiling at me again, he seems like a different person.

"Is everything okay? At the cottage, I mean…" I clarify my question, so he doesn't think I'm prying.

"Everything is perfect at the cottage," he says and I manage to drag my eyes away from his, looking down instead at the full basket he's carrying.

"Gosh… stocking up, are you?"

He chuckles. "Yes. It looks that way."

"I thought you were going to go to St Austell."

"I was, but when I came in here yesterday and saw how great it is, I decided I might as well buy locally. I don't want to waste my time driving to St Austell and pushing a trolley around a supermarket when I can be here…" He leaves his sentence hanging, although I sense there's something he's not saying, and I wonder if it's connected to whatever it was that made him so bad tempered this morning. That doesn't make sense though, because his face is a picture of relaxed happiness right now.

"Well, I'm all for buying locally," I remark, because I can't think how else to reply to him, and because it's the truth. Since my driving licence was revoked, not long after my diagnosis, I've come to rely on the local shop for most of my supplies and I don't regret that one bit. My mother takes me into St Austell once a month to stock up on larger, bulk-buy items that Amy and Nick don't have, and we usually make a day of it and go somewhere nice for lunch, which makes the new arrangement even better really. "I just came in to buy cookies." I nod down to the solitary item sitting at the bottom of my basket. "I've got to do my accounts this morning, and I'm afraid to say that cookies are an essential part of that."

He chuckles again, a little more loudly, the sound reverberating through my body, to the point where I have to concentrate really hard to avoid actually shuddering. "I don't blame you," he says. "I think I'd need wine – fairly serious quantities of wine – to get me to do accounts."

"I've considered wine in the past," I explain over my shoulder, as I walk towards the vegetable section, a warm glow filling me when he follows, "but I usually do my book-keeping in the mornings, and I'm pretty sure someone in the village would find out and talk... and besides, I need to be able to concentrate. Anything mathematical is a challenge, so adding alcohol into the mix isn't really the most sensible idea."

I pick up a box of mushrooms, dropping them into my basket and, then turn to the end of the first shelf unit, where the eggs are kept.

"Being sensible is vastly overrated though, don't you think?"

"Most of the time." I take half a dozen large free range eggs from the top shelf, where I know they're always kept, in a pale green box. "But not when it comes to my accounts."

"Fair comment."

Logan also picks up some eggs, adding them to his basket, and when I go to the refrigerator to get some milk, because I've remembered I don't have much left, he selects a couple of packs of bacon as well.

"Tomorrow's breakfast?" I suggest and he smiles at me.

"Don't get me wrong, I love the blackcurrant jam... I really do, but I'm on holiday. And this is one of those occasions when being sensible is definitely not required."

"Don't worry. I completely understand."

"Do you make the jams yourself?" he asks, taking a bottle of freshly squeezed orange juice and clutching it in his hand, because there's not enough space left in his basket.

"Yes. I don't grow the fruit, but I make all the jam."

"Well, I'll try the strawberry one tomorrow," he says.

"After the bacon and eggs?"

"Naturally." His smile widens and we turn together towards the counter. "Are you finished?" he asks.

"Yes. I think so."

"Well, you go first," he says, as Amy hops down from her stool, a cheeky grin on her face. "I'll be here much longer than you will."

I want to tell him I don't mind, and that I'd happily wait, but I don't. Instead I put my basket on the counter and glare at Amy while she totals up my purchases, glancing at Logan in a very pointed fashion, her eyes alight with mischief. I wish she'd stop her matchmaking exploits, but I can't say anything when the target of them is standing right beside me, so I lean on the counter, in silence, not taking the bait, and once she's finished, she notes down the total I've spent in the accounts book and I move my things aside to make room for Logan.

"Actually, Nick…" Amy says, looking over my shoulder at her husband, who's stacking the shelf behind me with tins of baked beans, "do you think you could serve Logan? I'd just like a quiet word with Hope."

Nick looks up, a little startled, it seems, but Amy shakes her head, just fractionally, and he says, "Yes, of course," coming around behind her and taking over the till.

I've got no idea what that was about, but I pick up my shopping, cradling it in my arms, being as I didn't bring a bag and I don't want to buy yet another one, and step to one side, Amy following me.

"Is something wrong?" I ask her, in a whisper.

"No. Not at all."

"So why all the furtive looks between you and Nick?"

"Oh…" she says, looking flustered now, "that's nothing. Look, I wanted to ask if you're going to be free sometime tomorrow to pop down for a chat."

"I'm free this afternoon," I point out, wondering why she doesn't want to take advantage of her afternoon off, if she's so desperate to see me that she feels the need to actually make formal arrangements.

"Yes, but I'm not. We're going to my parents' this afternoon."

"Oh, are they back from their holiday already?"

"Yes, they got back late last night."

Amy's mum and dad have been in Jamaica since just before New Year, and while I'm well aware that she's close to them, I'm surprised she and Nick are dashing over there so soon.

"Well, I'm probably going to be around in the morning."

"Great." She grins, putting her hand on my arm. "Come down whenever you've got a spare ten minutes."

"Is this something important?" I ask, because it seems as though it is. Our plans are usually a lot more spontaneous than this... to the point where they're not 'plans' at all.

"Yes," she says, her eyes twinkling.

Oh God... I hope this isn't something to do with Logan. I hope she's not trying to set something up between us. That would be so humiliating...

"Okay... but you do realise that the intrigue is going to keep me awake all night now, don't you?" I say, in the vain hope that she'll tell me what's going on in that pretty head of hers.

She chuckles. "Well, I like to be mysterious." *No such luck then.*

I shake my head, turning back to the counter, which is deserted, with no sign of either Nick, or Logan. "Oh, he's gone," I say out loud, wishing immediately that I could bite back the words.

"I assume you're not bemoaning the absence of my husband," Amy says playfully. I don't reply, embarrassed by my outburst, and she continues, "You did notice though, didn't you?"

"What, that Logan's gone?"

"No, silly... that he doesn't wear a ring."

"No, I can't say I did notice. That's not the kind of detail I tend to pick up on these days." I blame my condition for the fact that I was actually too busy trying not to make a fool of myself in front of the man in question. "And anyway, I was preoccupied with trying to remember why I came in here."

"Of course you were," Amy muses, her eyes narrowing impishly.

"And now I'm going home. I've put off the accounts for long enough."

"I'll try not to be offended by the fact that you're abandoning me in favour of your least favourite job in the world," she says, grinning now and moving back behind the counter to resume her position there.

"I'll see you tomorrow morning," I reply. "I can't say when, but I'll definitely come down at some point."

"I'm looking forward to it," she calls, as I open the door, and I give her a smile, and a half-wave with the hand that's holding the carton of milk, as I let myself out, pulling the door closed behind me.

I turn and stop dead, almost dropping my eggs, as Logan pushes himself off the wall beside the door and steps forward.

"Hello again," he says.

Logan

After the way my morning began, bumping into Hope at the store was like a ray of sunshine on the dullest and most dreary of days. But then, she does seem to have that effect on me.

I was so angry when I left the cottage. I'd like to say I've never been so angry before, but that would be ignoring the rage that coursed through me on Thursday evening, which I think is unlikely to be repeated in my lifetime.

Even so, Brianna's arrogance in her text messages, was astounding. Obviously Rachel's attitude didn't help, but it was Brianna I was really angry with.

And that's not a feeling I'm used to, because apart from Thursday evening, I can't recall ever being angry with Brianna before. She and I never really argued that much in the past, which thinking about it, was probably because I never cared enough to be bothered. But whenever we did quarrel, she always knew how to get around me, to make peace. It would usually involve her sexiest lingerie, her most seductive pout, and my complete capitulation.

The difference this time is, we haven't really argued, not in the conventional sense of the word. Well, I suppose I did shout at her on Thursday night, but she didn't respond, other than to make lame excuses, not even when I dumped her belongings in the living room, and thrust the airline tickets in her face. I don't think there's a man alive who would say I wasn't entitled to do that, in the circumstances, but if she thinks her usual tricks are going to work this time, she can think again, because I'm immune to her now. I would be, even if I hadn't met Hope... but being as I have...

Oh God... Hope. Seeing her again confirmed everything I'd been thinking last night. Not that I really needed to have it confirmed. I already knew I'm completely and utterly in love with her. I've never felt like this before, and while it may be inconvenient – although I'm not completely sure that it is – I don't care. I mean, what does timing matter anyway?

Of course, being in love has its drawbacks. It's very absorbing and equally distracting, and makes you inclined to forget yourself, like I did just now, when Hope was asking about why I hadn't gone to St Austell to do my shopping and I very nearly told her that I'd rather not waste my time in the supermarket when I could be spending it here with her. I stopped myself from actually saying that out loud, but only just.

Having seen that perfect smile, heard her soft, tinkling voice and noticed, for the first time, that her hair isn't just honey coloured, but is shot through with occasional strands that are ash blonde, and that her skin is dusted with just the lightest sprinkling of freckles, it didn't feel right to walk away and leave her there. So I didn't. I waited for her while she spoke to Amy, and when she came out, I just said, "Hello again," because I couldn't think what else to say.

"Oh, hello," she replies, seemingly startled by my still being here.

"I—I thought I could walk you home." I don't think I've stuttered in my life, but evidently my mouth has chosen this moment to start, which is helpful.

"Okay," she says, smiling, and I reach down and take the carton of milk from her hand.

"Are you okay with everything else?" I ask. "My bags are kind of full, otherwise I'd offer to…"

"I'm fine," she says, interrupting, as we start to walk back in the direction of Orchard House. I can't help noticing that she says she's 'fine' quite a lot. She did it in the shop just now, but I realised even then that she doesn't say it with any conviction. I also can't help noticing how much that thought bothers me. It does. A lot.

Taking a step back, I switch to the other side of her, so I'm on the roadside and she's next to the wall, and she glances up at me, seemingly confused, although it soon passes, and she asks, "Have you got any plans for while you're staying here?"

Seeing if I can make you fall as deeply in love with me as I have with you? "Just relaxing, reading, walking," I say aloud.

"Well, hopefully the weather will warm up a bit." She looks up at the sky, bringing up her free left hand to push a stray hair behind her ear and I notice, as she straightens the box of mushrooms that are balanced on her right arm, before letting her hand drop again, that there isn't a ring on her finger. Not a wedding band, or an engagement ring. There's been no sign of a man around the house either, or another car, other than my own. I'm clutching at straws, I know that… but that's what you do when you're in love. Evidently.

I'm deliberately taking small steps, in the hope of making the walk last longer.

"I don't mind the cold," I tell her.

"I hate it," she says.

"So you're a summer person?"

"I'm an anything but winter person," she says, looking up at me again.

I instinctively move a little closer, which I can only assume is a gut reaction; a need to protect her, even if only from the cold, and just at that moment, my phone beeps in my back pocket. I'm inclined to ignore it, but Hope shifts away.

"You should probably check that," she says, taking back her milk so I've got a free hand.

I don't reply, but pull out my phone and unlock it, knowing that at least the message can't be from Brianna, being as I've blocked her number now.

I'm right. It's from Rachel.

— Just thought I'd let you know that I've told Brianna you're changing the locks on your flat. Before you get cross again, she called me because she'd had a message from you, saying you'd gone away, and she was upset that you'd gone without telling her. In the end it seemed only fair to let her know about the locks too. She didn't take it very well, and said she's going to sort things out with you when you get back. She's definitely not giving up, and God knows why, but she still loves you ;). Sorry about being a bitch to you earlier, but you know I've only got your best interests at heart. I'll text tomorrow when the locksmiths have finished. R x

For Christ's sake. I let out a sigh. Why can't Brianna just get the message? And why does Rachel have to keep feeding her information about me? *Because they're friends, I suppose.* Even so, it's not helping. Well, it's not helping me, anyway. It feels like Rachel is giving Brianna false hope… *Damn.*

I suddenly recall that Hope is still at my side, and ignoring my bad mood, I type out a quick reply.

— Thanks for the update. L x

"Sorry about that." I turn back to Hope, replacing my phone at the same time.

"It's fine… don't worry." And there she goes with 'it's fine', again.

"That was my sister," I explain, perhaps unnecessarily, although I want her to know that I'm not getting text messages from another woman, even though I was a couple of hours ago. "She's getting the locks changed on my flat for me, in my absence."

"I see," Hope says, although I don't understand how she can. Not really. After all, I haven't explained why I need to get my locks changed, when I'm not even there.

"I'm sorry I was so rude."

"You weren't. It's fine."

Seriously? Again? I frown at her, wondering how long it's been since someone made her feel better than 'fine'.

We go in through the gate of Orchard House, our walk over much more quickly than I'd have liked, especially since so much of it was wasted by Rachel's text message.

I know we're going to have to part in a minute, her to the pale blue front door, and me to the yellow one. But the thing is, I don't want to.

"Do you run this place by yourself?" I ask, positively grabbing at straws now and hanging on for dear life. Short of asking 'is there someone in your life?', I'm not sure how I could be more obvious.

"Yes," she replies simply, but doesn't elaborate.

I suppose that could mean she's got a boyfriend, or a partner, who doesn't take an active role in running her business, although if that's the case, he's been very good at keeping himself to himself since I arrived.

We've come to a standstill now, halfway between her house and the cottage, and we're both standing, neither seemingly willing to part from the other – at least I hope that's what this is.

Looking down into her dazzling eyes, I can't help thinking that she doesn't seem the type of woman who'd stare at a man out of her window for a breathtakingly long time, or let him flirt with her, or smile at him in the way she smiles at me, if she had someone else waiting for her indoors.

"Would you like to come in for coffee?" My question leaves my mouth before my brain has had the chance to think it through.

After all… what if I'm wrong? What if she really does have someone?

"That would be lovely." She startles, as though she didn't expect to say that, despite the fact that her words are already floating in the air between us.

"Well, it gets you out of doing your accounts for a bit longer," I say, in the hope of putting her at ease, and it seems to work because she relaxes noticeably and smiles at me.

"I'll just put my shopping away, and I'll come over," she replies, taking a step towards her house.

"I'll put the kettle on."

She nods. "Give me five minutes…"

Five minutes? I'd give her a lifetime, if that's what she wanted.

Chapter Seven

Hope

Why did I say 'yes'?

Because you don't want to do the accounts? I muse to myself, and then I shake my head. No… although that is a very sound reason. I said 'yes', because I want to spend more time with Logan. Standing on the driveway, thinking about saying 'goodbye' to him, and maybe not seeing him again for the rest of the day, was like having a part of me wrenched away. And if that sounds over-dramatic, then bring on the drama.

I put the milk in the fridge, along with the mushrooms and leave the eggs and cookies on the table, leaning over it, my hands resting on the edge.

I've never done anything like that before. I've never accepted an invitation from someone I don't know, and certainly not a guest.

"It's just coffee," I say aloud, standing upright and sucking in a deep breath.

Yes, it's coffee… with a man who, last night, you contemplated falling into bed with.

I clasp my hand to my mouth. I really did that, didn't I? Amy asked the question and I didn't deny that the prospect was appealing. I thought about it… I really did.

The thing is… in the cold light of day, I know I couldn't do it. Because, as enticing as Logan Quinn is – and he really is, believe me –

I wasn't kidding when I told Amy that I'm not the kind of woman who has casual sex. I'm the kind of woman who needs romance and commitment in her life. My relationship with Greg taught me that, if nothing else. And these days, as much as I crave the romance part of that, I probably need commitment even more – given what my future holds. All of which makes a holiday fling with 'luscious Logan' completely out of the question. No matter how good, how satisfying and deeply pleasurable it might be in the short term, the long term cost would be just too great for me.

I glance down at Archie, who's sitting beside his basket expectantly.

"It's not walk time yet, but I won't be too long and I'll take you out when I get back, I promise." I go and crouch in front of him, clasping his head between my hands. "Do you think he'd cheat?" I ask, as though my unerringly faithful border collie can understand the concept of cheating – or any of my words, for that matter. "Do you think he'd have invited me for coffee, if he had a wife, or a girlfriend waiting for him at home?" Archie blinks a couple of times. "What am I saying?" I get to my feet, shaking my head. "It's just coffee. He's not suggesting we have wild, passionate sex on the kitchen table…" I feel a shiver run through my body, right to my fingertips, at the thought. "Honestly, I need to stop spending so much time with Amy. She's a bad influence." Archie lowers his head and then raises it again, which looks remarkably like he's nodding in agreement, and I chuckle to myself. "I'll be back soon," I tell him and, picking up my keys, I go back out, closing the door behind me.

I knock on the door of Orchard Cottage, even though I have a spare key on my keyring, because I couldn't possibly let myself in when there's someone staying here.

Logan answers within seconds.

"You didn't have to knock," he says, standing back to let me enter. "I was expecting you."

"I know," I reply, as he holds out his hand, directing me into the kitchen. "But you're entitled to your privacy while you're a guest here. I wouldn't dream of using my key."

I take off my coat, placing it over the back of one of the kitchen chairs. "If you insist," he says, bringing the cafetière to the table, along with two cups. "Have a seat."

"Thanks."

He fetches the milk and the sugar bowl and then sits opposite me, pouring the coffee and I help myself to milk, declining the sugar and taking a quick sip of the scalding liquid, in an attempt to hide my ludicrous nerves. *It's just coffee.*

He picks up his cup, although he doesn't drink, but gazes at me over the rim and for a moment, I wonder if we're just going to sit in silence, staring at each other again. Part of me wouldn't mind in the slightest, because the view is perfection, but another part of me feels embarrassed, given the intensity of his gaze and the way my thoughts had been turning before I came over here. He knows nothing about that, of course, but the fact that that we're sitting at same kitchen table on which I'd contemplated us having wild, passionate sex, isn't helping.

"So, you're a vet?" I blurt out, desperate to say something to break the strangely potent, almost tangible, stillness between us.

"Yes." He puts his cup back down, still not having drunk anything, and smiles at me.

"You enjoy it?"

"I love it." His smile is infectious and I return it with one of my own, feeling more at ease now, for some reason.

"Was it something you always wanted to do?"

"Since I was about eight or nine, yes." He sits forward, leaning on the table with his elbows, his eyes flashing with a boyish enthusiasm, which just makes me smile even more widely. "We never had any pets at home, but one day, I was walking back from school, and I found a cat lying by the side of the road. It looked like it had been hit by a car, but I could see it was still alive and struggling to breathe, so I picked it up, really carefully, and carried it to the vets, which was on the corner of our road. The vet came out straight away and took the cat into his consulting room, but I didn't want to leave, so I waited… and waited… and eventually the vet came back out again. He was surprised I was still there, and told me the cat was going to be okay. It was lucky to be alive, he said."

"You'd saved its life?" I ask.

"No. The vet saved its life," Logan replies, the left hand side of his mouth twitching upwards. "I just put 'A' in touch with 'B', so to speak."

"Oh… that's *all* you did, was it?" I tease. "And that's why you waited around for hours to find out if the cat was okay?"

"Well," he says, trying desperately hard not to smile, "it was a very cute cat."

"So it made a full recovery?" I take another sip of coffee, which has cooled slightly now, although I keep my eyes fixed on him.

"I don't know. It had a collar on, with a name tag attached, so the vet's receptionist phoned the number printed on it, and about fifteen minutes later, a woman arrived, with a little girl. She'd have been about five years old, I suppose, and when they found out what had happened, and that the cat was going to be alright, the little girl burst into tears."

"Did they thank you?"

He shakes his head. "No. They wanted to see their cat, which was understandable, so the vet took them through to his consulting room, and that's when I left…"

"You didn't wait to be thanked?" I'm surprised.

"No. It wasn't about being thanked. It was about saving the cat."

I smile at him. "So that's when you knew you wanted to be a vet?"

"Yes. I worked it out on the way home."

"And your parents didn't notice you were late, or worry about where you'd been?"

He lets out a half laugh, although there's no humour to it. "I was lucky if my parents noticed I was alive… so no, they didn't worry that I was late."

I'm not sure what that means, and I don't want to pry, so I take another sip of coffee and he mirrors my action, his eyes never leaving mine.

"Is this a full-time job for you?" he asks. "Looking after your guests, I mean…"

"Yes, it is. Well, it's not full-time, per se. Out of season, there isn't really that much to do at all, but when it's busy, it's very busy. Saturdays are the most frantic, because that's changeover day, but the rest of the time I manage to keep myself occupied."

"And how does someone as young as you wind up owning such a beautiful place as this?" he asks. "I always thought renting out holiday cottages was something people did in their retirement."

"I fell into it by accident," I explain. "Accident and inheritance."

"Inheritance?" he queries.

"Yes. I inherited the main house from my grandmother when she died, seven years ago…"

"So you're not a native of the village then?" he interrupts.

"No. I'm from just outside of Truro, which is about half an hour away."

He nods. "I see. So you moved here seven years ago?" he prompts.

"Yes. At the time, I was working for an estate agents in Truro and living in a one bedroomed flat, and although I could have sold the house and bought another property somewhere else, I didn't want to. I had happy childhood memories of coming to visit my grandparents here and I thought this would be the perfect place to live."

"It is, really… I mean you've got the sea on your doorstep, and you're surrounded by countryside. What more could you want?"

I can't help smiling, being as I recall saying something very similar to Greg when we moved here, and he was arguing about the merits of remaining in Truro.

"I couldn't agree more," I say. "Of course, I didn't intend turning it into a business to start with, and the house needed decorating, so that came first, but after a couple of years, when I finally got around to clearing out the barn, which is what this cottage used to be, I realised the potential for converting it, and I mentioned it to my parents. My dad is an architect and he drew up some plans, and the rest, as they say, is history…"

"So, you gave up your job and became a full-time business woman?" Logan asks.

"I don't think of myself as a business woman, but I did give up my job," I explain. "Running this place and working five days a week was too much. Obviously it was a risk at the time, but it was a calculated risk. We had my husband's income, you see, so…" I stop talking, feeling flustered, probably because I've just mentioned Greg for the first time, even if not by name.

Logan puts down his cup. "Your husband?" he queries, and I notice his eyes drop to my left hand, to the place where my ring used to sit, until just over a month ago, when I finally decided to remove it.

I wonder if I should explain about Greg, whether I should tell Logan that my husband has been dead for nearly two years, and that even when he was alive I was never happy with him. I also wonder if I should tell him about my Retinitis Pigmentosa, about the early symptoms, the diagnosis, the initial fear, the coming to terms with it all…

Logan looks out of the window, even though there's nothing but the view of my barren garden to capture his attention, and as I take in the blank expression on his face, the dullness behind his eyes and the tight line of his mouth, I realise there's no point in explaining anything. I'm nothing to him. And why would I be? He's a guest. A guest who's staying in my cottage for two weeks, after which he'll return to London, or wherever it is he lives, and he'll get on with his life. He probably only invited me in here for coffee, because he's feeling a bit lonely and wanted someone to talk to.

And let's face it, I know how that feels.

Logan

She's married.

She's actually married?

Oh hell.

I'd lulled myself into a false sense of security, a false sense of hope –

ironically, being as there seems to be quite a bit of that going around at the moment – that because she doesn't wear a ring, she must be free. But then I suppose not everyone wears rings these days, do they? Hope Nelson certainly doesn't.

Even though she's married.

I stare out of the window, the stark, bare branches and matt grey sky matching my now sombre mood.

How the hell can she be married?

Quite easily... because there's a really lucky man, living in her house, who was smart enough to ask her.

I turn back to her, and swallow down my shock at the sadness in her eyes.

"So, what made you go into the estate agency business?" I ask, because I can't think of anything else to say, but equally, I can't just sit here in silence either, not when she's looking at me with that dejected expression on her face.

"I got the job by accident really, through a friend of my dad's," she replies, although her voice doesn't hold any of the enthusiasm or buoyancy that it did earlier. "I started working there on Saturdays when I was at college, just for something to do, although it wasn't that interesting. I only did the filing and answered the phones if everyone else was out on viewings, but then, when I'd finished my A-levels, they offered me a full-time job."

"And you accepted, even though you clearly weren't that interested in pursuing it as a career?"

"Well, it was a living," she says. "Not a career."

"And you didn't want to go to university?" I ask, intrigued now by why she seemingly 'settled'.

She shakes her head. "No." she admits, her cheeks reddening beautifully. "I'm actually quite a shy person... I didn't want to leave home, or even Cornwall, to be honest. Th—the furthest I've ever been from here, is North Devon." The blush has spread to the roots of her golden hair, and she seems so unsure of herself that all I want to do is hold her and tell her it'll be okay. Except it won't. Not for me. And I have to actually clench my fists under the table, reminding myself that

I can never hold her, and I'll never be able to make it okay… and that she can't be mine. Ever.

"Really?" I manage to say.

"Yes."

"Was that for your honeymoon?" I ask, wishing I could learn to engage my brain before opening my mouth. "Sorry," I add quickly. "You don't have to answer that."

She smiles, very briefly. "It's fine," she says. Again. "No, Greg and I didn't have a honeymoon." *Greg…* her husband… I try to ignore the jealousy burning inside me and focus on her lips, which is probably the worst thing I could do at the moment, being as that just makes me want kiss her. I can't though, so I concentrate on her words instead. "I'd just blown a huge amount of money on converting the barn, and still had all the internal work to complete, so the wedding was small, and we skipped having a honeymoon." There's definitely a hint of regret in her voice, but she continues, "We went to Devon for our first anniversary."

"Oh… I see." I'm not sure I want to know any more about that, and we sit in silence again for a few moments, all the easy friendliness that there had been between us, now gone, it would seem.

It's Hope's turn to gaze out of the window, or at least in the vague direction of it, because her expression is kind of blank, to the point where I'm not sure she's seeing anything really, and I take the opportunity to study her. I can't deny that she's incredibly beautiful, regardless of the fact that she belongs to someone else. I just hope he appreciates what he's got. I know I would, if she were mine. I'd wake up every morning and give thanks that her face was the first thing that greeted me. The thing is, I know I won't get that chance now, and that thought is starting to mess with my already messed-up head.

Maybe Rachel is right about me. Maybe I am too impetuous for my own good. My experience with Brianna ought to have shown me that. But I suppose what's happened today proves it beyond any doubt. Should I give up on this holiday and go home, I wonder. The thought of dealing with Brianna and her histrionics doesn't appeal, but I'm not sure I can stay here for much longer and take the chance of seeing Hope with another man. She may never have been mine, and she never will be now, but just the idea of her with someone else is so much worse than the reality of what I witnessed on Thursday evening.

"I should probably get back," Hope says, bringing me back to reality with a start. I've been gazing at her, but now as she turns back to me, her eyes fixing on mine, I really see her – deep inside her – and she looks desolate. "I promised Archie I wouldn't be too long, and that I'd take him out for a walk when I got back."

She stands, and so do I. 'Archie'? Who's Archie? Her son, perhaps? And with that thought I'm pushed even further into depression.

"O—Okay. Thanks for stopping by." God, even I can hear the dismissal in my voice.

Stop it, Logan… it's your fault, not hers. Don't treat her like this. She didn't make you fall in love with her. You did that all by yourself.

She glances up at me, a look of confused rejection on her face and I want to take back the last four words that left my lips and tell her I'm sorry. But what would I say after that? How would I explain that I'm in love with her, without making things unbearably awkward? How could I tell her that, for the first time in my life, I've really fallen for someone with my whole heart, but that I can't have her? And that it hurts.

"I—I'll see you… sometime," she says, stuttering herself now.

"Yes."

I'm not sure she will. I think it's probably best if I go home and do whatever it takes to forget I ever met her. Somehow…

Just for a split second, I contemplate getting on with that old ambition of mine to start up my own practice. But then I realise, it doesn't matter anymore. Nothing matters anymore. Except Hope.

She moves towards the door and I follow, feeling as though I'm almost kicking her out now, in my haste to be alone, or at least to not be faced directly with the sum of my own mistakes.

I wish that she would just go… go back to her husband and her son, and leave me to myself.

"Bye," she says on the doorstep, and I nod my head, unable to even speak now, as she turns and walks down the path.

I feel terrible, wishing I could call her back and explain, that we could laugh over my stupidity… except it's not a laughing matter.

I close the door, unwilling to watch her go back into her house; unwilling to risk seeing her with the man she loves, or the child they've created. And instead, I go into the bedroom and fetch my walking boots, sitting down and pulling off my shoes.

I can't be here. Not knowing she's there. With him.

Properly booted, I grab my coat, and the keys, and head straight out of the door, my head down, making my way through the gate, where I turn to the left. There's a sign ahead – a wooden one, which reads 'public footpath' – and I turn, entering a narrow, slightly muddy pathway, flanked by wire fencing on one side and a tall hedge on the other… the boundary of Hope's property, I suppose.

After a short distance, the hedge comes to an abrupt end, and the path widens slightly, and I can see that it turns to the right, leading onto the cliff path, with a grassy knoll to one side and a low fence, bordering the sheer drop onto the rocks on the other.

I stand for a moment, admiring the view, the craggy coastline stretching before me, dotted with the occasional cottage or abandoned mine building in the distance. It's breathtaking. Quite literally, being as the wind is ferocious, catching in my throat and making my eyes water. At least I think that's the wind…

I turn again and start walking, at a slow but steady pace, weighing up the prospect of returning home and facing Brianna, against the idea of staying here and seeing Hope on a daily basis, knowing she'll never be anything other than the woman I've rented a cottage from… and the woman I've fallen hopelessly in love with. 'Hopeless'. It seems an appropriate description of how I feel, considering her name.

I walk for hours, wishing the wind would blow away the cobwebs in my head, or at least give me some clarity. But at the moment, all I can see, regardless of the wild, beautiful view in front of me, is Hope's face.

By the time the icy drizzle starts, and I turn to go back to the cottage, I still haven't decided what to do, other than to get back and get warm. After that? Who knows?

I'm frozen to the core, and soaked to the skin, and I take off my coat before I've even entered the cottage. I don't look over at the house, because I can't, but I let myself in and, standing on the doormat, I take off my muddy boots, and then I close the door.

The cottage is warm, but there's no fire in the hearth and I debate with myself whether to make one up, or shower. The fire wins and, depositing my boots and coat in the kitchen, I go through to the living room and crouch down in front of the fireplace, cleaning out the ash from last night and re-laying it with some screwed up newspaper and kindling wood. I'm about to put a match to it, when I notice there are only three logs left in the basket and, before I shower and get myself warm and dry, I put my shoes back on and carry the basket over to the wood store, which according to the card that Hope left, is alongside her house. I find the covered store easily, right beside the hedge. There's a gate, set in an archway in the tall evergreen, which has a sign marked 'Private' painted on it. I assume this leads to a separate area of the garden, reserved for Hope and her family and with that thought in mind, and I make light work of gathering up a basketful of fresh logs, before hastening back inside, telling myself that it's the rain that's forcing me to move so quickly, and not my fear of seeing Hope again.

Once the fire is alight, with a couple of logs burning well, I make my way into the bedroom, removing my wet clothes and putting them to one side, before going straight into the shower and turning it on. The water is hot and I'd like to say it's soothing, but I don't think there's much in the world that could soothe me at the moment, and once I feel warmed through, I step back out again, wrapping a towel around my hips, and pad through to the bedroom, where I find some clean jeans and a thick sweater, and put them on.

I wander back into the kitchen, and notice, by the clock on the microwave, that it's nearly two-thirty. I should probably eat something, although I'm not really hungry, and I open the fridge, checking out the contents, which I stashed quickly while waiting for Hope to come over earlier.

I bought cold meats, salad, cheese, fruit, some more vegetables, bacon, eggs, orange juice, some chicken breasts and a pack of minced beef. And I don't feel like eating any of it. Shutting the fridge door, I fill the kettle, turning it on, and cut myself a slice of Hope's fruit cake, putting it on a small plate, and while I wait for the kettle to boil, I wash out the cafetière from this morning, and put the cups in the dishwasher, trying hard not to remember the look on Hope's face when our conversation died… when she revealed she's married.

I lean back on the edge of the sink, lowering my head. It's odd, but I can't fathom why she accepted my invitation, if she's got a husband and a child at home. Obviously, I was only inviting her for coffee, and not to spend the rest of the day letting me make love to her in as many different ways as my very vivid imagination would permit – just the thought of which makes me groan out loud. But surely, with a family of her own, she could have switched the invitation around, and suggested I might like to go and have coffee with her, to meet her husband and son, couldn't she? Wouldn't that make more sense? Wouldn't that be more 'normal'?

Turning, I glance out of the window, frowning as I notice that there isn't a single child's toy in sight… not anywhere in the garden. There's not a cricket bat, or a bicycle, or even a football, lying abandoned on the lawn. But then I suppose, this is the 'shared' part of the garden, and maybe Hope has rules about her child not playing out here, and insists he sticks to their more private area instead.

With a cup of coffee in one hand and my cake in the other, I go back into the living room. The fire is blazing now and it's snug and warm, and I take a seat on the sofa, placing my mug and plate on the table in front of me and switching on the lamp on the low table at the end of the couch.

I'm not in the mood for television, and I doubt there will be anything on at this time on a Sunday anyway, so I get up again and wander to the bookshelves behind me. I could go and fetch one of my own books, but I'm intrigued by Hope's choices… not surprisingly.

The range is diverse, from classics to romance, from historical fiction, to a few reference books on the pre-Raphaelites, and several memoirs and biographies on famous political and entertainment figures. Feeling as though I've stepped into a library for the first time in years, I choose a book at random, from the second shelf down, a fairly new novel in the crime thriller genre, and take it back with me to the sofa.

A while later, my cake is eaten, my coffee is drunk and I'm lying along the length of the couch, one arm behind my head, engrossed. The book is absorbing, if confusing, and when I glance up, I'm surprised to see that it's completely dark outside.

I make a mental note of the page number and put the book down, getting up and stretching my legs, before going to the fire and adding a couple of fresh logs, and then picking up my plate and cup, carrying them through to the kitchen.

It's dark out here too, but I notice a light coming from Hope's house, from the window to the right of her front door. It's the window she stood at when she stared at me last night, when our eyes met and neither of us could look away.

Why did she do that?

I shake my head, put my cup and plate down and flick on the light, making it easier to block out the view. It doesn't matter why she did that, or why she does anything.

She's married.

End of story.

Chapter Eight

Hope

I wake with a heavy, depressed feeling.

I suppose that's normal for a lot of people on a Monday morning, but it makes no sense for me, being as in my life, one day is pretty much like any other – except for Saturdays, that is. As I was explaining to Logan… *No. Stop it.* I can't think about him…

Tears brim in my eyes again and I blink them away, remembering yesterday morning, which started so well, and ended so badly.

One minute he'd invited me for coffee and we were talking, quite freely and happily, just like normal, friendly people, and the next, he was quiet and sullen, and it felt like he was throwing me out of my own cottage. And when all's said and done, it is my own cottage.

I managed to make it back here before the tears actually fell, which was a relief. I'd have hated for him to see me crying. After all, he's got a perfect right to change his mind about wanting to spend time with me. Just because I read more into the situation than there was, and had decided to behave like a stupid, infatuated schoolgirl, isn't his fault, is it?

Even so, the change in him was astounding. He wasn't the same warm, amiable man I'd spent ages staring at the night before. He wasn't the same man I'd suddenly felt able to reveal my shyness and insecurities to. No… he was cold, distant, aloof. And I wanted to be anywhere but in his presence.

I cried for a while when I got back here, I'll admit that, and then I remembered that I'd promised to take Archie for a walk, so I snapped his lead to his collar and we headed out, sneaking past the cottage. I felt a bit silly doing that, but the thought of seeing Logan again was too much for me, especially as I knew my eyes would be swollen and my nose pink from all the tears I'd shed.

Archie and I turned right at the gate and I took him up into the woods. That was intentional. Even in January, there's usually someone walking along the coastal path and I really wasn't in the mood for seeing anyone. Not when I was still struggling to hold back my tears, remembering the way my thoughts had been turning, that I'd contemplated a 'fling' with Logan, that I'd gone so far as to imagine having sex on the kitchen table with him. I mean... what's the point in daydreams and fantasies? It's not as though I have any choice in how he feels about me, is it? Not that he feels anything at all. Evidently. What a joke.

Except it's not funny. It hurts.

The walk was cold, but then it is January. My least favourite month of the year. It always was, even before Greg was killed. But to make matters worse, Friday will mark the second anniversary of that fateful evening when the policeman knocked on my door, and broke the news that would change my life forever.

That wasn't the reason why tears kept filling my eyes as Archie and I hacked through the woodland pathway, or why I had to keep wiping them away with an old tissue I'd found in my coat pocket. After all, the memories of Greg hadn't bothered me earlier. I hadn't felt tearful when I'd woken up yesterday morning, or when I'd taken Archie for his walk first thing, or when I met Logan at the shop, and he walked me home again afterwards. I'd felt happy then. I'd felt alive, and hopeful, like there was something truly worthwhile to look forward to... and it was staying in my cottage.

And now that's all gone.

I glance from my bed over to the window, wishing I could see sunshine, or even daylight peeking around the edge of my curtains. I think that's one of the things I hate most about the winter; waking up to darkness. I've always felt like that, even when I was little, but I suppose I hate it even more now, because it gives me a sense of what my life might be like in a few years' time. Filled with darkness. I shake my head. "Stop being melodramatic," I mutter out loud, consoling myself that at least yesterday afternoon's storm seems to have passed. I was lucky and got back with Archie just before it started, and then we spent the rest of the day curled up on the sofa in the living room, watching old DVDs.

I remember closing my curtains when I came to bed last night though, and looking over at the cottage as I did so. The bedroom light was glowing and, for a moment, I wondered what Logan was doing, before I realised it was none of my business. That was when I resolved to avoid Mr Quinn for the rest of his stay. I always say my guests are entitled to their privacy, and the same applies to him. So, I'll keep myself to myself, and when it's time for him to leave, I'll wave him goodbye… and I'll go back to being lonely again.

Mondays are washing days. It's a routine fact, partly because I refuse to do it on Sundays, when I can spend time with my parents, or with Nick and Amy, or curled up on the couch feeling sorry for myself, but also because the guests have had the weekend to settle in, to come over and ask their questions, and work out any problems they might have with the cottage. That means that they tend to either go out for the day on Monday, or spend it tucked up in bed together, away from the world… depending on the purpose of their visit. Their absence, or pre-occupation, means I'm free to spend my morning up to my elbows in bedding, towels, linens and detergents, and my afternoon drying, ironing – where strictly necessary – and folding, before storing everything away again.

Today, I don't have any laundry to do for the cottage, being as there haven't been any guests there for the last two weeks, but I'm a creature of habit, so after Archie and I have returned from his early morning walk, and we've had breakfast, I go back upstairs and strip the bedding from my bed, bringing it back downstairs and putting it in the machine in the small utility room, at the back of the house, beyond the kitchen.

Throughout all of that, I manage to avoid looking out of the windows. In fact, since last night, I haven't glanced at the cottage at all, not even when I took Archie for his walk. I've made my resolution now and I intend to stick to it.

With the washing machine on a long cycle, I've got a choice. I can either get on with doing my accounts, which I never got around to yesterday, for obvious reasons… or I can keep my promise to Amy, and go down to the store for that chat she wanted.

It's not a difficult decision, and I go through to the lobby, sitting on the bottom of the stairs to put on my shoes. Archie jumps up from his bed, which is a surprise, being as we only came back from our walk about forty-five minutes ago.

"What's up, boy?" I ask, cradling his head. He nuzzles into me. "You want to come too?"

I'm about to tell him 'no', when it dawns on me that he might be a good 'get out of jail' card. I've got no idea what Amy wants to talk about, but part of me is still worried that she might have cooked up some kind of scheme to do with me and Logan. I was already dreading that prospect, but after what happened yesterday, I'm really not sure I could cope with it at all. And if I've got Archie tied up outside the shop, I've got a good excuse to make a quick getaway. I know it's underhand, and probably not fair on Archie, but I also know he wouldn't mind, not if he could understand the circumstances, because he's loyal to a fault.

"Okay," I say and he jumps up, his front paws on my knees, his snout buried in my hair. "Okay… okay. I get it. You're pleased."

He backs off and I stand, reaching for his lead and snapping it to his collar, before grabbing my coat and keys.

I keep my head down, passing the cottage, and once we're at the store, I tie Archie's lead to the hook outside.

"I won't be long," I tell him and he sits, obediently, knowing he's not allowed inside, but that when I do bring him here, I never leave him outside for any great length of time.

Inside, there are no customers, and Amy looks up at the sound of the bell, a smile forming on her lips.

"Hello," she says, jumping down from her stool.

"Hi."

She frowns as I approach, looking closely at me. "Are you okay?" she asks.

"Yes, I'm fine."

Her frown deepens, but instead of pushing for more information, she calls, "Nick?" over my shoulder. I turn just as he appears from behind the end of the aisle, a bottle of olive oil in his hand.

"Yes, sweetheart?"

"Can you cover for ten minutes, while I take Hope out the back?"

"Of course," he says and makes his way towards us. "Are you okay?" he says to me as he gets closer.

"Yes, I'm fine," I repeat.

His frown reflects that of his wife, and I know I'm not fooling either of them. One look in the mirror this morning told me that my eyes were still swollen from all the crying I did yesterday, but I'm not in the mood for explaining and hopefully they'll put it down to the impending anniversary of Greg's death.

"Leave her alone," Amy says, defending me and Nick holds up his hands in surrender, letting me step behind the counter ahead of him. It's a tight squeeze behind here with three of us, but Nick leans down and kisses his wife's cheek, which makes her sigh and look up into his eyes, before she opens the door into the back part of the shop.

"Come on, Hope," she says. "Let's leave him to it."

I follow her through into the kitchen, where we sit together at the small table, Amy leaning forward on her elbows, a sparkle in her eyes. I'm intrigued and slightly scared now.

"So… what's all the mystery about?" I ask, desperate to get this over with.

"I'm pregnant!" she blurts out, grinning broadly.

I hadn't expected that in the slightest, but my face instantly forms into a huge smile, regardless of my own problems.

"Oh Amy, that's fantastic." I get up again and go around the table to her. She stands and we hug. "How far gone are you?" I ask.

"It's due at the beginning of August," she says as we both sit again, with me beside her now, "which let's face it, is absolutely appalling timing, being as that's our busiest time of the year, what with holiday-makers and passing tourists, and everything."

Despite the issues she's raising, I can see she's overjoyed.

"We found out just after New Year," she admits, taking a deep breath, "and I've been dying to tell you, but we didn't feel like we could let anyone else know until we'd told both sets of parents... and with my mum and dad being away..." She looks contrite and I reach over and place my hand on her arm.

"Don't worry about that... I'm just thrilled for you. For both of you."

"You're going to make the best auntie in the world, you know that, don't you?" she says.

"I'll do my best," I reply, even as her expression softens, although I don't mention, and nor does she, the fact that, by the time her child turns ten, I'll be struggling to see him or her.

"Nick's been amazing," she adds, changing the subject that neither of us had actually raised yet. "He insists I sit down all the time, and I haven't stacked a shelf, or cooked an evening meal since we found out."

"Do think he can keep that up for nine months?" I ask, and she chuckles.

"I think he'll try, although he might drive me insane first." She stops talking and turns in her seat, so she's facing me. "Now... with that piece of news out of the way, are you going to tell me what's bothering you?"

"Who says anything's bothering me?" I reply, trying to sound as nonchalant as possible.

"I do. You look like you spent the night crying."

I did.

I blink a few times, to halt the tears that are threatening to fall again.

"Hope? What is it? Nothing's happened with your eyes, has it? Nothing's changed?"

I shake my head. "No. And I will tell you about it," I whisper through the lump in my throat. "But not today. Okay?"

She hesitates, just for a moment, and then nods her head. "Okay. But promise you'll call me if you need to chat."

I nod this time. "I—I'd better be going. I left Archie outside. He was desperate to come with me." That's not actually a lie, although I know I could have made him stay behind, if I'd wanted to.

"Probably because he's got a sixth sense for when there's something wrong with you," Amy says, getting to her feet.

"Probably," I reply, and she gives me a firm hug.

"Remember, call me if you want to talk," she says.

"I will."

I will. Just not yet.

We make our way back out into the shop, which is still empty. I'm grateful for that, being as I'm fairly certain most of the other villagers wouldn't respect my privacy in the same way that Amy and Nick do, and that rumours would be rife within the hour about my tearful state.

"Congratulations, Dad," I say, and Nick turns around, grinning.

"Thanks," he replies.

I go around the other side of the counter and Amy steps up beside her husband, nestling into him as he puts his arm around her. They look the picture of happiness and I feel genuinely thrilled for them.

I start moving towards the door, and Amy says, "Call me," in a firm, knowing voice.

"I will," I repeat, giving her my best attempt at a smile, before I let myself out into the chill morning air, and close the door behind me, turning around to Archie, and letting out a small yelp of surprise when I find Logan crouched beside him, rubbing his head.

So much for avoiding him…

Logan

I managed to tear myself away from the book long enough to make myself some supper last night, although I only had cheese on toast, because I still wasn't feeling very hungry, and afterwards, I went back to the book again, enjoying the distraction of the convoluted plot. It stopped me thinking about anything else at least. Then at about eleven o'clock, I went to bed, and presumably because of the emotional and physical exertions of the day, I fell fast asleep. Again.

This morning, after my shower and breakfast, on coming back into the living room to straighten the sofa, I've discovered that the book, which I'm about three chapters away from finishing, is actually the first in a series of six. I feel kind of relieved that at least I managed to start on book one, and also pleased that the story will continue to keep my mind occupied for the foreseeable future. I decide that, although the weather is better today, and I probably should be outdoors, I'd rather stay inside and read. Not only is it a good distraction, but there's less chance of seeing Hope if my head is buried in a book.

With that in mind, I go back to the kitchen to make myself a cup of coffee, only to discover I'm nearly out of milk. I don't know why I didn't notice it at breakfast, but then I suppose I have got a lot on my mind, and while I know I should have bought some yesterday, running into Hope was a bit of a diversion, not to mention my earlier text messages from Brianna and my argument with Rachel, both of which put paid to me actually writing a shopping list, which I suppose would have been useful.

I decide not to worry about wearing a coat, especially as mine still feels a little damp after my soaking yesterday, and putting on my shoes, I pick up the keys, make sure I've got my wallet, and head out to the store. I don't even glance at Hope's house, but keep my head down until I'm out on the main road. It's very different out here today, with even a hint of blue in the sky and the promise of sunshine, although it's nowhere near bright enough to lift my mood.

That said, I can't help the slight smile that forms on my lips as I approach the store and see the most beautiful border collie, tied up to a hook on the wall beside the door. I know, as a vet, I'm supposed to be impartial when it comes to animals, but I have a soft spot when it comes to border collies and this one is absolutely perfect, the markings on his face completely symmetrical, the white elements utterly pure and his eyes a deep rich brown. As I approach, he notices me and stands, raising his head, clearly wanting to be petted.

I crouch beside him. "Hey, boy," I say, tickling behind his ears, which he seems to like, as he nuzzles into me for some more attention. "Who's your lucky owner then?"

He seems very pleased to see me, even though he's never met me, and I'm just feeling for the name tag on his collar, to find out what I should call him, when I hear a squeal – a very female squeal – sounding from behind me. I turn and jump to my feet, almost wanting to squeal myself, at the sight of Hope, halted in the shop doorway.

"Hello," I manage to say.

"H—Hello." She's stuttering again, and her eyes lower to the dog, who's still standing by my feet, although he's gazing at her.

"Is he yours?" I ask and she smiles. *Dear God.* No-one has the right to look that beautiful. And yet, she does… despite the fact that her eyes seem different, somehow…

"Yes," she replies, coming closer and resting her hand on the dog's head. "This is Archie."

I try really hard not to show my surprise. Her dog is called Archie? I quickly run through our conversation yesterday in my head, when she said Archie would be waiting for her and that she'd promised to take him for a walk. Of course, it makes perfect sense…

I can feel a smile spreading across my lips, but I hold it in check. Just because her son isn't called Archie, doesn't mean she doesn't have children… and, whichever way I look at it, she still has a husband. She said so herself, so I seriously need to control my reactions to her.

"He's lovely," I say, focusing on the dog. "How old is he? I'd say he's around two, or three, but that's just a professional guess."

"He's two," she replies. "I bought him when… I mean, I—I got him just after…" She stops talking, hesitates, opens her mouth to speak and then closes it again. Then she squints at something over my shoulder, further down the road, I think, and I turn to see what's distracted her, but there's nothing in sight, other than the empty road, a handful of houses, the church with its surrounding graveyard, and a few bare trees. Looking back at her again, I'm stunned to see tears in her eyes, and instinctively take a step closer.

"What's wrong?" I ask.

"Nothing," she replies, her voice barely audible. She bends to untie Archie's lead from the hook and, acting on impulse alone, I take her hand in mine. She glances at the connection, and I let her go, realising it's wrong to hold her hand, even though every bone and sinew in my body is aching to touch her. *I can't. She's married. She's off limits.*

"Sorry," I say quietly. "I didn't mean to upset you."

"It's fine," she replies.

"No, it's not. Why would you say that, Hope? I mean… why do you keep saying that, when you're so obviously not fine?"

"It doesn't matter," she says, because that's so much better than 'fine', and then she looks at me, directly into my eyes, her own overflowing with tears now. "I need to go," she mutters, and I reluctantly step back, letting her pass, Archie walking obediently beside her. I stand and watch them, until they disappear through the gate of Orchard House, wondering what on earth just happened.

After a minute or two, I come back to my senses, and turning away, I let myself into the shop, glancing over to the counter, where Nick and Amy are cuddled up together. I try not to feel jealous of them. I try even harder not to wish that could be me and Hope, because I know it can't, and instead of dwelling, I go over to the fridge and pick up a carton of milk, taking it to the counter, with the intention of getting out of here as soon as possible, getting back to the cottage and burying myself in that book again, before anything else goes wrong.

"How are you getting on?" Nick asks, as I hand him a five pound note in payment. "Settling in alright?"

"I suppose," I mutter, without thinking.

"Is something wrong?" Amy asks. She sounds concerned, rather than nosy.

I wish I could tell them. I'd like to. Partly because it would do me good to get it off my chest, but also because I know something's very wrong with Hope. She needs someone to talk to and I don't think that's me at the moment. But they're her friends. Maybe they can help? I open my mouth to explain, but stop myself just in time. The fact that they're her friends is the very reason I can't say a word to them. I can't tell them how much I care about Hope, or how worried I am, any more than I can tell them I've fallen in love with her. They'd probably feel obliged to tell her, and then where would we be?

"No, everything's fine," I reply, echoing Hope's mantra, as I pick up my carton of milk from the counter.

"It doesn't look fine," Nick says. "Has something happened between you and Hope?"

My head shoots up. "What makes you say that?"

"Just the fact that she looked like she'd spent half the night crying, and you look as though someone just ran over your pet cat..." His voice fades into the background. She'd been crying? Of course. That's what was different. Her eyes were swollen.

"Did she say what was wrong?" I ask, interrupting Nick's flow, even though I imagine that, whatever Hope's problem was, it was almost certainly something personal, and therefore none of my business.

"No."

I shake my head. "Well, I think I might just have made things worse," I reply and Amy steps forward.

"How?" She frowns at me.

"I didn't mean to upset her," I explain, in the face of Amy's searching expression. "I was just asking about her dog, that's all. I asked how old he is and she started to tell me about when she'd bought him, and then she went quiet and looked over my shoulder, towards the church, and it seemed like she was going to cry. I've got no idea why though."

"Oh, I see. Well, that makes perfect sense," Amy says, relaxing a little, although I notice she's still not smiling.

"It does?" It doesn't to me.

"Yes. She was probably upset because she was remembering that she'd bought Archie as a puppy, a couple of years ago, so she'd have some company after her husband died. Looking at the church would have set her off, because he's buried..."

I can see Amy's lips are still moving, but I have no idea what she's saying. I can't even hear the sound of her voice, because of three words: 'her husband died', which are repeating, over and over, in my brain.

"Sorry," I blurt out, and without waiting for a reply, I run from the shop.

Chapter Nine

Hope

How much more humiliation do I have to take?

And why on earth can't I just tell Logan the truth about my life? That was the perfect opportunity to do it, so why didn't I?

Well, I suppose the reason is obvious. It's because I know, deep down, it's none of his business. I don't mean anything to him, after all, so my personal life and my personal problems don't mean a thing to him either. He's a guest here, plain and simple.

The only problem is, even thinking like that hurts like hell.

I make it back to the house and let myself in, taking Archie's lead off and letting him settle into his basket, while I grab some kitchen towel to wipe away my tears. I've got to stop crying. It's pathetic and pointless, and it's not going to get me anywhere.

I'm startled by a knocking on my door, and clutching the tissue in my hand, I take a breath, and open it.

"Why didn't you tell me?" Logan says, before I've even had the chance to properly take in the fact that he's standing on my doorstep, breathing heavily and clutching a carton of milk in his hand.

"Tell you what?"

"About your husband."

I take an even deeper breath. "Because it's personal." *And because you're not interested in me… not like I am in you.*

He pauses and then says, "Okay," while tilting his head, first one way, and then the other, "but when people are trying to get to know each other, don't they usually reveal personal things? Isn't that how it works, when you're making friends?"

I stare at him, trying to understand what he just said. 'Making friends'? 'Getting to know each other'? Is that what he wants? Is that what *I* want? If it is, I should also tell him about my RP, as well as my late husband, shouldn't I? *If* we're going to be friends, that is.

"If they want to get to know each other, I suppose," I reply, uncertain of what else to say.

He moves forward, leaning his hand on the doorframe, right beside my head. "Don't you want to get to know me?" he asks.

I can't reply, because at the moment, I'm so confused, I don't know what I want, but my body clearly has other ideas, because I take a step back, letting him in. He glances down at me, and without a word, moves inside and I close the door behind him.

"W—Would you like a coffee?" I ask, stuttering. It's a habit I seem to have developed since his arrival.

"I'd love one." He smiles and, despite my best intentions, my heart flips over in my chest, and we go through to the kitchen.

Archie looks up, his tail wagging, and Logan kneels down to stroke his head. "You really do have a lovely dog," he says.

"Thank you."

He stands again. "Would it be okay if I store my milk in your fridge for the time being?" he asks and I nod my head, taking the carton from him and placing it on the shelf inside the door.

"I—I'll put the kettle on," I say, turning back to him.

"Okay," he replies. "And then maybe we can sit down, and you can tell me about your husband… or, if you'd rather not, I'll tell you about my fiancée."

I feel as though all the air has just been sucked from my lungs, all thoughts of coffee and kettles and baring my soul forgotten in an instant. "F—Fiancée?" I mutter.

"Yes."

"You're engaged?"

He's still smiling. "No. And that's rather the point."

I've got no idea what he's talking about, but he pulls out a chair at the kitchen table for me to sit, and within moments, he's right beside me.

"I think we've both got stories to tell, and I think we both need to hear what the other one has to say, but it's entirely up to you…" he says. "Do you want to go first? Or shall I start?"

"I'll go first." I decide that I'd rather get my story out of the way, at least as far as Greg is concerned. As for my RP… well, I'll see what happens, and where this fiancée of his fits in, before I decide about that.

"Sure?" he says, tilting his head again, just slightly this time. "You don't have to."

"No, it's fine." His smile drops and he frowns, although I don't know why, and before I can spend too long thinking about it, I clear my throat. "My husband's name was Greg…"

"I know… you mentioned him yesterday."

I blush, recalling our conversation, how difficult that was, and how much I cried afterwards. Even now, tears prick my eyes and Logan reaches over, placing his large, warm hand on mine.

"I'm sorry," he whispers and I look up to see the concerned expression on his face. "This must be hard for you."

"N—Not for the reason you're probably thinking," I manage to say, using my free hand to wipe away the tear that's just trickled onto my cheek. Logan takes a deep breath, and so do I, focusing on our entwined hands, as I continue with my story. "We met at college," I explain. "We started going out at the end of our first year."

"How old were you?" Logan asks.

"Seventeen."

"That's very young," he says quietly.

"Yes," I reply, adding, "He was my first boyfriend." I don't tell him that Greg talked me into having sex with him after we'd only been together for a couple of weeks, although I feel myself blush at the memory. "After college," I continue, "neither of us wanted to go to university. Greg didn't see the point and… well, I've already explained my reasons… so, we both got jobs. I carried on at the estate agents, and Greg went to work at a local pharmaceutical company, in their sales department. Then, when I was twenty-two, my grandmother died and I inherited this house from her, and Greg and I decided to move in together. I'd been renting a flat in Truro, for about a year by then, and Greg used to divide his time between there and his parents' place, depending on how much washing he needed doing at the time." I look up and manage a smile, and Logan smiles back, encouragingly. "We fixed up the house first, and then started work on the barn… which became the cottage."

"And I'm guessing that, at some point, Greg proposed?" Logan prompts.

"Yes. The builders had just started working on the barn, but we were still decorating the house at the time," I explain. "We were finishing off painting the living room, which we'd left until last, and he turned around, with a paintbrush in his hand and said, 'Why don't we get married?'."

Logan stares at me for a moment. "Just like that?"

"Yes," I reply. "I said yes, obviously," I add, before he can make any remarks about Greg's unromantic proposal, "and we were married five months later."

"How old were you by then?" he asks.

"Twenty-four."

"That's still very young," he replies.

"Yes, I suppose it is."

"And had you given up working at the estate agents by then?"

"I gave it up a couple of weeks before the wedding. The builders still hadn't quite finished, but giving up work meant I could focus more on the renovations at the cottage. We got married in the November, and I wanted to have the cottage ready to take bookings for the following spring… it was hard work."

"But Greg helped?" he suggests and I try hard not to laugh.

"No. Greg said he'd had enough of decorating by then, and as far as he was concerned, the cottage was my project… my business. And in any case, he was away quite a lot with work, and he spent his spare time playing golf, or going into Truro or St Austell with his friends."

"Were you lonely?" Logan asks, perceptively.

I shrug my shoulders. "I was fine," I say, almost to myself.

"No you weren't. You were lonely."

"How did you know?" I look at him more closely.

"It's written all over your face. You were lonely. You still are. And you certainly weren't happy with him," he adds. "Were you? That's what you meant just now when I said about you finding this hard. I don't know why you had tears in your eyes, but it had nothing to do with your husband... did it?"

"No," I reply, without thinking. "No, it didn't. Not really. Like I said, talking about this *is* hard, but not for the reasons you might think."

"I know. It's hard because it means opening up about yourself, and you've got used to hiding behind a wall of 'I'm fine', to mask your unhappiness, haven't you?"

I stare at him, stunned. "Yes," I admit.

He shakes his head. "You don't have to look so surprised. It's not difficult to work out. You've had years of practice, from the sounds of things."

"What does that mean?"

He leans forward. "It means that Greg liked to have his cake, and eat it," he says, sounding almost bitter. "He continued to live the life of a bachelor, but with all the advantages of having a wife at his beck and call, whenever he wanted."

"It wasn't quite like that," I say, defending myself, as much as Greg.

"Really?" he replies. "So how was it then?"

"Well, he wasn't that interested in having me at his beck and call, if you must know." I lower my head, wondering why I blurted that out. It may be true, but what on earth possessed me to say it aloud?

"Do you mean he cheated?" The bitterness in Logan's voice has turned to anger now, which rather surprises me, being as this really has nothing to do with him. It's my marriage we're talking about, not his.

"Not as far as I know. He just... he just wasn't interested." Why am I telling him all this? I honestly have no idea. But the thing is, now I've started talking, I can't seem to stop. "I sometimes used to ask him," I continue, looking up at Logan again, to find he's staring at me, his eyes soft and filled with kindness… and something else… "I used to ask him if he loved me."

"And what did he say?" His anger has gone, and his voice is much warmer now.

"He'd either say 'yes', or 'of course', but he never said the words himself, and it didn't feel like love to me. Not the kind of love I wanted." I stop talking suddenly as it dawns on me that I've just told him more about my marriage and myself than I've ever told anyone else. Including my mother and my best friend. "Sorry," I say suddenly.

"What for?"

"I probably shouldn't have told you all that."

"Why not?"

"Well, because it's not the sort of thing you say to a stranger, is it?" I reason, and he smiles, looking down for a moment, before raising his head again and staring directly into my eyes.

"Ahh, but I'm not a stranger, am I? Not any more." I smile myself now, and shake my head slowly from side to side, admitting the truth behind his words, because sitting here like this, he feels like the opposite of a stranger to me. "What kind of love did you want?" he asks.

"Sorry?" I can feel the blush creeping up my cheeks.

"I asked what kind of love you wanted… or you want." His face is completely serious now.

"Um…"

"Hope?" he pushes.

"Well… I suppose I've always felt that it should be more than two people agreeing to live together and not argue too much, simply because neither of them is willing, or able, to admit they got it wrong." I'm keeping the conversation about me and Greg, rather than admitting that what I'd really like is the thrill of knowing that, when Logan looks at me, there's more behind his gaze than friendship.

I know I'm still blushing, and he's still staring at me, and I wonder if he can read my mind. But instead of pushing me further, he says, "So what happened to Greg?"

I sit back in my seat. "It was a normal Wednesday evening, as far as I was concerned," I explain, recalling that night, almost exactly two years ago. "We'd had a big row the previous day, because I'd been looking into us going away on holiday before the cottage got too booked up, but when he'd come home from work and I'd made the suggestion, he'd flown off the handle and told me it was out of the question. I tried to reason with him that we hadn't had a holiday in all the time we'd been married, other than our short break in North Devon for our anniversary, and his golfing and business trips – which didn't include me, obviously – and he said that was my fault, because my life revolved around the cottage. I didn't think he was being very fair, considering he was never here, but he said some horrible things to me, and I went to bed really upset, while Greg slept in the spare room. The next morning, he came into our bedroom before going to work, and apologised for calling me names, and said we'd talk about it that night, and maybe ask my parents to look after this place for us, so we could have a few days away together. It seemed like a reasonable compromise, and was probably more than I'd expected. But then, when he didn't come home by nine o'clock, I started to worry. He used to hate me checking up on him, but he was never normally so late home without texting to let me know, so I was just about to call his mobile, when someone knocked on the door, and I opened it to find a policeman standing there. He came inside and told me that Greg had been involved in an accident and had been seriously injured. He took me to the hospital…" I stop talking just for a second, and then start again, the thoughts whirring around my head. "It's funny," I say, without a trace of humour. "I didn't love Greg. If you were to ask me why I married him, I honestly couldn't tell you. I know that, because I've asked myself that question over and over… even before he died. And – you're absolutely right – I wasn't happy with him… but when that policeman stood in the hall, with such a grave look on his face, I think I knew then that my life was about to change, forever. I couldn't realise how much, or what would happen to me afterwards…" I let out a long sigh, knowing I've almost strayed from the self-imposed confines of my story, but Logan doesn't seem to have noticed and doesn't interrupt. He doesn't move at all. "The journey to the hospital was horrendous," I recall, returning to my recollections of that fateful evening. "It was freezing cold and there was ice on the roads because it had rained earlier in the day, so we had to take it slowly. I remember the policeman apologising, telling me about every five minutes that it wouldn't take much longer, and thinking to myself that I didn't care how long it took, but then feeling guilty for being so heartless. Greg was my husband, after all... I ought to have at least cared about him." I feel a tear fall to my cheek and pull my hand from beneath Logan's to brush it away. "He was dead by the time we arrived," I manage to say, before the sob leaves my mouth and I start to cry, loud, wrenching tears. The kind of tears I probably should have cried when Greg died, but somehow never managed to. Until now.

I hear the chair scrape across the floor, and the next thing I know, I'm being lifted to my feet and into Logan's arms. I bury my head into his firm chest, inhaling the soapy vanilla scent of him, and although I have no idea how or why, I feel like I've finally found my safe place. I've finally come home.

Logan

I let her cry on me. She clearly needs this, perhaps more than even she knows.

It feels good to hold her, and to comfort her. It feels even better to know that she's free, and that the last twenty-four hours of hell have been nothing more than a misunderstanding. But at the moment, that doesn't matter.

I want to help her. I want to take away the pain and sorrow in her eyes, and stop it hurting. Because even if she and Greg weren't happy – and it seems they weren't, or at least she wasn't – losing someone who's been such a big part of your life for ten years has still got to hurt.

I also want to stop her from hiding, from saying she's 'fine', when she so clearly isn't. Not all the time, anyway. That much is obvious.

Eventually, she shifts in my arms, and pulls away, leaning back and looking up at me.

"Sorry," she whispers, her eyes still glistening and her cheeks damp with tears.

"Don't apologise," I reply and then glance around, spying a roll of kitchen towel beside the draining board. "Stay here," I tell her, and go to fetch her some, bringing it back and handing it to her. We both sit back down, while Hope wipes her eyes. "Are you okay now?" I ask, once she looks up again.

"Yes, thank you. And I really am sorry."

"What for?"

"For crying," she says, as though it should be obvious to me.

"Hope, you've just told me about your husband's death. You're entitled to cry."

She gazes at me, her head tilted just slightly to the right. "Even if I didn't love him?" she murmurs. "Even if I wasn't happy with him?"

I suck in a breath and reply, "Yes. Who knows, if he'd lived, maybe you would have had the time to understand that pretending things are 'fine' isn't all it's cracked up to be, and you'd have talked it through with Greg and been able to work things out… or perhaps he'd have come to his senses and realised all by himself that you're worth so much more than 'fine', and that he had it better than most men dream of, and then he might have put in a bit more effort, tried harder, and given you the kind of life – the kind of love – you deserved. But you didn't have the time to do that… either of you. And no amount of regret is going to change that."

She's staring at me now, wide eyed. "I'm sorry," she says, yet again. "What did you just say?"

I smile. "Which part?"

"All of it."

I shake my head, still smiling, and take her hand in mine. "I just said that, if Greg had lived you might have had the opportunity to realise that you should never pretend things are 'fine' when they're not, which might have meant you'd have been able to work it out with him… one way or the other. Or that maybe he'd have woken up to how utterly amazing you are, and given you a life that was so much better than 'fine', because you're worth it… or words to that effect."

"I—I thought that was what you said," she whispers, as though she's in a trance.

"I did. Twice. And that means I must be right."

"But… but you can't say that." She's frowning now, more doubtful. "You don't know me. You don't know anything about me."

"No, but I'm getting to know you. That's what this is all about, remember? And I know you well enough to understand that you're worth so much more than spending ten years with someone who won't put you first. Plain and simple. All the time. Every time."

Her frown slowly clears, and she blinks until her eyes aren't brimming with tears anymore, and then a miracle happens. She smiles, that most perfect of smiles. And it's aimed right at me.

I wish I could kiss her, but I can't. Not yet. Not until she knows everything. So instead I ask, "Do you want to hear my tale of woe now? Or do you want a break?"

She hesitates for a moment, making me wonder if she's finished her story yet, but then she sighs and sits back in her chair. "No, I'd like to hear your story," she says. "But I think I should probably make us that coffee first, don't you?"

"Yes. I think we might need it."

"Why? Is your story that bad?" She gets up from her chair.

"I don't know. I'll let you be the judge of that."

She's holding the kettle under the tap and turns, frowning at me again. "Sounds ominous," she says.

"It's meant to."

"Oh," she replies, switching off the tap. Then without another word, she busies herself preparing coffee, and I watch, admiring her curves when she reaches to fetch the mugs from the cupboard, and the way her hair bounces and shimmers under the down lighters, every time she twists and turns. Her husband must have been mad to have neglected her in the way he did, because I know that if she were mine, she would be the sum of my world… because as she already is, and she's nowhere near being mine. Yet.

She comes and sits beside me again, and it's only then that I notice the cafetière is already on the table, with two mugs, the milk, and a sugar bowl. I missed her putting those out, so absorbed was I in her, and her alone.

"I don't know where to start," I say as she pours the hot, dark liquid into the cups.

"Why don't you tell me why you decided to come here?" she suggests. "I'm assuming that's got something to do with it... after all, my cottage is a very odd choice for someone on their own."

I smile. "Yes, I suppose it is. Although to be fair, I wasn't overly interested in the decor, or the setting, or the price. I just wanted to get away for two weeks."

"I'll try not to take that personally," she says, and I'm relieved to hear that teasing humour back in her voice. It's been absent since yesterday morning, since our misunderstanding, but it's there again now.

"Please don't," I reply. "It's really nothing personal at all. It's just that I needed to be anywhere but at home."

"Because...?" she says, prompting me.

"Because, being at home was only going to remind me that I was due to get married... except my fiancée had unilaterally decided that monogamy wasn't part of the deal."

"Oh God." She plonks the cafetière back on the table with a thump. "That's awful, Logan." Her hand comes to rest on my arm. "How long had you been engaged?"

"Ahh... well..." I say, facing the moment of truth. "I'd love to say we'd been together for years, and that she was the only woman for me, but I'd be lying if I did that. The truth is that I met her last September." I can see the surprise on Hope's face, made obvious by the widening of her eyes, and confirmed by the fact that she pulls her hand away from my arm, which is a shame. "Until I met Brianna – she was my fiancée, by the way," I continue in the hope of salvaging the situation somehow, "I'll admit that I'd never really thought of settling down." Judging from the way her brow is furrowing, I'm not sure I'm helping my cause, but I carry on nonetheless. "I'd always considered myself to be young, free and single... well, free and single, anyway. The young part was rapidly passing me by. But then I met Brianna at my sister's thirtieth birthday party…"

"Is this the same sister who sent you a message yesterday?" Hope asks and I smile. At least she's interested and her frown has faded.

"Yes. I've only got one sister… and she's more than enough."

She chuckles and puts a splash of milk into her coffee, offering the jug to me. I copy her action and then take a sip.

"So you met your fiancée four months ago?" Hope clarifies.

"Yes. I'm not sure which of us swept the other off of their feet, but we were engaged within six weeks."

"Who proposed to whom?" she asks.

"I proposed. But there were no paintbrushes involved, in case you're wondering."

She shakes her head, looking up at me through her eyelashes and smiling. "What was involved, if you don't mind me asking?"

"Well, I didn't make any grand gestures. I didn't hire an aeroplane to fly around with a banner hanging out of the back, or put a sign up on the scoreboard at a football match…"

"I'm glad to hear it," she says, grimacing slightly.

"I just took her out to dinner," I continue. "It was romantic, I guess… and at least, after all my careful planning, she said 'yes'." She didn't actually say anything, if I recall. What she did was to leap off the chair and throw herself at me. I only just had time to get up from my seat – having decided against going down on one knee in a public place – before she was smothering me with kisses. The 'yes' was a given.

"I don't know why you sound so surprised," Hope replies and then blushes, and lowers her head, realising the compliment she's just paid me, I think. Even if she didn't intend it, I'll take it. At the moment, I'll take pretty much anything she's offering.

"Hindsight?" I suggest, as a plausible answer and she looks up again, smiling sympathetically. "Still," I add, going back to my story, "at the time, everything seemed rosy, and we talked things through later that night and decided we didn't want to wait to get married, so we fixed the date for the last Saturday in January…"

"*This* January?" Hope queries. "You mean… the weekend after next?"

"Yes."

"Oh. You weren't kidding when you said you were due to get married, were you?"

"No. No, I wasn't. We called and visited our respective families that weekend, and the first thing my relatives assumed was that Brianna was pregnant. She wasn't. And once I'd made that clear, they set about telling me how impetuous I was being, how mad I was, that we barely knew each other. The most vocal of the lot was my sister, Rachel, which was a bit rich, considering Brianna is a friend of hers and that she'd introduced us in the first place… but as it turned out, Rachel was right." I pause for a moment, remembering our argument at the time, and thinking about the fact that, although she's been quick enough to call me an idiot, she's never actually said 'I told you so', which is an achievement for Rachel. "Brianna and I agreed right at the outset that we'd sell our individual flats – mine in Richmond and hers in Chiswick – and that we'd buy a house together after the wedding, because there wouldn't be time to get that organised in advance, and I took the opportunity to have my place decorated, because it needed it, and I knew I'd probably get a better price if it looked a bit less like a third year uni student lived there, rather than a reasonably responsible, fairly well house-trained adult. Because of that, I'd been living at Brianna's flat for a couple of weeks, but on the night in question, I left work early, because my last two appointments cancelled. I let myself into her place and heard the noises coming from the bedroom…"

"What? You mean you actually caught her… with her lover?" she says, stunned.

"Yes. I knew what was going on before I got into the room. It was obvious from the noises they were making."

"I know how that feels," Hope says and I stop, sitting back and staring at her.

"I thought you said Greg didn't cheat?"

"He didn't," she replies, smiling. "Not as far as I know. But you're forgetting about the cottage."

"What about the cottage?" I ask, feeling confused.

"Well, I've made a point of promoting it as the perfect romantic getaway for couples, in case you didn't notice."

"I did," I say, rolling my eyes.

"And that means I hear all sorts," she says, pursing her lips and trying not to smile. "I've learnt to keep my head down and not look," she adds, "just in case I see something I can't un-see."

Her face clouds over for a second, but quickly clears and I watch while she sips from her cup. She looks thoughtful, like she wants to say something, but then she focuses her eyes on me again.

"You were saying?" she prompts, although I can't remember anything at all now. I'm just enjoying looking into Hope's eyes. "You were telling me you'd caught them together?" she says, after an unreasonably long pause.

"Yes. I was. Although I wish I could un-see the scene in Brianna's bedroom," I remark and Hope puts her cup back down, placing her hand in mine. I give hers a squeeze, feeling the warmth and reassurance of her small fingers in mine. "They were in her bed... she was on top..."

"You don't have to give me the details," she says suddenly, then adds, "I mean, you can, if you want to... if it helps. But you don't have to..."

"Would you mind if I did?" I ask her. "It's just... I haven't told anyone else this. Not even my sister. But I want to tell you, if that's okay?"

"If it's what you need to do..." Her voice fades, but she keeps her eyes fixed on mine.

"Brianna was on top," I repeat, "and I could tell from the amount of noise she was making that she was... well, approaching a vital moment, shall we say... I couldn't see who the man was though, because Brianna was obscuring my vision. At the time, I wasn't sure I wanted to know. But then, I heard his voice. I heard him urging her on, telling her how close he was... and I knew exactly who it was..."

"Oh God. You mean, you knew him?" Hope whispers.

"Yes. I'd have known his voice anywhere. It was my little brother, Zach."

Chapter Ten

❦

Hope

His little brother? Did he really just say that the man he caught in bed with is fiancée was his little brother? That's even enough of a bombshell to deflect me from the fact that I've almost interrupted his story twice, by revealing my other little – okay, not so little – secret. But I'm glad I didn't now, because judging from the expression on Logan's face, I think I need to focus on him for the time being, and forget my own problems.

"Your little brother?" I say out loud.

"Yes. He's three years younger than me. And he was supposed to be my best man…" He almost manages a smile. "I guess he was just proving that point… to all three of us."

He's still gripping my hand and, although I'm tempted to just let him, after that comment, I feel like holding hands is not enough. It's nowhere near enough. So I pull free of him, my heart heaving in my chest at the look of disappointment on his face as I stand up beside him.

"Do you want a hug?" I ask, because I'm not physically capable of pulling him to his feet, like he did with me.

He stands himself now. "Yes," he replies and I go to put my arms around him, but he clasps them in his hands, just above my elbows, holding me away from him. "But can I say something first?" he adds.

"Of course." I take a half step back, waiting.

"I need to make it clear to you that, while I really want a hug, it's not for the same reason as you did just now." I can feel the confusion etching itself onto my face, but before I can say anything, he answers my unasked question. "I'm not heartbroken," he says.

"Neither am I," I explain and he smiles.

"Maybe not, but I think you've got a lot more pent up emotions going on inside you than I have… I don't feel anything other than hurt and angry. And in all honesty, that's just a male pride thing, because she had sex with my little brother. I'm not interested in seeing her, or talking to her again, and Zach hadn't better come near me anytime soon, but I'm not heartbroken. Not at all."

Why is he telling me that? "But you were engaged, Logan. You must have loved her," I reason, trying to get him to understand his own feelings.

"I thought I did, but looking back, I think I was more in love with *being* with her. She was beautiful, at least on the outside, and I was blinded by that, into thinking there was more to her than what was visible on the surface. There wasn't."

I nod my head, because I understand what he's saying a lot better than he probably thinks I do. Greg was handsome. He was very handsome indeed. It's what attracted me to him in the first place. It's certainly what made me sleep with him so early on in our relationship, and it's probably what kept me with him, even when I realised things weren't what they might have been. But it wasn't enough.

I lean into Logan, without any further words, and put my arms around his waist, my head on his chest, and he pulls me close. Even through his thick sweater, I can hear his heartbeat, and I swear to God, it's matched by my own.

We stand together for quite a while, and I just breathe him in, until he pulls back and smiles, keeping hold of me.

"Well, at least I understand why you wanted to come away, regardless of the destination, or the price, in the middle of January," I remark, smiling back. "It makes sense that you'd want to avoid being around when the wedding was due to take place. But when did this all happen? When did you actually discover them together?"

My eyesight may not be great, but I'm certain that his skin has just paled, slightly. "Last Thursday evening," he says.

I feel for a moment as though I'm spinning. Or maybe the room is. I can't tell which, and I don't care. I step out of his grip and away from him.

"Last Thursday?" I glare up at him. "Are you kidding?"

"No," he says, as though it's the most natural thing in the world to discover your fiancée in bed with your brother one minute, and hold another woman in your arms the next.

I mean, obviously he's only here in the spirit of friendship. That's what he said when he came in here… and he only held me, and let me hold him to feel the solace of a fellow human being, who cared enough to let it show… but *last Thursday*?

He made it sound as though it happened a while ago, didn't he? At least I think he did. But in any case, what's the matter with him? He should be moping around, feeling sorry for himself, crying into a bottle of whisky or something. Not making friends with my dog, sitting in my kitchen, drinking coffee, looking utterly gorgeous and like he doesn't have a care in the world.

Who does that, four days after they've ended their engagement?

I want to yell at him, or at least to raise my voice and ask that exact question, but I don't, because it's none of my business. We're just friends. In fact, I'm not even sure we're that.

I resume my seat, and he copies me, sitting sideways on and resting his arm on the back of my chair.

"What did you do?" I ask, deciding to get back to his story, because I sense there's more to come, although I'm dreading to think how many other revelations he could have, and I'm not sure I can stand the shock. "After you'd caught them together, I mean?"

"I left," he replies.

"You didn't confront them?"

"No." He shakes his head.

"Why not? Isn't that what most people would do? I know I would."

"I wasn't sure how I'd react," he says, thoughtfully, "especially not to Zach, so I thought it best to leave. I sat outside for a short while…

in shock, I think. I decided, there and then, to cancel the wedding – or at least to leave Brianna to cancel it – and then I went round to Rachel's. She doesn't live too far away from Brianna, and I thought it might help if I could tell someone what had happened."

"What did Rachel say? It must have been difficult for her, what with Brianna being her friend and Zach being her brother."

"I didn't get around to telling her that the man involved had been Zach," he explains and I feel my mouth pop open in surprise. Again. "She didn't give me a chance. As soon as I told her I'd caught Brianna in bed with someone else, she laid into me about being so impetuous, as though the whole thing was my fault. She told me that I only had myself to blame for getting engaged so quickly in the first place… and then added that she thought I shouldn't compound the felony by making any more hasty decisions, and should take some time to think about it before calling the engagement off."

"She said that?" I can't believe it.

"Yes." He nods. "I suppose she felt her loyalties were divided between Brianna and me. Needless to say, we argued. Loudly. And then I stormed off and went back to my place, in spite of having to clamber over the decorators' equipment. I sat there for a while, on top of the dust sheets on my sofa, but then decided enough was enough, so I packed up all of Brianna's things that she'd left at my flat over the months I'd known her, looked out the tickets I'd bought for our surprise honeymoon to Antigua, and went back round to her place."

"So you did confront her?"

"Yes. Zach had gone by the time I got there – which was a good thing – but I dumped Brianna's things and told her our engagement was over. She was stacking the dishwasher when I arrived, acting perfectly normally, as though it was the end of another average Thursday… maybe it was for her. Maybe it wasn't their first time. Who knows? Anyway, she claimed she had no idea what was wrong, or why I was behaving like that. I told her then that I'd come back earlier in the evening. She went as white as a sheet at that point. I told her what I'd seen, that I knew she'd been with Zach. She tried to tell me it didn't mean anything, that it was a one-off, that it was just sex… you know, all the usual lines people come out with at a time like that. But I wasn't interested and told her to forget it, that I didn't want to marry her anymore. She seemed surprised by that, and even more so that I expected her to deal with the fallout. I told her I'd pay my share of any compensation the venue or suppliers wanted, but I wasn't going to be the one handling it all… not when she'd clearly been having so much fun handling my brother behind my back. She just stared at me, with her mouth open, so I gave her the honeymoon tickets and told her she could change the name on mine to Zach's if she wanted to… which I guess might have been a low blow, but I was past caring by then. And then I left and went home. And that was when I decided I needed to get away, to somewhere just like this. Somewhere I could just kick back and be myself for a while…"

Good lord. I let out a sigh. This is too much. It's impossible to get my head around everything he's telling me. I'm so confused by him, by his responses to the things that have happened to him, and to me. And now I'm starting to wonder who on earth he is, and why he's *really* here. Not here at my cottage… he's just explained that. But here in my kitchen…

Logan

Looking at her now, with her eyes wide, her mouth open just fractionally, and slight hints of pink on her cheeks, I wonder if I've gone too far. In telling her everything, have I told her too much?

"Be yourself?" she mutters, after an uncomfortable pause.

"Yes."

"And who exactly is that?" she asks. "Who are you?"

I contemplate her question. "You really want to know?"

"Yes, I do." She sounds almost angry with me. "Who are you, Logan?"

"Well, I'm a vet." That seems like a reasonable – and safe – place to start.

"I know that already."

"And I'm thirty-five years old." I ignore her remark. "I've got a small flat in Richmond, which is in the process of being decorated, and which I was about to sell, but which I'll probably hang onto now. I have two siblings… both younger than me, although I'm not really talking to one of them at the moment, for obviously reasons." She settles back in her chair at this point, clasping her hands in her lap and tilting her head to one side, like I'm a prize specimen of something… something she's really not sure about. "My parents divorced when I was in my early twenties," I continue, because I've started now, so I may as well finish. "And my mum went back to Ireland, to the village where she grew up, and she lives there now with my step-father, who is actually only two years older than me." Hope's eyes widen again, and I struggle not to smile. I know my family history can be a bit shocking to some people, and I make allowances for that whenever I talk about them. It's not shocking to me of course. I'm used to them.

"And your dad?" she asks, with a note of trepidation in her voice.

"He's had a string of lovers," I explain, "most of whom are barely legal, and who only stick around until they realise that his money is staying firmly in his own pockets.

"You sound cynical." She unclamps her hands again, sitting forward, just slightly.

"No. I'm just realistic. Maybe that's why I got engaged to Brianna on a whim – because I didn't have any great expectations of marriage…"

"Well, neither do I anymore," she blurts out, and blushes to the roots of her honeyed hair, before pushing back her chair, scraping it harshly across the floor, getting to her feet and going over to the sink. She leans against it, looking out of the window, and it dawns on me that she must have been standing right there on Saturday evening when we were gazing at each other.

Her whole body is tense, emotion pouring off of her. I imagine she regrets her own marriage, but at least she made it down the aisle, which is more can be said for me.

127

I stand up and walk slowly over to her, hesitating as I approach, wondering if I should touch her, or not. She seems more hostile since I revealed my story, but I can't just stand here and do nothing, so I place my hands on her shoulders and turn her around to face me.

I'd expected to be met with tears, but instead I'm greeted with a blank, stoney expression. Even then though, she can't hide the anguish in her eyes.

"I'm sorry," I say, sincerely, inching closer. Whatever I've said, or done, it's hurt her, and that hurts me too.

She shrugs her shoulders and mutters, "It doesn't matter," and I place my fingers over her lips.

"Don't you dare say you're fine, Hope. I can see in your eyes that you're a long way from being fine, so don't say it."

"I wasn't going to."

"I really am sorry." I can't bear the way she's looking at me, and decide to take a stab at what it is that's upsetting her, hoping I won't be shot down in flames, because if I'm right, then it's promising. It's very promising. "I know my story sounds a bit bizarre…"

"A bit?" she says, and I try hard not to smile, because I think I was right. She's struggling with what I've told her about myself and Brianna – and while I don't want her to be hurt, at least it means she cares enough to be worried about it.

"Okay… a lot," I allow. "But you have to realise, I come from a truly dysfunctional family. I'm used to rolling with the punches when it comes to relationships."

"Are you?" she says, suspiciously.

"Yes. Insofar as I've had any relationships," I admit. "Because like I told you earlier, before I met Brianna, I lived my life doing pretty much whatever I wanted… devoid of any kind of commitment."

"So you said."

"But that doesn't mean I wasn't committed to her," I point out. "I'm not a cheat, Hope. I'd never have done to her what she did to me. I'm not the sort of man who says one thing and does something different. I have a lot of faults – far too many to mention, as I think you're starting to work out for yourself – but I am at least honest."

She stares at me for a moment, her brow furrowing. "Y—You were telling me about yourself… about your family," she stutters, her face clearing again.

"You want to know more?" I ask and she nods her head, making me wonder if that means she just wants to change the subject, or whether she wants to understand me better. I hope it's the latter, and if that's the case, then it's fine by me, because as far as I'm concerned, when it comes to Hope, I'm an open book. "Okay… well, my parents both had affairs throughout their marriage. To begin with they tried to hide it…"

"From you and your brother and sister?" she interrupts.

"Well, yes. But also from each other. Once it became clear they were both cheating, though, they made no secret about it at all, and they argued quite vocally most of the time."

"Why did they stay married?" Hope asks, frowning.

"I have no idea. But when Rachel left to go to university, they finally decided to split up. I suppose to them it seemed like they were doing the right thing by the three of us, in staying together for as long as they did. But I'm not sure they did any of us any favours. I think all they really did was taint our view of relationships, especially for Zach and myself. Zach's thirty-two and I'm thirty-five, and until I met Brianna, neither of us had been in a serious relationship at all. Zach still hasn't been, as far as I know… not unless his 'thing' with Brianna is more long-term than she was prepared to admit."

"Do you think it was?" she asks.

"I don't know. I don't care either. Not now…" Instinctively, I move my hands up to cup her face, stepping closer to her at the same time, so our bodies are touching, and my lips are barely an inch from hers.

She gasps at the intimacy, although she doesn't pull away, and whispers, "Um… Logan?" instead, just quietly, then adds, "I thought… I thought we were…"

"Friends?" I interrupt and she nods. "We are. Really, we are. But what if I told you I only mentioned us being friends, because if I'd said what I really want, I was scared you wouldn't talk to me? And I really needed you to talk to me… for both our sakes. What if I told you that when you started talking about your husband yesterday, it was like a knife to my heart? That's why I went quiet on you, by the way. And I'm sorry about my behaviour afterwards. I know I was rude to you, but you have to understand I wasn't expecting to hear that. I wasn't expecting to have to think about you with someone else."

She frowns, then opens her mouth to speak, and then closes it again. "I don't understand all of this, Logan," she says. "It's too confusing. One minute you're talking about friendship and the next minute, you're… you're saying all of that. A knife to your heart? What does it mean? W—What is it that you want from me?"

"I don't want anything *from* you," I reply. "I just want you."

She's shocked. Not surprised. Shocked. And I'm not sure that's a good thing, especially when she raises her hands, pulling mine away from her face, then leans away from me, as far as she can, allowing for the fact that the sink is right behind her, and says, "Stop it, will you? Just stop it."

"Stop what?" I ask, trying to stay calm.

"Being ridiculous. Your sister's right about you. You are impetuous. You've just told me that you only broke up with your fiancée four days ago, in very traumatic circumstances, having caught her in bed with your brother, and now you're saying that you want me? To what? Fall at your feet? Jump into bed with you, to make you feel better about yourself?"

Wow. For all my faults, I'm not sure I deserved most of that, and as she stops talking, breathing hard now, I clasp her shoulders again, holding her still and staring into her eyes, fixing her. "I don't want you to do either of those things. You never have to fall at my feet, Hope, and as for jumping into bed… well, we can do that some other time, when you're ready to trust me, which you're clearly not right now."

"Do you blame me?" she says.

"No. No, I don't. But none of that detracts from the fact that I want you. I've wanted you since you came out of your front door on Saturday afternoon, looking like my idea of perfect, and then smiled at me, and stole my heart… and I'm afraid there's damn all I can do about that, because even if I leave here right now, I'm still going to want you. Every. Single. Day. For the rest of my life."

There's a moment's pause, while she looks at me, confused and frowning, like she's trying to see where the catch is in all of this.

"Can you let go of me?" she says, her voice soft and quiet, as she finally stops examining my face and glances down at my arms, my hands still clenching her shoulders, and I release her, stepping back and putting some space between us. "What do you want from me?" she repeats, then before I can reply, she adds, "And don't just say you want me."

"Why not? It's the truth."

"Even if is is," she says, doubt clouding her voice, "what does that actually mean?"

I push my fingers back through my hair, and sigh. "It means I want to get to know you better," I explain, giving her the detail I think she needs. "I know I said that earlier, and it wasn't a lie. It wasn't a line either. I really do want to know everything about you… the good, the bad and the ugly. I want to hear all of your stories, no matter how hard they are to tell, or to hear. I want to hold you…" I take a step closer to her again, first one, and then another, my eyes locked on hers. "I want to make you smile, every minute of the day, because you have the most perfect smile I've ever seen. I want to make you feel like you're my first priority. Always. Because you are… and you always will be. And I never want to hear you say you're fine. Ever again. Because 'fine' isn't good enough for you."

We're still gazing deeply into each other's eyes, but she blinks, breaking the spell. "Is that all?" she says and I have to laugh.

"Isn't that enough?"

She's shaking her head now, still looking confused. "What I mean is… don't you want anything *else*?" She blushes, emphasising the last word, and bites her bottom lip, and I know, just from her physical reaction, exactly what she's talking about.

"Honestly?" I say, closing the gap between us, my body almost touching hers, my fingertips tracing delicate lines down her cheek. "No, that's not all. I want everything, Hope. I want all of you… but we have to start somewhere, don't we? And I can't think of a better place to make that start than right here, right now… getting to know each other."

Chapter Eleven

Hope

I'd have to be insane to say 'no' to him, wouldn't I?

He wants to get to know me… all of me.

That thought makes me shudder and my skin tingles at the prospect. I know I'm blushing, and I don't care… because Logan wants me. And I want him.

He wants to make me smile, and to put me first.

God, that's tempting. I've got no idea what that feels like, but it sounds joyous. It sounds miraculous.

And even more miraculously, I've stolen his heart?

I'm so tempted to tell him he's stolen mine too, and I wish I could.

But the problem is, no matter how much I want him, or how much I like the sound of what he's offering, or how good it feels to have his body so close to mine, or how convincing his words are, the memory of his recently broken engagement is a palpable spectre… the original elephant in the room.

I want to be sure about him. I really do. But more importantly, I *need* to be sure of him. Given my condition, I can't set myself up for a fall. Equally, I feel less certain about telling him my secret now, than I've ever felt about anything. Because whatever it is he's offering, I want it to be about me – about us – and nothing to do with the fact that I'm slowly going blind, or any pre-conceptions that he might have about that. The last thing I need is his pity, when what I'm craving – more than anything – is his love.

The thing is that, while I'm flattered that he seems to be offering himself to me – and I'm not going to say I'm not tempted to grab him with both hands – there's a part of me that's yelling, screaming into my head, to run for the hills. Assuming I could see them clearly enough, that is…

"I can't," I whisper, the words leaving my lips, even as I was preparing to say 'yes please'.

"You can't what?" He doesn't move an inch, the heat from his body radiating into me, his eyes fixed on mine, although he's frowning now, not smiling.

"I can't do all of that," I reply. "It's too soon." *And I'm too scared.*

"After your husband's death?" he queries.

"No." How could he think that, after I told him about the nature of my relationship with Greg? "No… after you found Brianna in bed with your brother."

He looks crestfallen now and turns away, moving back towards the table. I miss him already and wish he'd come back, but after just a few steps, he turns around and faces me once more.

"Okay," he says, pushing his fingers back through his hair again, "I get that I'm impetuous, or at least you think I am…"

"Yes, and so do your family," I interrupt, because I don't want him to think I'm judging him. I'm not. I'm just reacting to a series of facts, in the same way as everyone else would, I think.

"What have my family got to do with this?" he asks, his brow furrowing.

"Well, I assume they know you," I point out and he shakes his head.

"No. They just think they do. I don't show them the real me." He stops talking, seeming to think for a moment. "Actually, I'm not sure I've ever shown anyone the real me… until now."

"You expect me to believe that?" He'd started to move back towards me again, but he stops in his tracks, staring at me.

"Yes," he says, lowering his voice. "It's the truth. I've never opened up to anyone like that before."

"Not even the woman you proposed to?" I ask, wishing I didn't sound so jealous, or at least suspicious. It's not in my nature and I don't want him to think of me like that, because it's not who I am.

"No," he says, quite reasonably. "I mean, I told her I loved her, because at the time, I thought I did… but I've never told anyone how I really *feel*."

"And how do you feel?" I ask, aware that – to a certain extent at least – we're going around in circles here.

"Scared," he replies instantly, and with startling honesty, taking my breath away.

"Of what?" I manage to whisper.

"Of losing you before this has even started." He blinks a few times and then shrugs slightly. "But that's not the point."

"What is?"

"That while I may be impetuous… and scared… I'm also stubborn. Like a mule. And I'm not letting you go. I'm not giving up that easily." He steps nearer to me again, more resolutely this time, although he stops before he gets too close. Even so, I can see what look like chestnut coloured flecks in his eyes, sparkling in the combined reflection from the down lighter that's right above us, and the window behind me. "Apart from your fairly obvious refusal to believe that I'm serious about this, is there any other reason you've got why we can't get to know each other better, spend some more time together, discover whether you might come to think of me as worthy of you, and then maybe see what happens?"

"I never said you weren't serious," I reply, latching onto his initial statement.

"You implied it."

I suppose I can't deny that. "Okay, but I didn't say you weren't worthy of me."

"No. I did. So? Is there another reason?"

Other than my impending blindness, which I haven't told you about yet? "You mean, apart from the fact that four days ago, you were engaged to someone else?" I say out loud, because at the moment that feels more important than anything else and I know we're going to keep coming back to it. It's too hard to get away from.

"Apart from that, yes."

"What kind of reason?" I ask, wondering if he might give me an opening to tell him about my condition – and whether I'll take it.

"Oh, I don't know," he says, looking up at the ceiling for a moment, before moving just a little closer, lowering his head and gazing into my eyes. "You're not secretly training to become a nun, are you?"

I giggle, in spite of myself. "No."

"And there's no-one else in your life? No-one in the background that you haven't told me about? No-one you're interested in…?"

I can tell he's holding his breath, and I'm almost tempted to tell him that the only man I've been interested in for years is standing right in front of me. But I don't.

"No," I reply simply, and he smiles. Beautifully.

"And you don't find me physically or personally repellent?"

As if… I shake my head.

"Okay," he says, taking my hand in his and pulling me back to the table, where he sits us both down again, side by side, although he turns the chairs so we're facing each other, our knees touching, my hands in his. "In that case, I'm going to prove to you that I can be both impetuous and cautious at the same time."

"Is that even possible?" I ask, intrigued, my secrets forgotten, at least for the time being.

"Yes." He starts to brush along my knuckles with his thumb, which is distracting, in a nice way. "I want to be with you, Hope," he says, "and as far as I'm concerned, the timing is irrelevant. But I get that, for you, it's a problem."

"Just slightly," I mutter, and he shakes his head, although the corners of his lips are twitching upwards in a half smile.

"If I'd broken up with Brianna, say six months ago, would that make a difference?" he asks. "Allowing for the obvious fact that I didn't even know her six months ago, which for the sake of this hypothetical question, I'm going to ask you to ignore."

"Yes," I reply, without the need for thought. "It would make a huge difference." His smile widens, lighting up his face.

"Okay," he says, "then why don't I spend the next six months proving to you that I'm not the man you think I am? Why don't I show you that I'm trustworthy and honest and very, very loyal… and that these impetuous feelings of mine aren't going anywhere, and that it's just the timing that's out of kilter, and not us."

"Us?" I repeat, in a hoarse whisper, my voice refusing to cooperate properly.

"Yes," he says, shifting forward slightly on his seat, his grip tightening on my hands. "I know I don't have the right to ask this of you, and I'm sure you have no shortage of men falling at your feet, begging for your attention, but do you think that for the next six months, you could just bat them to one side and let me – for want of a better word – woo you?"

I can't help the smile that tweaks at the edges of my lips as I wonder if I've just stepped into the pages of a Jane Austen novel.

"Woo me?" I repeat. "You want to woo me?"

"Yes," he says, quite seriously. "If you'll let me. If you think you can keep your other suitors at bay.

Did he really just say 'suitors'? That's confirmed it, I'm officially Elizabeth Bennett. In which case, I'm very pleased to say that Logan must be Mr Darcy.

"Suitors?" I struggle to say, because, despite my enjoyment of my new-found role, I'm also trying not to laugh.

"Yes."

"I don't have any suitors."

He seems a bit taken aback by my response. "None?" he queries.

"No."

He shakes his head. "I suppose I should be glad of that," he says. "But I am starting to doubt the sanity of the men around here."

"Most of the men around here are in their sixties," I explain.

"So?" he says. "Being in your sixties doesn't make you dead from the neck up… or the waist down, for that matter."

I laugh, and so does he. "You… you really want to woo me… for six months?" I ask him, still feeling a little stunned by his suggestion, and the manner in which he made it.

"Yes. Of course, you can cut to the chase, if you want to… any time you like." He winks at me, and wiggles his eyebrows, and I have to laugh again, knowing I've stepped out of that Jane Austen novel and am back in the real world now, and that the real world is just as much fun, it would seem. At least it is when I'm with Logan, anyway.

"And what about you?" I ask. "Can you cut to the chase too?"

"No." His reply is emphatic but as I go to reply – to apologise for doubting him, actually – he puts his finger on my lips, stopping me. "I've never felt anything like this before," he says softly, and with disarming sincerity. "You're different, Hope. I knew that the first moment I set eyes on you."

No matter how sincere his words, or how hard I try, I can't escape the fact that he's been engaged… which I know means nothing, considering I've been married. But the difference is that my marriage ended when Greg died, nearly two years ago, although I'm not sure it ever really got started, whereas Logan was engaged until just four short days ago. "But…" I murmur.

"I know," he says. "I know you need time. And thats exactly what I'm going to give you… and while I'm doing that, I'm going to prove to you that you can trust me. Honestly." He sits back, looking into my eyes again. "You don't have to believe me when I say I'm honest, because it's one of the things I intend proving to you, but I can tell you that I learned a good lesson in honesty from my parents."

"What was that?" I ask, intrigued, considering that – based on what he's told me – his parents seem to have cheated and lied their way through their entire marriage.

"Well," he explains, "as I've already said, both of my parents had affairs. At the beginning, they used to sneak around behind each other's backs, but my dad got caught out, because he used to lie to my mum… and that was mainly because he had such a shocking memory and couldn't remember the stories he'd told her. Apart from my hair colour and my height, my appalling memory is one of the few character traits I've inherited from my dad."

"Given his propensity for infidelity, I'm glad to hear that," I interject, without thinking, and then blush to the roots of my hair. "I'm sorry. I shouldn't have said that."

"Why not? It's true. My dad was – and still is – a serial philanderer of epic proportions. I, however, have never cheated on anyone in my life. But the point of what I'm trying to tell you here, is that I learned very early on in life, that the best policy is to tell the truth and live with the consequences. So, if I tell you that you can trust me not to hurt you… if I tell you that I won't do anything you don't want me to… and if I tell you I've never felt like this before about anyone, regardless of the fact that I was engaged to someone else, then I'm telling you the truth."

I bite my bottom lip, feeling ashamed for doubting him. Because looking at him now, I can't help but believe him… and fall for him, just a little bit more.

Logan

Did I actually say the word 'woo', out loud, to Hope?

I must have done, because she repeated it back to me, with a smile on her lips and a hint of doubt – or was that incredulity? – in her voice. I can't blame her for being surprised. After all, what self-respecting twenty-first century man offers to 'woo' anyone?

This one does, I suppose.

Because he's desperate. And he's in love. He's desperately in love. And when the woman he's desperately in love with looked like she was going to reject him, he knew he had to do something about it. So he did.

"What do you say?" I ask her, once we've been sitting in silence for longer than feels comfortable.

"About you wooing me?" she asks, with that impish smile forming on her lips again.

"Yes."

She tilts her head to one side, thinking. "You're serious about this?" she clarifies.

"Deadly. Never been more serious about anything in my life."

"And you want to do this for six months?"

"Yes."

"But I can… how did you phrase it? I can… cut to the chase, if I want to?"

I smile at her. "Yes. Anytime you want."

"And if I decide I want you to stop, because it's just not working for me?" she asks, nibbling on the corner of her bottom lip, more in doubt than amusement, I think.

"Then you'll break my heart," I reply honestly, and her eyes widen. "And I'll probably try and persuade you to reconsider. But if you've really decided you don't want to be with me, I'll accept your decision."

She nods her head, thoughtfully, then says, "And what about if we get to the end of the six months and we're still where we are now?"

"If you mean that you feel like you might need more time, then you can have it."

"Really?"

"Yes… but you won't."

She shakes her head, although she's smiling, and she pulls her hand from mine, slapping me playfully on the arm. "You're hopeless," she says.

"Please tell me I'm not that. Please say I'm not without Hope."

She stills and sighs, and bowing her head just slightly, whispers, "You're not."

I place my finger beneath her chin, raising her face to mine. "Do you accept?" I ask.

"Yes."

I'm so tempted to pull her into my arms, to kiss her, to hold her and never let her go. But I don't, because that would hardly be 'wooing' her, would it? That would be sweeping her off of her feet, and being impetuous, reckless and impulsive… and all the things I'm trying to prove to her I'm not. So, instead, I just smile at her and whisper, "Thank you," and then lean back in my chair.

She looks a little disappointed, which is nice, and while I'd like to stay and discuss that with her, I've got plans, so I get to my feet, pushing my chair back under the table.

"You're going?" she asks, looking up at me.

"Yes."

"Already?"

"Yes." She stands herself now. "But I was wondering if you'd like to come to dinner with me tonight?"

She looks up at me a little warily. "Where?"

"At the cottage. I'll cook us something."

She smiles. "That sounds lovely."

"You haven't tasted my cooking yet," I acknowledge, and her smile widens.

And I fall, just a little bit harder.

I'm back in the cottage now, a smile permanently etched on my face, floating around on cloud nine and wondering what to cook this evening, when my phone rings. It's Rachel, so I answer straight away.

"Hi."

"Hello," she says. "I'm glad I've caught you. I'm just about to leave for my dress fitting, but I wanted to let you know that your locks have been changed."

"Thanks," I reply.

"The problem is that the locksmith gave me two keys," she continues, barely drawing breath, "and I've had to leave the spare one with the decorators, so when you get back from wherever you are, you're going to have to come to my place... otherwise you won't be able to get in."

"Okay. I'll text you when I know my movements." I smile to myself, thinking about the fact that just yesterday I was considering going home early, and now I'm not sure I'd care if I never went home again.

"Fine." She sounds a bit stressed. "Oh," she adds, "and I've had another couple of calls from Brianna, begging me to tell her where you are. I explained to her that I didn't know, so I couldn't tell her, but you really need to deal with things, Logan. She's starting to sound desperate."

"I don't care. And I have dealt with things. I've told her it's over. What more does she need to know?"

"She claims she's been trying to text you and call you, but she can't seem to get through."

"That's because I've blocked her number," I explain. "I don't want anything to do with her. I did tell her that. Why can't she just get the message?"

"Because she wants another chance," she says, like it's obvious. "I mean, wouldn't you, if it had been you who screwed up?"

"Yes… if I'd made a mistake, if we'd argued and I'd said or done something to hurt her. But she did a bit more than that. She cheated. There's a big difference between screwing up and screwing… another man." I'm not ready to tell her who the other man was yet. I think that's probably best done in person, not over the phone, when I'm hundreds of miles away. I've always been Rachel's hero, ever since she was little and struggled to say my name, resolving on 'Gan' in the end, which I suppose was better than the alternative of 'Log'. I'm the one she looks up to and comes to when she's in trouble, but in spite of all that, Zach's her friend. They're closer in age and hung out together more as children and teenagers, than she and I ever did, and I'm not sure what her reaction will be when I tell her what's happened.

"I know," she sighs. "But she's so unhappy."

"Well, maybe she should have thought about that before." I pause, catching my breath and controlling my rising anger. Today is a good day, after all. Hope said 'yes', and that makes it the very best day. "Anyway," I add, calmly, "thanks for seeing to my locks. I appreciate it."

"You're welcome," she replies.

"What do I owe you?"

"Call it a grand."

"What?" Seriously? What did she do? Fit solid gold locks to my front door?

She chuckles. "You're so easy to wind up," she says. "It was one hundred and twenty four pounds, and a few pence."

"That's more like it," I muse, shaking my head, although she can't see me. "I'll transfer you the money."

"No rush," she replies. "God… I've just seen the time. I must dash.

See ya!"

And with that, she's gone.

I transfer the funds, via my banking app, and then settle down on the sofa, browsing a few cookery websites, until I find a recipe that looks good, and quite easy. It's a variation on something I've made before – a linguine dish, with king prawns, chilli, lemon and parsley. I've made plenty of seafood pasta dishes in my time, and this one looks straightforward enough, and being as I'm already quite nervous about this evening, I don't want to make the cooking element any harder than it has to be.

I had to take a trip into St Austell in the end, to get the prawns and the parsley. While I was there, I picked up a very nice bottle of Chablis, and I found a florist, and bought Hope some flowers. I know I could have got them from the supermarket, but I wanted them to be special. And they are. They're not nearly as special as she is though, when she arrives, looking absolutely stunning in a long, dark blue dress, with embroidered flowers at the waist, which shows off her hourglass figure to perfection. She's put her hair up loosely behind her head as well, leaving just a few strands framing her face, and she's wearing the merest hint of make-up.

I resist the temptation to tell her that she could have arrived with her hair in a mess, no make-up, and wearing a sack, and I'd still have thought she was the most beautiful woman in the world. Instead, I hand her the flowers, feeling nervous, and she sniffs the blooms, smiling at me.

"You didn't have to buy me flowers," she whispers, her eyes sparkling.

"Yes I did… I'm wooing you, remember?"

She giggles, shaking her head, as though she doesn't believe I'm going to see this through. Little does she know me.

"I feel a bit silly inviting you through to your own kitchen, but I'm going to have to finish cooking the pasta, so would you like to join me?"

She nods her head. "Thanks," she says, walking through ahead of me. "I'll put these in some water too. There's a vase under the sink."

"There is?"

"Yes."

"Is there anything you don't supply for your guests?" I ask and she pauses for a moment, looking back over her shoulder at me.

"I don't know. You tell me?"

"I can't think of anything."

"Good," she says, smiling. "I must be getting something right then."

She finds the vase, just where she'd said it would be and, after filling it with water, places the flowers carefully inside and puts them on the draining board, after which I invite her to sit at the table while I finish cooking.

"I hope you like seafood," I say, suddenly realising that I should probably have asked.

"I love seafood," she replies and I smile at her.

"That's a relief. It would've been disastrous if you'd been allergic."

"Is there anything you're allergic to?" she asks, and I turn from my place by the stove, where I've just put the pasta into the boiling water. She's staring at me, her eyebrows raised, enquiringly.

"No. I don't think so."

"So I can cook you anything I want?"

"You can. Why? Have you cooked us a back-up dinner, in case mine proves inedible?" I ask, teasing her.

"No." She blushes profusely. "I wouldn't dream of doing that."

I've embarrassed her now, and abandoning the pasta, I walk around the table, crouching down beside her. "I'm sorry," I say, with utter sincerity. "That was very insensitive of me."

"No, it wasn't," she replies, turning to look down at me, her blush fading slightly. "But… I… well, I wanted to invite you to dine with me tomorrow evening."

"You did?" I'm surprised, and it shows.

"Yes," she says.

"In that case, I accept."

She smiles, looking beautifully shy now, and before I end up kissing her and blowing this whole 'wooing' thing right out of the water on our first date, I get up and go back to the cooker, adding the prawns to the garlic and chilli, that are sautéing gently in the pan, being as the fresh pasta is nearly cooked now.

"Whatever you're doing with those prawns, it smells delicious," Hope remarks.

"You'll be able to tell me how it tastes in a moment," I reply and I drain the pasta, adding it to the prawns, and giving it a good stir, before pouring the whole mixture into the two bowls I've put out on the work surface, which I then bring to the table.

"Wine," I say, mentally kicking myself. "I'm sorry. I should have offered you a drink earlier." My only excuse for not doing so is my nerves, but I'm not about to admit that, and instead, I open the chilled Chablis and pour some into the tall stemmed glasses, before taking my seat opposite Hope.

"This looks lovely," she says, studying the dish before her, as I offer her some water from the jug I poured earlier and put on the table, with some ice and sliced lemons. She declines, but I help myself, needing to keep my wits about me, in case I say the wrong thing.

"Nowhere near as lovely as you," I reply, deciding it's safe to say what I'm really thinking, now that I know I'm not going to have to get up and wander off; now that I can focus on her, and her alone.

She looks up at me. "Thank you," she mutters, and although I'm pleased she's accepted my compliment, I sense it made her feel self-conscious. Heaven knows why. She really is beautiful.

We start to eat, and after Hope has offered more praise than my simple dish deserves, I ask her about her family.

"I told you all about mine," I explain, "so what about yours?"

"Well, my father's an architect," she says, and I remember she mentioned that.

"And your mother?"

"She stayed at home and looked after me."

"You were an only child?" I guess, and she nods her head. "And did you mind that?"

"No," she says. "I never really noticed not having any brothers and sisters. But then I suppose you can't miss what you've never had, can you?"

"No. You can't." I say, sipping my wine. "What was your childhood like?"

"Idyllic?"

"You sound doubtful." I pick up on the tone of her voice and put my glass down, leaning forward.

"No. I'm not doubtful. I'm just trying to find the right word."

"It was happy?" I ask and she smiles.

"Yes. Very. The village where I grew up, on the outskirts of Truro, was very much like Portlynn. The kind of place where everyone knows everyone else… and their business."

"And that doesn't bother you? Your neighbours knowing all about you?"

"No. I like that," she says. "I like the feeling of security it gives you… that the people around you know you, and care about you. And you can choose what to reveal, and what not to…" Her voice fades and I wonder if she's thinking about her husband, but even if she is, I don't want to talk about him tonight. Tonight is about us. Not about our past mistakes.

"It sounds like the polar opposite of my childhood," I remark, twirling my pasta onto my fork.

"In what way?" she asks.

"Well, I don't remember ever feeling very secure. But that's not surprising, I suppose. Not when my parents were at each other's throats all the time. Still, on the bright side, it taught me to be independent, to stand on my own two feet."

"Where did you grow up?" She's looking at me now, full of interest.

"Various parts of South West London," I reply. "We never stayed anywhere for very long… usually because my dad had slept with someone he shouldn't have, and there was either a husband, a father, or an older brother who wanted to take a piece out of him."

"It sounds horrendous."

"You can get used to anything, if you have to. As a child, I had to. But once I'd left for university, I decided I was never going back. And I never have."

"Not once?" she asks, shocked now. "I can't imagine not seeing my parents on a regular basis, especially—" She stops talking abruptly.

"Especially what?" I prompt.

"Nothing." She shakes her head, and looks down, concentrating on eating her food.

I sit in silence for a moment, wondering if she's going to elaborate, but when it becomes clear she's not, I decide to let it go. I imagine she was going to say something about her husband, her unhappy marriage, or the time surrounding his death and its aftermath, and how her parents supported her through that, but then she changed her mind, and I'm not going to complain about that. "Well," I continue, "I still see my mum and dad when I have to. Mum comes over from Ireland once or twice a year, and we meet for dinner, and then there are birthdays and Christmas, although I do my best to avoid any big family gatherings, if I can… especially if both of my parents are going to be there. They struggle to be in the same room without throwing furniture, even now…" I chuckle. "We'll have to nail the chairs down at my sister's wedding…"

Hope looks up as I talk, relaxing and taking an interest again. "Your sister's getting married?"

"Yes. In May. In a swanky Mayfair hotel. From what I can gather, it's going to be the society wedding of the year. According to my sister, anyway."

"And your parents are both going to be there?"

"Oh yes… Rachel's insisting."

"Is that wise?"

"No, but Rachel was never top of the class when it came to wisdom."

Hope chuckles now. "What do they do?" she says, finishing her pasta and laying the fork in her dish. "Your parents, I mean."

"Mum doesn't do anything," I explain. "Her husband is a businessman of some sort, although I've never really worked out in what capacity. Mum has become one of those 'ladies who lunch', and it seems to suit her."

"And your dad?"

"He's in antiques," I reply. "He's a sort of dealer, I suppose."

"Why does that sound a little bit dodgy?" she asks, sitting back and taking a drink of her wine.

"Because it is?" I suggest, just as I notice something moving out of the corner of my eye… something large and dark, scuttling across the floor. "Don't move," I whisper.

"Sorry?" Hope says.

"Don't panic, but there's a spider."

"Oh?" She looks around, squinting just slightly, but completely calm. "Where?"

"Over there." I nod towards the back corner of the kitchen.

"Do you want me to get it?" she says, but I put my hand over hers, before she can get up.

"No. I just assumed you'd freak out, that's all."

"No." She smiles and shakes her head. "I don't mind spiders."

"Wow." I get to my feet. "You really are one of a kind."

She blushes, and watches as I walk over to the spider, bending down to pick it up in my hand.

"I'll just deposit this little fellow outside," I tell her, as she stares at me wide-eyed, and then I go through to the front door, open it, and carefully place the spider onto the grass outside.

When I return to Hope, she looks up at me. "Well, that was impressive," she says.

"What was?"

"Picking the spider up with your bare hands. Was that for my benefit?"

I frown at her. "Um… no. I always pick up spiders with my hands."

"You… you don't use a glass, or a tea towel to catch them then?" She's stuttering again, probably because she's worried she just insulted my manhood.

"No. But then I am a vet."

She nods her head now. "Where did you put him?" she asks.

"Well, I didn't run over to your house and dump him in your living room, just so you could call me over later to save you."

"Well, no… because I've already told you, I'm not scared of spiders, so that wouldn't work, would it?" She smiles sweetly.

"No… it wouldn't. Worst luck. I put him on the grass outside," I admit. "He didn't bother to say thank you, though."

She giggles, then asks, "Why would he? After all, he was nice and warm in here, and you just dumped him outside in minus two degrees, or something."

"At least I didn't crush him."

"Would you have done, if he'd been a moth?" she asks, shuddering almost visibly.

"No."

"What would you have done?"

"Roughly the same thing."

"Oh God…" She really shivers now. "You mean you'd have touched a moth… with your bare hands? How can you do that?"

"With great care," I explain, smiling. "They're very delicate creatures, moths."

"They're horrible."

I sit back down opposite her. "So, can I assume that, while you're not scared of spiders, moths don't share the same favour in your eyes?"

"That's one way of putting it," she says. "Another way would be that they terrify me… and before you think about putting one in my house and then coming to save me, I have to warn you that I'd never forgive you if you did that."

I hold up my hands. "I wouldn't dream of it. But if you should happen to come across one while I'm here, then call me. I'll come and rescue you."

"Thank you." Her relief is almost palpable, and I do my best not to laugh.

Over coffee, which we drink in the kitchen, still gazing at each other between sips, we talk about other fears and phobias, and I learn that she's never flown, which I suppose shouldn't be a surprise, being as she did tell me that she's never been anywhere further from here than North Devon. I reveal my fear of heights, which isn't extreme, but it's enough, and I notice the smile forming on Hope's lips.

"What's funny?" I ask.

"How can you be scared of heights?" she says. "Being as tall as you are?"

"Six foot three isn't that tall," I reply. "And anyway, that's not really the point with being scared of heights. I think it's more about not being in control. At least, it is in my case."

"How so?" she asks.

"Because it's very specifically a fear of climbing ladders," I explain. "I never feel safe on them. I don't like the fact that they could collapse, or give way at any moment."

"I see," she says, with a questioning, slightly teasing tone to her voice, which I'm starting to like. A lot. "So you like being in control, do you?"

I manage to keep a straight face and reply, "In certain circumstances, yes."

"Such as climbing up ladders?" she asks.

"Among other things."

A smile plays on her lips and she looks up at me through her eyelashes, which is incredibly alluring, and I have to use all of my willpower to remember that, for the time being at least, I ceded control to her. I may be wooing, but I'm not chasing.

She glances away, lowering her head slightly and looks down at her clasped hands, and presumably she notices the time on her watch, because she suddenly says, "Goodness, did you realise it's gone eleven o'clock? I need to go home and let Archie out." She gets to her feet as she's finishing her sentence. "I'm sorry," she adds. "I should have paid more attention to the time. I normally let him out at ten-thirty."

"I'm sure he'll be fine," I reassure her, standing up myself. "But I'll see you home."

She turns, looking up at me. "You really don't need to. I only live a few yards away, remember?"

"Of course. But I'll still see you home." She hesitates and then nods her head before going over to the draining board and retrieving her flowers from the vase. "You didn't bring a coat, did you?" I recall her arrival a few hours ago, and how she looked standing on the doorstep, the bright outside lights shining behind her, giving her an ethereal glow.

"No. It didn't seem worth it."

"Here…" I grab my own jacket from the hook on the back of the door. "Put this on. It's freezing out there now."

"I'll be…" she starts to say, even as I lower my coat around her shoulders.

"Don't argue," I whisper into her ear and she leans back into my chest, just slightly. "And don't say you'll be fine." She twists and looks up at me, and it's all I can do not to kiss her. "You were going to say that, weren't you?"

"Yes," she murmurs, turning away again and saying, "Thank you," as she pulls my coat on properly.

"Just let me get the keys." I keep them on the window sill in the living room, and it takes me just a second or two to pocket them and rejoin her.

"You'll get cold without your coat," she remarks, looking at the open neck of my shirt, and then at the rolled up sleeves.

"I know… but my coat looks so much better on you than it's ever looked on me."

"It's enormous on me," she says, looking down at herself, and I follow her gaze. She's not wrong. The sleeves are a good four or five inches too long for her arms, and the jacket itself comes down almost to her knees.

"Still looks good," I tell her and give her a wink, which makes her giggle. And I wonder then if I'll ever need a coat again.

Half an hour later, I'm lying in bed staring up at the ceiling, having cleared up the kitchen, switched everything off, and taken a quick shower.

Tonight was a good night. I was more nervous than I can ever recall being on any first date in my life. But then, none of my previous first dates have mattered as much as this one did. And I think it went well. Actually, I know it did, because not only did Hope invite me back to her place tomorrow, before the night even got started, but we learned a lot about each other, and I told her things I've never told anyone, which felt good. And on top of that, we ended the evening on a happy, flirtatious, teasing note, which I think bodes well for the future. I've never had a relationship like that before, where I can be myself completely; where there's nothing other than total honesty and openness. Nothing hidden. No secrets. No games. Nothing held back. But I think that's what I've got now, and I know it's what I've been looking for.

I turn over in bed and remember the moment we parted, when Hope handed me back my coat on her doorstep, and I was sorely tempted to lean in and kiss her. I didn't. Obviously. It's too soon. And I've got six months of wooing ahead of me, so I didn't want to rush things.

But that doesn't mean I didn't want to.

I smile to myself as I think about the fact that, despite all of my openness and honesty tonight, there is something I'm hiding from Hope. There is one secret I'm keeping…

Because I can't yet say say 'I love you', even though I do, more than anything.

Chapter Twelve

Hope

I've spent the whole morning in a dreamy haze, my mind filled with images of my evening with Logan; the way his eyes seemed to sparkle when he gazed at me, the quirky smile that lit up his face when he looked at me wearing his coat, the way his shirt clung to his body, showing off his broad shoulders and muscled arms. I've never been a great one for admiring that kind of brawny male frame before, but maybe that's because I've never seen one in the flesh... until last night. I'd obviously seen Logan prior to our meal, but only wearing thick sweaters, not a neat, white button-down shirt, which revealed how perfectly formed he really is.

I wipe down the draining board, shaking my head at my own shallow thoughts, and glance out of the window. There's no sign of him, and there hasn't been so far today, and I'm overwhelmed with disappointment at that thought, even though I know I'm going to see him tonight.

What's the matter with me? The thought whirls around my head.

I drop the dishcloth into the sink and move away from the window to sit down at the kitchen table. My laptop and the accounts are beckoning, but I ignore them. I'm not in the mood, mainly because I can't stop thinking about Logan... even now. Dear God, I'm behaving like a hormonal schoolgirl, but even as I mentally chastise myself, I can't help smiling, and I let out a gentle sigh, as I recall some of our conversations last night. He was the perfect mix of sweet gentleman and gentle flirt all evening, and I have to admit, coupled with the realisation of how good he really looks, it was a heady combination. I'd never admit this to him, but there were a couple of times last night when I was sorely tempted to 'cut to the chase' – as Logan had put it – even though I'd said I needed time; even though it was only our first date.

I sit back in my seat, shaking my head, the blush rising up my cheeks. "What's the matter with me?" I say it out loud this time.

Even if it wasn't for the fact that every time I think about Logan – which is pretty much every minute of the day, it seems – I'm constantly reminded of his recently broken engagement, I also have to remember that I've made the mistake of rushing into things myself, before now. And surely once is enough, isn't it? After all, I jumped into bed with Greg very early in our relationship – well, not 'bed' exactly, being as our first time was on his parents' sofa, but the principle is the same. It's a decision I came to regret, because in my own stubborn, seventeen-year old, romantic, pig-headed way, I failed to understand that, giving him my virginity wasn't as big a deal as I assumed it was, and certainly didn't mean I had to stay with him forever, not if he didn't make me happy. And he didn't. I didn't make him happy either, but then I think he was more prepared to 'settle' than I was. Especially if 'settling' meant he still got to live the life he wanted. It certainly seemed that way, anyway.

"Why am I thinking about Greg?" I mutter, getting up and going through to the hall to put on my coat and shoes. "Logan isn't Greg."

I know that much already.

After just a few days, I know that Logan isn't anything like Greg. If nothing else, I feel more alive just looking at Logan than I ever did when I was lying in Greg's arms. Not that I actually did much lying in Greg's arms. He wasn't a great one for cuddling up, either before, during or after sex… on the rare occasions that we had sex, that is. And as for other times… well, he usually had something better to be doing.

I let my hands rest on my upper arms, hugging myself, and wonder for a moment, if Logan is a cuddling up kind of person?

God, I hope so.

Then I grab my keys from the hook and put them in my pocket, check that Archie's still asleep, which he is – and judging from the way his paws are twitching, I'd say he's having a fantastic dream – and then head out of the door.

I walk past the cottage, as though I don't have a care in the world, trying not to think about what Logan might be doing, whereabouts he might be, what he might be wearing, whether he might be thinking about me… and I turn right at the gate and make my way to the store.

Inside, there are a couple of customers standing at the counter, so I pick up a basket and fill it with carrots, onions and a packet of stewing steak, before going to the wine section and taking my time over selecting a decent bottle of red. By the time I've finished, the shop is empty, thank goodness and I wander up to the counter myself.

"What's happened?" Amy asks, removing my items from the basket and ringing them up on the till.

"Nothing's happened." I frown at her. "Why?"

She stares at me. "You look different."

"In what way?"

"Happier?" she suggests, her lips twitching upwards.

I can feel myself blushing. "Well… maybe I am," I say quietly, just as Nick comes in through the door behind her. He smiles, but doesn't interrupt our conversation.

"And would this have anything to do with a certain handsome guest who's staying at your place?" Amy teases.

I'm aware of Nick shaking his head and glance in his direction to see him smiling, although he's pretending to be occupied with his iPad.

"It might," I reply, doing my best to sound mysterious. "But don't go reading anything into it."

"Why not?" Amy says, her eyes sparkling. "It's exciting."

"Well, it might be, if it wasn't for the fact that he only broke up with his fiancée last Thursday night."

"Oh." Amy's face falls and I almost feel sorry for having taken the wind out of her sails.

"Yes, 'oh'." I reply and she reaches across the counter, taking my hand in hers.

"That's a bummer," she says, sympathetically.

"Sorry, ladies." Nick puts down his iPad and moves closer. "I know I'm only a man, and therefore I can't be expected to know anything about anything, but I'm not sure I can see what the problem is. What does it matter when he broke up with his ex? The point is that he's not seeing her now, isn't it?"

"Spoken like a true man," I say, narrowing my eyes in mock exasperation.

"Hmm… a deliberately dense one," Amy adds. Oh, I'm glad she said that, and not me.

Nick comes up behind her, putting his arms around her and bending down to kiss her cheek as she turns and looks up at him. "Deliberately dense?" he repeats, grinning playfully.

"Yes." Amy nods, but leans back into him.

"Thanks," he says, then looks back at me. "Don't get me wrong… I get that it's only a few days ago, but if his previous relationship wasn't right, then it wasn't right. And if he's ready to move on already, then why shouldn't he?"

Amy sighs and glances up at me. "Men really are a whole different species, aren't they?"

"Why do you say that?" Nick argues, still smiling. "I mean, why should Logan deny how he presumably feels about Hope, just because he had the misfortune to break up with someone else a few days ago? It's just timing, and that can't be helped, can it?"

"Funnily enough, that's almost exactly what Logan said," I reply.

"Which just proves my point that they're an entirely different breed," Amy comments, shaking her head and looking a bit smug, in a very cute way.

"Why?" Nick perseveres.

"Because there's such a thing as waiting?" Amy turns to him, her eyes widening, like she feels she's stating the obvious.

"Waiting for what?" Nick replies. "It's not his fault that he met Hope so soon after his engagement ended, is it?" He drags his eyes away from Amy and turns to me. "He broke up with his fiancée, right? Not the other way around?"

"Yes."

"In which case, he's hardly likely to be moping around, all broken hearted because she left him, is he?" He pulls Amy in for a tighter hug. "So, my beloved, tell me… having met Hope, and taken a liking to her, why should poor Logan have to live like a monk for six months, just because you've decided that he needs to wait?"

I choke, and then start to cough, and the two of them look at me, concerned.

"Are you okay?" Amy asks, as I start to recover.

I nod my head. "Yes, I'm fine," I manage to say, clearing my throat.

"Was it something I said?" Nick asks, tilting his head and giving me a very knowing look. Amy joins him, her head tipping the other way, and I'm almost tempted to laugh. They look like a couple of inquisitive cats, gazing at me.

"It might have been," I answer, trying not to sound coy.

"You're making him wait, aren't you?" Amy says slowly, a smile settling on her lips.

"I'm not *making* him do anything." I start to gather up my shopping, wishing I'd remembered to bring a carrier bag with me, so I could make a quicker getaway. "It's his decision."

"What is?" Amy asks.

"To… to do what he's doing."

"Which is?" Her voice is loaded with mischief.

I dump my things back on the counter and let out a huff of breath. "He's going to woo me, if you must know."

"He's going to what?" Nick's incredulous.

"He's… he's going to prove to me that I can trust him," I explain.

"No… wait a minute. You said the word 'woo'." Nick's trying very hard not to smile.

"Yes. I did."

"Wow." Amy sighs. "Did he actually say that, or are you just being a bit 'Jane Austen' about the whole thing?"

"Did he say what?" I ask.

"That he wanted to woo you?"

"Yes, he did."

"Oh," she says, and sighs again, dreamily.

"Heavens," Nick cuts in. "He has got it bad, hasn't he?"

"Oh, be quiet." Amy slaps him playfully on the arm. "I think it's simply lovely."

Nick holds her even tighter still. "Wife… you are so contrary. Five minutes ago, Logan was the villain of the piece, for falling for Hope too soon after dumping his fiancée, and now he's the hero of the hour, just because he used the word 'woo'?"

"Don't get me wrong, the timing still sucks," Amy says, screwing up her nose and poking out her tongue at him, "but it's very romantic, don't you think?"

Nick chuckles, shaking his head. "Don't tell me you want wooing as well?" he whispers, loud enough for me to hear.

Amy looks up at him, smiling, and murmurs, "Oh, I think you've done quite enough wooing already, don't you?"

They kiss, just briefly and then turn back to me, in perfect symmetry.

"I still think it's lovely," Amy says, handing me my carrots.

"So do I," Nick adds, giving me a smile and a wink.

"Well, don't tell him I've told you," I say, picking up the rest of my purchases again. "He'll probably die of embarrassment."

"I doubt that," Nick replies, kissing the top of Amy's head. "One thing you need to know about us men is that, when it's right, it's right… and we don't really care who knows about it."

I shake my head, although I can't help the smile that's twitching at the corners of my lips.

"And he's okay about your RP, is he? It didn't faze him?" Amy asks, sitting back up on her stool again and stretching her back into an arc, her hands on her hips.

I pause, just long enough for them to stare at me, and for Nick to tilt his head again. "You have told him, haven't you?" he says.

I shake my head, looking down at the top of the counter. "No," I mutter.

Amy jumps down again, coming closer and standing right beside her husband. "Hope?" she says, with a scolding note to her voice. "Why not?"

I stare at the two of them, first one and then the other. "Because, if he and I are going to be together, I want it to be about us... about *our* relationship. Not about my RP. Not about my future blindness, or his pity."

Nick frowns. Amy sighs. And then they both nod their heads. "I can see why you'd feel that way," Amy says, speaking for both of them.

"I will tell him," I add. "Once I'm sure about him."

Nick chuckles, just briefly. "So the guy telling you he wants to woo you for six months wasn't enough to convince you then?"

"Yes... and no," I reply and he laughs out loud this time.

"And you say *we're* a different species," he mutters.

"It's... it's just that... it's early days. I mean, he might go home and forget all about me," I explain, revealing the depth of my fear, and noting the looks of sympathy and surprise on their faces.

"I very much doubt that," Nick says. "But I do understand."

"So do I," Amy adds, taking my hand in hers and giving it a light squeeze of support, and I find myself smiling again as I make my way to the door and let myself out.

I hadn't expected to tell anyone about Logan and me, or about the fact that I'm keeping things from him. I know I can trust Amy and Nick, though. I know they'll keep my secret for me, and they'll be there to help me, should I need them. And that's what matters where friends are concerned.

I walk back home with a spring in my step and a smile on my face, to find Logan sitting on my front doorstep. He's wearing a thick jumper again, on top of dark blue jeans, and is perched with his elbows resting on his knees. He turns on hearing my footsteps on the gravel, his smile matching my own.

"Hello," he says, getting to his feet and coming towards me, taking the wine and the bag of carrots from me. "You've been shopping?"

"Yes." I look up into his chocolate coloured eyes and feel my stomach melt, before I remember my duties as his host. "Sorry, was there something you needed? Have you been waiting here for long?"

He smiles. "No. I just wanted to see you, that's all." My stomach turns to a molten mass, heat pooling at its base and I gaze up at him, unsure whether to breathe in, or out. "But in any case," he adds, turning towards my front door again, "I thought you understood."

"Understood what?"

"That I really don't mind how long I have to wait for you," he whispers, leaning into me.

I'm blushing profusely, wondering why it is that I suddenly feel so shy around him. I didn't last night. Well, not after we'd got over the first few minutes, anyway. So what's wrong with me now? Is it the close attention he's paying me? Or the intensity of his voice? Or that I've just been talking to my friends about the fact that I'm keeping something fairly momentous from him? Or all of the above…? When I look up at him, he's studying me, his eyes grazing over my hair, my neck, my cheeks, and finally settling on my lips, which I lick, nervously as he lets out a slow sigh.

"W—Would you like to come in?" I stutter.

"I'd love to," he replies, and without waiting to make even more of a fool of myself, I let us both into the house, taking him through to the kitchen, where we dump my provisions on the table.

Archie gets up from his basket, greeting Logan warmly, before coming to me, bouncing enthusiastically.

"Yes… hello," I coo softly, stroking him, before he returns to Logan for yet more attention.

I remove my coat, hanging it over the back of one of the chairs and then turn to him.

"To be honest, I wasn't sure about coming over here," he says suddenly, getting up from his crouched position, where he was petting the dog, and I feel self-conscious under his sudden, intense gaze, plunging my hands into the pockets of my jeans, so he won't see them shaking. "I didn't want you to think I was crowding you. But the need to see you again got too much, I'm afraid." He does his best to look contrite, but only succeeds in looking even more gorgeous than normal.

I'm not sure what to do with compliments like that, mainly because I'm not used to receiving them, and certainly not from someone who's made it very clear that he wants to be with me.

This is a very new, very strange experience.

"I—I was going to make us a stew for tonight," I say, a little randomly.

"That sounds lovely." His voice is soft and I wonder if, perhaps, he's sensed my discomfort.

"I'll need to put it on soon."

He nods. "Okay. Well, why don't you get on with that, and I'll make us a coffee? If that's alright with you?"

"That's just fine with me." I manage to smile at him, and he smiles back, and for the next few minutes, I make myself busy chopping onions, carrots and potatoes and putting them into my slow cooker, along with the meat, some stock and a little of the red wine.

"I can't wait until tonight," Logan says, once he's started the coffee brewing in the cafetière, coming up behind me, so close I can feel his breath on my neck. "That already looks delicious."

"By the time it's been cooking in here all afternoon," I reply, "the smell with have driven me insane. Luckily, I have to take Archie for a walk, so I'll get some respite."

"Oh," he says, stepping back a little so I can turn around, "can I come?"

"To take the dog for a walk?"

"Yes."

"If you want to."

"I want to," he says. "As long as I'm not crowding you."

"You're not."

I move to the other side of the kitchen, reaching up into the cupboard and pulling out the travel mugs that are stored on the top shelf.

"Why don't we put the coffee into these?" I suggest. "And we can head off."

"Okay," he replies. "I'll just pop over to the cottage and get my coat."

I nod my approval and he disappears, while I pour the coffee, fastening the lids tight on the travel mugs, put on my own coat, grab my keys and put on Archie's lead, all the while trying to remain calm.

I use Logan's absence to give myself a serious talking-to. I know I really ought to tell him about my condition – and its consequences – but I don't want to spoil the time we've got together. After all, these two weeks might be all we ever have. As I said to Amy and Nick, he might go home and forget all about me, and if he doesn't, well… I can tell him then, can't I? But why should I ruin a perfectly happy fortnight with my depressing news, and risk changing his perspective of me, for no good reason? There'll be plenty of time to do that, if it turns out we have a future together… and as much as I'm dreading his reaction to my news, and how it might change us, I really do hope he doesn't forget all about me, and that I do get to tell him, and that we can build something out of this. Because I want him more than anything. I really do.

The sun's out today, so I'm wearing my sunglasses, which although they look quite normal, are specially designed to block as much brightness as possible and avoid me having too much difficulty adjusting when I go back indoors again. Even so, I can still make out the clear blue sky reflecting on the sequinned, sparkling sea.

"So beautiful," Logan murmurs, reaching over and tucking a stray strand of hair behind my ear.

"It is, isn't it?" I turn from the view, to see he's looking directly at me, and try my hardest not to blush.

I'm just about to ask him if he intends saying things like that too often, when Archie pulls on his lead, dragging my attention away from Logan, towards another dog, about fifty yards ahead.

"Ahh… looks like Archie's spied a lady friend," Logan says, pursing his lips.

"I'm not sure Archie's meant to care anymore," I reply. "He's been neutered."

"It doesn't necessarily follow that he won't be interested," Logan says, taking a sip of his coffee and eyeing the way Archie keeps pulling on his lead. "Especially if the female dog is in heat."

"Can he tell that from here?"

"Possibly," he replies. "Collies can be particularly sensitive to all kinds of things. More so than a lot of other breeds."

"Oh God… that's the last thing I need."

Logan chuckles. "I wouldn't worry. If he's been neutered, it's not as though he can do any damage, is it?"

"No, but I'm not sure I want him mounting random dogs, just for the hell of it."

"Oh, I don't know… why shouldn't he have some fun?" His eyes twinkle and I find it hard not to smile.

"Because I doubt the other dog's owners would appreciate it?" I deliberately slow our pace, so the other dog and its owner can move out of range.

Logan shrugs, slowing too. "Maybe not. Although it does remind me of the time at the surgery, when the owner of a female King Charles Spaniel went to answer the call of nature, rather stupidly leaving her beloved pooch to its own devices. What she didn't appreciate was that the owner of the Airedale Terrier, who was sitting three chairs away, wasn't that interested in keeping an eye on her slightly excitable hound either, and was more interested in her social media status, and when Spaniel lady returned, all hell broke loose."

"Was the terrier…?" I ask, leaving my sentence hanging.

"Oh yes," he replies, nodding his head. "We had to drag him off."

"Sounds horrendous." I shudder.

"It's an occupational hazard," he says.

"At least you've only had to deal with rampant dogs, and not human beings," I remark.

He stops abruptly, looking down at me. "What on earth does that mean? Surely you've never had to pull an over-amorous husband off of his wife, have you?"

"Oh God, no. But… well, let's just say, it's quite hard to… to look someone in the eye, when you've heard him and his wife screaming in the throes passion the night before."

"Men? Screaming?" he says, his eyes widening. "Real, actual, grown men? Screaming?"

"Well, maybe groaning loudly in the case of the men, but you get what I mean."

He smiles. "Yes. I do."

I wonder for a moment, how on earth we got onto the subject of men groaning and women screaming. And why I let that happen. And then it dawns on me that I don't care. I don't even feel uncomfortable about it. My self-consciousness of earlier seems to have disappeared. Logan has put me at ease, and I just feel completely relaxed with him. Relaxed in a way I've never felt before, to the point where I'm starting to wonder whether Logan groans in the throes of passion, and what it would be like to scream his name, if suitably aroused.

"Archie seems to have forgotten his lady friend already." Logan nods towards my dog, who's now rummaging in the hedgerow.

"That's the male of the species for you," I comment, my thoughts quickly pulling back to reality. "As soon as the female is out of sight, she's out of mind."

Logan lets his hand rest on my arm and I can feel the heat of him even through my coat.

"We're not all like that, you know," he says, seriously.

"I know you're not."

I look up at him and he smiles once more. "Good," he says, as we start to walk again, Archie trotting along between us.

Logan

I stand in the shower, my hands flat on the white tiles, my arms braced, the warm water cascading over my head and down my back, as I try to control my body's reactions to just thinking about Hope. I suppose I should be getting used to this by now, being as I've been reacting to her like this since the first moment I saw her, nearly a week ago now, but it seems I'm not, and it's getting more and more difficult to fight this burning need I have to take her in my arms and kiss her… and then to just take her.

God, I wish I hadn't said I'd wait.

I shut off the water and reach for the towel on the heated rail, wrapping it around my waist and padding out into the bedroom, smiling to myself.

I'm glad I said I'd woo her though, because these last few days have been incredible.

That first evening together was fun. It was kind of flirty and exciting, but I'll admit I felt really nervous the next morning, when I went over there to see her. She wasn't in, so I decided to wait, because I wanted to see her, more than anything else in the world. And when she walked through the gate with that huge smile on her face, I thought my heart was going to burst. I wasn't prepared for the fact that she seemed a little self-conscious in my company. She hadn't been the night before, and I started to wonder if she was having second thoughts about us, but I think maybe she was just nervous too, because when we went for a walk with Archie, she seemed to settle down, and even ended up making that comment about the people who come to stay in the cottage. How I kept a straight face when she started talking about men groaning and women screaming, I've got no idea, because all I could think about was what it would be like to hear her scream my name, and how much I wanted to make that happen.

Looking back, I think that walk might have changed a lot of things between us. I don't know how exactly, or even why, but since then, Hope has been a lot more relaxed around me. She hasn't been at all tense, even when I've paid her compliments, which I do, all the time… because she's everything I've ever wanted.

We've spent every single day together this week and I've taken Archie for his walks with Hope – morning, noon and night – and like most Border Collies, Archie can certainly walk. Well, he can run, most of the time. To start with, we walked side-by-side, sometimes with Archie between us, looking up from Hope to me and back again, as though wondering what was going on, or maybe checking we were both still there, but early this morning, when we were in the woods, and he was off his lead and racing through the trees, she took my breath away, by slipping her hand into mine. It was a very uncertain and hesitant move on her part, but it came entirely from her, with no encouragement from me at all, although I smiled down at her as soon as I felt the contact and she smiled back, with that slightly shy, sexy smile, that I've fallen in love with a little more each day.

We've eaten together every night too, alternating between her place and the cottage. We don't bother to get dressed up anymore, and I much prefer to see her as she really is, in her tight jeans and fitted sweaters, or blouses, which show off her curves to perfection.

I sit on the edge of the bed, still struggling for some control, even though I know it's impossible, because the only way that's going to happen is if I stop thinking about Hope. And why would I ever want to do that? I'm in love with her.

The problem is, I need to do something about my obvious arousal, for two very good reasons. Firstly, it's Friday night, and she's due here for dinner in less than half an hour now, and I'd really hate for her to know how hard I find it to control myself around her, because I think it might make her uncomfortable. I'd also hate for her to think that sex is all I want from her. It isn't. I want more. I want everything. The second reason is that I know I've got six months of this, unless she decides otherwise, so I really need to take myself in hand – metaphorically, if not physically. Or maybe both…

I suppose there's a third reason too, which is that, after we spent the whole of Archie's lunchtime walk holding hands, as we strolled along the cliff path, I decided I wanted to do something a little different tonight. So, earlier this afternoon, I told Hope I was going into St Austell. She didn't seem to mind, and explained that she had a few things to do herself, and I drove to the supermarket, where I picked up everything I needed. Now though… now all the preparation is done, and as I start to get dressed, I'm beginning to wonder if I've read too much into that hand-holding, and whether I've gone too far.

At eight o'clock on the dot, Hope knocks on the door and I go to answer it. I tried to persuade her earlier this week that I really didn't mind her letting herself in. It's her cottage, after all. But she explained that she didn't want to catch me in an embarrassing situation. I assumed she meant coming out of the shower, or something even more compromising, perhaps. But then I also wondered whether she thought that her letting herself in here might make me think that I had the right to let myself into her house. I don't, but I decided not to press the matter.

I hold the door open and smile down at her.

"You look lovely," I tell her, honestly.

She's still wearing her skin-tight jeans, but has changed from the short multi-coloured sweater she had on earlier, to a floral blouse, that's nipped in at the waist, and hugs her hips.

"Thanks," she replies, and steps into the house.

"Come into the kitchen." I lead the way, holding my breath, waiting for her reaction as she takes in the scene before her, and hope to God I haven't overdone it – not that I've ever done anything like this before, so I've got no idea… that is, until I turn to look at Hope and see her eyes sparkling in the candlelight, which isn't surprising, being as there are candles everywhere, and no artificial light at all. There are fresh flowers on the table, in three small vases, and soft music is filtering through from the living room.

"Did you do all this?" she whispers, looking up at me, as she moves further into the room and clasps the back of one of the chairs, a little uncertainly.

"Yes."

"For me?"

"Of course. Is… Is it okay?"

"It's lovely," she replies, although her voice is a bit subdued and her smile a little half-hearted.

My disappointment is almost overwhelming. I thought this was the right way to go, after she held my hand this morning, and then at lunchtime too, but I guess not. I must have read too much into that after all.

"Wine?" I suggest, breaking our first awkward silence since she said 'yes' to me wooing her.

"Thank you," she says, and I hold out a chair for her to sit, and then pour her a glass of chilled Sancerre.

"We've got lobster," I tell her, putting the wine on the table. "I hope that's okay."

"That's lovely," she replies, and although she's merely repeating her earlier praise, I suppose I should feel grateful she didn't say 'fine'.

Our meal is very quiet, although she manages a smile when I serve our food, and lets me help her crack the claws, but her sombre mood has me worried. I've moved too fast... too soon. That much is clear. I'm just even more relieved now that she remains unaware of the effect she has on me, because I know for sure that, if she found out, she'd call a halt to whatever it is we've got going on here.

"Shall we have coffee in the living room?" I suggest, once we've both finished eating.

She nods her head, not even bothering to reply now, so I prepare the cafetière, put it on a tray with the cups, milk and sugar, and carry it through, Hope leading the way this time, her footsteps slow and steady, as though she's dragging her feet, which makes me wonder if she's more comfortable in the kitchen than she might be in the living room, where we'll have to sit together on the sofa.

I regret filling this room with candles now, wishing I'd not bothered to try and create a romantic atmosphere. It seems so wasted.

As we sit on the couch, the tray before us on the table, I know I have to say something.

"Sorry." It's the first thing that comes into my head.

"What for?" She turns to me, startled.

"This." I look around the room at the smouldering fire, and the candles that fill literally every surface. "I got it wrong. In case you're wondering, I hadn't intended this as a big seduction scene... you know, starting with the romantic meal in the kitchen, leading through to the soft candlelight in here, and winding up in the bedroom." She seems to be blushing, although her eyes are glistening too. "I just wanted you to have a nice evening," I explain. "And I know the last four evenings have been nice.... they've been really nice, but I wanted to do something special for you... I just got it wrong."

"No you didn't," she says, her voice cracking slightly, and tears forming in her eyes. *God... what's that about?* "I'm grateful... for everything you've done. It really is lovely."

"Then why haven't you enjoyed it?" I move a little closer. "And why the tears?"

"I'm sorry." She gulps, blinking and clearly trying very hard not to cry. "It's just that today's a difficult day for me."

"It is? Why?"

She blinks even harder now, staring into the fire. "Because it's the anniversary of Greg's death."

Her voice is barely a whisper, but I feel like the world's biggest idiot. I *am* the world's biggest idiot. I move right next to her and, without saying a word – because I can't think of anything to say – I pull her into my arms. She rests her head on my chest and I stroke her hair, as she cries, the dampness seeping through my shirt and onto my skin.

"I'm sorry," I murmur into her, after a while. "If I'd known, I'd have done things differently."

She leans back, although not so far back that I can't keep hold of her. "How?" She looks into my eyes, hers searching mine.

"Well, I'd still have wanted to spend the evening with you… if that's what you'd wanted too…"

"It is," she says quickly, and I have to smile. She sucks in a breath, letting it out slowly.

"But I'd have steered clear of the romantic touches," I add. "I'd have made it more about you and Greg, somehow."

She shakes her head, vehemently, wiping her cheeks with the back of her hand. "No," she says. "No, that's not what I'd have wanted. Greg's my past, and there's no point in pretending he made me happy, because he didn't." She pauses and lowers her head for a moment, before looking back up at me. "I'll admit I went to visit his grave," she says quietly. "He's buried in the churchyard here, although I rarely go to see him. But I went this afternoon, just to pay my respects… it seemed like the right thing to do."

"Hey…" I brush my fingertips down her cheek. "You don't have to account to me for what you do. Especially not on a day like today."

"I know," she replies, "I know I don't. But the thing is, I want to. You see, even when he and I were together, we never really were, not in the way that we should have been." She leans into my touch, just slightly and gazes into my eyes. "I love what you've done here this evening," she murmurs. "I really do… but I suppose it's just reminded me of all the years I missed out on having evenings like this, when I was with him."

I pull her close again and lean us back into the couch, holding her. "There's no point in looking back like that. You know that, don't you?" She doesn't respond, so I continue, "You can't change your past, Hope, any more than I can change mine. The point is, that we're here now, and I just want to make you happy."

"You do," she says, without even a second's hesitation, and although I want to smile about that, I can't.

"Then why are you crying?" I ask. "Can you explain it to me?"

"I'll try," she mumbles and sniffles a couple of times before she says, "Greg may not have been the right man for me, and I might not have been the right woman for him, but we kind of settled for each other, I suppose, and for good or bad, for whatever reason, we were together for a long time… and then he died."

"I know… and you're sad." I hate that thought. I hate the idea of her being anything but happy, especially when she's with me, but there's no getting away from it.

"Yes. I'm sad. For today. And… and I feel guilty."

"Why?"

"Because, up until just after lunchtime, I'd forgotten it was the anniversary; and because I never should have married him in the first place… because I knew we were settling and that something was missing, because we made each other miserable…" She shrugs. "Do you want a list?"

"No. But I'd like you to stop beating yourself up over things that aren't your fault."

She rests her hand on my chest, looking up into my face. "Thank you," she whispers.

"Don't thank me. I'm just… well, I'm sorry."

"What for."

"Because you're sad."

I place my hand over hers, and she rests her head on my shoulder and we sit for a while, and I don't move a muscle... not even when I feel her tears dampening my shirt again, as she cries silent tears of regret for the man she once loved, and for the happiness they should have had together.

Chapter Thirteen

Hope

Yesterday was hard.

It was really hard.

The day started well. In fact, I even forgot what day it was to begin with, and Logan and I took Archie for his walk, which has become a habit since Tuesday morning. The decision to take his hand while we were walking in the woods, was pure instinct. It was something I wanted to do, not for him to guide me, or to lead me, because I was struggling to see in the dim early morning light, but just because I wanted to feel the presence of him. And it felt right. I don't regret it, not for one instant.

It only dawned on me that it was the anniversary, when I got back home after our lunchtime walk, during which Logan had held my hand for the whole time. As I was checking my e-mails, I noticed the date, and at that moment, a dark cloud descended. I'd forgotten. What kind of widow does that, just two years after her husband's death? I suppose the kind who thinks she might have found happiness with another man. The kind who was never happy with her husband in the first place. The guilt was overwhelming.

So, when Logan came over early in the afternoon and announced that he needed to go into St Austell, I told him I had some errands to run too. I didn't. But it seemed only right that I should visit Greg's grave and pay my respects. I stood in the churchyard, staring down at his headstone, the engraved words meaning nothing, the man beneath them meaning less… and that was when I realised I couldn't remember the last time Greg had held my hand, or looked me in the eyes, or made me smile, or done anything at all that was just for me. I don't think I've ever felt as sad as I did in that moment. The guilt didn't go though, because I realised I was as much to blame as he was. I let it happen… to both of us.

Obviously, I had no idea that Logan had planned such a special evening for us, and I suppose it would have been helpful if I'd told him, before he'd left, about the significance of the day, but I didn't want to spoil things. I didn't want him to think that Greg still matters to me. Not in that way. He's part of my past, obviously. He's a big part of it, because I was with him for so long, but in just a few short days, Logan already means so much more to me.

I didn't tell him that, of course. But I did try to explain everything else. I don't know if Logan understood, but he held me while I cried, and that felt good. And then, later on, he took me home. We stood on my doorstep for a while, and he asked if I was okay. I was tempted to tell him about my condition… that getting around the cottage by candlelight had been difficult, that I'd had to get him to help me with the lobster because I couldn't see it properly in the dim, romantic lighting, and that there will come a day when evenings like the one we'd just shared will be a thing of the past. But I didn't. Because the last thing I want to do now is to spoil what we have… just in case it's all we have. So instead I told him I was a lot more than okay, and it was the truth. Just being in his arms, somehow made everything okay again.

This morning, I wake feeling better, but I suppose that's not difficult after yesterday, and after a quick shower, I race downstairs, eager to see Logan… oh, and to take Archie for his walk, of course. It's only when I'm pulling on my walking boots, that it dawns on me that Logan might not want to come out with us anymore. My revelations of last night, my having cried all over him about my late husband, might have been too much for him. I hook on Archie's collar and open the door with a certain amount of trepidation, and smile out my relief, when I see Logan waiting for us.

"Good morning." He smiles back and takes a step towards us.

"Hello."

He holds out his hand and I take it in mine and, together, we walk out through the gate, across the road and up into the woods.

"Sleep okay?" he asks, after a few paces.

"Yes, thank you."

"Good."

"You?" I ask.

"Like a log."

"Sorry about last night," I say, as I bend to let Archie off his lead, and straighten up again.

"You have nothing to apologise for," Logan replies, his voice soft with concern, his thumb brushing against my knuckles.

I look up at him. "You were right about one thing…"

"I was?"

"Yes. It's in the past. So, do you think we can forget about it?"

"Of course." He smiles and I go to turn away, to start on our walk, but he pulls me back, looking deep into my eyes. "But if you want to talk about him, Hope, I won't mind. Honestly."

I lean into him and he puts his arms around me, just like he did last night. "Thank you," I murmur into his chest.

"You're welcome," he says, and then takes my hand, and we stride off after Archie.

We've only gone a short distance, when I remember what day of the week it is. "It's Saturday."

"And?" He turns to me.

"I'll have to come over to the cottage later, to change the sheets and give you some fresh towels. You don't mind, do you?"

"No. I'll help."

"Oh, you don't have to do that."

He nudges into me. "If it means I get to spend some time with you, I'll gladly help," he says, and I smile up at him. "What do you normally do when people stay for two weeks? Do you have to wait for them to go out and sneak over to the cottage? Or do you make an arrangement with them?"

I shrug my shoulders. "To be honest, no-one's ever stayed for two weeks before. I think they're too tired to stay for more than one..." I let my voice fade and he chuckles lightly.

"Well, based on what you've told me, they probably need to go home for a rest, and to catch up on their sleep."

It's my turn to laugh now, although my mind can't help wandering, and I contemplate whether a week at the cottage would be long enough if I were staying there with Logan. Somehow I doubt it...

We managed to spend the whole day together, firstly changing the sheets on the bed, then clearing up the cottage a little bit – not that it needed it. Logan is quite a tidy kind of person, from what I can see. Then we had lunch together at my place, after which Logan did the truly honourable thing and helped me with my accounts, reading out the figures on my receipts as I entered them into my accounting package, which made it a whole lot easier than it usually is. We made the process more fun by including lots of coffee and cookies and then a little later, I made us dinner.

After we've finished eating, I suggest we move into the living room to drink our coffee.

"This is a lovely room," he says, following me in and carrying the coffee things on a tray, and it dawns on me that he's never been in here before.

"Thank you." He puts the tray on the table and then we sit together on the sofa.

Once I've poured our drinks, I snuggle up next to him. He doesn't say a word, but moves his drink to the other hand and puts his arm around me. Far more so than last night, when I was crying and feeling guilty, I'm aware of how it feels to be held by him. I'm aware of how strong his arms feel, the hardness of his chest beneath me, and even the rippling of his stomach muscles, whenever he moves. I'm also aware that we've now held hands, and we've cuddled... and that I'd like to do more. A lot more.

Alternating between the cottage and my house, we spend all of our evenings together, and most of our days too, come to think of it.

I've grown accustomed to his company, to sitting opposite him at dinner, and at lunch, to drinking coffee with him, to watching him cook, to hearing his laughter and matching it with my own, to seeing the way he plays with Archie, and how much my stupid dog loves him for it. I love having him here. I love his company. And I'm a very long way to being very much in love with him. He makes me feel safer than I've ever felt before, and happier than I can remember being in my entire life.

But, as we get to Wednesday, the end of his holiday approaches like a dark shadow. It's not something we've discussed yet, but it's there, in the background, all the time now. I can feel it, and so can he.

"How would you feel about coming to visit me?" he says out of the blue after we've finished dinner and are clearing away the dishes. "I mean, obviously I can come back to the cottage whenever it's free, but do you think you could come to me?"

I stand, staring at him for a moment, the hope in his eyes almost overwhelming. I suppose now would be the perfect time to explain that a journey like that wouldn't be as straightforward for me as it would for most people… and to tell him why. But I can't. Not yet. Instead, I just say, "But… but I've never been to London," sounding pathetic.

He steps slowly towards me, his eyes never leaving mine. "I don't live in London, Hope," he replies, taking my hands in his when he reaches me. "Not really. I live in Richmond."

"Oh yes. I remember you saying now." I frown. "But that's close enough to London, isn't it?"

He smiles. "It's not far," he says, "but I promise you, Richmond is nowhere near as scary as London and there are all kinds of ways to get there, if you're going by train, some of which don't take you anywhere near Central London."

I think for a moment, wondering if it would be possible. I've been on the train to the Royal Devon and Exeter Hospital for my initial diagnosis and check-ups. And that was okay… "C—Can I think about it?" I ask, feeling incredibly feeble.

"Of course you can." He gently kisses my forehead, his lips lingering for just a second before he pulls away again.

"And in the meantime, we can call each other?" I say gazing up at him. "And text?"

"Text?" he says, frowning slightly and looking doubtful now, although I'm not sure why.

"Yes."

"Okay." He shrugs. I've got no idea what that's about, but I don't query it, because my mind is too full of long train journeys, interspersed with complicated changes and too many people on station platforms, with signs that I won't be able to see properly…

For the next couple of days, Logan doesn't mention me visiting him again, but when we're together on Friday – the day before he's due to leave – it dawns on me, as we're finishing lunch, that the only meal we haven't shared together yet, is breakfast, and that if I do go to stay with him, that will change. Of course, having breakfast with someone implies spending the night with them, so I don't bring it up in conversation, but I look at him across the table, and wonder if he's been thinking the same thing. I wonder if that's why he asked me. But then I mentally slap myself for doubting him, even for a second. Logan's not like that. He wouldn't try and trick me into sleeping with him. That's not who he is.

We're just getting ready to take Archie on his evening walk, a stew bubbling away in the slow cooker, when Logan's phone beeps. He checks the screen and his face darkens, before he turns it off and puts it in his pocket.

"Is everything okay?" I ask.

He shakes his head. "That was Zach," he replies.

"Oh."

"It's the first time he's been in touch since… since… well, you know."

"I see. Does he know that you know what happened? I mean, he'd left by the time you went back and confronted Brianna, so…"

"He knows," Logan says grimly. "His message makes that very clear. But why send it today, of all days?" he mutters. I stay silent, because I don't understand the significance of this day, more than any other. He looks down at me, then closes the gap between us, standing right in front of me. "Tomorrow would have been my wedding day," he says softly and I feel my heart actually constrict in my chest.

"Do… Do you want to talk?" I ask him.

"About Zach's message. Not particularly. I was planning on ignoring it."

"No… I meant about the fact that tomorrow would have been your wedding day."

"Not particularly. That's in the past, as far as I'm concerned." He reaches out, cupping my face with his hand. "The last two weeks have shown me all kinds of things," he murmurs gently, "one of which is that I'm better off without them… both of them."

"Do you want to stay an extra night?" I ask him on impulse.

A slow smile forms on his lips and he looks directly into my eyes. "I'd love to," he says.

"I know you'll still have to go home on Sunday, but we could have one more day together before you do, couldn't we?"

He nods. "Yes. And there's no-one else I'd rather spend the day with than you."

"Well, I don't like the idea of you spending tomorrow travelling… and thinking too much."

He steps closer still, so we're almost touching. "The only person I'd be thinking about tomorrow is you," he says. "I promise you that."

"It would have been your wedding day, Logan," I reason, not wanting to say out loud that it makes perfect sense to me that he'd spend the day thinking about his ex-fiancée, the time they spent together, their broken engagement, and all the 'what ifs' that go with that.

"Would have been," he repeats. "That's the point." His thumb grazes gently against my cheek and it's all I can do not to sigh. "Have breakfast with me tomorrow?"

I lean back, staring up at him, stunned. "H—Have breakfast? What are you suggesting? I—I'm sorry, but when I asked you to stay the extra night, I meant for you to stay on at the cottage… I—I didn't mean…" I blush, feeling flustered.

He smiles. "Hey… I'm just suggesting we have breakfast together," he clarifies. "That's all."

"Oh." I feel a little foolish now, for reading too much into his suggestion, based entirely on where my mind had been wandering earlier on.

"Don't get me wrong. I'd love to wake up with you first," he says, moving his thumb slightly, and letting it brush across my bottom lip, "and *then* have breakfast. And I'd like it even more if we'd just spent the whole night together… not necessarily sleeping… but I'll make do with breakfast. For now."

His voice is low, deep, and sexy, his eyes like molten chocolate, boring into mine and my body quivers at his words. For a moment, I wonder about saying 'yes', to a lot more than breakfast, but then I'm hit by the instant, ice cold shower of the memory that it's only two weeks since he broke off his engagement, and that tomorrow would have been his wedding day.

"Breakfast would be lovely," I say, although my voice sounds a little strangled, and I clear my throat. "Why don't you come to me? It'll be easier."

He nods his head, smiling and says, "Thank you," and I lean into him again, as he adds, "Sorry," and I look up at him. "I wasn't playing fair then, was I?"

"No."

His arms come around me, as he whispers, "Still, let's not dismiss the idea completely," and I chuckle into him.

We spend the whole of Saturday together. It's our last day, and after we've walked Archie, Logan takes us out in his car, with Archie as well. This isn't something I'm used to these days, having become a creature of habit, but Logan is very solicitous of me. He's a very competent, safe driver, and after a long walk in the countryside, we go to a lovely pub for lunch, before returning home with fish and chips in the evening. Sitting in the living room, curled up beside Logan, his arms tight around me, with Archie nestling at my feet, I can't help thinking how perfect this is... or that it would be, if Logan wasn't going home tomorrow morning.

Logan's very quiet and hasn't even drunk his coffee, and I lean back slightly looking up at him.

"Are you alright?" I ask.

"Not really."

I pull away from him and he lets me go. "What's wrong? Are you thinking about the wedding?" I'd rather he wasn't, but I suppose it would be understandable. Especially today.

"No." He looks at me, then sits forward slightly, turning and taking my hands in his. "I'm thinking that I don't want to go home."

I smile, blushing slightly. "I was just thinking the same thing."

He stares into my eyes, shifting sightly closer, as his gaze moves to my lips and I know he's going to kiss me. I inch forward, parting my lips, my eyes fluttering closed, just as I feel a nudging in my back, between me and the sofa.

"What?" I turn, and see Archie, trying to force his way in. "What is it?"

He moves further forward, trying to settle in the tiny gap between myself and Logan.

"I think we've got ourselves a chaperone," Logan says, smiling.

"He just doesn't like to be left out of anything," I say, rubbing Archie behind his ears, to which he closes his eyes, in apparent ecstasy.

"Who does?" he remarks, petting Archie on the head.

Logan

It's hard to think this will be my last shower here... at least for the time being anyway.

We had such a lovely day yesterday, getting away from it all and just being a couple, like any other. I honestly didn't think about the wedding at all, not once, not until Hope mentioned it in the evening. And at the time, all I'd been thinking about was going home, and that I really didn't want to. I'd been thinking about how much I love her house, and how easy it would be to make a home there with her. Being in her living room with her, seeing her in her own space like that, it made me want to be there with her all the time, to spend our evenings curled up on the sofa like that with Archie, watching a movie, or snuggled up on her love seat in the corner, reading a book, or maybe just kissing. God... kissing Hope. What a thought. We came close last night too. We really did. Would that one kiss have led to more? Might I have ended up staying the night, and maybe not sleeping too much, like I'd suggested earlier, when I managed to embarrass the heck out of her so easily, teasing her about breakfast? Who knows? But judging from the expression on Hope's face, she at least wasn't averse to the kiss. And that's a good thing.

Speaking of breakfast, I'd better get on. I'm supposed to be over at Hope's by eight, because I'm on a tighter schedule than I'd expected. Rachel was obviously expecting me to go home yesterday – as was I – but when I sent her a text message late on Friday night, to say I'd changed my plans, she informed me that she was going to be out today from three onwards, so if I wanted my key, I'd need to get there before then. As a result, I'm going to have to leave here before ten, which is a shame, because I'd rather stay longer, even if it was just a few hours.

I switch off the shower, dry off and fold the towel neatly, leaving it over the rail, and then head out into the bedroom to get dressed, putting on jeans and a thick sweater, before I make my way over to Hope's, knocking on her front door.

She lets me in, smiling, although I can see a sadness behind her eyes, which I guess might reflect my own.

"Breakfast is nearly ready," she says.

"I could smell the bacon from the cottage," I tell her and she chuckles. "I'm going to miss that sound."

"What sound? Bacon cooking?"

"No. You. Laughing."

She turns, tilting her head. "I'm going to miss you too."

"Good."

She offers me a seat and I sit down, while she dishes up bacon and eggs, followed by toast and home-made preserves, washed down with coffee.

We talk while we eat, both scrupulously avoiding the topic of my imminent departure, and I don't push Hope about her visiting me either, because I know she's nervous about it and I don't want my last few hours here to revolve around her uncertainty. We can talk about it over the phone, and if she really isn't sure about coming up by train, then I can always come back here again. Anytime she likes.

Once we've finished breakfast, I go back over to the cottage to finish my packing, hurrying a bit, because I don't have much time left, and I'd rather spend what little there is with Hope.

When I come back outside to put my holdall into the boot of my car, Hope appears from her house, carrying a small box, which she hands to me.

"It… It's just something to remember me by," she murmurs, ducking her head, although there's a strong emotion in her voice that touches my soul.

I look inside the box, to see it contains a fruit cake and a couple of jars of home-made jam.

"Thank you." I turn and put the box alongside the holdall, before closing the boot, and stepping up close to her. "I appreciate that… but I don't need a cake, or jam, to remember you. I'm not going to forget you, Hope. And we're going to talk, every single day."

She looks up, her eyes brimming with tears and I put my arms around her, pulling her close to my chest. God, this is hard.

"Do you really want to give me something to remember you by?" I ask, resting my forehead against hers, so that I feel her nod her head, even though she doesn't actually reply. "Then can I kiss you?"

I lean back a little, studying her face, feeling shy all of a sudden, although I don't know why, considering how close we came to kissing last night. She raises her hand, brushing her fingers through my short beard.

"Yes," she whispers, and I lower my head, until our lips meet, holding them there for a few moments, feeling the softness of her lips on mine, the intensity of that simple connection, reaching right down to my core, before I pull back again. Her eyes are still closed, but she slowly opens them, perhaps wondering why I kept that so brief. It was intentional, mainly because if I'd done anything else, if I'd lengthened the kiss in the way I want to, I'd never have been able to leave her.

As it is, I have to, but kissing Hope isn't something I'm ever going to forget. It's like nothing I've ever felt before.

Leaving Hope is the hardest thing I've ever done. Harder than leaving Brianna, or realising that she and my brother were cheating on me. Harder than breaking off my engagement... Harder than anything.

Even so, I'm driving home grinning to myself.

Okay, so I don't know when I'm going to see Hope again – not exactly – but I know that I will. And obviously I'm going to miss her like mad, but at least we can talk all the time, so it could be worse.

I manage to make it to the services at Sparkford, roughly two and a half hours into my journey, before the need to hear her voice becomes too overwhelming and I pull up outside the petrol station, where I buy myself a coffee, while calling Hope. She answers straight away, before I've even paid for my drink and I smile to myself.

"Did you know it was me?" I ask, handing the guy behind the counter a ten pound note.

"Yes. I saved your number into my contacts," she replies. "But surely you can't be home already?"

"No." I take my change, pick up my coffee and head back out of the door. "I've stopped for coffee, or more accurately... I've stopped because I needed to hear your voice. I miss you already, Hope."

"Oh... that's a lovely thing to say."

I can hear her smiling, and smile myself. I don't care how stupid I look, walking back to my car, with a dumb grin plastered on my face. I'm in love, and I don't care who knows it.

"Well, it's true," I reply, getting back behind the wheel of my car and closing the door. "I'd better be going again, or I won't get back in time for Rachel, but I'll call you when I get home. Okay?"

"Okay. Take care, won't you?"

"I will."

"Goodbye," she says, softly.

"Goodbye."

We both wait. "Are you going to hang up?" she asks eventually.

"Yes, but only because I have to."

She giggles. "Go on then."

"Okay. I'll talk to you in a couple of hours."

"Alright."

The words 'I love you' are on the tip of my tongue, scrabbling to get out of my mouth, but I can't say them now, sitting in my car, by myself, in a petrol station. That's not romantic at all. And it's certainly not the actions of a man who's doing his best to woo the woman he loves.

"Goodbye, beautiful…"

She sighs. "Goodbye."

I hang up, before I can change my mind, and start the car, pulling out of the parking space and driving out of the garage and around the roundabout to rejoin the main road.

It's just after two-fifteen by the time I get to Rachel's flat in Kew and I park in the area at the front, in one of the visitor bays. There's an intercom system to get in, which I ring, pressing on the buzzer for flat ten, waiting until Rachel's face comes onto the mini screen and she smiles, which is nice.

"You're back!" she almost screams and I hear the click of the door, letting me into the lobby.

"Cheers, sis," I call out, passing through the door, which slams behind me, before I open the interior door to my right, leading to the stairs, which I take two at a time, leading up to the second floor, of three. I've still got that stupid grin on my face, but I can't help it. I think it's a permanent feature now.

Rachel's flat is one of five on this level and when I get up there, she's waiting outside her door for me. At around five foot five, Rachel's tiny by comparison with me, and with Zach, but she shares our dark colouring. Naturally slim, she's bordering on unhealthily skinny at the moment, having decided for some unknown reason that she needed to lose weight before the wedding, and I have to say, I don't think it's done her any favours. Her cheekbones are now protruding, and her eyes seem to have almost shrunk into her head. She looks unwell, if you ask me, but then no-one's asking me, and I'm certainly not offering an opinion. I'm not a complete fool.

"I was starting to think you were never coming home," she says, leaning up and kissing me on both cheeks, her lips not quite making contact.

"You'll never know how tempted I was not to," I reply, as she steps aside and we enter her perfect apartment, which is all whites and creams, all angles and lines, and way too sterile for me.

She stops, halfway into her living room and turns to face me, looking up at me closely. "You're different," she says.

"I am?"

"Yes."

She takes my hand and positively drags me into the centre of the room, facing the large floor-to-ceiling windows, the winter sunshine falling onto my face. "Your eyes," she muses, standing in front of me. "They're not the same."

"I think my eyes are pretty much the same as ever they were."

She frowns. "And you're feeling okay?"

"I'm feeling absolutely bloody perfect."

Her shoulders drop and she rolls her eyes dramatically. "Oh, Christ Almighty," she wails. "Please tell me it's not true."

"What?"

"Please tell me you haven't met someone else?"

I take a step back from her intense gaze. "So what if I have?"

Her eyes darken and her lips form into a thin line, and I know I'm about to get hit with both barrels. "Don't you ever learn, Logan?" She raises her voice, her hands perched on her narrow hips.

"This is different," I reason, although I don't know why I feel the need to justify myself to her.

"Yes, and I seem to remember you said that about Brianna, not that long before you walked out on her, leaving her to deal with cancelling *your* wedding, which should've been yesterday, in case you've forgotten, while you've been so busy playing hide the sausage with whoever the fuck it is you've shacked up with now."

"Don't talk about Hope like that, Rachel," I warn. "For your information, I'm not playing at anything, and we haven't 'shacked up' as you so charmingly put it. We've only known each other for two weeks."

"That's never stopped you before," she counters.

"What the hell does that mean?" Her not so veiled insult towards Hope has me more angry than I've ever been with her before, and I can't hold back now. "You know perfectly well that, until Brianna, I'd never lived with anyone, so stop making me sound like some kind of lothario. Besides, Hope lives in Cornwall, so we can hardly move in together just like that, can we? *And* it would be nice if you could remember that I'm not the one who walked out on your friend…"

"Yes, you did," she interrupts. "You left. Remember?"

"Yes, but only because I came home and found her shagging Zach."

The air between us positively crackles and Rachel takes a half step back, almost stumbling, and I grab her arms to stop her falling.

"Careful, sis." It seems I do still care about her, despite my anger.

"Zach?" she mumbles.

"Yes."

"It was Zach?

"Yes."

She sighs and pulls away from me, going to sit down on her white, angular sofa. "No wonder he's been so weird the last couple of times I've spoken to him," she says, pushing her fingers back through her shoulder-length hair. She looks up at me again. "Why didn't you tell me this before?"

"Well, at the time, you didn't exactly give me a chance," I reason. "You jumped down my throat that night, if you remember?"

"And afterwards?" she asks, ignoring my accusation. "We've spoken over the phone. Why couldn't you have told me then?"

"Because I didn't think this was the kind of thing to tell you over the phone. You and Zach are close, and I didn't want to hurt you."

She looks down again, shaking her head slowly from side to side, struggling to take it all in, I think. Well, I know how that feels.

When she looks up again, her eyes meet mine. "I wish you'd told me," she mutters, sulkily, before she rallies and adds, "but when it comes down to it, it doesn't really matter who the man was, does it? It was just sex as far as Brianna was concerned, and she still wants you back. She's not going to give up that easily, Logan. She calls and texts me several times a day, and she keeps coming down to my floor at work to ask about you and talk about it. So, don't be surprised if she tries to contact you again."

"I'm not interested in her. Or in anything she's got to say. She's history."

"Well, if you want my opinion, I think you're making a mistake breaking up with her, without even trying to work things out. You were good together."

"That's not what you said when I came and told you we were getting engaged."

She frowns at me. "No, but I was wrong about that."

"You told me I was being a fucking idiot, if memory serves."

"I know… and I just said, I was wrong. You and Brianna were right for each other."

"Yeah, we were perfect." I can't hide my sarcasm. "Right up until she decided to jump on our brother."

"That's as may be. But you're not even giving her a chance to explain. Everyone makes mistakes…"

"This is a bit more than a mistake, Rachel. And, in case you haven't noticed, I don't have to give her a chance. I've already walked away."

She stares at me for a moment and then shakes her head. "At least don't get involved anyone else just yet… not when things aren't really over with Brianna. Can't you see? It's not fair on anyone. Not Brianna, and not this new woman… Hope, was it?"

"But things *are* over with Brianna. At least they are for me. And I'm already involved with Hope, so Brianna's just going to have to deal with it."

"Hmm, well good luck convincing Brianna of that," she says, letting out a long sigh as she gets up to fetch my key.

By the time I get home, I'm feeling a bit disgruntled. The smile has certainly faded after that conversation – well, argument – with Rachel. I suppose I knew from the tone of her text messages to me that Brianna wasn't going to give up, but to be faced with the reality of it, coupled with my sister siding with my ex, and her evident lack of understanding for how I feel, after such a lovely time with Hope, is all a bit depressing.

I open the door to my apartment, using my new key, and let myself in, before sucking in a breath as I take in my surroundings.

"Wow…" It looks amazing in here, and I walk from room to room, marvelling at the change.

The decorators have done a fantastic job, replacing my old, dull beige and magnolia coloured walls with soft, muted blues, greens and yellows, brightening the whole apartment and making it feel much more homely. To be honest, I'm really glad I'm not selling the place now, because it's just how I've always wanted it to be.

And with that in mind, I sit down on my navy blue sofa, in my duck-egg blue living room, and call Hope.

She answers on the second ring, and I instantly feel better, just hearing the word, "Hello."

"Hi," I reply.

"You're home?" she asks.

"Yes. I just walked in. How are you? What have you been doing?" I bombard her with questions.

"Not much. I took Archie for his walk this afternoon. He missed you… he kept looking around for you."

"That's nice to hear," I reply, smiling at the thought. "Did you miss me too?"

"Yes. But I didn't keep looking for you. I knew you wouldn't be there." She sounds sad.

"I will be," I tell her. "It won't be long before we see each other again." At least I hope not, anyway.

"I hope not," she says, as though she's read my mind, and I grin like a Cheshire cat. "So, how was your journey home?"

"Not bad." For a moment, I contemplate not telling her about my visit to my sister, but then I remember that our relationship is about complete honesty. "That is, until I got to Rachel's."

"Oh." I can hear the inquisitive note to her voice, tempered with disappointment, I think.

"She noticed something was different about me."

"She did?"

"Yes. I think it was the smile plastered on my face that gave me away."

"Why were you smiling?" she asks.

"Because I was thinking about you."

She sighs and I lay back on the couch, staring up at the ceiling, picturing her, and smiling once again. "What did she say?" Hope asks.

"Oh, just that I'm being impetuous... you know? Being me."

"I see."

"I told her you're different, but I'm not sure she took me very seriously. I suppose my history goes against me."

"I suppose it does," she replies.

"Even if you are different," I add quickly, because I can hear the doubt creeping into her voice. "You're completely different to anyone I've ever known before."

"I hope so," she whispers.

"You are. I told you that already, Hope. I meant it. You are different."

There's a brief pause, before she asks, "Was that all you talked about?"

"No. I told her that it was Zach who'd been in bed with Brianna... although maybe not in those precise words, being as I was losing my temper with her at the time."

"Oh dear... and how did she take the news?"

"Not very well. She was shocked, I think. But she made a point of telling me that it made no difference to the fact that Brianna wants me back." There's a silence on the end of the phone. A long, stony silence. "Hope?"

"Hmm?"

"Brianna is a friend of Rachel's. They've known each other for years, and it's a difficult situation." I'm not sure why I'm skirting around my sister's disloyalty, but I can only assume that speaking with Hope – even for just a few minutes – has already soothed my anger, to the point where I don't really care about Rachel's attitude to the situation. "They have to work together too," I add. "But none of that means I want anything to do with Brianna, or that I'm going to speak to her. I can't stop her from doing anything with Rachel, or from trying to contact me, but I promise I won't respond to her. Okay?"

"Why are you telling me this, Logan?" Hope asks, her voice barely audible.

"Because I'm being honest with you. Completely honest. I'm proving to you that you can trust me and that I'll always tell you the truth, about everything."

The silence returns, deafening me.

"Are you okay, Hope?" I ask, refusing to let it stretch for too long.

"Yes," she replies, but I'm sure I can hear something in her voice. Uncertainty? Suspicion? Fear?

"Are you worried about Brianna?" I decide to get straight to the point. Or at least what I think is the point.

"Yes, in a way," she says. "But do you blame me? You say you want to be with me, but you were supposed to marry her… just yesterday. And, whatever you think, she's clearly not giving up on you. She wants you back, and I'm not sure how I feel about that."

"Okay. I can understand that. But just because she wants me, that doesn't mean I want her. Don't you remember? That first Monday I was with you, when we talked properly about our pasts, and I opened up to you. I told you how I feel about you, and that I want you… all of you. I meant it. I still mean it now. I want you so much, Hope, there isn't room in my heart for anyone else. We've only been apart for a few hours and I miss you, so much. I miss your sparkling blue eyes, and your scent… the way it lingers in a room, even after you've left. And the way your hair shines in the sunlight, and the softness of your hand in mine…" I hear her gasp, just slightly. "What's wrong?" I ask.

"Nothing… but that's… that's just so romantic." She whispers the last word on a breath and I smile.

"I know. I'm wooing you. Remember? You should probably try and get used to it."

Chapter Fourteen

Hope

I really, really didn't like hearing that Logan's ex wants him back. I mean, I doubt any woman wants to hear that. But the fact that he's hundreds of miles away, and she's just around the corner from him, isn't helping.

I've never felt threatened, or jealous before, and I didn't like it. It's not who I am. But it even overshadowed all the lovely things he said, when he told me that he missed me, although I'll admit that hearing him say there wasn't room in his heart for anyone but me did take my breath away. I mean, that's the next best thing to saying 'I love you', isn't it? Well, it is to me.

Of course, hearing all of that made me feel guilty for keeping my secret, but at the same time, the knowledge that his ex is still in the picture feels like a kind of justification of my actions too. After all, why should I burden Logan with my problems if we really don't have a future together?

This morning, my phone rings early, just as I'm stepping out of the shower and I race back into my bedroom to answer it, knowing the only person who's likely to call at this time of day, is Logan.

"Hello," I answer, throwing myself onto the bed.

"You sound out of breath," he replies.

"I've just run into my bedroom from the shower," I explain.

"Oh…" He pauses. "You really shouldn't tell me things like that."

"Why not?"

"It's distracting, thinking of you running around in nothing but a towel."

I chuckle and flip over onto my back. "Sorry," I mutter, although I'm not. Not even remotely.

"No, you're not," he says, like he can read my mind.

"No, I'm not."

He laughs himself now. "So, apart from running around in a towel, and fuelling my dreams, what else are you up to?"

I blush at the thought of what he might be dreaming about, but I don't remark on that. Instead, I just reply, "I'm about to take Archie for his walk. What about you?"

"I'm just about to leave for work."

"At this time of day?"

"Afraid so. It's a four mile cycle ride, which will take me about half an hour, and because my boss let me have the last two weeks off at extremely short notice, I agreed to get in early today and open up… oh, and take the next two weekends on call."

"Oh." I'm struggling to disguise my disappointment. "Does that mean we won't be able to see each other?"

"Not for a couple of weekends, no," he explains, sounding calmer than I feel. I'm not sure how to take that. Before he left, he seemed really keen to see me again, to 'woo' me, in fact, but now he's back home, is that wearing off? Was I right… were those two weeks all we were ever destined to get? "I mean," he continues, "I obviously can't come down to you, not if I'm on call, and I'd hate for you to come all the way up here, and for me to have to keep running out on you every time there's an emergency."

"I see." Even I can hear the dismay in my tone, so I'm sure he must be able to as well.

"Hey," he says. "Don't sound so sad. We'll work something out. I promise."

I try really hard to believe him and not to think about the fact that his ex-fiancée wants him back, and that she's there… and I'm here, hundreds of miles away, an ever-fading memory.

There's a moment's pause. "I'm sorry," he says, "I'm going to have to go, or I'll be late for work."

"Okay."

"Hope. Will you please stop worrying?"

"How can you tell I'm worrying?"

"I can hear it," he says.

"I didn't say anything."

"Exactly. I'll call you later."

"Okay."

"Now… hang up."

"No. You hang up."

He sighs. "Okay, but only because I'm going to be late for work." I can still hear him breathing. "Bye, Hope," he says, and after another few seconds, the line goes dead.

After I've finished breakfast and Archie's settled in his basket, I go over to the cottage.

I decided while I was walking Archie, that worrying about Logan and his ex isn't going to get me anywhere. I have to learn to trust him. At least I have to try, and thinking the worst won't help.

I strip the bed first, remembering doing this with Logan last weekend, him over by the window, and me on this side, gazing at him across the wide expanse of the mattress. It's nowhere near as much fun doing it by myself, although at least now he's not here, I can sit for a few minutes, hold the pillows to my face and smell his scent. Closing my eyes, I can picture him, my body tingling as I recall his kiss yesterday morning, the way his lips felt against mine, the intensity of his gaze, and the feeling that lingered behind them. I know it was there. I know it wasn't just me who felt something then. Was it?

I shake my head and get up, going around to the far side of the bed, and tripping over a pile of books that are lying on the floor. I manage to stop myself from falling, remembering as I do why I have the furniture, both here at in my own home, arranged in the way that I do… so that I have clear pathways and I know exactly where everything is, and don't end up flat on my face. Bending, I pick up the books, one at a time, being as they're quite hefty, and put them down on the bedside table. There are half a dozen here, three by the same author, but judging from the covers and titles, I'd say they all fall into the 'action/adventure' genre, which really isn't my scene at all. I know there are a few on the shelves in the living room, though, in case guests should want to read them, and I wander through and check the bookshelves, just to be on the safe side. No... there are no gaps. These aren't my books, so they must belong to Logan, and he must have left them here by mistake.

I finish stripping the bed, then gather up the towels, adding them to the pile of bedding, and then, with the books on top, I carry everything back across to my house, leaving the books on the kitchen table before I put the bedding into the washing machine.

There's no point in me trying to call Logan now; he'll be at work. But I'll maybe try giving him a ring at lunchtime, to let him know that he's left his books here, and in the meantime, I suppose I might as well go back over to the cottage and get on with clearing up.

I take my box of cleaning materials with me, and let myself back in, starting in the kitchen. I have to say, it doesn't need much clearing up, but I can't help feeling sad, with every wipe of my cloth, that I'm cleaning away the memories of our time together.

I'm just thinking about stopping for a coffee, at about ten-thirty, when my phone rings and I pull it from my back pocket, my stomach turning somersaults when I see Logan's name on the screen. I put down my duster and sit on the couch in the living room, connecting the call.

"Hello," I say.

"Hi."

"I didn't expect to hear from you until later." I'm smiling. I hope he can tell.

"Well, I've got a ten minute break between patients, so I thought I'd call you to see how you are. You sounded kind of... anxious this morning."

"I was. I'm sorry."

"Don't be sorry," he says softly. "Just tell me what's wrong."

"It's nothing," I reply, because I don't want to tell him how jealous and insecure I've been feeling since he left. "I'm fine."

"Don't say that," he snaps. "I told you. Hiding behind 'I'm fine' is never a good idea. Something's wrong, so tell me what it is."

"Okay." I bite back my tears, but carry on, "I'm worried about the fact that your ex wants you back. I'm scared that you'll forget about me now you're home, and I've got no idea when I'm going to see you again, and I don't like it… alright? Happy now?"

"No. Of course I'm not happy." He sighs. "You're not happy, so how the hell am I supposed to be?" There's a second's pause, before he continues, "I can't make you stop worrying about Brianna, but I can tell you – again – that she means nothing to me. And you mean everything. I don't want her back, Hope. I promise." I let out a long breath, and he says, "I don't want you to worry about when you and I will see other again either… because I miss you so much already, I'm going to have to see you again soon, just to stay sane…" His voice fades.

"Sorry," I whimper.

"There's nothing to be sorry for," he says, his voice so soft I'm surprised by how much it hurts. "I'd much rather you were honest with me and told me how you're feeling, than that you kept things from me."

I feel a pang of guilt, knowing that I'm being far from honest with him, but before I can say anything, his voice interrupts my train of thought. "I'm sorry," he says, "my next appointment has just arrived. I'll call you later on. Okay?"

"Yes."

There's a long pause, during which neither of us says anything. "I— I really miss you, Hope," he says eventually.

"I miss you too."

"Hang up… Please." There's a slight change of pitch in his voice, like he's struggling to control it, and my heart aches for him… well, for both of us. Because I'm struggling too.

"No. You."

"I can't."

I sigh. "Okay. Call me later."

"I will."

I don't wait to say goodbye, but end the call quickly, in the hope it'll be like pulling off a Band-aid, and will hurt less.

In a way, it does, because now, sitting here on my own, all I can think about are his words, the way he makes me feel safe, wanted, needed, cherished… loved. Even my guilt over keeping secrets is receding, because I know now that I will tell him. Soon. Very soon.

It's only an hour later, when I get back to the house, that I realise I forgot to mention the books.

Logan calls again at lunchtime… well, just after one-thirty.

"I've got half an hour," he explains. "It's been one of those days."

"You're busy?"

"Very. I've got some paperwork to do, but I wanted to talk to you. I wanted to apologise if I snapped at you before. I didn't mean to. I'm just finding it really hard being away from you."

"You don't have to apologise, Logan. I'm finding it hard too."

"Are you feeling better than you were earlier?"

"I am." I smile. "Much better, thank you. Oh… and I forgot to mention when we talked this morning, that you left your books behind."

"Oh God… did I?"

"Yes, they were on the floor in the bedroom."

"I don't know how I can have forgotten them," he says. "My only excuse is that I wasn't actually reading them."

"You weren't?"

"No. I was reading some of your books instead, and I tucked mine down on the floor, out of the way. In my haste to pack, I must have forgotten they were there."

"Why were you in such a hurry to pack?" I ask.

"Because I wanted to spend every second of my time with you," he says.

"That's a lovely thing to say."

"It's the truth."

"Well, I can post your books back to you, if you want?" I suggest.

"Good Lord, no," he replies. "That would cost a fortune. And anyway, we'll be seeing each other soon."

My stomach flips with excitement. "We will?"

"Yes… I told you, I'm going to go insane if I have to wait too long." I laugh. "You know?" he says. "I think that's about the most perfect sound in the world…"

"What is?"

"You… laughing. I think, in the absence of being able to see you, I'm just going to have to get you to laugh down the phone at me."

"And you don't think I might be mistaken for a crazy woman, if I start cackling down the phone at you for no good reason?"

"You don't cackle," he replies. "And I'm sure I can give you a reason."

"To laugh at you?" I tease.

"*With* me," he says and I quieten, thinking about a life of laughter and love… and Logan.

Our call last night went on for over an hour, and I was grateful I'd gone to bed by the time Logan phoned, because it was very relaxing, lying back on my pillows, while we talked and laughed and I listened to his soft voice and reasoned to myself that I can't tell him about my RP over the phone. It's something that's going to have to wait until the next time we're together, because I need him to understand what the condition means for me right now, what the consequences are for the future, and why I've held it back from him. And those aren't the sort of things you can discuss in a phone call. At least, I don't think they are.

This morning, my phone rang while I was walking Archie. Logan explained that he was able to leave for work a little later today, and I suggested we should perhaps set up a regular time to call each other, and that maybe I should phone him. He vetoed that plan right away, and when I asked why, feeling a bit put out, he explained, in the most soothing tones I'd ever heard him use, that he likes being spontaneous, he likes surprising me with random calls, and *he's* wooing *me*, not the other way around.

I get back from my walk, with a smile on my face, remembering Logan's words, and meet the postman at the gate. He hands me three white envelopes that look like circulars, and a cream coloured one with the address written in what seems to be a neat, handwritten print, although it's hard to tell without holding the envelope a little closer, and I never do that in front of other people. The postman gives me a nod and a 'Good Morning', before getting back into his van and driving off, and I make my way into the house, kicking off my shoes and taking off Archie's lead. Once I've removed my coat, I feed Archie and put the kettle on, and then return my attention to the post. The circulars hit the recycling bin, but the handwritten envelope makes me sigh in a warm-hearted kind of way. Every so often, I get an enquiry for the cottage like this and, although I like the convenience of using my online booking facility, and e-mails to communicate with people, I must admit, I rather like the fact that some people still communicate by letter. There's something rather comforting about that, I think.

I tear open the envelope, raising the letter much closer to my face so I can read it clearly and lean back against the work surface. Then I smile, then giggle, my hand coming up to cover my mouth as I read…

27th January

My darling Hope,

I hope you don't mind me calling you 'darling', but I wanted to find a way to address you that was appropriate for how I feel about you, so I used an online Thesaurus (because I'm a vet, not a writer, it seems). It turns out that the synonyms for 'darling' are 'dearest, sweetheart, beloved, love, lover…' and so on. And they all seemed most fitting for what's in my heart, so unless you tell me otherwise, I'd like for you to be my 'darling'.

I'm writing this letter to you at work, because I want to catch the post to make sure you get it tomorrow morning. Admittedly, I'm really supposed to be catching up on my admin, but I don't care about that. Writing to you is much more important. Telling you how I feel about you is much more important. You are much more important.

I hated the fact that you sounded so worried earlier on today when we spoke on the phone. It's been playing on my mind ever since. Please, please don't feel insecure about us. As I told you then, you have nothing to fear, not when you're with me. And before you say that you're not with me, let me reassure you that you are. You're with me all the time, in my memories, and my dreams, and in my heart, which belongs, entirely, to you. It has done since the moment you walked out of your front door on that fateful Saturday just over two weeks ago, when you stepped into my life and changed it forever.

These last seventeen days have been a rollercoaster, from the high of meeting you and discovering that dreams really do come true, to the low of hearing you say you had a husband, of believing you to be married and out of reach, which devastated me more than I'll ever be able to explain. I told you it was like a knife to my heart, but that doesn't do the feeling justice. To think that we might never have a chance to be together, that you belonged to someone else, that another man got to hold you, to touch you, to kiss you, to call you his, was too much for me, for my body, or my heart to tolerate. I know I've already apologised, but I'll do so again. My reaction to you at that time was appalling and I hope you will forgive me and forget my disgraceful behaviour. I can only plead insanity. I can also only thank you for pulling me back out of that low, for explaining the truth of the situation, which I know was hard for you, and for giving me a chance, despite your justifiable doubts, to prove myself worthy. I will. I promise.

I remember that you said during our call this morning, that you thought I might forget you now that we're apart, and I realised later on that I probably didn't address your fears fully, so I'm going to do so now, by explaining to you that it's simply not possible... because in everything I've done since returning home, I've thought of you, and nothing else. When making my coffee on Sunday afternoon, after I got back to my flat, I remembered sitting in your kitchen, having our first serious conversation about your past – and mine – and the net result of that, of my desire to woo you, and your hard-won consent, when I first dared to let my heart truly fill with Hope. When preparing my supper, and longing to be eating it with you, I recalled all our meals together, sitting across the table at the cottage, or in your kitchen, wondering what on earth I did to get so lucky, that I was even permitted to be in the same room as you, let alone spend my time gazing at you, hearing your voice and your perfect laughter, which echoes in my head, even now. When sitting on my sofa after I'd finished eating, watching a movie, I remembered our evenings, curled up together, with you in my arms, in those precious moments, when I honestly believed that life couldn't get any better. And when lying in bed last night, I used my imagination, rather than a memory *and pictured you beside me, my darling, while I gazed at you, your eyes closed fast in blissful and contented sleep. When I dreamt, I dreamt of you, and when I woke, I was smiling, because my first thought was of you.*

My only thoughts are of you. Always.

With that in mind, the time has come for me to end my letter, but even as I sign off, and seal the envelope, as I write your address and drop it through the postbox, I'll be smiling to myself, still thinking of you, knowing that you'll be reading this tomorrow, and hoping that my simple words might make you smile as well.

Your devoted

Logan xx

∞

Logan

I know Hope said we could text each other, but seriously… texting? Where's the romance in that? Even as she said that to me, I'd started to think about maybe writing to her instead, but then on Monday morning, when we spoke on the phone during my break, she sounded so insecure, so damn scared, and I knew exactly what I had to do. So, during my lunch break, I ran to the shops and bought some nice writing paper and envelopes, and I sat and wrote her a letter, before I called her. It meant I didn't have time to eat, but I didn't care. Writing the letter, making sure she understood… that was much more important.

I didn't have to try hard to make it romantic. I just had to tell her how I feel. Well, not exactly how I feel, because I didn't say 'I love you', although I did drop a few incredibly heavy hints, especially in telling her that my heart belongs to her, and calling her 'darling'… oh, and then explaining the synonyms of the word, which include both 'love' and 'lover'. Not entirely subtle, I'll admit, but I hope it brought a smile to her face, and probably made her blush too.

The letter I wrote to her yesterday lunchtime, was quite similar in tone, although I included a description of my ride to work. I know that doesn't sound very romantic, but I made a point of telling her that the frost on the grass reminded me of the way the sun shone on the sea at Portlynn, making it sparkle like jewels when we walked along the clifftops together, and how, when we were together, I'd noticed that her cheeks would get pink and rosy in the winter breeze, and that I loved the fact that her hair would sometimes get caught up, until I'd catch it and push it back behind her ears. There was something really intimate about doing that, and I liked telling her how much I enjoyed touching her. I also told her that on my morning ride, while sitting at some traffic lights, I caught a glimpse of the first snowdrops of the season, and how they reminded me that spring is just around the corner. February is just a few days away now, and the thought of seeing in the new season with her, seeing its beauty through her eyes, is something I dream of. She'll probably think I'm mad when she reads that, but it's the truth. All my words to her are the truth.

Having covered my journey to work yesterday, today I told her a little something about my flat. I know I could have taken a picture on my phone and sent it to her, but that would be cheating. I decided I'd much rather describe it to her, tell her what I do in each room, about the new colour schemes here, what my furniture is like, and how, even though she's never been here, it feels like she belongs. Because in my imagination, she's here with me all the time. I put it all into words, not pictures, because words matter to us. They make memories between us when we can't see each other. At least not all the time. Although I'm going to FaceTime her tonight, rather than just calling her. I don't know why I didn't think of it before, but we spoke about it earlier today, when I phoned her at lunchtime, after I'd finished writing my letter, and agreed that in the mornings and evenings, when I'm at home, it would be lovely to actually be able to see each other. We both agreed that when I'm at work, a phone call is better; it's more private, and I only really call her during the day to make sure she's okay, for a quick chat, and to hear her voice. Our morning and evening calls are the ones that matter the most.

I let myself into the flat at just after six-thirty, leaving my bike at the bottom of the stairs, flicking on the lights, picking up the post from the floor, and opening it as I start to climb. There's a letter from my credit card company, about a change in interest rates… an increase, needless to say. There's also a bank statement, which annoys me, because I specifically requested that they stop sending them by post, and just let me view them online, at least three months ago, which means I'm going to have to call them. Again. Finally, there's an envelope with a typed label. I'm fairly sure it's a circular and am about to consign it to the recycling bin, when I notice the postmark is St Austell and, smiling broadly, I unzip my coat, shrugging it off and letting it drop to the floor, along with the other post, as I go to the couch, sit down and tear into the envelope, pulling out the sheet of paper inside, the words neatly typed across it…

28th January

Dearest Logan,

I don't really know what to say, or where to start.

I suppose, I should start at the beginning and say that it would be my privilege to be your 'darling', as long as you will accept being my 'dearest', and if you are in any doubt about what that means, you could try looking it up in your Thesaurus… but as a hint, I'll offer up: 'beloved, cherished, and adored', just for starters. By all means check it out for yourself, and if 'dearest' works for you, then let me know.

Secondly, I feel I must apologise for the fact that my letter is typewritten. There is a very good reason for this, and I promise I will explain it to you when I see you next. I'm not trying to be mysterious, but my explanation really should be made in person. And I hope you'll forgive me.

I don't know how you can say you're not a writer. I'm looking at evidence to the contrary, with a really stupid grin on my face. I have no idea what kind of vet you are, although I imagine you are spectacular, simply because I haven't yet come across anything that you don't do well, but the world lost a truly talented scribe when you chose to be a veterinarian instead of an author. Still, the world's loss is my gain, I suppose… she said, shrugging and smiling to herself.

Your words definitely made me smile. In fact, I've been smiling since opening your letter, and reading its content, which have allayed any doubts or fears I might have had about you, or us to be more precise. I had to write back straight away, just to tell you how happy you've made me, especially as I was so sad when I cleaned up the cottage. I felt as though I was wiping away your time here. With every brush of my duster and sweep of the vacuum, it felt as though I was obliterating my memories of you and our precious time together. And then, this morning, I opened your letter and it was like you'd poured sunshine into my clouded heart. You knew exactly what to say, and how to say it, and what I needed to hear the most.

But tell me, do you have any faults? You once said you did. You said you had many. But I'm finding that hard to believe. If so, I'd like a list, please, just so I can refer to it every so often, to remind myself that you really aren't as perfect as you seem. A perfect man would be too hard to live up to... the expectation would be too high, I fear. So, even if it's just that you're a closet Barry Manilow fan, can you let me know?

I have to sign off now, because the post leaves at noon – the perils of living in a small village, I'm afraid.

Archie sends his love, and he asked me to tell you that he misses you... as do I. Your Hope xx

I sit back, grinning, thinking, sighing deeply.

I must admit that receiving a letter like this in a typed form is a bit strange, as is her lack of explanation, but she says she's got a good reason, and I'll wait to hear it from her own lips, because I've got more important things to think about... such as the fact that by now, Hope will have received her second letter from me, and we've spoken on the phone three times today, and neither of us has mentioned our correspondence at all. And that thought is what pleases me the most, I think... even more so than being called her 'dearest', which is an honour in its own right. And the reason it pleases me so much? Well, it means she might just understand the purpose of my letters... or one of the purposes, anyway. You see, I wanted them to become a private, personal, intimate way for us to say what we're really feeling. No holds barred. And maybe, when she gets her next letter, tomorrow, she'll work out that this is going to become a regular thing. That I intend writing to her every single day that we're apart, because although we speak on the phone several times a day, our letters mean so much more. Just like she does.

I look down and re-read her letter once more, smiling to myself. I don't need a thesaurus this time though. 'Dearest' works very well for me. For now, at least. And I chuckle out loud at the thought of Hope blushing as she wrote out the words 'beloved', 'cherished' and 'adored', not to mention the idea of my own simple words bringing her so much happiness, which puffs me up with a rather ridiculous male pride. I'd intended my letter to make her smile, and to reassure her, so it seems its purpose was served. It was more than served. Because she wrote back.

Now I just need to start work on that list of faults… I'll put it in tomorrow's letter, and hopefully make her laugh.

I stare at my screen, waiting for Hope to connect the call, and when she does, I notice she's in her living room, the bookshelves behind her.

"Hello." I can't help grinning, as her beautiful face comes into focus.

"Hello." She's smiling back at me. "How was your day?"

"Pretty good. Quite busy in the end. I had a couple of emergencies this afternoon, but that just makes the day more exciting really."

"I doubt the owners involved saw it like that." She's shaking her head at me, although she's still smiling.

"Probably not, but I always do my best to reassure them."

"I'm sure you do."

"Well, I suppose that's part of my job. I mean, I have to try not to get emotionally involved, because I wouldn't be able to function, but I also have to remember that, to them, their pet is everything."

"I know I'd be lost without Archie," she says, wistfully and I decide to change the subject, because she looks sad now, and I don't want that, not when I'm not there to hold her.

"How was your day?" I ask, and her expression changes completely, her eyes widening and another smile forming on her lips.

"I had a booking," she says, like it's an unusual occurrence, which I know it isn't. "It's another short-notice one." That explains her tone.

"Shorter notice than mine?"

"Good Lord, no." She laughs and so do I. "I'm not sure that's possible."

"Neither am I."

"They want to come next weekend, which means I'm booked solid from then until the beginning of November."

"That's amazing, Hope. Well done."

She sighs. "My bank balance is incredibly healthy, but…" Her eyes drop, her head following suit.

Looking at her, I'm so relieved we had this conversation on FaceTime and not over the phone. It makes it easier to read her thoughts, or at least to see the worry in her eyes, as well as to hear it in her voice, and being as I know she won't be fretting over her bank balance, or having guests to stay at the cottage, there's only one other thing I can think of that might make her look and sound so anxious. "And now you're wondering when we're going to see each other again?"

"Yes," she replies, looking up again. "How did you know I was thinking that?"

I smile. "Because I know how your brain works."

"Already?" she says, frowning slightly.

"Yes. And, in all seriousness, there really is nothing for you to worry about… we'll see each other soon."

She raises a hand, pushing a stray hair back behind her ear, and I wish I were there to do that for her. "But it's already nearly the end of our first week apart," she reasons, "and we haven't been able to make any plans yet."

"No, but we will. Have you thought any more about coming up here?"

She sucks in a breath. "Yes, I have. But I'm still a bit… worried." She seems to struggle to find the right word and frowns, properly this time.

"About the journey?" I ask, just to clarify that she's not worried about seeing me again, although I don't think she can be, given her earlier reaction. She nods her head, but doesn't say anything. "I promise, Hope, there really isn't anything to be worried about. As I told you, there are lots of ways to get here by train, and if the most convenient one ends up taking you into central London, then I'll meet you at Paddington, so you don't have to do the complicated bit by yourself."

Her eyes widen even more than they did before. "You... You'd do that? For me?"

I smile, shaking my head. "Of course I would. Look, why don't you give it a bit more thought? Would your parents be able to cover at the cottage for you?" I don't know why, but it's only just dawned on me that her weekends are not her own.

"Y—Yes." *Thank God for that.*

"Then maybe have a chat with them, and perhaps over the weekend, we can talk about it in more detail and work out some dates?"

"Okay," she murmurs, looking and sounding a little more enthusiastic, I think. I hope.

"And stop worrying."

She smiles. "I'll try."

"I promise I'll look after you."

"I know you will."

"And I'll keep you safe." She dips her head, although I know she's blushing. "And if you really don't want to come up here, then I'll come down to you," I offer. "It's just that I know you'll have a lot to do, what with handling the changeover and everything, and... well, if I'm being honest, I'm already missing you like hell, and I'd quite like to just spend a couple of days by ourselves... and not have to share you with your guests."

Her eyes dart up to mine again. "I'm missing you too... and I will speak to Mum and Dad. I promise. They've got my aunt visiting at the moment, but she's leaving on Friday morning, so I'll call them after she's gone." She sounds so earnest, it's really hard not to reach out and touch her, even though she's just an image on my phone.

We talked for over an hour, before we finally managed to say goodbye, and then I phoned her again before going off to sleep. I made it a phone call, rather than a FaceTime, because I knew she'd already be in bed, and I didn't want her to think there's anything voyeuristic about our calls. There isn't. I just like seeing her.

This morning, our conversation is brief, because Archie is to be desperate to get out of the door, evidently. I can hear him barking in the background, and although we could continue our conversation while Hope takes him for his walk, I've got to leave for work soon myself.

"I'll find some time to ring you later on," I promise.

"Okay… Archie, stop it!"

"What's he doing?"

"Running rings around my legs, when I'm trying to put his lead on. Honestly, he's the one who wants to go out, but you'd never know it… Come here."

"Put the phone near to his ear, if you can," I tell her, smiling at the harassed expression on her face.

"What?"

"Try and put the phone closer to his ear."

There's a moment's silence, and Hope's face disappears from my screen, replaced by a fleeting glimpse of the stairs, then a patch of wall, and then the front door, as she presumably chases her errant dog around in circles, during which all I can hear is the scuffling of paws on the tiled floor of Hope's hallway. "Archie!" I bellow down the phone, when it becomes clear she's getting nowhere. "Sit!"

The scuffling stops. "Bloody hell…" I hear in the background, and then Hope comes onto the screen again. "How did you do that?"

"It's one of my many talents." I smile.

"What are you, a dog whisperer?"

"Hardly." I chuckle. "Have you got his lead on now?"

"Yes."

"Okay. Then I'll let you go, and I'll call you later."

"Thanks. Archie will be waiting with bated breath."

"And you?" I tease.

"Oh, I'm always breathless waiting to hear from you…" She falls silent, blushing to the roots of her honey coloured hair. Then, before I can reply, she hangs up. And I can't help grinning as I finish the dregs of my coffee. I contemplate sending her a text, but I don't, because we're not about texting, and in any case, I don't want to embarrass her further. It's enough for me that she said it, so I don't need to make a big deal out of it, and instead, I go to my emails, checking through and deleting most of them, because they're junk, except for one, which is from a very well known London art gallery. I'm on their mailing list, because Rachel got me tickets to an opening there a couple of years ago, and I've never bothered to unsubscribe myself. They sometimes have some interesting things going on, and I usually read the information, thinking to myself that I'll make the time to go, and then forget all about it. But this time, the subject of the e-mail catches my eye.

'The Romance of the Pre-Raphaelite Brotherhood'

Opening the e-mail, I discover that there's due to be a special exhibition, starting on Valentine's Day, and running for three weeks. This is just perfect. In fact, it's better than perfect, and I quickly check my calendar, making sure I've got the dates right. Sure enough, Valentine's Day is a Friday, so if I can get tickets for the day after, I'm pretty sure it'll work out… I click on the link in the e-mail, which takes me to a website where I can book the tickets. They're already selling fast, but there are two available for noon on the Saturday, so I take them, paying by credit card. At the checkout, I'm given the option of having them as e-tickets, but I elect to have them sent by post instead, opting for special delivery. For a very good reason.

Chapter Fifteen

Hope

Archie and I have had a lovely walk today, and I had a definite spring in my step. Maybe that's because today is the last day of January, and I always feel better once the darkest month of the year is over and done with. Or maybe it's because I hoped we'd get home and there would be another letter from Logan. They've been arriving every day since Tuesday, so if I'm right, and he's going to send one every day – which seems to be the case – then today will be my fourth. Assuming I'm right, of course.

When we get back, there's no sign of the postman, but I let us in anyway, unable to disguise my disappointment that there's nothing on the mat today.

Maybe I got it wrong… maybe he's not going to write every day, although it seems odd to stop now, when he's written three days on the trot. And he did tease me in yesterday's letter that he was still working on his list of faults, because it's so long, which made me laugh. Even so, I suppose he's busy, and I shouldn't expect him to be able to find the time to write every single day. That would be too much to ask.

Archie comes over, nudging his head against my leg, and then barks at me.

"Yes… okay." He wants feeding, and since Logan left, he's become a lot less patient… a lot more demanding and a lot more mischievous. How Logan got him to sit down yesterday morning, over the phone, I'll never know, but I think I should get him to record his voice, and send it to me, just to calm my dog down.

I get up and give Archie his food, putting the bowl down, just as the doorbell rings, and I go to answer it.

"Sorry to trouble you, but you've got a special delivery." The postman holds out an electronic device. "You just need to sign in the box. But you'll have to use your finger. I've lost the little pen thing."

I do my best to sign my signature with my fingertip and hand him back the device, whereupon he gives me a long white envelope, and a now familiar looking cream coloured one, which brings a smile to my face.

"Thank you."

I close the door, floating into the kitchen. I don't care about the white envelope, marked 'special delivery'. I only care that Logan's written again, and I tear into the cream coloured envelope, leaning against the table as I pull out the sheets of paper from inside.

30th January

My darling Hope,

I've been thinking of you all day today. Literally all day. From the moment I woke this morning, with a smile on my face, because you'd filled my dreams, to our conversation over breakfast, and my attempts to calm your dog, which I'll admit did make me chuckle... right through my morning surgery, which I know isn't a good thing, because I should have been concentrating on my patients, not on images of your smile, or your laugh, or the way your hair glows in the firelight, or the sparkle of your eyes... or the memory of your lips on mine.

At least we can see each other during our calls now, because not seeing you was driving me insane. Not touching you is still a bit of an issue when it comes to the balance of my mind, but hopefully that's something we can rectify very soon.

And in the meantime, at the risk of scaring you off, giving you second thoughts, and having you running for the hills, screaming like a banshee, I thought I should fulfil your wish to know my many faults – or at least the worst of them. So, here goes.

1. I know this is a big deal with a lot of women (Rachel hates it), so I'll admit up front that I'm not great with putting the toilet seat down. I never was, even as a child. Sorry, it's just how I am. And I'll use the excuse that I'm used to living on my own most of the time, because hopefully that will count in my favour.

2. I'm not very good with separating my coloured washing from my whites. This might not seem like a big deal, but as a result of my ineptitude, I have an awful lot of pink clothing.

3. You may not think this a fault, but I actually look pretty good in pink. It's not very manly to admit that, and I'm not sure how you feel about being seen with a man in very pale pink t-shirts, but I thought I should put it out there, especially as fault number 2 doesn't give me much choice in the matter.

4. I am completely useless with most forms of technology. Even the 'record' setting on my TV remote control is a mystery to me. Call me a dinosaur, if you want to, but I'm beyond trying to work these things out now.

5. I take longer in the shower than the average fifteen year old girl. I only know this because I remember how long Rachel used to take in the bathroom when she was fifteen, and I give her a really good run for her money. I'd like to put it down to beard maintenance, but actually, I just like showers. So shoot me.

6. I can be quite quiet and grouchy until I've had my first cup of coffee of the day. Although I imagine that, if I woke to your smile every morning, that situation would soon change.

7. This is the last one, for now at least, but I suppose it's probably the most important, and it's that I can be a bit controlling. Some might call it domineering, but I didn't want to come straight out and use that specific adjective, just in case you got the wrong idea about me. We've already touched upon the fact that I like to be in control of certain things, like climbing ladders – or rather not climbing them – but in this instance, what I mean by 'controlling' is that, for example, I can sometimes take the initiative and just go ahead and try to plan things, without thinking to ask whether it's convenient first. Hopefully, when this happens, and I guarantee that it will, you'll forgive my occasionally overbearing nature, and accept that all I want to do is to spend my time with you – every single minute of it. I'm not trying to manipulate you into doing anything you don't want to; there is no artistry to my plans. I simply want to make you smile, to make you happy, to fill your heart with joy, in whatever way I can.

I think that's enough of my faults for one letter. If I list any more, you may never write to me again, or even speak to me, and that, my darling, would surely break my heart.

I'll close for today, so I can catch the post, but I'll write again tomorrow, rest assured.

In the meantime, I remain,
Your devoted,
Logan xxxxx
p.s. Who's Barry Manilow?'

I giggle to myself, re-reading his list of faults, which aren't really faults, if you ask me, especially not the last one, which seems kind of endearing and mysterious in equal measure. I'm pretty sure that what he's talking about is his request that I go and visit him, and his offer to meet me at Paddington station, if necessary, which was very kind of him and not at all controlling. Of course, he doesn't know the real reason for my fears over the journey, but in spite of my natural misgivings, I'm determined to speak to my parents about it later this morning, and then to look into the trains. Because I want to see him just as much as it seems he wants to see me. And I want us to have a normal relationship too… at least for as long as we can.

Standing up straight again, I put down his letter with some reluctance, and turn my attention to the other envelope, which has the stamp of a well-known London art gallery on the reverse. That strikes me as odd. I've never been to this gallery in my life, although I've heard of it, obviously. But why would they be sending me something… *and* by special delivery?

I rip open the envelope, and pull out a the single sheet of paper inside, unfolding it. Two tickets flutter to the table, and I pick them up, gasping when I read: 'The Romance of the Pre-Raphaelites' printed on one side, along with the date of the fifteenth of February, and the time of twelve noon. What's going on? I love the Pre-Raphaelites. I always have done. But why is this gallery sending me tickets – quite expensive tickets – to an exhibition of their work?

Studying the piece of paper in my other hand, I double-check that they're addressed to me, which they are, and then read down, sucking in a sharp breath, when I notice the payment details. The name given on the credit card, the last four digits of which are shown, is 'Mr L. Quinn'

Logan's done this?

With shaking hands, I put the letter and the tickets on the kitchen table and pull my phone from my back pocket, looking up Logan's contact details and connecting a call to him. He doesn't answer and his phone goes directly to voicemail, but then I suppose it would. He'll be working.

"Um… hello. It's me. Hope." God, I sound so silly. "Sorry… Can you call me when you get this message? Thanks."

I hang up quickly leaning on the table. So, this is what he meant when he mentioned being controlling and organising things without asking first? I shake my head, let out a long, deep breath and gaze down the tickets.

I've got no choice now, have I? I'm going to have to go and see him… no matter how scared I am.

Twenty minutes later, I'm still at the table, although I'm sitting down now, when my phone rings, and without even checking the display, I answer, "Hello?"

"It's me."

"Logan…" I sigh out my relief.

"What's wrong? You sounded confused… worried."

"I—I've just received two tickets." I pick them up, studying them. "For an exhibition… from you."

"Yes. I know. I wondered if you'd like to come up here on the fourteenth…"

"Valentines Day?" I query.

"Yes. We could go out for dinner, and then you could stay over at my place and we can go into London together and see the exhibition on the Saturday, and then I'll put you back on your train on Sunday afternoon."

My hands are shaking, my heart beating fast.

"Hope?" Logan's voice whispers in my ear. "Are you okay?"

"D—Did you plan all this?" I stutter.

214

"Yes. I know I should have asked you first, but well... I can be controlling at times." I smile, recalling fault number seven, although I don't mention it directly, and neither does Logan.

"It's not controlling. It's lovely." I do my best to put on a brave voice, because it is lovely for him to have arranged all this, for me.

I hear him sigh. "You're sure?"

"I'm positive."

"I didn't want you think I was trying to use the exhibition as a way of forcing your hand. I meant it when I said I'd come to you... but then I also meant it when I said I wanted us to have some time together, on our own... and when this came up, well, it seemed perfect."

"It is perfect."

"So you'll come?" he asks, with maybe a hint of residual doubt in his voice.

"Yes. Although I'm still not sure about the trains." That's the understatement of the century. I'm terrified about them.

He chuckles. "It won't be as bad as you think, I promise. And as I said before, if you do end up having to catch one that takes you into town, then I'll come up to Paddington and meet you there. In fact, I'll come anywhere you need me to. If you book your train and let me know when you'll be arriving, I'll make sure to be at whatever station you need me to get to, and then I'll take you out for dinner."

"Well, I just need to check with my parents first. I'll need to make sure they're free to come and stay here."

"Okay... I probably should have thought about that, before I went ahead and booked the tickets, shouldn't I?"

"I'm sure it'll be fine." I know it will. Especially when I explain why I want them to come. Okay, so they're probably going to throw a fit when I tell them where I'm going, and that I'm going by myself, but they've both been telling me for months that I should get out more and find someone else to share my life with, or even to just have some fun with, so they can hardly complain. Can they?

"Text me when you know what you're doing." His voice interrupts my thoughts.

"Text you? I didn't think we did texting?" I refuse to mention our letters, because he hasn't, and I like the fact that they're a kind of secret, romantic, separate part of our lives.

"We don't," he replies. "But I've got a busy day ahead of me, and I want to know for sure that you can make it."

I smile and wish I could feel his arms around me, rest my head against his chest, feel his lips on mine… and I smile as it dawns on me that it won't be long now, until I can.

"Mum! I was going to call you later." Sometimes I wonder if my mother comes from a long line of witches. She often turns up unannounced, just when I'm thinking about her, or phones as I'm about to call her. Less than an hour has passed since my phone call with Logan and I was just thinking of making a cup of coffee and telephoning my parents… and here's my mother on my doorstep.

She steps inside the house and I check behind her to see whether Dad's come with her today.

"Well, I had to drop your aunt at the station first thing, and then go shopping, so I thought I'd drop by and see how you are. I've left your father ripping weeds out of the garden for relaxation."

I close the door and take her coat, hooking it up alongside my own.

"Can I take it Aunty Jennifer's visit didn't go well?"

She turns to me and rolls her eyes. "Does it ever?" she smirks, coming into the kitchen and sitting down at the table. Archie gets up from his basket and pads over to her, resting his chin on her lap, and while she pets his head, she adds, "I know she means well, but ten days of having everything criticised, from my cooking, to my cleaning, to my choice of reading material… well, it starts to grate."

"I can imagine." I fill the kettle with water and put it on to boil, leaning back on the countertop and looking across at her. My mother is in her early fifties, but looks ten years younger, perhaps because, like me, she has blonde hair, and hers hasn't greyed in the slightest. "I don't know why you put up with her."

"Because she's your father's sister, and despite her many failings, he loves her." She smiles up at me, her expression altering, her brow furrowing slightly. "What's wrong?" she asks.

"Nothing." I turn and busy myself with the cafetière, measuring out the coffee. "Why would you think there's something wrong?"

"Because you look different."

"Different?" I'm playing for time, slightly embarrassed that I'm clearly so transparent. "In what way?"

I hear her chair scrape against the tiled floor and, the next thing I know, she's standing beside me, looking up into my face. "You look… happy," she says, searching for the word and finding it eventually. I turn to face her, but before I can reply, she smiles and says, "You've met someone, haven't you?"

I laugh, throwing my head back. "I do wish these psychic skills of yours were hereditary, Mother."

She giggles now and leans into me. "I'm right though, aren't I?" I nod my head and she sighs. "Hurry up with that coffee then, and come and tell me all about him."

I do as she says, pouring hot water over the coffee grounds, then placing it on the table, together with two cups and the milk.

"Who is he?" she asks, impatiently.

I smile. "His name is Logan Quinn. He's a vet and he lives in Richmond."

"Yorkshire, or Surrey?" she asks.

"Surrey."

She pales, but tries hard to smile. "And?"

"And he came to stay here for a couple of weeks, and…" I'm not sure how to finish that sentence, so I don't.

"One thing led to another?" my mother suggests, succeeding with the smile this time, her eyes sparkling mischievously.

"No, Mum."

"Oh. Sorry." She smirks. "What happened then?"

"We spent some time together." I don't explain that I'm not prepared to let one thing lead to another yet, not when he's only just broken up with his fiancée. I'm not willing to share that nugget of information with my mother, not when I haven't completely come to terms with it myself. "We got to know each other a little bit."

"I see," she says. "And I presume he's gone home now, has he?"

"Yes, but we're still in touch. Regularly." I'm not going to mention our letters, or the fact that Logan promised to woo me into submission. God knows what she'd make of that. But equally I don't want her to think Logan would have spent two weeks romancing me and then just walked away.

"So, when's he coming down again?" she asks and I smile, because at least she's understood that it wasn't a brief holiday romance – for either of us.

I pour the coffee, passing a cup to her. "Well... that's what I was going to call you about."

She adds milk to her steaming brew, raising her eyebrows. "Oh yes?"

"Yes. Logan's invited me to spend Valentine's weekend with him. He's bought us tickets to go to a Pre-Raphaelite exhibition in London on the Saturday..."

"London?" she interrupts, her face falling as she starts to blink rapidly, and I wonder if she's going to cry. "He wants you to go to London? By yourself?"

"Yes. And I want to go, Mum. I'm twenty-nine, not twelve." Even as I'm speaking, I can hear the slightly childish twelve year old tone to my voice, and I know my mother has the perfect counter argument; namely that my age is irrelevant... it's my ability to see properly that's the issue.

"I assume you're planning on taking the train?" she asks, surprising me.

"Yes. And Logan's going to meet me at the station. I'll be perfectly safe. Honestly."

She sucks in a long breath, and then lets it out again, placing her hand over mine. " I know. But I can't help worrying about you." Her eyes glisten slightly and I can hear that familiar note of guilt in her voice.

"You don't need to, Mum. I'll be fine." I try to sound more certain of that than I actually feel and she smiles at me, seemingly reassured.

"And can I assume you've got guests that weekend?"

"Yes. It's Valentine's weekend. The couple booked in ten months ago. So… I was wondering if you and Dad would mind coming and managing the changeover for me?"

They've done it before, especially after I was first diagnosed and they practically smothered me in tender loving care, until it drove me insane and we had a serious heart to heart about the situation, but that was a while ago now and I don't want to make assumptions.

"Of course we don't mind. Your father will love taking Archie for his walks, and despite Aunt Jennifer's criticisms, I'm sure I can manage to clean the cottage and change the sheets." She chuckles and the relief at seeing my mum behaving like her old pre-diagnosis self is almost too much for me.

"I'm sure you can. Logan's asked me to go up on the Friday afternoon, because that's Valentine's Day."

"Oh, how romantic…" Her eyes sparkle – but with excitement now, rather than regret, or guilt – and I have to smile, despite myself.

"Behave yourself, Mother."

"Why? It *is* romantic."

I chuckle. "Yes, it is, isn't it?"

"It's good to see you so happy, Hope," she murmurs. "I don't remember the last time I saw you like this."

"I don't remember the last time I felt like this."

She sits back, placing both hands around her coffee cup. "We'll come over perhaps the Wednesday before you go, shall we?" she suggests. "We can go through everything, just to make sure we don't make a mess of it."

"You won't make a mess of it. And I'll bake a Madeira cake on the Friday morning, and leave it ready, so you won't have to worry about that."

"I'll just have to remember to tell your father that it's for your guests, and not for him." Mum shakes her head. "He needs to lose some weight, but he's got absolutely no willpower whatsoever… especially when it comes to cake." We both take a sip of our coffee, and then she adds, "So, will your young man be coming down here again anytime soon?"

She's fishing now, and she's not very subtle about it.

"I'm not sure. We haven't made any plans yet. His work keeps him busy… and obviously I've got this place." I glance around the kitchen, although we both know I'm really talking about the cottage.

"Well, you know we'll help out whenever you need us to. And perhaps when he does come down again, we could meet him?"

I'm a little thrown by that. I hadn't expected it. But even as I contemplate my response, the thought of introducing Logan to my family seems absolutely right… assuming he doesn't freak out when I tell him my secret, of course. God, I hope he doesn't…

"Yes… I'd like that," I manage to say.

"Good. So, apart from being a vet and living in Richmond, what's he like?" Mum asks.

I feel my lips twitch upwards as I think about Logan, and notice the smile forming on my mother's face. "What?" I say.

"Oh… nothing. But you don't need to tell me what he's like. Not anymore."

"I don't?"

She shakes her head. "No. Because I know he's right for you."

"How?"

She taps the side of her nose with her forefinger. "Mother's intuition," she murmurs and after a couple of seconds, we both burst out laughing.

Mum stayed for another half an hour, during which we mainly talked about Aunt Jennifer. She's ten years older than my dad, has never married, and has always been what might be termed 'difficult', but as Mum said, he loves her dearly. We didn't talk about Logan very much more, but then I don't think we needed to. After all, Mum had already decided he's right for me, so what more was there to be said?

As soon as she's left, promising to call after the weekend, I go online and study the train journey I'm going to have to make. Logan was right, there are several options available to me, including ones that made several changes, at either Plymouth or Exeter. They're far too complicated for me and simply out of the question. So, in the end, the train that seems best, in terms of changes and timings, is one that leaves St Austell at one o'clock on Friday the fourteenth, and gets to Richmond at six fifteen in the evening, with just one stop, at Reading. That doesn't sound too scary to me, although it does mean that I'll be arriving after dark, but that can't be helped, so I book my ticket before I can chicken out and change my mind. Once I've had a confirmation e-mail, I send Logan a text message, detailing my arrival time, and confirming that my parents are fine covering for me for that weekend, adding at the end, that they want to meet him when he next comes down here.

It takes a couple of hours for him to reply.

— Hello, beautiful. Sorry for the delay in coming back to you. I was operating. I can't stop to talk as I'm running late going into surgery, but wanted to say that all sounds wonderful. I'll meet you at Richmond station… and I can't wait to meet your parents. I'll call you later, but it will probably be at the end of the day. It's crazy here today. Have a good afternoon. Logan x

I know that him telling me he'll call me is his way of saying that he doesn't want to get into a massive text conversation, because that's not who we are, so I don't reply to him and instead, I wait for his call, while sorting out some of my bed linen, and doing the ironing.

My phone lights up at six-thirty, just after I've started preparing my Thai green curry for dinner, and I connect the FaceTime call, waiting until Logan appears, before I say, "Hello."

"Hi," he replies.

"You sound tired." I sit down at the kitchen table, holding my phone in my hand and studying his slightly pale face.

"I am." He runs his hand across his bearded chin. "I thought today was never going to end. It's been non-stop since the moment I got in this morning. I'm sorry I didn't get the chance to talk to you at lunchtime." He flops down onto his sofa, although he keeps the phone so close to his face that I can't see very much around him. "How are you?" he asks.

"I'm fine."

He smiles. "Fine? Really, Hope?"

He wants honesty. "Okay… I'm nervous – and I'm excited – about coming up to see you."

"Why nervous?" he asks.

"Because of the journey." It's the truth.

He nods his head. "Is that the only reason?"

"Yes."

"Okay. And why excited?"

I hesitate, clear my throat and then whisper, "Because it's a Pre-Raphaelite exhibition, and I love the Pre-Raphaelites… and because I want to see you."

A slow smile forms on his lips, spreading to his eyes, which twinkle at me in the dim light of his living room. "I want to see you too," he replies. "And I'm sorry I didn't ask you before I booked the tickets. I wasn't trying to trick you into coming here. I promise. I just saw that the exhibition was on, and couldn't resist."

"You don't have to apologise. But I am intrigued."

"What about?"

"About how you knew I like the Pre-Raphaelites so much."

He chuckles. "Oh… that was easy. I noticed the books in your cottage, and then saw there were a couple more in your house. I put two and two together."

"And made four?" I suggest.

"For once in my life, yes."

Logan

When I booked the tickets for the exhibition and Hope made the arrangements to come up here, I thought the time would drag, but between work, phone calls, and letter writing, it's actually flown by. Hope's due to arrive tonight, and I've spent the last few evenings tidying my flat. I've sorted out some spare bedding, and this morning, I got up early and changed the sheets on my bed, so everything is prepared.

And now, having finished work as promptly as possible, I've dropped my bike at home, showered and changed at lightning speed, and am on my way to the station.

I completely understood Hope's nervousness about making this journey. It's got to be worrying for her, when she's never done it before, but with any luck it will have gone smoothly and she'll realise it's not as bad as she thought it was going to be. She sounded really anxious when we spoke last night, but I kept trying to reassure her, and I think I won her over in the end. As for myself… what can I say? My excitement is off the scale.

I spot her hair first, shining in spite of the dour surroundings, through a crowd of commuters, shoppers and teenage college students. I smile in anticipation of actually seeing her, and holding her again, almost unable to contain myself, right until I notice the middle-aged woman, wearing jeans, and a red raincoat, walking alongside her, holding onto her arm, talking to her, and then I'm struck by the anxious, fearful expression on Hope's face. My God… what's happened? My excitement dies in seconds, as my heart beats hard in my chest, my palms sweat with terror, and I wait impatiently for her to come through the barrier, whereupon, I walk right up to her, and she dissolves into tears, releasing the woman, dropping her bag to the floor and throwing her arms around my neck.

I hold her close. "Hope?" I murmur, but she just shakes her head.

"She'll be fine," the woman says soothingly, and I realise she's still there. "I think it was just a bit much for her…"

"Um…" I don't know how to reply, because I've got no idea what she's talking about, but Hope pulls away from me, turning towards the woman, and placing a hand on her arm.

"Thank you so much," she says softly. "I'm so grateful."

The woman shakes her head. "Oh, don't think anything of it. It was my pleasure." She glances up at me, a glint in her eye. "And I can see you're perfectly safe now, so I'll make my way home."

Hope thanks her again, and I smile at her, despite my confusion, before she walks away and I turn back to Hope again, my hands on her waist, pulling her close to me. I'm almost overwhelmed with fear, but I stay silent, waiting until she stops shaking and her tears subside a little, and then she leans back slowly and looks up into my eyes. Before I can ask her what's wrong, she simply says, "Not here… please," her voice little more than a cracked whisper.

I gaze down at her, confused beyond words, then nod my head, bend, pick up her bag and take her hand in mine, leading her from the station. We've only gone a few steps, though, when she pulls me back.

"Can you put your arm around me?" she mutters, gazing at me, her eyes still brimming with tears.

"Of course." I hold her close to me and we start the walk back to my place, my panic mounting with every step, to the point where even the feeling of her soft body against mine can do nothing to quell my anxiety.

Fortunately, my flat is only a short walk from the station, above a hairdressers, and we arrive within a few minutes. Hope tenses as I let her go to open the door, but she seems to relax again when I flick on the light and she looks up into my face, attempting a smile, which almost touches her eyes.

I lead the way up the stairs and into my flat, leaving her bag by the door and directing her into the living room, which is straight ahead, through the double doors.

I left the light on in here, so she goes straight through and stops, looking around, before she turns and lets her eyes settle on me.

"What's wrong?" I ask, unable to wait a second longer.

"Can we sit?" she asks, and I nod, taking her coat, hooking it up behind the door, and letting her sit down on the sofa before I join her. She pauses, placing her hands on her knees, and then turns to me. "I have a confession to make," she says softly, and I feel myself frowning.

"A confession?" I query.

"Yes. I—I haven't been entirely honest with you." She bites her bottom lip, but the only thing I'm really aware of is the deafening beat of my heart and the cold fear creeping up my spine.

"Hope?"

She blinks rapidly, then moves slightly closer, but I feel myself stiffen, preparing for the worst… even though I'm not sure what the worst is yet.

"Do you know what Retinitis Pigmentosa is?" she asks, taking me by surprise, and I struggle to focus on her question, wracking my brain.

"An eye condition?" I hazard.

She nods her head. "It's an inherited eye condition, known as RP for short. It—It usually affects night and peripheral vision and, in most cases, leads to the sufferer becoming legally blind." She stops talking like a text book all of a sudden and holds her breath, staring at me, with a look I can't work out, but I equally can't ignore.

"Hope?" I say again. "What are you telling me?" She doesn't answer, so I ask her outright, "Are you saying you have Retinitis Pigmentosa? Is that what you're trying to tell me?"

Very slowly, she nods her head, and I start to shake my own.

"But that's not possible. It can't be. I mean, we've done so much together… We've walked in the woods… I've watched you cook…"

"Yes. In places I'm very familiar with," she says softly, as though she senses my difficulty in understanding this.

"And now you're telling me you're blind?"

"No," she says quickly. "I'm telling you I'm *going* to be blind." She sighs. "I was only diagnosed fifteen months ago, but in all probability, I'll be legally blind by the time I'm forty."

"You keep saying 'legally blind'. What does that mean?"

"It means I'll still have some sight, but not enough to function like I used to… or like I do now, even."

Her voice falters, although she sounds very matter of fact, but then she's had longer to get used to the idea than I have, and I turn to face her properly.

"Can I ask you something?" I say, managing to keep my voice as calm as possible, although inside, I'm a boiling mass of emotions, most of which I can't begin to explain. Hope nods, looking worried, like she knows what's coming. "Why am I only hearing about this now?"

She sucks in a breath, and turns to me, so our legs are touching, reaching out with her hand and placing it on my knee. I don't object, although I'd still like an explanation.

"I'm sorry," she says, which I suppose is a good place to start. "I've thought about telling you so many times… and I've come close on countless others…"

"Then why haven't you?"

"Because I didn't want to tell you over the phone, or in a letter…" She falls silent and I know it's because she's just mentioned our correspondence, which we've avoided doing so far, by an unspoken agreement.

"And is this what you were talking about when you said you'd explain why you had to type your letters to me?" I ask her, completely blowing that agreement out of the water.

"Yes. Typing is so much easier for me than writing."

I suppose that makes sense. "Can you… can you see well enough to read what I write?" I wonder for an awful moment whether she's been having to get someone else – Amy, perhaps – to read my letters to her, and whether our private, personal correspondence isn't so private, or so personal.

She smiles and nods her head. "Yes, I can. It's my night vision that's most badly affected, and in the last couple of months, things in my periphery have started to become a bit fuzzy… that's all."

That's all? "How do you manage?" I ask what seems to be the obvious question.

"I keep the lights on most of the time at home," she explains, moving a little closer to me. "And I had the exterior lights fitted, so I can see outside at night."

I recall the fact that she even had the lights on during the day in her house and nod my head.

She lets her head drop slightly, but looks up at me through her eyelashes and I wonder what's coming next. "That's why I struggled so much, when you created that romantic evening for us at the cottage," she says softly. "I mean… obviously it was hard, because it was the anniversary of Greg's death…" her voice fades.

"But you couldn't see properly either?" I close my eyes, wondering how I didn't notice at the time, and feel her free hand come up, gently caressing my cheek. Leaning into her touch, I open my eyes again and whisper, "Sorry," and she smiles.

"It wasn't your fault. You weren't to know."

I take a deep breath, endeavouring to take it all on board… and failing miserably. "What happened this evening?" I ask eventually. "Why was that woman helping you?"

She lets out a long sigh. "I was doing okay. I really was. Until I got to Reading," she admits. "But it turned out to be a much bigger station than I'd expected, and it was busy, and there were so many signs, a lot of which I couldn't read, and it was getting dark… and…"

"It was a bit much for you?" I suggest, recalling the words of the woman at the station.

Hope nods her head. "I think that lady must have noticed me panicking, and she offered to help. It was very kind of her."

"It was," I agree. "But what if she hadn't been there?"

She leans back a little, looking into my eyes. "Don't treat me differently," she whispers, sounding desperate and desolate at the same time. "Please… please don't wrap me in cotton wool."

How can I not? "I'm sorry," I murmur, but she shakes her head.

"No. I'm the one who's sorry… if I'd told you before…"

"Why didn't you? I mean, I understand not wanting to tell me over the phone or in our letters, but I spent two weeks with you… we were together every day. You could have told me then."

"I know," she says, "but I needed to be sure…"

"About me?"

Her eyes are still locked with mine, and I wonder what she's seeing as she slowly nods her head. "I'm sorry, Logan, but at the time, I didn't know what I meant to you… whether those two weeks were all we'd ever have."

"Do you think I make a habit of going around offering to woo every woman I meet?" I struggle to conceal the hurt in my voice.

"No," she says, moving her hand a little further up my leg. "But please try to understand… I didn't want to be defined by my condition. I wanted you to want me for me, not just because you felt sorry for me."

"You think that's the sort of man I am?"

"No." She pulls her hand away and I get to my feet, wandering over to the window, although I'm oblivious to everything outside. My mind is a whirl of thoughts. Obviously, I wish she'd been able to tell me before now, but more than that, I'm in awe of how she manages to cope, how she gets on with her everyday life so normally and easily, how she can sit there so calmly and talk about an uncertain future that must scare her. And how the hell I'm ever going to be able to be as strong as she is.

"Are you angry with me?" Her woeful voice breaks into my thoughts, piercing my heart, and I flip around to face her.

"No."

"Disappointed?"

"No, my darling, never." I cross back over to her and sit down again, taking her hand in mine.

"But you'd rather I'd told you sooner?" She looks at me doubtfully, and I know I can't lie.

"Yes. Of course."

"I—I'm sorry," she mutters and tries to pull her hand away, although I keep a firm hold.

"Don't. I'm not making myself very clear, am I?" She stares at me through tear-filled eyes, waiting, and I suck in a breath. "Naturally, I wish you'd told me sooner, Hope, but only so I could have understood your fears a bit better, not expected you to travel up here by yourself... so I could have helped you more. That's all."

She blinks twice, and two tears fall onto her cheeks as I pull her into my arms, stroking her hair while she sobs against me.

It takes a few minutes for her to calm, but when she does, she pulls back and looks up at me. "I'm sorry," she whispers again, and I shake my head, then lean down and very gently kiss her lips, keeping it brief, because this isn't about wanting her – even though I do, more than ever. This is about reassuring her that she's safe with me. Always.

"I can't guarantee that I'm not going to be a little bit overprotective," I murmur, gazing into her eyes. "But I've wanted to keep you safe from the very first moment I saw you... and I'm not going to apologise for that. I'm not going to change either."

"You don't have to," she says and we sigh, as one, as she lets her forehead rest against mine and we sit in silence together.

"Do you still want to come out to dinner?" I ask, after a moment or two, struggling to think about anything other than her momentous news, how not to over-react to it, and settling in the end on my original plans for the evening.

"Can we?"

"Our reservation isn't for another hour, so…" I leave my sentence hanging, and she leans up, kissing me on the cheek. "What was that for?"

She smiles. "For thinking about dinner, and making things normal, rather than focusing on my RP."

"It was a conscious effort," I confess.

"Well, thank you anyway. For making the effort."

"Don't thank me." How can I accept her gratitude? How? When I feel so truly humbled… for a moment, I struggle not to be undone by her, fearful that she might misjudge my reaction, if I let it show, and misinterpret my heightened emotions as pity, rather than the overwhelming love that's threatening to completely bury me. I turn to practicalities instead. "Are you going to be okay in the restaurant?" I ask, barely in control of my voice.

"In what way?" she asks, tilting her head.

"It's Valentine's Day. I imagine the lighting will be fairly subdued…"

"I'll manage," she says softly. "You'll be with me."

Dear God… how do I reply to that? How to I respond to such faith? Such trust? I open my mouth to tell her the only thing I can… that I'm in love with her. Completely. That she's filled and owned my heart from the very moment I first met her, and that knowing about her condition makes no difference to me because all I want is to spend the rest of my life being with her… come what may. But before I can utter a single syllable, she grabs my hand and says, "At the risk of spoiling the moment, do you think I could use your bathroom?"

I chuckle at her idea of ruining the moment… if only she'd known what 'the moment' was going to be. And then I get to my feet and pull her up with me. "I'll show you where it is."

She follows me back into the tiny hallway, where I indicate the bathroom, and she ducks inside. I stand for a moment or two, feeling awkward, until I notice her bag, still lying on the floor by the front door.

"I'll just put your bag in my bedroom," I call out, picking it up and carrying it through to my room, where I leave it on the bed, only remembering at the last minute to turn on all the lights, so Hope can find her way around, if she needs to.

"Um… excuse me." I look up to find her standing by the door, her hands in her pockets, a puzzled look on her face. "Did you just say 'your' bedroom? I—I mean… I thought you had more than one." She bites her bottom lip and I cross the room to her

"Didn't I mention that?" I tease.

Folding her arms across her chest, she tilts her head to one side, frowning, and I guess she's not in the mood for being teased. "No… it must have slipped your mind."

I take her wrists, pulling them apart, and clasp her hands in mine, despite her obvious reluctance. "I wasn't trying to trick you into doing anything you're not ready for, Hope. I'd never do that to you."

"I didn't think you would either," she says, sounding sceptical still. "But, are you seriously trying to tell me that, in planning all of this, you just happened to forget that you've only got one bedroom?"

"No. I didn't forget. But I did neglect to mention it… because I didn't think it mattered."

"Of course it matters." She tries to pull away from me, but I hold on tight.

"No, it doesn't." I nod towards the chair in the corner of the room, which is piled high with pillows and a duvet. "Because I also sorted out some spare bedding, so that I can sleep on the sofa."

She relaxes, then blinks a few times in quick succession. "You're going to sleep on the sofa?"

I smile down at her. "Naturally. I would never make assumptions like that about you… or about us. And besides, I've already explained, you're the only one who can cut to the chase. You know that." She sighs and then bites her bottom lip again, but before I have the chance to do anything about that, she pulls her hands free of mine and throws her arms around my neck. It's the second time she's done this tonight. The first time, at the station was because she was scared, and she needed me. Even though I was scared too at the time, I liked that she turned to me. This time, I'm not sure if I understand her reasons, but I still like her reactions, all the same.

"Thank you," she whispers in my ear, standing on tiptoes to reach, before she lets her arms drop and pulls away again, much to my regret.

"You really don't need to thank me, Hope."

"Oh… I think I do."

"You don't." Ever.

She shakes her head, ignoring me. "I think I should apologise too."

"What on earth for?" I move slightly closer, so we're almost touching. "You've already apologised for not telling me…"

"This isn't about that," she interrupts, resting her palm on my chest. "I'm apologising for jumping to conclusions."

I smile. "Well, I can't blame you for that. Not in the circumstances."

"Even though you were being completely honourable?" She brings her hand up now, resting it on my cheek, in an action that is somehow even more intimate than it was when she did this earlier, while we were sitting on the sofa together.

"Well, I don't know if all of my intentions are honourable," I mutter, and she giggles, flushing just slightly, although she doesn't pull away this time. "But I promised I'd wait for you… and I will."

She dips her head forward, and I lean down and kiss it, just above her hairline.

"Now… would you like to take a shower?" I suggest. "You've just about got time before we have to leave."

"I'd love to take a shower." She looks up at me again, her eyes brightening.

"Okay. Well, you should find everything you need in the bathroom. There are towels in the cupboard behind the door… and while you're doing that, I'll just go and bury myself in my phone."

"You will?"

"Yes. It'll be a struggle but I'll try and find something to hold my attention… just so I don't see anything I shouldn't."

Her chuckle is still ringing in my ears as I settle onto the sofa and do my best not to think about her naked body, just a few yards away, standing under a cascade of water… and how tempted I am to go back on my word and join her.

The restaurant is very romantic, which isn't surprising, given the date. It's decked out with candles and fairy lights and as I'd predicted, the lighting is very dim indeed, and Hope doesn't object when I link her arm through mine and guide her towards our table, helping her to sit, and smiling up at me as I take my place opposite her. There's a single red rose on one of the place settings at our table, where Hope sits.

"Did you arrange this?" she asks, picking it up and holding the bloom to her nose.

"No." *I wish I had though.* "It's something the restaurant did, but it's a nice touch."

She smiles at me and puts the rose down next to her place setting.

She's changed her outfit from the skin tight jeans and fitted blouse she was wearing earlier, into a deep red knitted dress, which isn't skin tight at all, but touches her in all the right places, and I can't take my eyes off of her. The waiter is attentive, but not overly so and leaves us in peace with our menus, and it's then that Hope glances up at me over the top of hers.

"I can't see it," she whispers, her voice cracking. "You were right. It's too dark in here."

"Then I'll read it to you."

I take her menu from her, putting it down, then open my own and reach across the table, holding her hand at the same time, as I start to read each dish in turn.

Hope quickly chooses a starter of scallops, and I decide to have the same, and am about half way through reading the main courses, when the waiter returns, hoping to take our order. Without giving him a reason, I explain that we're not ready yet and he disappears once more, only coming back once I've closed my menu and am holding both of Hope's hands.

I place our order, thanking the guy for his patience and he gives me a knowing smile, assuming I guess that this is just some romantic gesture on my part. I wish it were that simple. I really do.

"It's so good to see you again," I say, once Hope and I are alone again, but even as the words leave my lips, I wish I could take them back. "Sorry... God. I'm so sorry. I'm such an idiot. That was a really stupid and insensitive thing to say."

She shakes her head and leans forward. "Stop it, Logan," she says firmly.

"Stop what?"

"Overanalysing everything you say. That's not how I want it to be... not between us. I'm not going to burst into tears, just because you mention seeing or looking, or sight, or blindness, in some way. And I can take a joke."

"About this?" *Seriously?*

"Yes... especially about this. I'm not going to lie and say it's always been easy, because it hasn't. And sometimes I still have really bad days, when I can't see a future for myself... excuse the pun." She tips her head and grins and I have to smile, as she continues, "When I was first diagnosed it was really tough. It was a huge shock for everyone, and my parents were awash with guilt, because they're both carriers, although neither of them had any idea until then, obviously. And, of course, there was the long-term prognosis, which was hard to hear."

"I know," I interject, because it was hard for me to hear too and I'm unable to keep the sadness from my voice. She clearly understands how I'm feeling, and her eyes glisten with unshed tears as she mouths, 'Sorry,' and I shake my head and mouth back, 'Don't,'.

"What happened?" I ask her, after a minute or so, during which we just stare at each other. "I mean, what symptoms did you have?"

She pauses while the waiter brings our wine, pouring a little into my glass to taste, and then half filling Hope's, once I've nodded my approval.

"My night vision went first," she says, as soon as he's gone. "But then almost straight away, I noticed that I struggled to adjust going from bright sunshine into a dark room."

"So you went to an optician?" I ask.

"No. I made the mistake of going to my GP, and because it was only a short while after Greg's death, he put it down to stress."

"You're kidding."

"No." She shakes her head. "Then a few months later, I noticed that I was walking into things, so that time I did go to an optician, who clearly didn't like my test results and referred me to the hospital…" She lets her voice fade.

"And you inherited this from your parents, even though they don't have it themselves?"

She nods her head, looking down at her lap. "It's a genetic disorder. In my case, the inheritance was recessive, so Mum and Dad are just carriers, but if I were ever to have children…" She doesn't finish her sentence, and I free one of my hands from hers and reach across the table, placing my finger beneath her chin, and raise her face to mine, the sadness in her eyes taking my breath away.

"They'd inherit?" I guess.

"Not… not necessarily. If… if the father carried the gene, even in its recessive form, then yes, they would. But if he didn't, then they would become carriers, like my parents."

I nod my head, taking in what she's just said. "I take it there are tests the… um… potential father can have done to find out if he has this gene… in whatever form?"

"Yes," she whispers and stares at me as I contemplate the fact that, although I've never even thought about parenthood before, the idea of the father of Hope's children being anyone but me is just wrong. Utterly wrong. I find myself letting out a breath I didn't even know I was holding, and then I smile across the table at her, just as the waiter brings our starters.

While we eat, Hope explains that her parents have struggled more than she has with her diagnosis, and that even Amy and Nick can sometimes be a little stifling in their attitude to her. "I know it's because they all care," she reasons, "but sometimes I just miss being normal."

"Whatever the hell 'normal' is."

"Precisely. But whatever it is, it's not being wrapped in cotton wool and treated with kid gloves…"

"Any more clichés you want to throw into the mix?" I ask and she chuckles.

"No. But I do want to make the most of what I've got, while I've got it. I want to spend as much time as possible looking at the most beautiful things in this world, like the sun sparkling on the sea, and the leaves in spring, and rosebuds about to bloom…" She lowers her head and her voice, just slightly, but not so low that I can't hear her add, "And you."

For a moment, I can't speak, but when I know I'll be able to, I take her hand firmly in mine and ask her, "Can you see me?"

She smiles. "Yes. It's harder in here, in this light… but yes, I can see you. That's why I said what I just did, about looking at the most beautiful things in the world." She blushes and I lean in closer to her.

"You're the bravest person I've ever met, Hope… and the strongest."

She shakes her head. "No, I'm not. I get scared, you know. A lot."

"You're entitled… but you're still brave. And you're so, so beautiful."

The waiter clears our plates and Hope smiles at me, looking shy, as I reach across the table and take her hand in mine.

"Can we change the subject?" she says.

"If you want to."

She nods her head, and before I know it, we're deep in conversation, stopping only to taste the wine, and sample the main courses that the waiter soon brings.

There's barely a break, as we chat about Archie, who it turns out seems to like our FaceTime conversations and sits listening to them, enraptured, every morning and evening. I make a mental note to try and include him, before we move onto discussing the couple who arrived at the cottage last Saturday, who she tells me, came over to see her on Sunday evening… to see if they could borrow some batteries, of all things.

"I learned my lesson a year or so ago," she explains, taking a sip of wine. "A similar thing happened, and I had to let them down at the time." She sniggers. "I honestly don't think I've ever seen anyone look so disappointed, so I put a stock of batteries in the kitchen drawer now, just in case. The thing is, that's not something I can tell people when I'm showing them around the cottage, so I just usually hope they'll discover them for themselves, should the need arise."

"Only this particular couple didn't?"

She shakes her head. "I'm not even sure they bothered to look."

"Did they say what they needed them for?" I ask, taking her hand in mine, once the waiter has cleared our plates again.

"No. But I didn't need them to draw me a diagram… I think it was fairly obvious."

"You mean, the TV remote had died?" I suggest, teasing her.

"Something like that, yes," she replies.

The waiter returns, offering us dessert menus, but we both decline. "Do you want coffee?" I ask Hope.

"I'm not sure… I'm quite tired."

"Okay… well, we can just go back to my place, if you'd prefer?"

She nods her head and I look up at the waiter and ask for the bill.

He smiles and darts away, making the incorrect assumption, I presume, that I'm about to get lucky. Little does he know that I already feel like the luckiest man on earth, because the woman I love is holding my hand and looking into my eyes… and for now, at least, she can see them. And that's more than enough for me.

It's only a ten minute walk back to my flat, and I keep my arm firmly around Hope all the way. It's dark, and I know that means she'll be finding it hard to see, but I'm holding her because I want to, not because she needs me to, and when we arrive, I take her into the living room, where I was clever enough to remember to leave the light on.

"I know you're tired, and probably all you want to do is fall into bed, but if you can just wait here for a second; there's something I want to give you…"

She looks up at me, confused, but I don't explain. Instead, I go into my bedroom, and grab the brown-paper wrapped parcel from the bottom of my wardrobe and take it back through.

"Happy Valentine's Day." I hand it over to her, then add, "I'd have given this to you earlier, but your arrival didn't go exactly as I'd thought it would. And then we got waylaid talking about my bedroom, and then you wanted to shower… and I didn't want to rush things by just throwing this at you before we went out…"

She looks down at the long, narrow, flat parcel in her hands, and then puts it down on the sofa beside her, holding up one finger. "Hang on a second," she says, and then disappears, returning a moment later with a much smaller, oblong box, wrapped in deep red paper, which she hands to me. "Happy Valentine's Day," she whispers, sounding shy again.

"Do you want to go first?" I nod towards her present.

"No… let's do it together."

She picks hers up again and we both open them at the same time, but she gasps as hers is revealed, and then turns to me.

"It's *Prosperine*," she says, even though only half of the picture is revealed, the rest still concealed by brown paper.

"Yes."

"Oh my God." She doesn't bother to unwrap the rest, but throws her arms around me. Again. I could seriously get used to this. "Thank you."

"It's not the original… you get that, don't you?"

She chuckles. "Of course I do." She pulls back and peels off the rest of the wrapping, to reveal the beauty of Rossetti's *Prosperine*; thoughtful, enigmatic, shrouded in rich blue drapes and clutching her fateful pomegranate.

"She's so beautiful," Hope breathes, studying the portrait closely. "How did you know she's one of my favourites?"

"I didn't. But I did my homework and decided I should buy you something by one of the original Brotherhood… and I really liked this one." I focus on Hope's spellbound features. "It is alright, isn't it?"

She pulls her gaze from the picture and looks up at me. "It's perfect."

I smile down at her, relieved and then finish opening my own present, discovering that Hope has given me a very expensive, very attractive fountain pen. I know this is for me to use when I write to her, but rather than mentioning our letters again, I simply turn to her and pull her close to me. "Thank you," I whisper, then kiss her lips just briefly. "I'll think of you when I use it."

She smiles and I know she understands exactly what I mean, and while she clears away the wrapping paper, I make us both a coffee.

Sitting on the sofa, curled up in each other's arms, she twists and looks up at me.

"Are you sure you're going to be alright sleeping on here?" she asks.

"Yes. It's very comfortable."

"I know… but I feel guilty for stealing your bed."

I wonder for a moment whether she feels guilty enough to ask me to share it with her, but I don't say anything, and instead I pull her closer to me, running my hand down her side, along the soft curve of her waist and hip, letting it settle there, while she rests her head on my chest, her arm tight around me and I smile to myself. It's been a momentous evening, but I know that, no matter what the future holds, this is where I belong.

Chapter Sixteen

Hope

My journey to Richmond turned out to be so much harder, and more terrifying than even I'd imagined it would be, and if it hadn't been for that lovely lady who rescued me at Reading station, and who fortuitously happened to be travelling to Richmond herself, I don't know what I'd have done. Well, I do. I'd have phoned Logan and asked him to come to Reading to help me. And he'd have done it too. I know he would. I especially know that after the way he reacted to me telling him about my condition. I mean, obviously I think he was hurt to start with, that I hadn't told him before, and looking at it with hindsight, that's completely understandable. I should have told him, and I regret not doing so. But he's not the sort of man to bear grudges or harbour regrets, or to let others do so either, and I genuinely think he was more interested in finding out about RP, my experiences of it, and my prognosis, than in anything else.

Obviously he's got some adjustments to make, like remembering not to leave things lying around on the floor for me to trip over; things like the pile of books he left behind at the cottage, and his shoes, that he'd obviously taken off last night and deposited behind the sofa, where I least expected to find them when I came into the living room after my shower this morning. He was so apologetic, helping me off the floor and holding onto me, while cursing himself for not thinking, until I reminded him that he's had less than twelve hours to accommodate my problems; I've had fifteen months, and I'm still getting it wrong. He made us both a coffee then, and before he showered, while I tried my best not to stare at how gorgeous he looked, in nothing more than shorts and a t-shirt, with his hair all mussed up, I explained to him that the need for clear floors and simple layouts is why I have the furniture in my house and at the cottage arranged the way it is, and why I'm a bit of a neat freak. I wasn't always like that, believe me, but I had help from an occupational therapist not long after my diagnosis, and she gave me some invaluable advice about simplifying my life to make the future easier.

The exhibition is everything I could ever have hoped it would be. And more. The rooms are well lit, meaning I can see all the exhibits clearly and just being able to gaze upon paintings by William Holman Hunt, John Everett Millais, James Collinson, Edward Burne-Jones, and above all, Dante Gabriel Rossetti, is like a dream come true for me. It's almost worth the torture of my journey up here. Almost. Because, I have to be honest, the feeling of terror I experienced, standing on the platform at Reading station, not knowing which way to turn, is unlikely to leave me.

Even so, I've spent the last two hours enraptured, staring at the canvases, admiring the way these amazing artists used light and shadow, the depth of colour in the subjects and their natural surroundings. It's been a revelation. And throughout our time at the gallery, Logan has stood beside me, listening to me wax lyrical, or joining me in awed silence.

Unfortunately, our timed tickets, and the overcrowded rooms necessitate that, after we've visited every exhibit, we have to leave, despite the fact that I'd love to start again from the beginning, and spend the remainder of the afternoon, just admiring.

"Do you want to look at the rest of the gallery?" Logan offers. "Or shall we go and get some tea?"

"Tea, I think. We can have a look around afterwards, can't we?" I feel like a child, asking to be permitted to stay up late on a school night, and he laughs and takes my hand in his.

"Of course we can."

He leads me to the lower ground floor, where the cafeteria is situated, and because it's early afternoon, the worst of the lunchtime crowd has dispersed, which is a relief. I could do with a break from people.

Logan fed me a full English breakfast this morning, including sausages, mushrooms and grilled tomatoes. It was a lot more sophisticated than the bacon and eggs I cooked him on his last day at Orchard Cottage, but I think we were both reminded of that earlier occasion, and Logan's comments about us having spent the night together prior to eating breakfast. Of course, I'd thought about that to myself too, but I wasn't about to admit that… and I'm still not. Even so, he made a very tasty breakfast, and I made a pig of myself over it, so I'm not in the mood for anything more than a cup of tea and a slice of cake, and they do have a very nice looking chocolate sponge sheltering under a glass dome, so I order that, while Logan asks for fruit cake, giving me a wink while the lady behind the counter makes our tea.

"London's very busy, isn't it?" I remark, once we've found a table and sat down.

"Yes." He sits opposite me, passing me my cake. "I don't particularly like it. I prefer to stroll, not run."

I chuckle. "Why do people rush up and down the escalators on the underground?" I ask, remembering how he held onto me so protectively on our way here, as people jostled past, and how much I liked it. "Surely it doesn't make much difference, does it? I mean, it seemed to me that there was a train every minute or so."

"There is."

"Then I don't understand why they waste their energy running."

"Neither do I." He gazes into my eyes. "Life's too short not to admire the beautiful things around us…" His words echo my own of last night, and I feel myself leaning into him.

"Yes," I whisper, and we stare at each other, until someone drops a plate and we're startled back to reality.

It's much busier on the journey back to Richmond than it was travelling into London this morning, and I can't hide my nerves. It's raining, and there have even been a few claps of thunder, and on the underground, there are people rushing everywhere, pushing and shoving, desperate to be first in the line.

A group of football supporters, wearing blue and white rush onto the platform, their shouting making me jump, and I let out a yelp of surprise.

"It's okay," Logan whispers directly into my ear, his arm tight around my waist.

I look up at him. "I don't like this. It makes me nervous."

He tightens his grip as the train arrives and the crowd surges forward, carrying us with them. "I've got you," he says, protecting me from the worst of the buffeting, and I let myself relax a little, because I know he has.

"Shall I cook tonight?" Logan says, as we walk up the stairs to his flat. We're both soaked through and, I don't know about him, but I'm exhausted. "I'm too tired to go out." It's as though he's read my mind, and I smile to myself.

"Why don't we both cook?" I suggest.

"Why don't we both shower… and then cook?" he offers, turning on the lights as we enter his living room.

"Both shower?" I turn to face him.

"Separately," he smirks and I smile. "You can go first."

"No, you can. You're soaked."

"I hate to tell you this, my darling, but so are you." I suck in a breath at his use of my pen name, the one he uses in his letters, but don't comment on it. I didn't when he called me that last night, when we were both awash with emotion, rather than rain, and instead I revel in the joy of hearing the words directly from his lips instead.

"You don't mind?"

He shakes his head. "No. I'll just get some dry clothes from my room, if that's okay?"

I nod and he goes into the bedroom, returning with what appears to be a pair of jeans and a t-shirt, which he deposits on the back of the sofa. "It's all yours," he says. "I'll stay in here until you tell me the coast's clear."

"Thanks."

I grab myself some clean clothes and go into the bathroom, where I enjoy a quick, hot shower, towel drying my hair and getting dressed again, in jeans and a blouse. When I rejoin Logan, he's perched on the edge of the sofa, his head bowed.

"You don't look very comfortable," I remark, pushing my damp hair back behind my ears.

He flips around. "I didn't want to get the sofa all wet," he says, putting down his phone, which I hadn't noticed he was looking at. "I've got to sleep on it later."

"Fair point." I indicate the bathroom with a wave of my hand. "Well, it's your turn now."

He smiles and gets up. "I've been checking out some pasta recipes… why don't you see what you think?" He goes to hand me his phone, but then stops. "Sorry," he mumbles, his cheeks flushing. "I wasn't thinking. That was really stupid of me. I'll get my iPad. It's larger."

I want to tell him that I can always enlarge the type on his phone, that he's not being stupid at all, he's being really considerate, and I can't possibly criticise a single thing he's doing, but he's already disappeared into his bedroom, returning a moment later with an iPad in his hand, his fingers dancing across the screen.

"This is probably more practical anyway," he says, handing it over to me. "It'll be easier to use in the kitchen. I've left it on the website I was looking at, but if you can't find anything you like, feel free to browse."

I lean up and kiss his cheek, just for being so wonderfully normal, and he smiles down at me as I turn my attention to the screen, which shows a photograph of a recipe for courgette and bacon linguine. "This looks lovely," I say, turning it around and showing it to him.

"It would look even lovelier if I had any courgettes." He comes to stand beside me. "That's why I was looking. I'd planned to take you out again tonight, so we're going to be limited by whatever's in my fridge."

"And how will I know what's in your fridge?" I ask, as he moves towards the bathroom, his clean jeans and t-shirt clutched in his hand.

"Just go through it for yourself," he says. "I don't think I've got anything embarrassing in there."

"Embarrassing?" I call out after him and he pops his head back around the door.

"Yeah, you know… three month old pizza, mouldy leftovers… that kind of thing."

I grin. "Well, if I find anything like that, I'll throw it out."

He smiles and disappears, and I make my way into his kitchen, which is tiny, the scant work surface cluttered with a coffee machine, a blender, a kettle and a toaster, leaving room for little else. I start scrolling down the screen on his iPad, studying it closely, and a recipe comes up for 'Marmite Carbonara', and I feel my stomach churn at the thought. "Do you like marmite?" I call out, loud enough for him to hear, being as the shower hasn't started yet.

"Um… no," he shouts back. "Please tell me there isn't a recipe that requires it."

"There is."

"Yuk."

I'm still giggling when I hear the water turn on, and for a moment, I let my imagination switch into overdrive as I picture Logan standing beneath the shower, his head tipped back, rivulets of water cascading down his toned, naked body, and I lean back against the countertop to steady myself.

"A bit of self control would be good, Hope," I whisper to myself and focus on his iPad again.

'Pasta with goat's cheese and spinach' comes up next and I go over to the fridge to check the contents. For all of Logan's worries, it's quite well stocked, and there's nothing mouldy or out of date in here. He's actually got some goat's cheese, but no spinach, and I wonder about adapting the recipe, using perhaps some peppers instead, but decide to scroll through some more ideas first, just in case there's something else that comes to mind.

A picture of 'Tender stem broccoli and lemon pasta' fills the screen and I open the salad tray at the bottom of the fridge to find a small pack of the required green vegetable and a net of lemons. It looks like we might be in business, so I click on the recipe, enlarging the type, to see whether it really is as easy as the brief description beneath the photograph would have me believe.

It claims to take a total of thirty minutes to make, and the most complicated element seems to be the roasting of the tender stem broccoli, which isn't complicated at all.

I'm just reading through the rest of the instructions, when a window pops up at the top of the screen. It's a message for Logan, and although I do my best not to read it, my eye is drawn to the first three words.

— *Logan, baby. Sweetness...*

'Logan, baby'?

'Sweetness'?

The box disappears and I drop the iPad onto the countertop, even as the kitchen starts to blur and swim around me. My heart is pounding, I can't catch my breath, but I run into the bedroom knocking my shoulder into the doorframe en route, and slam the door behind me, feeling lost and alone, and a very long way from home.

I left the light on in here, which is a habit I've developed, and I manage to get to the bed before my legs give way and I collapse down onto it, my mind racing. Who's sending him messages that start with 'Logan, baby'? Who calls him 'Sweetness' for God's sake? Who calls anyone 'Sweetness', for that matter?

I feel sick to my stomach, and clamp my hand over my mouth to stop myself from retching.

"I can't be here," I whisper, turning my head, desperately searching the room... for a way out, I think.

I haven't unpacked my holdall, although some of my clothes are lying over the back of the chair in the corner, and I go over and pick them up, stuffing them into my bag, which I dump onto the bed to make it easier.

My wet things are still in the bathroom, as is my shampoo and body wash, but I don't care. I can live without them, and I zip up my holdall, checking around the room and spying my phone on the bedside table.

I wander over and pick it up, contemplating calling my mum, or Amy perhaps. I'm terrified of making the journey home at this time of night, shrouded in threatening darkness, and although they can't do anything about that from where they are, I'll need someone to pick me up from the station. And, to be honest, just to hear a friendly voice would be good right about now.

"Hope?" Logan's voice makes me jump. "Where are you?"

I stay silent, waiting.

"Hope?" he calls again, and I can tell he's right outside the bedroom door, which is confirmed by the knocking that follows.

I still don't respond, and after a moment's pause, the door opens, just a crack, and then a little further, once he sees me standing there. He's dressed in jeans and a white t-shirt, his feet bare, his hair damp at the ends and I let out a small sigh of regret for what might have been.

"Hope?" he repeats for a third time, although he sounds worried now. "What's wrong?"

"Nothing." I know that's a lie, because everything's wrong, but I'm not going to give him the satisfaction of seeing how hurt I am. Or how much I wanted this... how much I wanted him. Not that it matters now. None of it matters. Because there's someone out there who calls him 'Baby', and 'Sweetness'. And that makes 'dearest' sound positively cordial in comparison...

He takes a step into the room, and I stumble backwards, falling onto the bed.

"Something's happened..." He looks around, his eyes settling firstly on my holdall and then on my phone, which is still clutched in my hand. "Why have you packed? What's going on? Did someone call? Has someone upset you?"

"No. No-one called me..." I mutter, regretting my words as soon as they've left my lips.

"In that case, I don't understand. Tell me what's going on, Hope." He steps closer still and I get to my feet, so we're on vaguely the same level, although I still have to look up at him, at the deep concern in those molten eyes.

"Nothing's going on."

"Well, clearly something is. You were perfectly happy when I went into the shower, and now… well, you're not."

"No."

He frowns. "So, what's happened?"

I drop my phone onto the bed beside my bag and place my hands on my hips, a bolt of anger darting through me as I glare up at him. "Why would someone send you a text message calling you 'baby', and 'sweetness'?" I ask. "And before you accuse me of checking your messages behind your back, I didn't. It came in while I was looking at one of the recipes on your iPad."

His face darkens, his eyes narrowing slightly. "Wait here," he says, and goes out of the room, returning moments later with his iPad clutched in his hand, his finger scrolling up the screen in rapid motions. "Jesus Christ," he mutters. "What is wrong with her?"

"With who?" I ask, raising my voice.

He looks up and then steps towards me. "I'm sorry," he whispers and my heart cracks open in my chest, pain seeping outwards and filling my body. Tears well in my eyes and Logan moves closer. "Don't cry," he says.

"Then tell me what's going on." I manage to hold back the tears, but I can't help sniffling a little.

"The messages are from Brianna."

I suck in a breath. "*Messages?* You mean there's more than one?"

He nods. "She's sent three in the last five minutes. The first one starts, 'Logan, Baby… Sweetness…'" His eyes fix on mine. "I'm going to guess that's the one you saw?" I nod my head and he pushes his fingers back through his hair. "God… I'm so sorry, Hope."

"How long has this been going on for?" I ask.

He tilts his head, his brow furrowing in confusion. "How long has what been going on for?"

"Well, I'm guessing you're back with her."

"Hell no," he blurts out and it's my turn to feel confused.

"Then why is she sending you messages like that?"

"Because she's certifiable," he huffs, and takes my hand, which I allow, although with some reluctance. "I'm not seeing her," he says, with heartfelt sincerity, and I want to believe him. I really do. "She sent me a few text messages when I first got to Orchard Cottage, before you and I got together, so I blocked her number. Then she started calling Rachel instead… just like I told you."

"Because she wants you back?" I interject and he nods his head.

"Yes. Evidently."

"But if you blocked her, how is she able to send you messages now?"

"She's obviously got herself another phone," he replies, shaking his head and glancing down at the iPad. "It's a different number."

I close my eyes for a moment, and when I open them, he's staring at me.

"If you don't believe me, look for yourself. Look through my messages, and my contacts. She's not on there." He holds the iPad out to me, but I refuse to take it.

"I can't," I whisper.

"Why not?"

"Because… because that implies I don't trust you."

He huffs out a half laugh, dropping the iPad onto the bed. "Well, you don't."

"I do… at least, I want to."

"Wanting to trust me, and trusting me are not the same thing."

I take a deep breath, because we both know he's right, then I ask, "What are you going to do?"

"What about?"

"About her messages?"

"I'll ignore them," he replies, without hesitation. "And I'll block this number too. She'll get the hint."

"You don't think she'll just go out and get herself another phone, once she's realised you've blocked her again?"

He shrugs. "She might do, but eventually she'll work it out. Even Brianna isn't that thick skinned."

I'm not convinced myself, but I don't say anything and I look down at our clasped hands instead. "And what are you going to do about us?" I whisper, holding my breath.

"About us?" he queries.

"Yes. You... you seem cross that I'm struggling with this... with trusting you and believing you."

I feel him release my hand, and blink back my tears as I prepare for the worst, for having survived bearing my soul to him, and revealing my darkest secret, only for his ex to still be the thorn in our sides... but then he places a finger beneath my chin and raises my face to his, and the sincerity I find there is breathtaking. "I'm not cross. Not with you. I'm livid with Brianna. But I'm not cross with you, darling. I understand why you'd struggle with this," he says softly, the darkness gone from his eyes now. "If I'm being completely honest, I suppose I'm disappointed that you still don't feel you can trust me, but I don't blame you for that. I know it's difficult, given the timing and everything... especially when my ex won't leave me alone."

"But that's not your fault," I reason, and he smiles.

"No, but that doesn't make it any easier for you. I have to earn your trust, Hope. I've always known that. And this is part of that process... showing you that, when things go a bit wrong, you can depend on me. Always. Because I won't let you down."

"I'm sorry," I whisper, feeling guilty for making such a fuss now.

"Don't be sorry. Please, don't be sorry. That's the last thing I want."

"What *do* you want?" I ask, instinctively, desperate to make up for my lack of faith, given that he's been so ready to forgive me for not being honest with him about my condition, a fact which he could have argued, he had a right to know.

"I think I'd like to kiss you," he whispers, although he doesn't move. In fact, he doesn't even seem to breathe. He just stares at me, waiting for my answer.

"I think I'd like that too."

He moves his hand and brings up the other one, clasping my face, his eyes locked on mine, as he edges closer, our bodies touching at the same time as he brushes his lips against mine. He takes a half step closer, so we're completely melded together, then changes the angle of his head, licking gently along my lips with the tip of his tongue. It tickles and my tiny gasp gives him entrance, and I hear his throaty groan as he starts to explore. There's fire in his kiss. Fire and longing and anticipation… and I match it with my own.

We break the kiss together, our foreheads meeting, and neither of us says a word, until eventually Logan asks, "Are you okay?"

"I'm fine."

"Please, Hope… Don't give me 'fine'. Especially not now. Tell me how you really feel."

"I'm a little breathless, if that helps," I manage to sigh out.

"Me too."

"And I'm scared."

"What about?" He leans back and looks down at me, concerned.

"Your ex?"

His hand comes around behind my head and he pulls me close to his chest, so I can hear the flutter of his beating heart. "You have nothing to be scared about," he whispers into my hair. "I don't want anything to do with her. I want you, Hope… no-one else but you." He leans back again. "I'll tell you everything… every time she contacts me. I promise. I won't keep secrets from you. I'll do whatever I have to, to prove to you that you can trust me… that I'm worthy of you."

"You are worthy of me."

He shakes his head. "No I'm not. Not yet."

This morning, Logan has brought me out for brunch at an American style diner about a fifteen minute walk away from his flat. It's somewhere he comes to often on Sunday mornings, evidently, and the proprietor – a man called Harry – seems to know him well, judging from their banter. Over a huge portion of buttermilk pancakes with caramelised bananas and maple syrup, while Logan and Harry discuss Harry's plans to create an extension at the back of the restaurant, I find my mind wandering back to yesterday evening. We cooked and ate our pasta, which was every bit as delicious as it looked in the photograph, and by a kind of silent mutual agreement, we didn't discuss Brianna any further. We also didn't talk about our intense kiss. Instead we relived our day, telling each other the parts we'd enjoyed the most about the gallery, and I revealed how stressful I'd found it to be in central London, even though Logan had been with me. The conversation moved around to the picture he'd bought me, which was lying against the wall by the door, and it dawned on me that I wouldn't be able to take it home with me on the train.

"I'll bring it when I next come down to see you," Logan suggested.

"But the cottage is fully booked for…"

"Does the cottage have to be available for me to come down?" he interrupted, looking confused, and he then reached across the table and took my hand. "I mean, your house has more than one bedroom, doesn't it?"

I nodded my head, and explained that it actually has three; my own, the guest bedroom, and a small third room, which used to be my office.

"Used to be?" he queried. "What is it now then?"

"It's just a kind of store room, I suppose," I managed to mumble and he clearly picked up on my discomfort.

"Why isn't it your office anymore?"

I looked up at him. "Because there's not enough light in there for me to see. When… when Greg was alive, he hated me having my business things around the house, especially when I first got started and hadn't got quite such a good system going, so the office was the perfect solution, but it's at the back of the house and the window in there is tiny, and of course, it's only got a single light in the middle of the room, which isn't enough for me…" I stopped talking – well, rambling really – and he got up from the table, came around to my side and crouched down beside me.

"I'm sorry," he whispered.

"Why? It's not your fault."

He shook his head then and took my hand in his, kissing it gently, before looking up at me and smiling. "I'm still sorry," he said. "In all kinds of ways. But the point is, that you've got a spare room, and we've already established we can sleep together under the same roof, so…"

I smiled at him then, seeing his point, and we agreed that the next time we met, he would come to me. I can't say I wasn't relieved.

When it came to bedtime, we stood by the door to his bedroom, and he kissed me goodnight, but his kiss was chaste, not passionate, and in a way, I was grateful for that, because it had been a very confusing and emotional evening, and I wasn't sure how I would react if he'd kissed me so deeply again. Would I have invited him to join me in his bed? I thought I probably would. Did he know that? Was that why he held back? I had no idea, but either way, he left me to my own devices and I surprised myself by falling into a deep sleep the moment my head hit the pillow.

"Hope?" Logan's voice interrupts my thoughts. "Are you okay? Sorry… I've been neglecting you."

"It's fine." He narrows his eyes at me and I smile. "Really. It's fine. I've been thinking."

"What about?" He takes a sip of his coffee.

"Yesterday."

"Daytime, or evening?" I lower my eyes. "Okay… evening," he says and I glance up at him to see a very contrite expression on his face. "I'm sorry about what happened."

"Which part?"

"Brianna's messages, of course." He smiles. "If you think I'm going to apologise for kissing you, you can think again."

I smile back at him and we both seem to relax. At least we've mentioned it now… well, he has.

He gets the bill and, after a playful argument over who's going to pay – which I win – I hand over sufficient cash to include a tip, and we leave the restaurant, making our way slowly back to Logan's flat. I've got just over an hour until my train is due to leave, and while I'm nervous, at least I'll be doing the hardest part of the journey in daylight, and my dad will be at the station in St Austell to collect me, so I'm sure it won't be as scary as my trip up here. I've already packed my things, so there's no need to hurry, and I don't want to. I want to savour every moment with Logan.

When we get back, we go into the living room and sit together on the sofa, and Logan twists in his seat to face me. "Will you be angry with me, and accuse me of wrapping you in cotton wool, if I suggest driving you to Reading?" he asks, taking my hand in his.

"Driving me?"

"Yes. It's about an hour from here, but I've checked the train times and if we left in the next twenty minutes, we'll get there in plenty of time. Then I can buy you a coffee and put you on the train directly to St Austell, so you won't have to make any changes."

I gaze up at him. "You'd do that?"

"Actually," he says, looking shy all of a sudden, "I was going to offer to drive you home to Portlynn, but I thought you might object to that."

"Yes, I might… because that would be completely over the top, and really would be wrapping me in cotton wool. But I'll happily accept your offer of a lift to Reading. Thank you."

I lean into him as I'm speaking, letting him pull me back into the sofa with him. And then he puts his arms around me, protectively, wrapping me up… and I don't mind one little bit.

"Do you remember last night, over dinner, we were talking about me coming down to see you?" he asks, leaning back slightly and looking down at me.

"Yes."

"Well, I wondered, are you going to be free next weekend?"

"No." I shake my head. "I'm sorry, but I promised Amy I'd go into St Austell with her."

"You don't have to be sorry," he says, although his disappointment is obvious.

"She's just found out she's pregnant, you see," I explain, in spite of my own, mirrored, frustration. "And before I left to come up here, she asked if I could go with her into St Austell next Sunday, once she and Nick have closed the shop at lunchtime."

"Any particular reason?" he asks.

"Retail therapy, with a little research on the side, I think." I smile up at him. "She wants to look at nursery furniture, because they'd like to make a start on decorating their spare bedroom. I think it's going to be quite hard for them, being as they only get Sunday afternoons off, and they've never actually done anything with that room, so it needs a lot of work. Nick's dad's offered to help, and they're planning of ripping out the carpet next weekend and, hopefully, stripping the walls too, but Amy wants to look at furniture before they decide on exactly what they're going to do. It didn't seem like a problem when she asked me to go with her. I mean… I didn't think you'd be able to see me again so soon…" I let my voice fade.

"Hey… it's okay. You don't have to explain yourself," Logan says hugging me a bit tighter. "I imagine they're thrilled, aren't they?"

"Oh God, yes. You should see them. They can't seem to stop smiling."

"And are you okay with it?" he asks and I twist in his arms, looking up closely at him.

"Me? With their pregnancy, you mean? Why wouldn't I be?"

"Well… you explained on Friday that it might not be such a straightforward decision for you, when it comes to having children."

"Oh, I see… Yes, I'm fine with it."

"Fine? Hope, give me a better word than that."

"I'm happy for them." I give him what he's asked for – namely the truth. "But thank you for thinking about it, and for asking, and for realising that it might not have been easy for me. It means a lot." It really does, because it's just dawned on me that, even though Amy's fully aware of the consequences of my RP, not even she thought about how I might feel on hearing her news. Logan did though. And that makes me fall in love with him, just a little bit more.

"*You* mean a lot," he whispers, bringing me out of my thoughts, and I lean back into him again.

"I'm sorry I can't see you next weekend…" I murmur, playing with the button on his shirt. "I mean, I suppose you could still come down, but we'd hardly see each other. Between the changeover on Saturday and going out with Amy, we'd only have a few hours together…"

"It's not a problem," he says, his arms coming tight around me once more. "Why don't I come to you the weekend after instead? Unless you're busy then too?" I tilt my head back and pretend to be thinking, biting my bottom lip and frowning.

"Well, I'm fairly sure I'm free. I don't recall any of my other suitors indicating an interest…"

"They'd better not." His voice is deep and growly, his eyes flashing, although not with anger, but with something much more intense than that. "You're spoken for."

I giggle, because I can't help myself and he leans down and kisses me, still keeping it light.

When he leans back, he stares down at me, the intensity still there in his glinting eyes. "You're mine." Although it's not a question, I feel as though he's waiting for an answer, so I nod my head, and he smiles. "Two weeks?" he whispers.

"Two weeks."

Logan

I made a point of blocking Brianna's new number straight away, or at least as soon as Hope had gone to bed on Saturday night. I didn't want to do it in front of her, simply because I wanted to focus on her, and nothing else. I wanted to make sure she was okay, after those few minutes of tension in my bedroom, because when I went in there and saw her holdall on the bed, packed and zipped up, I honestly thought I'd lost her. I went through so many emotions in those few minutes; pain, anger, fear, confusion, and finally relief and happiness... oh, and I suppose I have to mention the overwhelming longing that accompanied our kiss.

That kiss was something else. It was passionate and intense, but also it was like finally finding myself and realising my purpose in life... which I know now is loving Hope. And keeping her safe... while doing my best not to wrap her in cotton wool. Naturally.

I know some people might think that I was being overprotective in driving Hope to Reading and putting her on the direct train to St Austell, but those people didn't see her face filled with fear on Friday night when she came out of the station, or hold her shaking body in their arms. And in any case, regardless of Hope's condition, or cotton wool, I defy any man not to go that extra mile for the woman he loves.

I don't mind confessing that I spent yesterday afternoon and evening wandering around my flat, waiting for her to call me to let me know she'd got back to Portlynn safely. When she did, I simply stared at her image on my phone, and wished she could still be here; wished I could still hold her, kiss her, touch her, talk to her, laugh with her... be with her.

I've slept surprisingly well, dreaming of Hope, yet again, most especially of her lips on mine, and although it's not even six yet, so it's far too early to call, I get up anyway and, using my brand new pen, I sit down and write a letter.

17th February

My Darling Hope,

I'm writing this early on Monday morning, before work. Before even calling you. Because I can't wait another moment to tell you how much I miss you already. You were only here for two days, but my flat feels empty without you. I feel empty without you.

I somehow managed to sleep really well, even though you weren't here. But I think that's only because I didn't change the sheets on my bed, so they still smell of you. I know the scent will fade eventually, but until it does, I'll savour every moment.

Spending time with you this weekend has been magical and scary, and confusing... perhaps in equal measure, and with that in mind, there are a few things I need to get off my chest. I hope you'll forgive me for being so forthright, but I want our next time to simply be magical... and nothing else.

Firstly, I wanted to thank you for sharing your secret with me, and to tell you that I do understand why you kept it to yourself. I wish you hadn't. Obviously. I think I made that fairly clear when you were here. I wish you'd felt able to tell me before, but I promise I won't smother you, or stifle you, and I'll do my very best to control my overprotective tendencies. But that said, I have one thing to ask of you, which is that you must allow me to worry about you, and to try and keep you safe. It's what I do, when it comes to you. It's who I am. And I could no more stop doing that than I could stop breathing.

Secondly, I wanted to apologise (again), for what happened on Saturday evening. We'd had such a lovely day together, and I know Brianna's messages took the shine off for both of us. I would have done anything to make it different and the idea that you'd packed your bag and were clearly thinking of leaving me still fills me with fear, every time I think about it. I want you to promise me that if you ever feel scared like that again, you'll talk to me, rather than running from me. Write to me and promise, if you can. Please.

Thirdly, I want to explain my kiss. I realise that a kiss doesn't really need an explanation, or at least it shouldn't, but I wanted to explain the consequences, I suppose. I kissed you in my bedroom, because – as I said at the time – I wanted to. Plain and simple. I think I was scared I might have lost you, and the relief that I hadn't made me bolder, and more forward, than I might otherwise have been. I'm not apologising, because I'm not sorry I did it. I just want you to know that kissing you was the most magical part of the whole weekend, as far as I was concerned. But I didn't kiss you like that again afterwards, as much as I wanted to, because I need you to still feel safe with me; to realise that, as much as I want you, we're taking things at your pace, not mine, and to let you know that you can trust me. Honestly.

Finally, at the risk of coming across as completely controlling (although I would refer you back to fault number seven, for reference), I want to reiterate that you are spoken for. You're mine, Hope. And you are my hope.

Always,

Logan xxx

I'd love to say that the last two weeks have gone by in a blink, but they haven't. They've dragged, and my only consolations have been my memories of our kiss – although I've been starting to wonder whether that was all a dream – and the letters that Hope has sent me each day, starting with the one I received in reply to the early morning missive I wrote the day after she went home. She apologised – again – for not telling me her secret sooner, and told me that she didn't want me to worry about her... not too much, anyway. Like that's going to happen. I've done nothing but worry about her since the moment she left. Then she added that I didn't need to apologise for Brianna's text messages and that she knew it wasn't my fault, basically reiterating everything we'd said on that Saturday evening, before she promised that, in future, she would do her best to talk to me, but that sometimes her fears just overwhelm her. I suppose that's understandable, especially in her circumstances, and a promise to try is better than no promise at all. She didn't touch too much on the kiss, and hasn't done in our subsequent letters, but she did make my heart sing, by telling me that, yes… she is my Hope.

Being as today is Friday, the much anticipated day of my departure for Cornwall, I've driven into work, rather than cycling, with my holdall in the boot, and I've managed to arrange my appointments so that I can leave by four. No-one seems to mind, and as I wave goodbye, Betty and Ruth give me knowing smiles and wish me a 'lovely weekend in the country'. I haven't mentioned Hope at work that much, but they all know something's going on. They're not oblivious to my ludicrous good cheer.

The drive is busier than when I made it last time, but then it is Friday night. The long journey gives me time to think, and I wonder how good I'm going to be at behaving normally around Hope, and giving her the freedom she needs to be herself, when all I want to do is hold her in my arms and protect her from everything and everyone… forever. I know that's not what she wants though, so I'm going to have to put on the performance of a lifetime, and trust that she doesn't see through me.

It's nearly nine by the time I pull into the driveway of Orchard House, where a sleek silver Mercedes is already parked up, which I presume belongs to her guests, so I park alongside it, closer to Hope's house than the cottage.

Getting out, I go around to the boot to retrieve my bag, just as Hope opens the door. In the bright outdoor lighting, I have just enough time to take in her tight, light blue jeans, her pale grey sweater and her smile, before she comes down the steps, running directly towards me. She flies into my arms and I catch her, swinging her around and holding her body close to mine. As I lower her, she captures my face in her hands and, before I have a chance to say a word, she kisses me. Her tongue instantly demands entry to my mouth and I grant it willingly, groaning in reply to her soft sigh as our tongues clash. I know for sure now that everything I've been remembering about our kiss is for real. It wasn't a dream. Her touch is still electrifying, and yet numbing at the same time, and for a few seconds, I lose my mind, and myself, in her. Then, I slowly regain a little control, and with my hand in the small of her back, I pull her onto me. She knows I want her and I don't care anymore if she feels the physical evidence of that. I need her, and I don't think my feelings are entirely one sided.

We break apart, breathless and she gazes up into my eyes, a flush creeping up her cheeks, and her eyes sparkling… and there's something else. Something beneath the surface. A desire, I think, that mirrors my own.

"I wanted to be the one to do that," she whispers, biting her bottom lip.

"Why?" I release her lip with my thumb, then cup her cheek in my hand.

"Because I want you to know that I trust you to take this just fast enough that we can both keep up and enjoy it, but not so fast that I can't handle it. And that I like your kisses… I like the fire and the heat, and there's nothing about them, or about you, that makes me feel unsafe."

I can't keep the stupid grin off of my face as I absorb her words and recall my letter to her, and the fact that she didn't really mention our first kiss in her response. And, as I lean down and touch my lips to hers again, I wonder if she's been waiting all this time to give me her reply… in person. I'm not going to mention that, of course, because unless it's absolutely necessary, I'd still prefer us not to talk about our letters, but I have to admit to myself, that while I like our words, I really love her style. I also love the normality of this. I like the fact that we're just like any other couple, who've spent a few weeks apart, and can't wait to touch and kiss and hold each other again. I love the fact that her condition isn't part of this. Nothing is part of this, except Hope and me. And that's just how it should be.

Pulling away from her for a second time, I brush my thumb along her slightly swollen lips.

"Shall we go indoors?" She nods her head and I take her picture from the boot, along with my bag, before closing it and locking the car. With her hand in mine, we make our way towards the door. "Sure you trust me?" I ask.

"Yes." I smile at her simple response. "What's funny?" she asks.

"I'm not sure I trust myself."

She chuckles. "Then it's just as well there's a lock on my bedroom door, isn't it?"

I stop, pulling her back, releasing her hand and putting my arm around her instead. "Hope, you don't have to lock yourself in to feel safe. I'm not going to do anything you're not ready for… anything you don't want me to. You know that, don't you?"

"Of course," she says, looking crestfallen. "I already said, I trust you. I was only joking about the lock."

I pull her closer. "Good… because if you honestly think that locking your door would keep me out, you don't know me at all."

Her eyes widen and her mouth drops open, but the gentle moan that escapes her lips tells me everything I need to know. She's not scared; she's aroused, and she's curious, and that's an extremely potent combination. Too potent for me, anyway, and lowering my bag and the picture to the ground, I capture her face in my hands and we discover between us that kisses aren't always about fire and heat and ferocity; that sometimes, slow, steady and deliberate, can be even more erotic.

Hope's guest bedroom is compact, but comfortable, with soft cream coloured furnishings, stripped floors, thick rugs, a pine chest of drawers and a double bed. Hope has left me up here to shower, in the bathroom that's next to her bedroom, on the opposite side of the landing, and has gone downstairs to finish off the supper. I was tempted to ask her to stay, but after our kisses downstairs, I think it's probably best if we have a few minutes apart, just to calm down.

Once I'm dressed again, in jeans and a rugby shirt, I go back down and open the kitchen door, where I'm greeted by the smell of something delicious, and Archie, who jumps up from his bed and bounds over, his tail wagging so hard, that his whole body seems to follow suit.

"Hey, boy…" I crouch down and let him nuzzle into me, before glancing up at Hope.

"He seems to remember you," she says, smiling down at us.

"Looks like it. Either that, or he greets all of your guests like this."

She shakes her head. "No, he doesn't."

I feel rather pleased about that, and after a few more minutes of petting the dog, I get up and go over to her. "Ready to eat?" she asks, looking a little embarrassed, although I'm not sure why.

"Yes. But only if you kiss me first."

She tilts her head back and I take advantage, claiming her lips in a slow, tender moment.

"That's better," I breathe, as we both lean back again.

"Better?"

"Hmm… you looked a bit uneasy just then, and I don't want there to be any awkwardness between us, Hope."

"Neither do I." She looks at my chest, rather than my face. "I'm sorry," she mutters, "I suppose this is all just a bit new to me."

I place my finger beneath her chin, raising it until our eyes lock. "It's new to me too."

"It is?"

I move closer to her. "Yes." I let my forehead rest against hers, and although I want to tell her I'm in love with her, I'm aware that I might scare her if I do, so instead I just say, "It's never been like this before."

She swallows hard, and then I hear her whisper, "No, it hasn't," and my heart bursts with love for her.

It takes us a minute or so of silent embrace to pull apart, and then Hope clears her throat and looks up at me. "I made a stew," she announces, smiling.

"Sounds perfect. Smells incredible." I return her smile and we turn to the table, which she's laid for the two of us, a loaf of bread in the centre.

"Take a seat," she offers and I obey, while she gets a large casserole dish from the oven.

"Do you need any help?" I ask, hoping she'll see that as a genuine offer, and not me being overprotective.

"No, I'm fine." She glances at me as she puts the dish down between us, and smiles.

"Fine?" I query, smirking, not letting her get away with it.

"Really… I'm fine."

She sits opposite me and takes the lid from the dish, steam and a mouth-watering smell wafting upwards, filling the kitchen.

"Do you want to cut the bread?" she suggests and I oblige while she dishes up the chicken stew, after which I pour the wine and we settle down to eat.

"This is amazing," I remark, after the first mouthful.

"Because it's been cooking for hours and hours," she replies, smiling. "I couldn't be sure when you'd get here, so I just left it on a low heat for most of the afternoon. The smell has been driving me crazy."

I chuckle. "Well, it was worth it."

Her eyes sparkle into mine and she puts her fork down, reaching across the table for my hand, which I give her willingly. "Yes, it was," she says softly, and I lean forward, raising her hand to my lips and kissing her fingers.

She sighs and she picks up her fork with the other hand, and we continue to eat, our fingers clasped together across the table, unwilling to let go.

"Thank you for bringing my picture down," she says, after taking a sip of wine.

"My pleasure. Where are you going to hang it? Have you decided?"

"Yes. It's going in my bedroom." I nod my head, although I'm surprised. I'd expected her to say the living room. Her bedroom feels like a very personal choice, but in hindsight, maybe that's a good thing. "I might need some help hanging it though," she adds. "The walls here are like granite."

"We'll do it tomorrow, if you want."

She shakes her head. "I don't think we'll have time. Tomorrow's going to be silly enough as it is."

"It is?" I'm wondering if I've missed something. We haven't talked about doing anything.

"Yes. My guests are leaving at the crack of dawn," she explains. "So I'll have to be up before six to see them off. They're driving back to Yorkshire and have a family event to attend in the evening, or something."

"Oh, I see."

"And then I've got to get the cottage ready for Mr Blake and his girlfriend, whose name escapes me at the moment. They're due at four, or just after…" She pauses, and I sense she has something more to say, and that it's a great deal more important than the comings and goings of her guests at the cottage.

"And?" I prompt.

"And then Nick and Amy are coming to dinner… with my parents." She takes a breath, but only a short one and then continues, "I'm sorry I didn't check with you first, but my mum and dad are desperate to meet you, so when they found out you were coming down, they practically invited themselves, and I thought if I asked Nick and Amy to come too, it would make things easier, because you already know them, and…"

"Hope." I lift her hand to my lips again and plant a gentle kiss there. "Will you stop panicking?"

"I'm not… well, I am."

"Yes, you are. I'll be honest and admit that I'd forgotten your parents wanted to meet me, but I want to meet them too… so this is perfect. It'll be fun. I'll help out with the cooking, and anything else you need me to do."

"You don't mind?"

"Of course not. Look… I completely understand that they'd want to meet me. They've wrapped you up in cotton wool for the last fifteen months and I'm… well, they probably see me as the man who's trying to unwrap you." I can't help the smile that's twisting at the corners of my lips and it seems neither can Hope, who's also blushing. Again. "In their shoes, *I'd* want to meet me. And anyway, I'm happy to do anything with you, as long as we do it together."

"Well, I might just take you up on that," she replies, grinning properly, her embarrassment forgotten. "Changeover days are chaotic enough without adding a dinner party into the equation."

"We'll cope," I reply and she nods her head, as we start eating again, although we keep hold of each other's hands, because it would feel wrong to let her go.

We daren't go to bed too late, considering everything that's going on tomorrow, so once we've finished eating, had a quick coffee and cleared away, we make our way upstairs, pausing outside my bedroom door.

"May I kiss you goodnight?" I ask, putting my arms around her waist.

"Yes."

I start it slowly this time, with every intention of keeping it that way, but when I feel her hands slide up my arms, around my neck, and her fingers twisting into my hair, something flips inside my head, and everything changes up a gear. Breathing hard, I turn her around, pushing her gently up against the wall, one hand behind her head the other resting in the small of her back, as I nip at her bottom lip with my teeth and she arches her back, her breasts pressing hard into my chest. I place my feet either side of hers, our bodies fused, and I pull her close, letting her feel the effect she has on me. She sighs, then moans. Loudly. And at that point, I know that if I'm going to be the gentleman I've promised to be, I'm going to have to stop this. Now. I pull away, taking a step back, and look down at her flushed cheeks, her swollen lips and her glistening eyes and it's all I can do not to lift her into my arms and carry her into the bedroom. But I don't.

"Goodnight," I whisper.

"Goodnight," she murmurs in return. I'm almost sure I can hear a hint of disappointment in her voice. But all the while it's only a hint, I'll stick to my promise of wooing, not chasing. Even if it kills me.

Without another word, she pushes herself off the wall and goes inside her bedroom, closing the door behind her, and I listen. There's no sound of a lock, and a smile settles on my lips. I know she said she was joking... but I wasn't. There isn't a lock in this world that could keep me from her, if she was ready to be with me. But she's not. Not yet. And so, I'll wait.

Hope wasn't wrong about her guests wanting to leave early. I was up and dressed by six thirty, but they were already packing up their car, getting ready to go. Hope had gone through the shower before me, and was watching from the kitchen window looking nervous, worried that the timing of their departure meant she couldn't take Archie for his walk. I offered to take him for her and she accepted with an enthusiastic hug, clearly not reading anything overprotective into my suggestion, and Archie and I spent half an hour walking along the cliff path, before returning to find Hope had made toast and tea, her guests having already departed.

"I'd have made a proper breakfast," she says, taking Archie's lead from his collar and putting down his food bowl, which he tucks into heartily, "but there isn't really time today."

"Toast is perfect."

She smiles at me. "Good." And we sit opposite each other.

"I've finished all the jam you gave me," I tell her, helping myself to a spoonful of blackcurrant from the jar in front of me, and spreading it on my toast.

"I'll give you some more when you go home."

"Thank you." I start to eat. "So, what happens next? I take it there's a kind of cleaning frenzy, is there?"

"That's one way of putting it." She rolls her eyes, although she's smiling.

"Do you want me to help?"

She thinks for a moment and then bites her bottom lip, her brow furrowing. "Ordinarily, I'd jump at the chance, but would you hate me if, just for today, I said 'no'?"

I lick my fingers of blackcurrant jam and butter, wipe them on my serviette and then take her hand in mine. "I could never hate you, Hope, no matter what you said to me."

"It's just that, what with having the dinner tonight, I think it'd be better if I stuck to my routine… I kind of perfected one after my diagnosis and I think it'll just take longer, if I'm having to tell you where things go and what to do."

I nod my head. "That makes sense. Why don't I just keep myself busy over here, and bring you the occasional cup of coffee?"

She smiles. "That sounds lovely."

"And I'll try not to miss you too much," I add and she blushes, just slightly.

"I'll only be in the cottage," she whispers. "Not hundreds of miles away."

I squeeze her hand. "I know. That's what makes it bearable."

She smiles and we finish breakfast, while I tell her about my walk with Archie, and then Hope gets up and starts to clear away, before I stop her. "Leave that and let me do it. You get on."

She pauses for a second, then leans over and kisses me on my cheek, before bringing her hand up, her fingertips playing lightly over my beard. "This tickles," she murmurs.

"In a good way?"

"Yes."

"Thank God for that." I pretend to mop my brow in fake relief, although in reality, the sensation is real enough.

"What to you mean?"

"I've had a beard for nearly twelve years," I explain, standing now and rubbing my thumb along the length of her bottom lip. "I'd hate to have to shave it off."

"Shave it off?" She looks and sounds surprised.

"Yes. If you really didn't like it, I'd shave it off."

She stands up on her tiptoes, cupping my face with her hands. "I'd never ask you to shave off your beard, or to change yourself in any way."

I rest my hands on her beautifully rounded hips. "I know. But if you didn't like it, I'd do it anyway."

"Well don't. I like it."

She leans up a little further, kissing me briefly on the lips, and then steps away, and while I start to clear the table, smiling to myself, she busies herself, fetching a box from one of the cupboards, and filling it with various items, including milk and two jars of jam, some bread and a cake tin.

"You prepared all of that yesterday?" I ask her.

"Yes."

"What kind of cake did you make them?"

She turns, smiling. "A Victoria sponge. I cooked it yesterday morning, before I prepared the stew, and then filled it in the afternoon."

"Do you know, I was so disappointed when I worked out that you make cakes for all of your guests," I admit. "I honestly thought it was something you'd done specially for me."

She puts the lid on her box and comes over to me. "Well, if it helps, I haven't made a fruit cake for anyone since."

"Hmm… that does help. Just a little bit." She chuckles and moves away again, going to pick up her box. "Do you want me to carry that for you?" I ask her, as I start to stack the plates into the dishwasher.

"No, I'm fine." She glances at me. "Really."

"Okay." I'm not going to argue with her, or go over-protective on her, or even pick her up on saying she's 'fine'. Not today.

While she's gone, I finish loading the dishwasher, sweep the kitchen floor, clean down the work surfaces and vacuum the living room, picking up the book she left on the arm of the love seat, and folding the throw she left in a heap, placing neatly it over the back. I smile, imagining her sitting there, probably yesterday afternoon, waiting for me to arrive, reading her book, the throw wrapped around her legs… and only wish I could have been curled up there with her. With, or without the book.

I'm just making us a cup of coffee, when the front door opens and Hope breezes in. She's carrying a pile of bedding and comes into the kitchen, through to the door at the back, which I assume leads to a utility room. Returning, empty handed, a few minutes later, she looks flushed, but beautiful, and glances around.

"I know my eyesight isn't great, but it looks to me like you've cleaned my kitchen," she says, her hands resting on her hips.

"Yes, I have. I hope that's okay."

She purses her lips, smiling at the same time. "Okay?" She covers the few paces between us in a moment, and throws her arms around me, planting a brief, chaste kiss on my lips. "It's better than okay. Thank you."

I hold her close. She smells of bleach and furniture polish, and of Hope. That beautiful, light, floral scent that I've come to know so well, and to love so much. "You don't have to thank me."

"But I didn't ask you to do…"

I lean back, holding up one hand to cut her off. "You don't have to ask me. And you don't have to do everything yourself, while I'm here. I'm not going to sit back with my feet up and let you run around, doing all the work. And before you say anything, that has nothing to do with your RP. You've got guests coming to dinner tonight, and I know your parents and Nick and Amy are coming here to see you – well, and me, I suppose – and they're not coming to inspect your house, but I also know you well enough to know that, despite the fact that your house is always really tidy, you'd have insisted on making it perfect for them. So, I thought I'd help."

She leans up again and kisses me once more, taking a little longer this time, and when she pulls back, we're both breathless and it takes a moment before she sighs and says, "I'm not expecting guests for dinner tonight."

I frown down at her. "You're not? Have they cancelled?"

"No." She shakes her head slowly. "What I mean is *I'm* not expecting guests... *we* are."

I don't even give myself time to smile. Instead I place my hand behind her head, holding her still while I kiss her. Thoroughly.

The new visitors to the cottage, a man called Ryan Blake, and his girlfriend, Anna Townsend, arrive at just after four o'clock, as expected. Hope takes half an hour to show them around and then leaves them to their own devices, returning to the main house, and to me.

"They practically pushed me out of the door." She shakes her head, smiling, as she sips the coffee I've just made her.

"Does that happen often?" I ask from my position near the fridge.

"Yes. Most of the time." She sets her cup down on the draining board.

"Well, I wasn't pushing you out of the door when I came to stay," I point out.

"No. But then you were here alone. You didn't have anything to preoccupy you."

"Yes, I did."

Her face falls instantly as I speak. "Oh yes, of course… Brianna. Your engagement…"

I put my cup down on the table and, within three steps, I'm standing in front of her. "No. Not my engagement. Or Brianna. You." She blinks up into my face, tears hovering on the brink of falling. "All I could think about, from the moment I first saw you, was you." She blinks again and her tears fall, landing on her upturned cheeks, and I brush them away with my thumbs, before bending to claim her lips in the softest of kisses.

"Am I allowed to say I was pre-occupied too?" she says, as I straighten again.

"What with?"

She runs her fingertips from the corners of my eyes, down my bearded chin. "This," she whispers, her voice a note deeper than usual, more husky perhaps, before walking her fingers down my arms, letting them rest on my biceps for a moment. "And these…" And then she brings her hands across and places them firmly on my chest. "And this."

"In that case, you're definitely allowed to say you were pre-occupied."

She lets her head rest between her hands, in the centre of my chest and I hold her tight for a while, enveloping her in my arms, relishing the feeling of her body against mine, until eventually she pulls back slightly and looks up into my eyes.

"Sorry," she whispers.

"What on earth for?"

"I don't know."

"Yes, you do. Tell me."

She leans back and I give her a moment, although my grip on her makes it clear I'm not letting go. I'm not giving in either, and eventually she takes a breath and says, "For leading you on."

"When exactly have you led me on?"

"The kissing… the touching. It's not fair of me to do those things, or to let you do them to me, knowing… knowing that I can't… I can't… not yet."

I know what she means, even if she doesn't seem capable of saying the actual words. "I kissed you first, if you remember? And I think I probably touched you first, not that it matters in any event, because I like being touched by you... I *love* being touched by you. Have you heard me complaining?" She hesitates and then shakes her head. "I'm not complaining about any of it, Hope."

"No. It's just that, sometimes, when we're together, I really think I'm okay with everything, that I can put your past behind me, and think about the future, and then something happens... a word, or a gesture, or something, and it reminds me of the fact that Brianna is such a recent memory."

"She's a bloody nightmare," I reply, and Hope chuckles, and I cup her cheek in my hand. "It's early days, my darling. We both knew it would take time, and I'm happy doing exactly what we're doing, getting to know each other and taking it slow. Aren't you?"

"Yes. Of course I am."

"Then stop worrying. Just let it happen..."

"Let what happen?"

"All of it, whatever we decide we want 'it' to be. Because it will happen, you know? I don't think either of us is capable of stopping it. Not really." I pause, and then decide to go for broke. "And if we're both being honest, I don't think either of us wants to stop it... so just go with the flow."

She smiles, the shyest of shy smiles and I duck my head down to kiss her.

"What on earth are we doing?" She pulls back, startled as my lips touch hers and she glances at the clock on the wall.

"Well, I was about to kiss you, but..."

"We've got four people coming to dinner in a couple of hours; we need to stop kissing, and start cooking."

She goes to pull away, but I keep hold of her. "I'm never going to stop kissing you," I growl, surprised by the depth of my own voice.

Her lips part, her eyes find mine, and then she whispers, "Good," right before she gives me a quick peck on the lips, and then twists out of my embrace. "But if we don't get the lamb in the oven, we'll be eating at midnight."

"Okay… you deal with the lamb, and I'll make a start on the vegetables… deal?"

She glances over her shoulder as she opens the fridge. "Deal."

Once the meat is in the oven and I've prepared the potatoes, we take Archie for his walk, during which Hope answers my questions about her family, namely explaining why her mother didn't inherit Orchard House from her grandmother. I wondered if there had been a feud of some kind, but evidently not. It seems Hope's grandmother left her money to Hope's mother, but decided that Hope herself would make better use of the house, being as her mother and father are firmly settled in their home near Truro. She wasn't wrong, either. Hope is clearly so at one with this place, it's impossible not to somehow become a part of it myself, whenever I'm here.

On our return, I start work on the carrots while Hope lays the table, which makes sense, because she knows where everything is kept, although I make a mental note of where she stores her placemats, glasses and cutlery for future reference. Then she takes twenty minutes out to go upstairs and change, coming down, looking stunning in a deep blue floral wrap around dress. I've finished the vegetables now, and loaded them all into the steamer, and I'm clearing up after myself when she re-appears, and takes my breath away.

"You look beautiful."

She smiles. "Thank you."

She comes over to inspect my handiwork, plugging the steamer into the wall socket at the same time. "You've done all the vegetables, then?" she marvels.

"Yes, and the potatoes are in the oven, so I'll just go up and change my shirt, if that's okay?"

"That's fine."

"Hope…" I tease, and she turns to face me.

"What?"

"Tell me how you feel."

"I feel fine."

I shake my head. "Just 'fine'?"

She hesitates. "Well, okay then… I feel a bit apprehensive, and a bit excited at the same time. And I'd quite like you to go and change your shirt."

"Why?" I look down at the striped rugby shirt I'm wearing, wondering what's wrong with it.

"Because the sooner you go, the sooner you'll be back."

I take her hand in mine and raise it to my lips. "I won't be gone long. But first you're going to tell me why you feel apprehensive."

"Because you're about to meet my parents," she says, as though that should be obvious to me.

"Who I'm sure are very lovely people, if their daughter is anything to go by."

"And who are incredibly protective…" she muses.

I step closer to her. "Understandably. But that doesn't mean they can't be happy for you… if you're happy."

"I am." She smiles up at me. "Although I still feel nervous."

"Would it help if I promised to be on my best behaviour?" I do my best to sound like a contrite schoolboy and she giggles.

"Probably," she jokes.

"Okay. And why are you excited?" I wiggle my eyebrows, and she laughs properly.

"Because we're having a dinner party. It's such a 'couple' thing to do." She's positively bursting with enthusiasm, and it makes her even more adorable than she normally is.

"Well, we are a couple, so why shouldn't we do 'couple' things?"

"I don't know really." She sounds bemused, as though she's wondering why she ever thought this was a problem.

"Right then… so now we've cleared all that up, I'll go and change."

I don't wait for her reply, but start up the stairs, thinking about her nerves over me meeting her parents and smiling to myself that she seems more on edge that I am. Suddenly a thought occurs and I stop halfway, running back down again and straight into the kitchen.

"What's wrong?" Hope asks, turning to face me properly.

"Your name."

She frowns."My name?"

"Yes." I feel like such an idiot for not knowing this, but… "Your surname… Nelson… is that your married name, or your maiden name?"

"It's my maiden name," she replies, still frowning and evidently confused. "I went back to it after Greg died. His surname was Hobson and it had never really worked very well with my Christian name."

I can understand that, and nod my head going over to her. "Okay. I—I only asked because I didn't want to call your parents Mr and Mrs Nelson, and then find that their name was something completely different."

She smiles now. "No. I see what you mean. I probably should have told you that before."

"Or I should have asked. And I would have done, if I hadn't been so distracted."

I take a half step backwards, but still gaze into her eyes. "What have you been distracted with?" she asks.

"You."

Her smile becomes a grin, and before I'm tempted to kiss her again, which is bound to lead to us being interrupted by the arrival of her parents, I leave her staring after me, and run up the stairs, where I freshen up and change my top for a more formal button down, white shirt, marvelling all the while how much further we seem to have come in one short day. Okay, so we're still learning about each other, and I'm still trying to work out what the boundaries are when it comes to her condition and how far she'll let me go in terms of looking after her, but I think the understanding between us is so much deeper than it was, and that's enough to put a smile on any man's face.

Back downstairs, Hope is standing at the sink, and I go over to her and put one arm around her waist, using the other to push her hair aside, so I can kiss her neck. She sighs and leans back into me.

"I missed you," she murmurs.

"I was ten minutes."

"I still missed you."

"Well, I'm here now."

"Hmm…" She turns in my arms and puts her hands on my shoulders, leaning into my kiss, just as the doorbell rings and she jumps back. "God, they're early."

"Don't panic." I try to sound soothing, as she smoothes her dress and goes to the door, opening it wide. Archie bounds up, but stays inside, obediently greeting the middle-aged couple who come into the hallway. As Hope takes their coats, I use the time, and the ever-present bright lights, to study them before they come into the kitchen. Her dad is probably three or four inches shorter than me, with mid-brown hair, streaked with grey. I'd say he's in his late-fifties, and is casually dressed, thank goodness. His wife is like an older version of Hope, and she has exactly the same colouring as her daughter, the only difference between them, apart from their clothing, being that Mrs Nelson wears her hair in a shorter style.

Hope steers her parents into the kitchen and they stand before me, both looking at me with a hint of suspicion in their eyes.

"Mum… Dad… this is Logan." Hope sounds really nervous and I step forward, offering my hand, firstly to her mother.

"It's a pleasure to meet you," I say as she shakes my hand, before I turn to Mr Nelson. "Sir."

A slight smile forms on his face and I struggle not to show my relief. "Call me Jack…" he says.

"And I'm Maria," Hope's mother adds.

"Well, it's good to meet you both. Now, shall I get us all some wine?" I suggest, moving towards the fridge. I'm just opening the door, when I notice a look pass between Hope and her mother. It consists of Maria raising her eyebrows, and Hope shaking her head. I've got no idea what that's about, but I think I'd quite like to find out.

Nick and Amy arrived about fifteen minutes after Jack and Maria, and about ten minutes later, we sat down to a very enjoyable roast leg of lamb, with piles of vegetables, being as it seems I'd overestimated how many we would need. The meal was a huge success, not only because it tasted incredible, but because the conversation flowed continuously. There were no awkward pauses, no moments of wondering what to say next. We laughed. A lot. No-one mentioned Hope's condition, and, whenever I glanced over at her – which was often – I was rewarded with a smile, a twinkle in her eyes, and a look which spoke volumes.

Afterwards, we have some ice cream that Hope made earlier in the week, which is delicious, and then everyone adjourns to the living room for coffee, and I offer to help Hope prepare it.

While she fetches the cups, I fill the kettle with water and then, as she passes me, I grab her hand.

"Can I ask you something?"

"Yes."

She stands, leaning against me. "What was the significance of that look your mother gave you earlier?"

"Which look?"

"Just after they arrived, when I was getting the wine from the fridge, she looked at you and raised her eyebrows and you shook your head. What was that about?"

She smiles and purses her lips, like she's trying not to laugh. "It was just about something she'd said to me, when I first told her about you."

"Oh?"

She sucks in a breath. "You're not going to let this go, are you?"

"No."

"Okay then… well, she asked me to tell her about you, and I was about to, when she told me not to bother."

"Why?" I'm confused by that.

She smiles. "Because she said I didn't need to anymore…" She bites her lip. "She said she knew you were right for me."

I grin. Uncontrollably. "And how did she know that?"

Hope shrugs her shoulders. "Probably because the moment she asked me about you, all I could do was smile."

I kiss her, very deeply.

"You make me smile too… all the time. It seems to confuse people…" I whisper, resting my forehead against hers, once we come up for air.

"Hmm… it does, doesn't it?"

"I suppose we'd better make this coffee and take it through."

"Yes. Before they come looking for us." She nestles into me, just briefly, and then pulls back again, and between us we finish making the coffee, and I carry the tray through to the living room, placing it on the table.

Hope sits in the corner of the sofa, and I sit on the arm, beside her, my arm around her. It's the most affectionate I've been to her all evening, because we've been sat at opposite ends of the table, and there hasn't been the opportunity to touch her, but now that I can, I want to. Not just because touching Hope is one of my greatest pleasures, but also because I want her family and friends to see that caring for her, protecting her, and being right by her side are the most important things in my world.

When it's time for everyone to leave, the hallway gets crowded, with coats being pulled on and Archie wanting to say 'goodbye' to each and every person in turn. Twice. Nick and Amy head off first, and while Hope and her mother are talking in the kitchen doorway, Hope's father puts his hand in mine, giving me a firm handshake.

"It's been a pleasure to meet you," he says, with disarming sincerity. "I hope we'll do so again, very soon. And very often."

"I hope so too, Jack."

He looks me in the eye, his own now more stern, his voice much more serious as he says, "Good. Now take care of my girl."

"I will. I promise."

He nods his head and releases his grip, just as Maria joins us.

We say goodbye, waving to them from the doorstep, and then close the door and move back into the living room to clear away the cups.

"What was my dad saying to you?" Hope asks, stacking things onto the tray.

"He just said he hopes to see me again soon," I reply.

"And?"

"And he told me to take care of you."

She stands, staring at me. "He said that?"

"Yes."

"And what did you say?"

"What do you think?" I move closer to her and note the slight shrug in her shoulders. "I promised him I would." I lean down and capture her bottom lip between my teeth, nipping on it gently. "And I never break a promise."

Chapter Seventeen

Hope

I can't believe how well last night went. In spite of my nerves – and my dad coming over all heavy-handed with Logan, although he assured me when we went to bed that Dad didn't mean it that way. And he didn't take it that way, either. Mum and Dad are naturally protective of me, and they clearly loved Logan, not that I can blame them. I love him too. I really do.

The problem is that he's going home later today, and I have no idea when I'm going to see him again. We haven't had time to discuss it yet, but I suppose now that we've walked Archie and had breakfast, it's as good a time as any.

Pushing my plate to one side, I lean forward.

"When can I see you again?" I ask outright, trying not to sound too clingy or needy, even though I feel both of those things, most uncharacteristically.

His face falls and I feel my heart sink with it. "The next few weeks are going to be tricky." He tops up our coffee cups. "My sister's getting married in the middle of May, which is only two and a half months away now, as she keeps reminding me every time I speak to her." He rolls his eyes dramatically, and I smile at him. "Unfortunately, she's arranged a big gathering next weekend to go through some of the plans, because essentially Rachel's wedding is all about the wedding, not the marriage…"

"Really?" I can't help my surprise.

He nods his head. "It's costing tens of thousands, and is so glitzy and glamorous, you'd think it was being covered by one of those lifestyle magazines." He smirks. "It isn't. But I think she wishes it was." He takes a sip of coffee. "Anyway, it's not my thing at all, but she's panicking that something will have been forgotten, or won't be done in time, or to her exacting standards, and has summoned everyone to her flat on Saturday. Being as I'm one of the groomsmen – as well as her brother – I kind of have to attend."

"You're a groomsman?"

He smiles. "For my sins."

"How many groomsmen are there?" I ask.

"Four." He pauses and I can sense he's building up to saying something. "Zach is one of them."

"Oh. I—Is he going to be there on Saturday?" That's going to be a very awkward meeting if he is, and I think in Rachel's shoes, I'd keep the two brothers apart. But I'm not Rachel.

"I have no idea."

I place my hand on the table, moving it towards him and he takes it in his. "Is there a best man as well the groomsmen?" I enquire, because I've never been to a wedding that has so many attendants on the male side. "Or do you all act as pseudo best men?"

He chuckles, the deep throaty sound tickling along my nerves, just like it always does. "No, there's a proper best man as well. He's a guy Lucas went to university with."

"What about bridesmaids?" I ask. "How many of those are there?" I had one for my wedding – Amy.

"There's the maid of honour and four bridesmaids, so everything looks balanced and even." He shakes his head. "Everything's got to look right."

I feel a lump rising in my throat, but swallow it down as I whisper, "Is Brianna one of them?"

"No." He looks me right in the eye. "No. Rachel's acquaintance with Brianna doesn't stretch quite that far." I'm sure he must be able to hear my sigh of relief, which is confirmed when he squeezes my hand tightly in his. "I wouldn't care if she was, Hope. I still wouldn't be interested in her."

"I know." I really do, so I need to tell him that. "But it's nice to know she won't be at your sister's this weekend."

"No, she won't."

I suck in a deep breath and get back to the point in hand. "So, what about the following weekend? Can I see you then?"

He shakes his head slowly. "I'm on call. And unfortunately I've got to cover the weekend after that as well, because Ethan's on holiday, and he covered for me when I came down here in January, so I kind of owe him."

"Oh, heck."

"That's the polite way of putting it." He gives my hand another squeeze.

"Well, what's the date of the weekend after that?"

"I've got no idea. I've lost track." He pulls his phone from his back pocket and looks it up. "It's March twenty-eighth."

"Well, I can't make that," I say, feeling a cloud descend over me. He looks up, raising an enquiring eyebrow. "It's my mother's birthday."

His shoulders drop, but then he tilts his head. "Speaking of birthdays, when's yours?"

"October the nineteenth," I tell him. "And the next one is a big one…"

"Oh." He smiles. "The big three-oh?"

I nod my head. "Yes."

"It's nothing to write home about," he says gently.

"When's yours?" I ask.

"My birthday?" he asks, and I nod again. "November thirtieth."

"And that's when you'll be thirty-six?"

"Yes… and I feel like we've gone off topic."

"Because we have."

He smiles again. "And that was my fault," he admits. "But it was only because I wanted to be sure you hadn't snuck a birthday in while I wasn't watching." He looks down at his phone and taps on the screen a few times, before placing it on the table in front of him.

"At least you won't forget it…"

"What?"

"My birthday. You've just entered it into your phone, haven't you?"

He shakes his head. "No. October nineteenth…" He touches his forefinger to the side of his head. "It's stored up here now."

"Then what were you doing on your phone?" I ask him.

"Working out when we're going to be able to see each other again."

"And?" I sit forward.

"It's going to be the weekend of the fourth of April. That's five weeks…"

I can hear the distress in his voice and this time, there's nothing I can do about the lump in my throat, or the tears that well in my eyes, and before I know it, Logan's standing beside me, pulling me up and into his arms.

"Don't cry, Hope. Please don't cry. It's hard enough leaving you, knowing how long we'll be apart, without you crying."

"I'm sorry," I whisper.

He holds me tighter. "You don't have to be sorry. It's no-one's fault."

"It just feels like such a long time."

"We'll talk… every day." He doesn't mention writing, and neither do I.

"I know." I try to sound braver and stronger than I feel, and because he's asked me not to cry, I ask him if he can hang my picture for me, to distract us both.

"Of course." He smiles. "Do you have a hammer?"

"Hmm. There's one in the shed."

"And picture hooks?" He leans back, staring down at me.

"That might be a bit more tricky."

He smiles. "Okay. Well, you clear the table and I'll go out and take a look in your shed."

He goes to move away, but I pull him back by his arm and he looks down at me. "Promise we can survive five weeks apart," I whisper.

"We can survive anything, Hope."

"Mean it?"

He leans down and kisses me gently, his lips brushing repeatedly over mine, each stroke a tender balm to my troubled spirits.

"I mean it," he whispers against me, and I believe him.

Logan's not only found a hammer, but a brand new pack of picture hooks I didn't know I had, and carrying the picture, he leads the way up the stairs, standing to one side to let me enter my bedroom before him. He's never been in here, and for a moment I feel embarrassed, remembering that the only man who has, is Greg, and thinking back to the times we shared in here. There were conversations – stilted and awkward. There were arguments – loud and accusing. There was sex – quick and disappointing. *Please don't let life be like that with Logan. Please...*

I look up at him, as he places the picture on the floor, leaning it against the wall, and the hammer and picture hooks on top of the chest of drawers, then turns, his eyes darting around the room, and my gaze follows his, to the distressed pine furniture, the stripped floorboards with thick rugs scattered around, the low window seat, with it's comfortable cushion and a blanket, folded and set to one side, the deep cream painted walls, and, in the centre, dominating everything, the huge wrought iron bedstead. My bedding is deep blue in colour, with a cream and pale blue check throw over the end, and a blanket box at the foot.

"This is beautiful," he breathes, turning to stand in front of me, his eyes gazing deeply into mine.

"Well, it's nothing like it used to be. I—I changed it all, completely, after Greg died." I look around again. "He'd have hated this. He liked things to be more... functional. But after he died, I decided to make it more how I wanted it to be..." I let my voice fade.

"Was this after your diagnosis?" he asks. "To make life easier?"

"No."

"Then why are you telling me this?"

A blush creeps up my face. I know why I'm telling him. I want him to know that, other than me, no-one has ever slept in here, but that I'd like him to... one day soon, even though I'm still not quite ready yet. I want him to know that I do want this. I do want him. I'm not sure I can say that though, so instead I murmur, "Because I think it's important that you should know."

"Why?" he asks.

He's not going to make this easy for me. He's going to make me talk, just like he always does. "Because I want you to understand how different things are to when Greg was here."

"Are we talking about you, or your bedroom?" God, he's perceptive.

"The bedroom, definitely."

"And you?" He steps closer, so we're almost touching.

"I don't know yet."

His face falls. "You don't?"

Why is he so surprised by my answer? Okay, so our conversations are never stilted or awkward. In fact, they're the polar opposite; it seems to me that we always have something to talk about. And we haven't argued yet. Not really. So I don't know what that will be like. And as for sex... well, that hasn't happened yet either, so how do I know whether it'll be different with him, or not? "Well, no..." I mumble.

His brow furrows deeply. "But... I thought you said Greg made you unhappy."

Oh God. He's totally misunderstood... I press my hands against his chest, then move them up around his neck, pulling myself closer to him, my body pressed firmly to his. "He did, and I didn't mean that you do too. Nothing could be further from the truth. You make me so happy Logan. Honestly."

His frown fades slightly, although he still looks confused. "In that case, I don't understand..."

I suck in a breath and swallow my nerves... and my pride. "This wasn't a room I enjoyed sharing with Greg. We argued in here sometimes... although we argued in other rooms too."

"You argued a lot then?" He rests his hands on my waist.

"Yes. Well, it felt like it to me, anyway, but that's not what I wanted to say... not really." God, this is embarrassing. "I wish I'd never started this conversation now..." I pause, wondering how to phrase this. It's hard. But I have to say something, because I've sown a seed of doubt in Logan's mind, and that's not fair. "The thing is… being intimate with Greg, well it wasn't intimate at all."

"What was it then?"

"It was… impersonal. It became a routine, for both of us, I think." He's staring at me now, with a dark intensity in his eyes. "What's wrong?"

He shakes his head, as though coming round from a daydream. "I —I just can't imagine how making love to you could ever be impersonal, or routine."

"You can't say that." I lean back, but he doesn't let me go, keeping his hands firmly on my waist and holding on tight. "You don't know how it will be… I mean, how do you know it wasn't me who made it routine and impersonal? That's what I meant when I said just now that I didn't know yet whether I was different. How *can* I know when we haven't…" I can't finish my sentence, but I don't need to. Walking me backwards, until I hit the wall, he moves one hand up behind my head, the other resting where it is, his feet either side of my own. This is just like Friday night, out in the hallway, except it isn't, because this is so much more intense.

"We don't need to. I don't need to make love to you to know it's going to be magical." He breathes out the last word on a whisper. "And I don't care whether this room is completely different to when you shared it with Greg, or whether it's identical. That's no different to you having slept in my bed. It's not about the room, Hope. It's not about where we are. It's about you… and me."

"I know. It's just…"

"Stop worrying about how it used to be. The past doesn't matter. The future doesn't matter either… not really. It's now that matters. Us. Being together. That's what's important."

He leans down and kisses me, his tongue seeking and finding mine, and as he presses his body against me, I think about what he's just said. For some stupid reason, I'd placed so much importance on this room, and the fact that I'd shared it with Greg, it hadn't occurred to me until just then that the bed I'd slept in at his flat was the same one he'd have shared with his previous girlfriends. Thinking about it now though, he's right. None of that is important. Not compared to what we've got… or at least to what we're becoming. I tilt my head and let him kiss me more deeply, his soft groans reverberating through my body, imprinting this memory into my brain, because the thought of five weeks without him is almost too much to bear.

∽

Logan

It was torture driving away from Hope last weekend, especially after our conversation in her bedroom. I hadn't expected her to be so unsure of herself, not when her kisses are so breathtaking, but then I guess it must have been different between her and Greg. Just as it's different between Hope and me. I've never been with anyone like her before… which is how I know I love her.

I'm waiting for our FaceTime call to connect, with bated breath, needing more than ever to hear her voice and see her beautiful face, to calm my nerves… and my temper, both of which have been on the very edge, all afternoon.

"Hello?" I sigh at that perfect sound.

"Hi."

Archie barks and Hope smiles and looks away. "I know it's Logan, but there's no need to get so excited," she says, before looking back to me and rolling her eyes.

"Archie, sit!" I raise my voice, just fractionally and Hope frowns at me, even though she's smiling.

"I wish you didn't make that look so easy."

I shrug my shoulders. "Some of us have it…"

"Hmm…" She narrows her eyes, playfully. Our calls have been quite lighthearted all week, I think because we know we've got a long way to go before we're going to see each other, and we can't afford to get into anything too deep and meaningful. That said, this call might change everything, and I think we both know it. "How did it go at Rachel's?" Hope gets straight to the point.

I think back over my afternoon at my sister's flat, which started badly, and got worse.

"Terribly."

She tilts her head, looking sympathetic. "Tell me about it."

I lie back on the couch, trying to get comfortable, even though I know that, without Hope here to hold in my arms, that's not remotely possible.

"Zach was there when I arrived."

"And how did that go?" she asks.

"We ignored each other to start with, while Rachel went through her plans. But when we stopped for coffee, he came over and asked me why I haven't answered his message."

"You mean the one he sent when you were here?" I nod my head. "What did you say?"

"You want the unedited version, or the polite, censored, one?"

She manages a half smile. "I might as well hear it in all its unedited glory."

"Okay… if you insist. I'll admit that it took me a few seconds to recover from him having asked such a stupid question, but once I did, I pushed him out onto Rachel's balcony, and asked him if he didn't think that fucking my fiancée was a good enough reason for me not to have replied to him… or to ever want to speak to him again, for that matter." I keep my eyes on Hope as I speak, but her expression doesn't alter at all. "Sorry about the language," I add, as an afterthought.

"Don't worry about it. What did he say?"

I shake my head, because I still can't believe what happened. "He said that he's my brother."

"And? What was his point?"

"Precisely. I pushed him up against the balcony railing… I think he thought I was going to push him over it at one stage, but he's not worth it. I—I said that, being my brother isn't an excuse for what he did. It just makes it worse. I didn't understand – I still don't understand – how he can't see that. I mean, as if Brianna cheating on me wasn't bad enough, she had to cheat on me with my own brother. And not only did he seem to think that was all perfectly okay, he didn't seem to understand why I might be hurt, or angry, or upset by what they did, for crying out loud."

I stop talking, breathing hard, and then notice that Hope's face has paled, and in the light from the lamp beside the sofa that she's sitting on, I can see a glistening in her eyes, and I sit up myself now.

"Oh… don't cry, darling. Please."

"Tell me honestly, are you over her?" she whispers, sounding so uncertain that my heart aches for her.

"Yes. Oh God, yes. You mustn't think I meant anything by what I just said. I'm completely over her. I promise. I don't love Brianna. I'm not sure I ever did. And I certainly don't want to be with her. It's just…"

"It's just what?"

"I'm still so bloody angry with Zach. He's my brother, and forgiving him is… well, at the moment, it's impossible." She blinks rapidly, and swallows hard. "Please don't think my feelings about Zach have anything to do with Brianna, though. They don't."

"It's fine," she mutters.

"No, it isn't. It's anything but fine. I want to be with you, so I can hold you. I know you're feeling scared about all this, and if it wasn't for the wedding, and Rachel's plans, I'd be there with you, and I wouldn't need to have anything to do with Zach."

"Did it bring back memories? Of times when you were happier with him, I mean," she asks, in a soft whisper.

"Yes. But that doesn't mean I want to try and fix it. It also doesn't mean I want to turn back the clock and go back to how it was before. I want you, Hope. I want us."

She sucks in a breath, a long stuttering breath, and I know she's only just managing not to cry. "I know," she murmurs, "and I'm sorry if I seem to be doubting you. I wouldn't be if you were here, or if I were there with you. It's just hard when we're having to do all this over the phone."

"I know it is." God, don't I know. "I could use a hug right now."

She smiles. "Me too." We both pause, just for a second, and then Hope says, "So, did you push him off of the balcony?"

I shake my head, managing to smile. "No. Like I said, he's not worth it. He wanted to talk... to explain, he said. I didn't want to listen. So we agreed, in the end, to bury the hatchet until after Rachel's wedding."

"Can you do that?"

"I can be polite, yes."

"And after the wedding?" she asks.

"I made it clear to him that if he comes near me once the wedding is over, I'll bury the hatchet... right between his shoulder blades."

Hope giggles and I laugh myself, for the first time today. "So, what else happened?" she asks.

"Not much. Rachel spent the whole afternoon barking instructions at everyone, especially her maid of honour, who I think is fairly close to having a nervous breakdown. Lucas spent most of it hiding in the kitchen, on the pretence of making coffee... and one of the bridesmaids decided my day wasn't bad enough already and thought she'd drive me insane by flirting with me... incessantly." I stop speaking and wonder for a moment if I should have mentioned that. But then, I'm being honest... and judging from the smirk on Hope's face, I don't think she minds at all.

"Oh?" she says, with that lovely teasing note to her voice. "Is there anything you'd like to tell me?"

"No. Because there's nothing to tell. But I would like to know why you could barely stop yourself from crying and you sounded so scared at the thought of me not being over Brianna, but you seem to find it amusing that one of the bridesmaids spent the whole afternoon flirting with me."

"They're two entirely different things, Logan," she says, looking bemused, as though she thinks I should understand, and that I'm being dense for not doing so. "You were engaged to Brianna. You were two weeks away from marrying her. You shared something intense and meaningful..."

"Not that intense and meaningful," I interrupt, but she shakes her head, so I add, "Drinking coffee with you in your kitchen is more intense than anything I ever did with Brianna," and she manages a smile.

"Even so, you have a history with her, and we both know she wants you back."

"That doesn't mean I want her… or anyone else… other than you."

"I know. And that's why I'm not bothered about the bridesmaid. I trust you, Logan. I really do." Why does that make me feel about ten feet tall? I have no idea, but it does. "I don't trust your ex though," she adds.

"Neither do I."

"Do you think she'll try anything else?" she asks, although she sounds inquisitive, rather than scared.

"Probably. But I'll tell you if she does. And I won't do anything about it."

"Good."

We spend a moment just staring at each other, until Archie starts barking and Hope tells me that he needs to go for a walk, so we end the call, promising another later, before bedtime. Staring at my phone, though, I feel guilty for not being completely honest with her, for not telling her about the conversation I had with Rachel as I was leaving her flat. It's a conversation I can never repeat to Hope. Ever. It consisted of Rachel asking if I was still visiting my 'latest model' in the country, and me telling her not to refer to Hope like that, while confirming that I am, indeed, still seeing her, whenever I can – whether that be in the country, or up here. She seemed surprised, although not as surprised as she was when I stupidly told her about Hope's RP. I don't even know why I did that, other than that maybe I hoped my sister might find it in her heart to be supportive for once in her life. But I got that wrong. *Really* wrong. And I regret it now. Because all Rachel did for the next ten minutes was to go on – and on – about how much of a 'burden' Hope is going to become in my life… if I let her. She focused heavily on the fact that, right from the outset, from the time I first qualified as a vet, I've always wanted to set up my own practice at some point in the future, and that having Hope 'around my neck' would make that ambition of mine impossible. I said I didn't care about that anymore –

because I don't, to the point where I haven't even thought about it for ages, simply because, in meeting Hope, I've realised there are more important things in life. But Rachel insisted that I should 'cut Hope loose' while I still can, before she 'drags me down' completely. I managed to stop short of boiling over, and left before I said something I highly doubted I'd regret. And then I drove home, wondering how I'm even related to my brother and sister.

I feel the need to shower, to wash off the day and, wandering into my bedroom, my phone still in my hand, I know I've done the right thing in not telling Hope about that conversation, because I know it would bother her. I know she'd start to worry about what Rachel thinks, and whether other people – me included – might feel the same way. And the fact that we've still got four weeks until we're going to see each other again, wouldn't help with that. Of course, she'll never be a burden, no matter what. And I can't imagine ever cutting her loose, or even thinking about it. Persuading Hope of those facts, however, might prove difficult, especially with hundreds of miles between us...

I sit on the bed, trying to block out those thoughts, thinking instead about when she was here, and imagining her lying beside me, her head on my pillows... and suddenly, I have an idea. It's a really great one, and I lie down myself, and start browsing the internet on my phone, wondering why I didn't think of this before...

The last two weekends have been frustrating beyond words.

Being on call is one of the banes of a vet's existence, but all it basically means is that I have to be available for emergencies at work, and while that only means being on the end of my mobile phone, and being able to drop everything to go into the surgery at a moment's notice, it can be intrusive. I'd thought it would be awful to ask Hope to go through the hassle of coming up here, even though I would have picked her up from Reading, and the evenings are a bit lighter, so she wouldn't have been travelling in the dark, only to risk her sitting in my flat by herself all weekend, so I'd decided we wouldn't do anything, and at the time, that felt like the right decision. Except that, for both weekends, absolutely nothing happened. Not one single call out.

We spent a lot of time talking on the phone, but it was no compensation for being together, for touching her, or holding her… or kissing her, and by the time we get to the last weekend of our enforced separation, I'm missing her so much, I can feel it, like a physical ache.

Today being Sunday, our morning call is slightly later than usual, but we can at least talk for longer than during the week, and Hope starts our conversation with a broad grin, and profuse thanks for the bouquet of flowers I had sent to her parents' house, for her mother's birthday, which was yesterday.

"How on earth did you find out their address?" she asks.

"I called Nick."

"And how did you get Nick's number?"

"It's on the shop's website."

She nods her head, still grinning. "Mum was so touched. It was such a lovely gesture."

It wasn't a gesture at all, but I don't say anything, and instead we spend the next half an hour talking about the day before, and how much fun she had with her mum and dad, how they wished in hindsight that they'd invited me – which was nice, and would have meant I could have gone to see her this weekend, instead of waiting another five days until we can be together – and how we can't wait for next Friday. Being apart for this length of time is killing both of us, in equal measure, I think.

Once we've finished our call, I go into the living room and sit at the dining table, taking out the writing paper and pen, and start composing a letter…

29th March

My darling Hope,

This letter is briefer than usual, but I had to write to you straight away. What I needed to say couldn't wait, and I don't want it to get bogged down with any other messages, because this is important.

I wanted to explain to you that sending those flowers to your mother wasn't a gesture. It was something I wanted to do, to make _you_ happy, in the same way that I want to hold you in my arms and feel your body against mine, or walk with you in the rain, or kiss you in the moonlight, or sit with you on your love seat, our heads buried in books, or in each other, or hold you while you sleep. I want to breathe you in, my love, because to me, you are the very air that sustains me. You are the ground beneath my feet, steadying me when I need you. I know I can't always see you, but I can picture you in my head. I can't always touch you, but I can still feel you all around me. I can't always talk to you, but the sound of your voice echoes through me all the time.

You might not be with me, Hope, but you're with me. Everywhere.
Until the next time,
Logan xx

Both of us have been aware that, while we'd set a date for our next weekend together, we hadn't decided where it would take place, and during our more recent conversations, we've talked it over and agreed that Hope would come up and stay with me again. We went through all the pros and cons, all of her fears and anxieties, and some of mine too. I think she wanted to prove to herself that she was capable of making the journey, and as much as I want to protect her, I have to let her do this. Even so, I told her that I'd meet her at Reading on the Friday, and although she demurred to start with, I could tell she was secretly relieved at the idea. After my gift of the flowers, her mother was only too pleased to hold the fort for another weekend, so today I've managed to finish work early, go home, change and have driven out to Reading to meet her.

Standing, waiting for her train to arrive, I think back over the last week, over our letters and phone calls and my little idea which came to fruition, and arrived on Tuesday. I don't know whether Hope will even notice it, but if she does, I hope she understands the significance.

Our eyes meet as she exits the platform, and we both smile and step forward, and then she's in my arms. She smells of Hope, of flowers and sunlight, and I crush her against me, before leaning down and kissing her deeply. She doesn't object, and for a full five minutes, we're absorbed in each other, oblivious to the crowds milling around us, even to the jostles of commuters trying to get to their evening trains.

"God, it's good to see you." I brush her hair back from her face and gaze into her eyes.

She smiles. "It's good to see you too."

We both take a deep, simultaneous breath. "Before I get tempted to do that again, shall we go?"

She nods her head, and I bend down to pick up her holdall, which she dropped at her feet a few minutes ago, before putting my arm around her and turning us towards the station exit.

"I thought we could stay at my place this evening," I suggest. "I mean, obviously, if you want to go out, we can, but to be honest, it's been so long since I've seen you, I'm not sure I want to share you... not even with a waiter."

She giggles, that delightful tinkling sound that reverberates through my body. "Eating in sounds perfect," she whispers, looking up at me.

"Good."

The drive home is surprisingly quick for a Friday evening, and Hope spends it filling me in on Archie's latest adventures, and how Amy's pregnancy is developing. I listen intently, not really caring about the subject, just feeling overjoyed that she's beside me and I can reach over occasionally and take her hand, and feel the warmth of her soft skin against my own.

Back at my place, I hand over her bag, and suggest she puts it into the bedroom, going through to the living room while she does and wondering if she'll notice the change. It's quite subtle, I suppose, and all of a sudden, I feel nervous about it. I hope she doesn't think that it means I have any expectations of her. Because I don't. That's not why I did this... but if she thinks I did...

"Something's different." Her voice interrupts my train of thought, and I turn to face her. She points over her shoulder in the direction of my bedroom. "I can't put my finger on it, but something's different in your room. It is, isn't it? That's not my eyes playing tricks on me..."

I take her hand in mine. "No, it's not. I bought a new bed."

A smile crosses her lips, twinkling into her eyes. "Of course. That's what it is. But... but there was nothing wrong with the old one, was there?"

"No..." I pull her over to the sofa and sit down, bringing her with me, so we're side by side. "But I realised when we were in your bedroom, when I was last staying at your place, that you'd made all those changes, and that you'd made a point of telling me about them."

"And we went through why that was," she says, blushing, probably recalling the turn of our conversation that morning.

"I know… and then I made that stupid remark about you sleeping in my bed, which was unbelievably insensitive of me… so I decided to replace my bed. The room itself was redecorated when I did the rest of the flat, and now the bed is new too, so I can promise you faithfully that no-one but me has ever slept in that room as it is now."

I'm aware I'm rambling, just like Hope did when she gave me her explanation about her own bedroom, and for a moment, she just stares at me, but then she leans into me slightly, gazing into my eyes.

"It's okay, you know? I'm a grown-up, and I know you'll have shared your bed with other women."

I twist slightly so I'm facing her, and take her hands in mine. "I know, but I don't want you to have to think about that, not when you're sleeping in there on your own."

Her brow crinkles into a slight frown. "On my own?" she murmurs.

"Yes…" My heart skips a beat. "Unless… unless you've decided you don't want to be on your own?"

She bites her bottom lip. "I'm not sure."

"If you're not sure, then we'll keep waiting until you are."

"I'm sorry."

"Don't be."

"It's just that it's still only ten weeks since it would have been your wedding day, and…"

"And what? There's something else, isn't there?" She nods her head. "Is it something to do with me?" Has something changed over the last five weeks? God, I hope not.

"No." Thanks heavens for that.

"So it's to do with you?" She nods again and I wait. And wait. When it becomes clear she's not going to talk, I ask, "Are you scared?" because I suppose that might be one reason why she'd be prevaricating.

"Not of you, no. I mean, I'm nervous, because it's so new, and… and everything, but I'm not scared."

Well, that's a relief. "Can you tell me?" I ask, wondering now if perhaps it's something medical that's holding her back, something to do with her condition, or maybe even something else, something more 'feminine' that she'd rather not share with me, although even if that's the case, I wish she would. I hate the idea of her keeping something from me.

"Yes... I..." She sighs and turns to face me, staring at my chest, her cheeks flushed. "Look, if you must know, I made a huge mistake with Greg. I slept with him far too soon, and... and regretted it, only I was too stubborn to admit it."

She doesn't come across as stubborn, but I guess the teenage Hope may have been very different to the adult one, who's learned her lessons the hard way. "How soon is too soon?" I ask.

"We'd only been together a couple of weeks. I shouldn't have done it."

"Not if you weren't ready, you shouldn't have."

"No... especially as it was my first time."

I let out a long breath, full of regret. "I'm sorry," I whisper, letting my head rest against hers for a moment. "I'm sorry your first time couldn't have been something more memorable... more special. But, I'm not Greg. I won't hurt you. I won't take anything you're not ready to give."

"I know."

"Then why don't you trust me?"

"I do."

"Okay. Prove it." The words are out of my mouth before I can stop them, and she leans back, staring at me, wide eyed.

"P—Prove it?" she stutters. "How?"

"Sleep with me." She tries to pull her hands from mine, but I hold on tight.

"Sleep with you?" she whispers, shocked. "But you just said... I mean..."

"I know I said we'd wait until you're ready, and that we've agreed you're not quite there yet. And I know I said you could be the one to cut to the chase, and that still applies. I'm asking you to sleep with me,

Hope, as in *sleep* with me. I promise, I won't touch you, I won't even kiss you. I'll just sleep beside you, because… well, because we get so little time together, and I don't want to spend a single second of it apart… and, if I'm being completely honest, being right next to you is where I belong."

We stare at each other for what feels like forever, and then, very slowly, she nods her head

Chapter Eighteen

Hope

I have no idea how we've got through dinner. Logan cooked it while I showered, my hands shaking, as I washed myself, and then we sat opposite each other at the table and ate the stir-fry he'd prepared, although how I managed to swallow anything, I don't know.

I wasn't scared. I wasn't even worried. I was nervous. And now that we've had coffee and he's switching off the lights, my anxiety has reached a new peak. It's got nothing to do with not trusting him to stick to his word. I do trust him. I'm not worried about that. I'm worried that, when he sees me without clothes on – or at least with a lot less clothes on – he's going to change his mind about us, and that will be the end of everything.

Logan takes my hand and leads me down the short hallway and into his bedroom, flicking on the lights. "Why don't you change in here," he suggests, "and I'll go to the bathroom?"

"O—Okay."

He opens a drawer, pulling out a pair of grey shorts, then turns back to me. "And don't look so scared. We're just going to sleep."

I nod my head. *And you're going to see me in my pyjamas… for the first time. And maybe the only time, if you don't like what you see.*

Before I can say anything, he's gone, closing the door behind him, and I stand, staring at the space he's just vacated, wondering if this is all a big mistake. Even if it is, there's nothing I can do about it now, other than change my clothes, I suppose, because I don't want him to come back in here in a few minutes to find me staring at the door.

I open my bag and pull out my pyjamas, holding them up and wishing now that I'd bought a longer pair with me, preferably ones that started at the neck and finished at the ankle. Why did I choose these short ones with the lace trim? I mean, I know I like them, and they're comfortable, but they're also quite revealing. I quickly undress, giving myself a mental talking to. I'm not shy or embarrassed about how I look… not any more. I used to be, when I was with Greg, but looking back, I think that was only because he never said or did anything to make me feel good about myself. He seemed to think his continued presence should be enough, and maybe for some women, it would have been. But I always imagined that loving someone meant more than just being there.

I pause, my shorts halfway up my legs, a smile forming on my lips, and I think for a moment about all the times Logan has shown me in his kisses, and told me through his words, how he feels about me, and about us, both when we're together, and when we're apart. Okay, so I'm no catwalk model, and I never will be. I'm curvy, and I like that… and, thinking about it, Logan must like that too, or he wouldn't be wooing me so avidly, would he?

I pull up my shorts and am just straightening my top, when there's a gentle knocking on the door and I hear Logan's voice, calling, "Are you decent?" from the other side.

I glance down at my exposed legs, and then reply, "Yes," holding my breath as he opens the door and steps inside.

He's wearing his grey shorts and carrying his clothes, folded in his arms, but he stops dead on the threshold, staring at me, with his mouth slightly gaping, and then all of a sudden, lowers his hands, so his clothing falls in front of his shorts, and I try my best to disguise my smile, as I duck past him. "Back in a minute," I murmur.

"O—Okay," he stammers, and I rush next door to the bathroom, smiling broadly now and thinking on the fact that I might not be such a disappointing sight after all.

Once I've finished in the bathroom, I switch off the light, and go back to the bedroom. The door is ajar, and I go in, closing it, and then turn around, to see Logan lying on the far side of his wide bed, facing me, the covers pulled only half way up his chest. I didn't notice when he came in just now, but his shoulders are broad, defined, and muscular, and there's a dappling of fine, dark hair on his chest. This is the first time I've seen him without clothes either, and it's hard to take my eyes from him.

"You're not wearing a top." I state the obvious, and he smiles.

"No. But I can put one on, if you want me to."

I shake my head. "Not on my account. It's just, when I stayed here last time, you wore a t-shirt at night. I assumed…"

"That was normal practice?" he interrupts.

"Yes."

"Actually, I normally don't wear anything at all. But the last time you were here, I wore shorts and a t-shirt, so you'd feel more comfortable."

"So, you're slowly divesting yourself of nightwear, are you?" I tease, although I'm not sure that's entirely sensible. "Does that mean next time…?"

"Shall we let next time take care of itself?" he murmurs and pulls back the covers a little further, inviting me to join him, and I do, climbing in and pulling up the duvet, before turning over to look at him. "I won't do anything… I promise," he says, resting his head on the pillow.

"Well, can you do one thing?" I ask.

"Of course. What?"

"Can you hold me?"

He smiles, then reaches behind him to turn off the lights, and pulls me close to him. I rest my head on his chest and, as our breathing matches, I fall into a deep sleep.

There's something hot behind me, and a heavy weight resting on my hip. There's another on my thigh, and something very hard pressing into my behind. For a moment, I start to panic. Where am I? What's going on? I open my eyes and glance around… and then I smile. I'm in Logan's bedroom. The hot thing behind me is his body, which is nestled against mine, and the weight resting on my hip is his forearm. The other one on my thigh is his leg, which is thrown across me… and as for the hard thing that's pressing into my behind… my smile turns into a grin, and I decide against making any movements for the time being, and just stay exactly where I am, enjoying the feeling of his very obvious arousal.

I don't know how long it takes for Logan to wake up, but I become aware of the change in his breathing, and then his leg moves from mine, and I decide the time has come to turn over myself, which I do, although my breath catches in my throat at the sight of him. God, he looks so gorgeous first thing in the morning, all mussed up and sleepy.

"Sorry," he says, pulling his hips away from me.

"It's fine," I tell him and he frowns.

"Please… please will you not say that, especially not now. I can't help the fact that you turn me on, or how my body responds to you, but please can you tell me how you actually feel about that, and not just say 'it's fine'?"

I lower my eyes, feeling self-conscious, but then look up at him again. "I like it," I whisper. "I like that you feel that way, and that your body responds to me in the way it does."

He smiles, his eyes sparkling. "That's good," he says, "because I can promise you, there's damn all I can do about it. Seeing you in your pyjamas nearly killed me last night, but waking up beside you… well…" His voice fades and I lean in and kiss him. He goes to pull way after just a moment or two, but I pull him back and run my tongue along the seam of his lips. He groans, loudly, but leans back, shaking his head. "Please, Hope," he mutters. "I promised you I wouldn't do anything… but I'm only human and we're both nearly naked, and you're even sexier in reality than you are in my dreams. I don't think I've ever wanted anything more than to make love to you, but I said I wouldn't touch you, so until we've got some clothes on, can we try to keep our kisses as brief and as chaste as possible… unless you want me to go back on my word?"

I can feel myself blushing, and lower my head again, murmuring, "No, I don't want that."

"You don't want me to go back on my word? Or you don't want me to make love to you?"

"The first one," I whisper. He places his finger beneath my chin and raises my face to his. He's grinning.

"So you want me to make love to you?"

I nod my head, but then place my hand on his bare chest, marvelling at the strength, the power of his muscles. "But not yet," I add. "I'm sorry… I'm not being a tease, or leading you on… I'm just not ready."

He leans in and kisses the tip of my nose. "I know. And it's okay, honestly. I get that you need a bit longer… and like I said, I'll wait."

Without saying another word, he pulls back the cover and jumps out of bed, and despite my best efforts, I can't keep my eyes from wandering south. When they reach their destination, my mouth drops open, and I gulp. Audibly. And then Logan laughs. Out loud.

"I'm going to take a shower," he says, leaning over the bed and kissing my forehead. "A cold one. Would you mind making the coffee?"

"Um… sure. Fine. I—I mean. Yes. N—Not a problem. Absolutely." What's wrong with me? Why won't my mouth engage with my brain?

He chuckles. "You know… if you want to change your mind about cutting to the chase, you can. Anytime you like."

"I know…" I glance down again, just to make sure my eyes weren't deceiving me, and I'm pleased to discover they weren't. "And it's very tempting, believe me."

"I'm glad about that," he murmurs, his voice deep and distractingly sexy. "And I'm really glad you're tempted. Because I *am* being a tease."

With that, he pushes himself up off the bed and wanders over to the door, closing it behind him.

God, I've never felt so flustered in my life. Actually, 'flustered' feels like an understatement for all the thoughts that are rushing through my brain right now, and as I flop back on the bed, my heart pounding, I roll to my side, doing my best to ignore the voices in my head that are screaming at me to follow Logan into the shower, and focusing instead on the nervous knot in my stomach…

By the time we sit down to breakfast, we're both suitably calm, although in different ways. I've managed to restrain my nerves – because logic tells me I have nothing to fear from Logan, no matter what the situation – and he seems to have his arousal in hand. Thinking about it, that may not be the best way of putting that, but in any event, he's outwardly in control of himself.

"Have you remembered that next weekend is Easter?" he asks, pouring me some coffee, before helping himself.

"Yes."

"And do you have any plans?" He stares at me across the table.

"No. Unless my boyfriend would like to come for a visit?"

A smile beams across his face, and I return the gesture. "Your boyfriend would love to come for a visit," he replies.

"You've got nothing planned yourself, then?"

He shakes his head. "No. I'm not on call, and Rachel's got her hen party booked at some flashy spa hotel in the Cotswolds, or something, so there won't be any wedding dramas. Well, none that concern me, anyway."

"What about the groom?" I ask.

He shrugs. "The best man booked everyone into an activity hotel somewhere, although I can't remember where. I was invited, but I declined."

"The thought of spending four days with Zach was too much for you?" I suggest.

"I wouldn't have relished it. But it's Easter, which means four days off, and I'm not on call, and I know where I'd rather be… namely with my girlfriend." He chuckles. "I like the sound of that."

"What?"

"Calling you my girlfriend."

"Well, it's accurate."

"Hmm, isn't it?"

We finish breakfast, then clear up and go for a walk in Richmond Park, after which we have lunch at a pub, and spend the afternoon shopping, before returning to the flat for dinner. Afterwards, we watch a movie, over homemade popcorn, and finally make it to bed at just after midnight. This time, there's no embarrassment, and we just get changed separately and fall into bed, and asleep, in each other's arms, like we've been doing it all our lives.

And I wish we had been.

This morning, Logan wakes before me, but as I come to, I'm aware of his arousal, and I wiggle my behind into him.

"You're going to have to stop doing that," he murmurs, although I notice that he doesn't move away, and instead he brushes my hair aside and kisses a tender spot behind my ear.

"Why? I told you, I like it."

"Hmm… it likes you too," he says, and we both laugh, before I roll over in his arms and he kisses me, much more deeply than yesterday.

"Feeling more subdued this morning, are we?" I ask, teasing, as we break the intimate connection.

"Do I seem subdued?" He nudges his hips into mine and I giggle, shaking my head.

"Not really."

"Not at all," he replies, tapping the side of his head. "I'm just taking a mental cold shower, that's all."

"And how's that working for you?"

He throws back the covers and we both glance downwards. "Not very well, it seems." He climbs out of bed. "I think I'd better go and do the real thing, before I get carried away."

"Maybe you had." I lean up on my elbows and he glances downwards, his eyes glazing over slightly.

"Oh, I wish you hadn't done that."

"What?" I look down at myself.

He shakes his head. "Lying like that… it does incredible things to your breasts."

"It does?"

"Yes…" He moves around the bed towards the door, pulling open the second drawer of his chest and grabbing some jeans and a top, while shaking his head all the time. "I'll be in the bathroom. If I haven't come out in twenty minutes, come and find me. I might have frozen solid. And, if that's the case, just pray you get to me before anything vital falls off."

I chuckle as the door closes and lie back, letting out a sigh. I'd love to just lie here and wallow… to think about how much my life has changed in the last few months, how perfect every moment is with Logan, and how much I love him. But I don't have time. I'm catching the ten o'clock train, because I need to be home earlier than usual, being as Mum and Dad have an evening commitment today. We knew this was going to happen when we made our arrangements, but I wouldn't change a moment of the last two days with Logan. Not a moment.

Sleeping with him has been a revelation in all kinds of ways. I love falling asleep on him, and waking up in his arms, and I haven't slept so well in years. And as for his reactions to me… well, they couldn't be more flattering.

Realising that lying here isn't getting my packing done, I jump out of bed, going over to the chair and grab the clothes I've been wearing since I got here, putting them on the bed, together with my holdall. Before putting my things away, I pull out the clothes I intend wearing today – a clean pair of jeans and a pale blue blouse, and I'm just delving for a pair of clean knickers, when I feel Logan's hands coming around my waist, pulling me into him, my back to his front.

"I thought you were freezing to death in the shower?" I murmur, leaning into him.

"I was. But I cut it short and got dressed instead. I missed you. And I remembered there was something I forgot to ask you."

"Oh?" I turn in his arms and look up at him, his hair all wet and messy, his t-shirt slightly askew.

"Yes." He drags his thumb across my bottom lip and gazes deeply into my eyes. "Next week, when I come to see you, can I sleep with you? I mean, I know you have the spare room, and I'll understand—"

I rest my hand on his chest. "I want you to sleep with me," I interrupt.

He takes a step forward, moving me with him, until the backs of my legs hit the bed, and then he gently pushes me down onto the soft mattress, so I'm on my back, looking up at him as his knee comes up between my legs and he leans over me, his hands either side of my head. "I'm so glad you said that." He bends closer and kisses me with a new-found intensity, using soft, gentle, enticing brushes of his lips and glancing licks of his tongue, all promise and temptation, with just a hint of fire. After a while, once I'm breathless, panting and needing more, he leans back, his eyes dark with mirrored desire. "I'm glad we've only got to wait until Friday, because I think I'd spontaneously combust if we had to go for another five weeks."

"Me too," I breathe.

And he kisses me. Again.

Logan

I wrote to Hope the moment I got back from taking her to Reading station, telling her how incredible it had felt to have her in my bed, how much I loved waking up with her in my arms, that I wasn't looking forward to trying to sleep without her, and that I couldn't wait until Friday, when we could do the whole thing again… over and over, for four days… well, three nights, anyway. I also told her that, if sleeping was all we got to do, then I was happy with that. I felt that needed to be said, just to reassure her that, no matter how aroused I am around her, or how much we might joke about cutting to the chase, she doesn't have to feel pressured.

Her reply arrived today while I was at work, and I open the envelope while removing my jacket, pulling out the single sheet and sitting down on the sofa as I start to read her typewritten words…

Dearest Logan,

I feel exactly the same way as you do. I loved sharing your bed, falling asleep in your arms and waking up with you, and I haven't slept well since. I'm almost breathless with anticipation, waiting for Friday, for the moment you get here and we can be together again. But I have to question one thing. Is sleeping together really enough for you? I know you say it is, but I've experienced your reactions now – first hand – and I need to know the truth. I don't want you to feel frustrated waiting for me, so if it's not enough, then I'd rather you told me…

I stop reading, her letter falling to my lap, and I pull my phone from my pocket, going to my FaceTime app and connecting a call to her. She's not expecting to hear from me for about an hour yet, but I don't care. This needs saying, and it needs saying now.

After a few seconds of the annoying warble, she picks up and then her face appears on the screen.

"It's enough," I say, before she can even open her mouth.

There's a moment's hesitation, while she seems to gather her thoughts, probably taking on board that I've just broken our unspoken rule and mentioned something from our letters, and then she says, "How do you know?"

"Because this is the first time in my life I've ever waited for anyone."

"Ever?" she queries, her brow furrowing.

"Yes… well, unless you count waiting until the third date?" She smiles, although there's a sadness behind her eyes, and I wonder if that has some significance for her. "Did I say the wrong thing?" I ask.

"No." She shakes her head.

"Then why so sad?"

She swallows and closes her eyes, before opening them again and murmuring, "It was on the third date that I slept with Greg."

I nod my head. "I wondered…"

"And that was a huge mistake."

"Well, this isn't. Look… as I said, I've never really waited for anyone. Except you. And I know that it's enough because waiting for you is so much better than being with anyone else."

"But… when it comes down to it, I could be a huge disappointment."

I huff out a laugh. "That would be humanly impossible."

"How do you know?"

I sigh. "I just know."

"Because you're so experienced?" There's no denying that I am more experienced than Hope, but there's an edge to her voice that sounds horribly like fear, and I know I need to rein that in.

"No. Because I know you."

"No, you don't. Not in that way."

"Yes, I do. I know that you're fun, and you're funny. After last weekend, I know you're pretty hard to shock too. You're intense, and you're sexy as hell… and if you put all of that together, couple it up with how absolutely gorgeous you are… well, I know you could never disappoint."

She bites her bottom lip, rather than smiling, like I'd hoped she would. "I—I just don't want you to go through all this, only to find that it wasn't worth it in the end."

"Not worth it?" I let out an exasperated sigh, pushing my fingers back through my hair. "Would it be okay if I told you, before we go any further with this, what your only real fault is?"

She frowns. "I suppose so… if you want to."

"It's just that, I did use up an entire sheet of paper listing out my faults, and that wasn't even all of them… so it seems only right that I point out that you worry too much, my darling. You fret over things that haven't happened yet, or that might never happen, and in doing that, you forget to live in the moment, to just go with it."

She stares at me, and although we're hundreds of miles apart, I can see her eyes glistening with unshed tears. Have I said too much? Gone too far? Why can't we be together, so I can hold her and tell her I love her? "I know," she whispers. "You told me to just let it happen…"

"Then stop worrying. I promise you, I'm not going anywhere. I'm not going to get frustrated and I'm never going to be disappointed in you. Ever."

She smiles, properly this time and dabs her eyes with a tissue. "I'm sorry," she says.

"No, *I'm* sorry."

"What for?"

"For calling, rather than writing. I wouldn't normally have done that, but it seemed important to let you know that you've got nothing to fear. Because you haven't."

"I'm glad you called. It's good to hear you say that… it's good to hear your voice, and to see you." She reaches out and touches the screen with her finger.

"Well, it's only two days, and you'll be able to touch me properly."

"Oh God…" There's a tremble to her voice that echoes through my body. "I can't wait…"

I chuckle. "Believe it or not, neither can I."

It's Good Friday morning and I've just arrived in Portlynn, and I don't even care that it's overcast and looks like it might rain. I set off early, to make the most of our long weekend and, pulling into Hope's driveway, I smile at the sight of her kneeling over the flowerbed by the front door, a trowel in her gloved hand. She glances up, pulling off her gloves and stands, stretching, as I park the car and climb out, before she runs over and throws herself into my arms. It's so good to hold her, to feel her body against mine and for a minute, we just stand, until I lean back and look into her eyes.

"Hello."

She grins. "Hello."

"I've brought you something."

Her brow furrows. "You have?"

I nod my head and lean into the car, over to the passenger seat, pulling out the enormous hand-finished Easter egg, in its presentation box, and hand it to her. She gasps and takes it from me.

"Oh, that's beautiful," she says.

"Too beautiful to eat?" I ask, teasing, and she looks up at me.

"I wouldn't go that far… it's chocolate."

We both chuckle and, with my arm around her, we walk to the back of my car, where I grab my bag from the boot, and then we proceed into the house, closing the door behind us.

Archie comes to greet me and I kneel down, petting him and letting him nuzzle into me for a few minutes until he gets bored and returns to his basket, his tail wagging ferociously.

"I—I've got something for you too," Hope says, as I stand up and take off my jacket, hanging it up.

"Oh?"

She takes my hand and leads me into the kitchen, then steps aside so I can see the large dark chocolate egg, sitting on the table. It's decorated with white chocolate swirls and looks incredible.

"I made it for you…" she murmurs.

"You *made* it?" I glance at her, and then back at the egg.

"Yes."

She looks so unsure of herself, and without hesitating, I pick her up and she squeals as I swing her around. "You're amazing, you know that?" She shakes her head, and I lower her to the ground again. "Well, even if you don't, I do. You. Are. Amazing."

"Because I can make chocolate eggs?" She narrows her eyes, teasing, I think.

"No. Because you're you."

We gaze at each other, just enjoying the fact that we're here again, at last, and then she sighs and says, "Shall we take your bag upstairs?"

"Okay."

Back in the hallway, I pick up my holdall and let Hope lead the way upstairs. At the top though, I pull her back, her hand in mine.

"Can you be honest with me?" I ask, voicing the fear that's accompanied me on my journey down here.

"Yes."

"I know you've had some doubts about me during this week, so can you tell me where you want me to sleep? If you'd prefer to slow things down again, and that we slept in separate rooms while I'm here, I won't mind. It won't make a difference to us, or to how I feel about you…"

I let my voice fade, wondering if that's too much of a clue as to how much she means to me.

She steps closer, her body moulded to mine, and I drop the holdall, and release her hand, cupping her face instead.

"I haven't had any doubts about you," she whispers. "If anything, the doubts have been about me; about whether what we're doing is enough for you… about whether I'll be a disappointment."

"And we've covered this already, haven't we?" I step even closer, letting her feel the effect that just being with her has on my body. "I can only repeat what I've already said. It's enough… it's more than enough. I love everything we do, and even if this is all we ever have, it will still be enough." I lean down and gently brush my lips across hers. "So?" I murmur. "Where am I sleeping?"

She reaches behind her and twists the handle, opening the door to her bedroom. "With me?" she says, like it's a question.

I nod my head and kiss her again, more deeply, walking her backwards at the same time. With each step, she gets more breathless, her hands working up my arms, across my shoulders and up into my hair, fisting there and holding me still. I'm vaguely aware of my surroundings and move us across the room until Hope hits the bed, where I lower both of us onto the mattress, her perfect body beneath my own, and gasp in a breath as she wraps one of her denim clad legs around me.

Changing the angle of my head, I take her mouth with my own, and run a hand down her side, skimming over the swell of her breast, and letting it come to rest on her rounded hip.

I only pull back when it becomes absolutely necessary, and I lean up on my elbows, looking down at her flushed face, her sparkling eyes and swollen pink lips, and I smile. She wants more, that much is obvious, but until she says the word, this is where we have to stop.

I kiss her, more gently, although I do nip at her bottom lip, before leaning up once more.

"You really thought I might find you disappointing, when you make me feel like this?"

I flex my hips into her as I'm speaking, teasing her, and she moans, closing her eyes, as though in rapture, but bites her lip, battling with herself, I think.

"It's okay," I whisper, leaning down, placing my mouth directly beside her exposed left ear. "Until you're ready, this is where we stop."

"It is?"

"Yes."

"And you're okay with that?" The uncertainty behind her voice is almost my undoing, but I take a breath and gently trace a line of kisses from her ear, back to her gently pouting mouth.

"Yes. I'm quite capable of wanting you, of kissing you…" I quickly dust my lips across hers. "Of holding you, even touching you…" I let my hand roam back up her body, from her hip to her neck, and hold it there, my thumb brushing against her soft skin. "Of feeling your perfect body beneath mine… and of stopping."

She moans, just softly, and, with her fingers twisted into my hair, pulls me in for another kiss.

Our weekend has flown by far too quickly.

We've been more physical than ever, the sexual tension positively crackling between us, and I'll admit it's been a real test of my willpower. One which I've survived… but only just.

Whenever we've taken Archie for his walks, instead of holding hands, we've walked with my arm around her waist and with Hope's hand tucked into my back pocket. That's not something anyone has ever done before – not with me, anyway – and I'll admit, I really liked it. It felt familiar and intimate, and yet kind of friendly at the same time. An intoxicating combination, at least where Hope's concerned.

On Saturday, I helped with the changeover, being as we didn't have an important dinner to cook in the evening, and I made a start on tidying the cottage while Hope baked a cake and sorted out all the food and supplies. It turned out that we worked well together and it gave me plenty of opportunities to sneak kisses and cuddles, when she least expected them.

Saturday evening was spent fulfilling one of my fantasies, being as, after we'd eaten, we adjourned to the love seat in the living room. We started off curled up together, with Hope's head on my chest, both reading individual books, but before long, we abandoned our books and discovered that just kissing was the perfect way to spend an evening.

On Sunday it poured with rain. All day. Archie still needed his exercise though, and when we came home from his evening walk, absolutely soaked through, we dried off in the kitchen, me towel-drying Hope's hair, and kissing her neck in the process, while she decided that I should remove my 'damp' shirt, with which she offered to help, taking her time, and resting her hands on my bare skin at every opportunity.

Her condition hardly featured in our weekend at all, and that felt so wonderfully normal… for both of us.

Each night, we've fallen asleep, tired but happy, in each other's arms. And each morning, we've woken entwined, aroused, and in my case at least, just a little bit more in love.

Unfortunately, I'm going home again today, and Hope's just dishing up our breakfast, when she turns to me.

"How are you fixed next weekend?" she asks.

I feel like the life has just been sucked out of me. "Let me check, but I think I've got something on…" I pull my phone from my back pocket and go into my calendar, my heart sinking when I read the entry for next Saturday. "I thought so. Unfortunately, I'm booked up for the final suit fitting, for the wedding. All six of us are going together, so it's probably going to take most of the afternoon. That's assuming I don't kill Zach, of course."

She chuckles, bringing over our bacon and eggs and sitting in the chair opposite me. "Try not to," she says.

"I'll do my best."

"So, what about the weekend after?"

"I'm on call." I hesitate. "I mean, you could come up, if you want, but there's always a chance that you'll end up sitting in the flat by yourself, while I go and deal with some emergency or other. It's… well, it's unpredictable at best."

She pulls a face, like she's not overly enamoured with that idea, and I can't say I blame her. It would be different if we were here, but being abandoned in a strange place, where she doesn't know anyone isn't something that would make Hope very comfortable. And who can blame her for that?

"The weekend after?" She's sounding desperate now.

"I'm free." I smile at her and she smiles back. "That's only two weeks before Rachel's wedding, but if she springs anything on me, I'll tell her I'm out of the country." Hope giggles and, on hearing that sound, I make a snap decision. "Come with me," I blurt out.

"Where to?"

"Rachel's wedding."

Her eyes widen. "You... You want me to come with you to your sister's wedding?"

I nod my head. "Yes."

"But I haven't been invited," she reasons.

"I'm inviting you."

She shakes her head. "I think the invitation is supposed to come from the bride and groom... or even from the bride's parents, if they're being completely traditional about it."

"They're not. They've issued the invitations themselves, and if you want to come, then I'll talk to Rachel. She won't mind." Well, she might, given our recent conversation, but I can be very persuasive, when I have to be.

She frowns. "This is the same Rachel who's trying to create the perfect wedding?"

"Yes."

"And you think she won't mind having a stranger there, on her special day?"

"You're not a stranger."

"I am to her, Logan."

I reach across the table and take her hand in mine. "I want you there... actually, I need you there."

"Why?"

I manage a half laugh. "If you'd met my family, you wouldn't have to ask that question." She falls silent, lowering her eyes to the table. "Are you worried about Brianna being there?" I ask and she nods her head. "Then don't." Hope raises her face again, looking at me. "Obviously she was invited, as my fiancée…"

"She'd have been your wife by now," she interrupts, reminding me of the mistake I so nearly made.

"Yes, but the point is, she's not my wife, or my fiancée, and she's not invited to the wedding. Not anymore. Even Rachel isn't that insensitive, given that both Zach and I are going to be there." I'd like to say that her concern for my feelings was the main factor in her cancelling Brianna's invitation, but the reality is that she didn't want her friend to make a scene in the middle of the service. She admitted that to my face, but I'm not about to tell Hope that.

She stares at me in silence for a moment, then says, "Can I think about it?"

"Of course."

"I won't take too long… and I'll call and let you know. I'm sure the last thing Rachel wants, other than a stranger turning up at her wedding, is a stranger turning up at the last minute."

I run my hand up her arm, caressing her skin with my fingertips. "I've said it once, but I'll say it again. You're not a stranger, Hope. I don't think you've ever been that… even before I met you."

Chapter Nineteen

Hope

I accepted Logan's invitation. Apart from wanting to spend as much time as possible with him, which was a major factor in my decision, I was haunted by the way he'd said he 'needed' me there. It made me wonder if the idea of facing his family on his own after what happened with Brianna, and especially of dealing with Zach by himself, was too much. Obviously I'm not overflowing with enthusiasm at the idea of meeting his cheating brother, and his seemingly appearance-conscious sister, not to mention his bickering, divorced parents, or of travelling into central London, but I love him, and I want to support him, so I've said I'll be there, and to be honest, just hearing the relief in his voice when I told him my decision was worth it.

During that phone call, we decided, being as the weekend of the wedding will be spent at his place, for obvious reasons, that he's going to come down here again next time. I have to admit that I couldn't help smiling, and when Logan asked me why, I told him outright, that we'd had such a good long weekend together, I was looking forward to repeating it. He laughed at that, but then told me he felt the same way, in a voice so deep and sexy, my whole body shuddered.

Logan's letters keep arriving, every morning. They're becoming more and more romantic, if that were possible, and I look forward to them every single day. At night, I sometimes take a stack of them to bed, and re-read them, just so I miss him a little less, although even his words don't make up for having him in my bed, or lying in his arms, or feeling his lips on mine...

The days are passing quickly, thank goodness, and each time I go into the shop, whenever we're alone, Amy quizzes me on Logan, and on how things are going between us. To be honest, I think she's enjoying the romance of it all, almost as much as I am. She's got a very neat little bump now, which makes me smile every time I see her, and our conversations drift between babies and Logan... and I enjoy them both in equal measure.

Because she's such a good friend, Amy agreed to take me into Truro to find the perfect dress for the wedding, but having scoured every single shop, we admit defeat.

"Come back to my place. We'll pinch Nick's laptop and have a try on the internet," she says, on the drive home.

"I hate buying clothes online... they never seem to fit."

"Well, it's still a few weeks until the wedding, so you've got time to try it on and return it, if it's not quite right."

She has a point and when we get back, we settle down on her sofa, with Nick's laptop balanced between us.

Miraculously, we find the absolutely perfect dress on only our second attempt, both of us pointing to it and yelping at the same time. Nick smiles indulgently from his seat on the chair, and I'm tapping in my credit card details before they sell out in my size.

"Now we just have to find you shoes and, probably a wrap or a scarf, just in case it gets chilly in the evening," Amy says, and Nick rolls his eyes.

"I'm going to make coffee." He gets to his feet and walks behind our sofa, kissing the top of Amy's head as he passes, and she and I go back to our searching.

As usual when Logan's due to arrive, I'm trying to keep myself occupied, so I don't spend the entire time looking at the clock and trying to work out when he'll be here, or why he hasn't arrived yet, or how many more minutes I've got to wait. This evening, rather than just reading a book or watching the television and second guessing his arrival, I'm cleaning out my cupboards in the kitchen and I'm just putting back the jars when I hear the sound of tyres on the gravel and jump down from the chair I've been using to reach the top shelf, running to the door and pulling it open.

Because it's early May, it's still vaguely light out here, but even so, the outside lights ore on, to help me see, and Logan's parked in his usual spot, and is already walking towards the boot, when I run up to him and launch myself into his arms. He catches me, just like he always does, spinning me around and burying his head in my neck. He inhales, like I'm his form of oxygen, and I throw my head back, relishing the feeling of his strong arms around me. He lowers me eventually and my feet hit the ground, although he keeps hold of my hand, while he opens the boot and retrieves his bag, and then I lead him into the house, where Archie comes to greet him and, abandoning his luggage at the foot of the stairs, Logan kneels to pet him as usual.

I'm impatient for a kiss though, and I haul him to his feet after just a few minutes, then, with one hand behind his head, the other on his shoulder, I kiss him. He cups my face in his hands and returns my kiss, walking me backwards, into the living room, until I feel the arm of the sofa behind my legs. Logan applies just the slightest of pressure and, with a giggle, I topple backwards, landing on the seat of the couch. He follows, crawling up over me, his body lying along the length of mine, his lips tracing a line from my mouth to my ear.

"Hello," he says, his voice rumbling through me, making me shiver with anticipation.

"Hello." I reach up, pulling on his jacket. "Are you going to take this off?"

He leans up, gazing down at me. "Just this?" he teases, wiggling his eyebrows, and without even a second's hesitation, I shake my head.

"No... not just that."

He stills, not even blinking, just staring. "What are you saying, Hope?"

I take a breath, then tuck my hands inside his jacket, resting them on his chest, feeling the heat of him through his shirt. "I—I know the six months isn't up yet, but I was wondering if we could cut to the chase… if you don't mind, that is?"

"Mind?" His gaze roams down my body, then back up to my face, resting for a moment on my lips before settling on my eyes. "No, I don't mind," he says. "But do you think we could move this upstairs?"

"Of course."

Smiling, he gets up and holds out his hand to me. I take it and, without a word, he leads me back into the hallway, kicking his bag out of the way, and we go up the stairs and into my room.

He closes the door behind us and then turns to me.

"You're sure about this?" he asks.

"Yes."

"Only… I'm not going to ask again."

"I'm sure. I've never been more sure of anything in my life. It's time, Logan."

He smiles and, reaching out, unbuttons my blouse, pushing it from my shoulders and letting it fall to the floor. Then he undoes my jeans, kneeling before me to pull them down.

"This is where I belong," he says, looking up at me, "kneeling at your feet, worshipping you."

I feel myself blush, but then suck in a gasp as he tucks his fingers inside my knickers and lowers them to my ankles.

"You're so beautiful," he whispers, and then I feel his fingers on me. "Move your legs," he mutters, and I do, kicking off my underwear and parting my feet. He settles on the floor and I clasp the back of his head, trembling, as his tongue licks across that most sensitive part of my body; hard and fast alternating with slow and tender.

"That feels so good," I manage to whisper, between my clenched teeth, just as Logan sits back, and then stands and cups my face in his hands, kissing me. Hard. I taste of me, a kind of salty sweetness.

I like it.

He breaks the kiss eventually, but maintains his grip on my face, his eyes locked with mine.

"I want you," he growls. "Now."

With that, he picks me up in his arms, walks the few paces to my bed, and drops me on my back, my head on the pillows, then leans over, reaching around behind me. I sit slightly to give him access and he undoes my bra, releasing me, and then stands again, letting the garment drop from his hands as he just stares at me. I feel slightly self-conscious, being as he's still fully clothed and I'm stark naked, but the hunger in his eyes is enough to light any flame and I lie back again, watching as he unbuttons his shirt. It hasn't even hit the floor before he's undone his jeans and I turn onto my side, propped up on one elbow, taking him in, as he lowers them to the floor, along with his trunks. He stands again and is revealed to me in all his perfect, naked glory... and a slight gasp comes, unbidden, from my mouth.

Logan smiles and climbs onto the bed, rolling me onto my back, then kneels between my legs, parting mine with his own, before he settles back on his ankles, his face falling.

"Shit," he whispers, letting his head fall into his hands.

I lean up on my elbows. "What's the matter?"

He looks down at me, a picture of contrition. "I'm so sorry," he murmurs and my heart sinks. What did I do? "I don't have any condoms." He pushes his fingers back through his hair, sighing. "I wasn't expecting this to happen, so I didn't bring any." He looks up at the ceiling. "I can get some tomorrow though... if you... if you don't mind waiting?"

I smile up at him, then reach out and touch his chest, the contact sparking off a tingling sensation through every nerve in my body. "I think we've waited long enough, don't you?" I whisper.

He tilts his head, frowning and clearly confused. "Hope?" he mutters.

"I'm on the pill," I explain. "I was... before..." I'm wary of saying Greg's name at a time like this, so I don't. "I haven't stopped taking it, and... well, you know I haven't been with anyone else."

He leans forward, his hands either side of my head. "I promise you, I've never in my life been with anyone and not used protection. So, do you trust me?"

"You know I do."

He sucks in a deep breath, then reaches down between us and I feel the tip of his arousal against my entrance, and then… I wince at the intrusion, and he holds still. "Is that hurting?"

"A little."

He nods his head. "We can take our time. There's no rush, darling. I know it's been a while…"

"I'm not sure it's got anything to do with that," I try to explain and he lowers himself onto his elbows, so his face is just an inch or two from mine.

"What's wrong?"

"I—It's just that… well, it's going to take me some time to adjust."

"Would you like to stop? Maybe try again later?" he offers.

"No," I say quickly, and he smiles broadly. "I'm not complaining. But let's just say the reality of you is so much more than I'd anticipated."

He chuckles now. "Why, thank you," he murmurs and, keeping our eyes locked, he starts to push inside me, just an inch at a time, kissing me and caressing my cheeks, in the tenderest of moments, until eventually, I'm filled up with him, and I revel in the wonder of being his at last. We lie still, for a long time, just breathing and staring at each other, perhaps unable to believe that we've finally arrived in this place; that we're now one. Letting out a low sigh, he raises himself up, and brings his right hand down behind my hip, lifting me slightly off the mattress, while his other hand caresses my cheek, his fingers laced in my hair, his forehead resting against mine. And then he starts to move, slowly, deliberately, and with an aching tenderness, his body claiming mine. Demanding, yet giving. Controlling, yet loving.

"Take me," I whisper, and he grinds his hips into mine. "I'm yours."

"Yes, you are." His voice is deep and husky, filled with emotion. "And I'm yours."

I have no sense of time or place. I only know pleasure. Over and over. The ecstasy of losing myself in him. Repeatedly. And yet I know I'm never really lost, because with him, I'm safe. I'm always safe. I don't know how many peaks I've reached, or how many times I've cried his name, but just as I'm toppling on the the precipice again, his body stills and stiffens and then… we fall together, his loud groans and my heartfelt screams filling the empty corners of the room, our bodies tumbling, entwined, through wave after wave of light and heat and longing.

Slowly – very slowly – we come back to reality. Logan leans down and kisses me gently on my lips, before turning us over onto our sides. I can barely breathe, let alone focus, but I'm very aware of the fact that I've never felt so thoroughly and completely satisfied in my life and I lie in his arms, not wanting this moment, or this feeling, to ever go away.

He gently runs his fingertip along my jawline, his lips following, in tender kisses.

"Can I ask you a question?" he whispers, resting his hand in the small of my back and pulling me close to him.

"Yes."

He thinks for a moment. "Actually, I have two questions…"

"Okay."

I wait, and eventually he says, "Are you insane?"

I frown at him and try to lean back in his arms, except he won't let me. "Sorry? Was that one of your questions?"

"Yes. I mean, how could you ever think I could be disappointed in you?" He swallows. "I—I never make comparisons, and I never will, but at the risk of appearing to do so… it's never been that good before. Not with anyone."

Although I don't want him to make comparisons either, I can't help smiling, and he smiles back.

"Well, I don't think I need to tell you that it's never been that good before for me either," I murmur, feeling shy.

"So, not impersonal, or routine then?" he teases.

"No. Far from it. And I'm sorry I made so much noise. I didn't mean to keep screaming and calling out your name like that."

He chuckles. "Don't apologise. I like that you screamed. I especially liked hearing you cry my name. And I've got every intention of making you do it again… as soon as possible." My insides clench at the thought and I grin at him.

"What was your second question?" I ask, nestling into him a little.

"That's a bit more intimate, I suppose, but I just wondered whether you took the pill when you were with Greg for medical reasons? Or was it because you didn't want to have kids?"

I look up at him, stunned. "That's a serious question for a time like this."

"Well, there's no time like the present. We've talked about your RP and the impact that might have on your decision to have children in the future, but that wasn't a factor then, was it?" He keeps his eyes fixed on mine, waiting for my response.

"It wasn't medical," I explain.

"So you didn't want kids?"

"I did, at the beginning... but Greg was ambivalent, to put it generously, so I decided to play it safe, rather than putting another problem into our marriage."

He nods his head, and lets out a breath. "And now?" he asks. "How do you feel now? Bearing in mind your condition and everything?"

"About having children?"

"Yes."

I raise my eyebrows, wondering how we got onto such a momentous topic at this precise moment. "Why do you want to know?"

He moves his hips forward and I feel his arousal, still hard, and still distractingly deep inside me. "Because, given our current situation, I think these things are important to know, don't you?"

"I suppose..."

"And the answer is?"

"I always wanted to have children. And I suppose that was another of the disappointments in my marriage to Greg... facing the fact that I wouldn't have any. Since my diagnosis... well, obviously it's not something that I've really thought about that much, not being in a relationship or anything, but I suppose, given the risks, I'd have to think very seriously about it, and..." I stop rambling and let my voice fade, not wanting to say that clearly he would too, because I can't take that for granted. I can't take anything for granted. I've learned that much in the last fifteen months, if nothing else.

Logan nods his head, staring at me, and as his lips start to twitch upwards, a smile settles across his face, touching his deep brown eyes and making them sparkle. "Good," he says.

"What do you mean, 'good'?"

"Just that. Good. I mean I'm glad, because at least we're both on the same page."

"We are?"

"Yes," he says, rolling me onto my back again and settling between my legs. "I can understand why you might not have thought about it before, but I'd like you to think about it now. Not as a matter of urgency. But please… give it some thought. Because you are in a relationship. With me. I get that there will be tests involved, and people to talk to, and decisions to be made. I get that it might not be easy… but for the first time in my life, I want to have children. With you."

And as he says that, he starts to move inside me again, and takes me back to heaven. With him.

Half an hour later, we're lying side by side, limbs entwined, facing each other, still catching our breath.

"Are you hungry?" I ask, running my finger down the centre of his chest, and twirling it through the curled hairs centred there.

"For you? Yes."

"Again?" I frown, although I'm smiling.

"Yes." He leans forward and kisses me. "I can't seem to get enough of you." He grazes his fingers along my jawbone, down my neck and between my breasts, his eyes following the movement, before they dart back up to mine. "Unless you're sore, of course," he says.

I chuckle. "No, I'm not sore… but I did make a stew which was probably ready to eat about an hour and a half ago. I dread to think what the time is."

"I don't care what the time is."

"Well, we ought to eat something." He wiggles his eyebrows, and starts to move down the bed, as I struggle not to laugh. "Not that," I chide, slapping his shoulder, playfully.

"Spoilsport." He looks up at me, faking a pout, then moves back up again. "Okay, why don't you go and get us some stew, we'll eat it in bed, and then… we'll see about dessert?"

"You're incorrigible, you know that, don't you?" I mutter, climbing out of bed and picking up his shirt from the floor, shrugging it on and turning to look down at him, lying sprawled across my bed.

"Yes. That and impetuous are my two middle names," he replies, smartly, his eyes roaming over my exposed body. I quickly do up a couple of buttons of his shirt and roll up the sleeves.

"I'll be back in five minutes," I tell him. "Try and keep yourself occupied."

"Without you? How?" he says as I head out of the door.

"I'm sure you'll think of something," I call over my shoulder, and skip down the stairs, feeling lightheaded, a smile etched on my face.

In the kitchen, I get the casserole from the oven, and set out two bowls and some cutlery on a tray, humming to myself, feeling better than I have in years – well, in my life, actually. I love the fact that Logan is so relaxed, and so much fun, that he finds the humour in almost any situation, but that he never makes light of my problems, and is always willing to listen. That said, I also love the romance of his words, his fierce passion and his intense need, especially now I've experienced them first hand. Actually, I don't know why I'm bothering to list his qualities. Because I just love Logan. Completely and utterly. Pure and simple. And I'm just wondering if I should go upstairs and tell him that, when I feel a pair of hands on my waist.

"You couldn't wait five minutes for me to come back?" I say, trying to sound disappointed, although I'm secretly pleased he's here.

"I was struggling after five seconds, to be honest," he replies, and I chuckle, leaning back into him, aware of his naked arousal, as his hands come up and undo the buttons of his shirt, before reaching inside. I wiggle my behind against him and he kisses my neck. "You should probably stop that," he warns. "You already look sexy as hell in my shirt, so unless you want me to take you back upstairs… or better still, make use of your kitchen table…"

I twist in his arms and turn to face him. "Are you teasing me?" I ask, playing with fire myself, I think, judging from the heat in his eyes.

"No. Not this time."

"So, this is the real you, is it?"

He frowns. "I've always been the real me with you," he says, serious now. "More so than with anyone else in my life. Ever. I've never pretended to be anyone other than who I am, when I'm with you."

"So, you're really this insatiable?" I ask.

"With you, yes. Just with you. I told you, I can't get enough… and I meant it." I nod my head, but he clasps it between his hands, staring at me. "Is that a problem for you, Hope? Do you need me to slow it down? I can if you need me to… although I've got no idea how, not now… but if you need me to take things slower, then I'll work it out."

I shake my head, just once. "No, that's not what I need."

"Then why did you go all doubtful on me?" he asks, and I look up at him, biting my bottom lip.

"Because I was trying to work out how to keep the stew warm for another half an hour…"

He smirks, then smiles and pats me gently on the behind, before pulling his shirt from my shoulders and leading me over to the table, so he can make good on his suggestion.

Logan

I'm not sure I'm ever going to stop smiling again. Although the contrast with how I felt on the drive down here, after my conversation with Rachel, is almost too great to believe.

Knowing that she and Lucas were both off work today, doing some last minute wedding things – well, last minute by Rachel's standards, anyway – I finally plucked up the courage to call her, just before I left work at three o'clock, to let her know that I'd invited Hope, and that she'd agreed to come, and my little sister basically freaked out at me. Actually, there was nothing basic about it, other than her language, which can be ripe at the best of times. She laid into me for not asking her permission, before issuing my invitation to Hope, telling me I had 'no right'. I started off being placatory, and even apologised, but that fell on deaf ears, and our conversation quickly became an argument of fairly epic proportions. Again. I hung up in the end, right after she pointed out – not for the first time – that she thinks I'm mad for getting involved with 'someone like Hope', although she made it clear this time that she felt that way, not just because of Hope's 'disability', as she rather charmingly put it, but also because Hope isn't Brianna, and isn't evidently as 'good for me' as Brianna was… right before she reminded me – yet again – that my ex is still interested in 'working things out' with me. They both need to get the message that I'm not. But I wasn't sure I'd picked the best moment for telling Rachel that. Even so, I was surprised when Lucas called me back just ten minutes later and told me that, of course Hope must come to their wedding. His powers of persuasion were obviously greater than mine, and I thanked him profusely for his intervention, although what it cost him, I dread to think. And then we spent five minutes talking through how Hope's presence would affect my groomsman duties. Lucas was very understanding of the fact that I'll need to help Hope, being as we'll be in a strange place, and she won't know her way around, and he bent over backwards to accommodate that, but I could hear Rachel muttering in the background and was glad not to be around when we ended our call. My sister has a foul temper, but I think Lucas probably knows that by now.

As I say, the contrast between then and now is enormous, and the smile that's etched on my face this morning feels like a permanent fixture.

When I told Hope last night that it had never been that good before, I wasn't lying. Nothing in my life has ever felt so fulfilling, so satisfying, so deeply, intensely rewarding, as making love to her. I'll probably find the words eventually to describe how it made me feel and what it did to my heart, but at the moment, I'm just lost.

I'm also exhausted. I've never had sex so often, or for so long, in such a short space of time, but even now, having made love to her four times last night, including that spectacular moment on her kitchen table, and again, right before we went to sleep, then twice more this morning – once in bed and again in the shower – I still want her. I don't think this need will ever fade. I can't see how it will, not when it runs so deep in me.

We've just taken Archie for his walk, and Hope is seeing off her guests while I make the breakfast. She's been quiet, and kind of ponderous, since we came downstairs, but I think that's mainly due to tiredness… and perhaps the knowledge that we've got a busy day doing the changeover, and that our time together will, therefore, be limited.

Once Hope's back and the toast is ready, I bring it to the table, and then pour the coffee, handing her a cup. She doesn't make eye contact with me, and mumbles her thanks.

"Is everything okay?" I ask, wondering if this is just tiredness, after all.

"Everything's fine."

There's no way I'm listening to 'fine', not this morning, so I get to my feet, going around to her side of the table, and crouch beside her. She looks down at her hands, clasped in her lap, and after a moment, I cover them with my own. "Don't give me fine… not after all the things we've done together. If something's wrong, I need to know." She continues to stare at our entwined hands. "Hope? Will you look at me?" I give her a moment, and eventually, she turns to face me, the sadness in her eyes snatching at my breath. "We're lovers now, my darling. That means we don't have any secrets. Not one. So whatever it is, will you tell me?"

Her eyes soften and she sighs, "I'm scared."

I stand, pulling her to her feet and into my arms, my heart thumping in my chest. "What on earth are you scared of?"

She rests her hands on my biceps, looking up into my face. "It dawned on me earlier, after we'd finished in the shower… I'm scared that everything's going to change between us. I mean, you've wooed me now, haven't you? And you've won me… so you won't be the same anymore…"

I smile and shake my head slowly. "Of course some things are going to be different." I feel her shoulders slump.

"What things?" She stares into my eyes, fear and doubt clouding her own.

"Well, we'll spend our time differently, for a start. I mean, obviously we've got to deal with the changeover today, but I doubt I'll be concentrating as hard as I normally would on what I'm supposed to be doing… because, believe me, all I can think about at the moment, is how incredible you felt last night, and this morning… and how soon we can do all of that again." She tilts her head, but before she can say anything, I continue, "You arouse me more than anyone I've ever known, and I want you all the time… to the point where I'm struggling to think about anything other than making love with you… over and over… and over." I let my voice drop and she gasps, just slightly, her cheeks flushing. "I'm still the same man, Hope. And if you seriously think I'm going to give up the pleasure of wooing you, just because we're now lovers, then you need to think again."

She purses her lips, just for a second, and then breaks into a perfect smile, throwing her arms around my neck and nestling into me.

"Promise?" she whispers.

"I promise."

We kiss, just briefly, and then sit down and eat breakfast, although we don't take our eyes from each other, not even for a second.

"I assume I'm on tidying up duty over at the cottage, like last time," I ask her, licking jam from my fingers and taking a sip of coffee.

She purses her lips and then bites the bottom one. "Well, probably not," she replies and I feel myself frowning. "It's just that I've already baked the cake, so I can make a start on the cleaning, if you wouldn't mind staying here and emptying the dishwasher, and giving the kitchen a bit of a tidy?"

"Of course I don't mind." I reach over and take her hand. "Other than the fact that I won't be with you, of course."

She smiles. "I know. But this way, we'll get everything done a bit quicker, and once it is…" She hesitates, blushing.

"We can go back to bed?" I suggest and her smile widens into a grin, matched by my own.

Once we've finished eating, Hope starts to pack up her things into her box, going upstairs to collect the bedding and towels. While she's gone, I quickly write out a note on the kitchen notepad, shoving it into her box, between the carton of milk and the jar of blackcurrant jam. I know she tends to stock the fridge quite early on in her routine, so I can be fairly sure she'll read it – and hopefully act on it – within a few minutes of getting to the cottage.

She kisses me goodbye, even though she's only going to the other side of the driveway, and I can't help smiling, wondering how long it's going to take her to find my note, and what she'll do when she does.

I've just finished unloading the dishwasher, when I hear the front door open, clattering against the wall behind it, and she comes in, breathless, her cheeks flushed, her eyes alight with expectation, the note clasped in her hand. She waves it vaguely in my direction and just says, "Yes?"

"God, you're beautiful," I murmur, crossing over to her and placing my hands on her hips, pulling her closer to me. "I think I must be the luckiest man alive, do you know that?"

"No." She slowly regains her breath.

"Hmm, well, I do."

"How?"

"Because I love you."

There's a moment of stillness, an almost smothering silence, and then she whispers, "You love me?"

"Yes."

She looks perplexed, leans back in my arms and holds up the note between us, studying it. "You… You wrote me a note, saying, '*Come back here. Now*', to—to tell me you love me?"

"Yes." I lean forward, pushing her hair aside, and whisper in her ear, "Still scared that things are going to change between us?"

She shakes her head. "No… because I love you too."

I close my eyes, letting her words wash over and engulf me in perfect oblivion, and then I kiss her, gently sucking on her bottom lip, teasing her with my tongue, keeping it soft and gentle, but because it's Hope, incredibly intense at the same time.

"I so wanted you to say that," I murmur, finally resting my forehead against hers.

"I've been trying to find the right time to tell you for ages."

Does this get any better? "So have I." She smiles at me, leaning in for another kiss, but I place my fingertips against her lips. "Uh-huh… Before I kiss you, I want to know why you thought I wrote you that note." I nod down towards it, still gripped between her fingers.

She blushes deeply, then looks up at me. "Well," she whispers, "I assumed you wanted something else…" God, she's cute. Especially when she's embarrassed.

"And would this 'something else' have anything to do with us going back to bed?" I tease. She nods her head, quickly, with enthusiasm, and I laugh. "Oh, the irony, that you should come bolting through the door like you did, so eager and excited, with that in mind, when all I wanted to do was to express my undying love for you."

"Undying?" she queries, wide-eyed.

"Yes." I kiss her. "Undying. My love for you will never cease, or diminish. No matter what happens. No matter what the future holds." We both know what I'm talking about, without either of us having to mention her impending sight loss.

She sighs and leans right up against me, her hands clasped behind my head. "I love you so much, Logan Quinn."

"I love you too, Hope Nelson…" I look down into her eyes. "And now, about going back to bed with me…"

She takes a half step back. "I don't think I have time," she murmurs, but I take her hand, leading her towards the stairs.

"Yeah, you do." She's trying to pull away, although she's giggling at the same time, and I turn towards her, walking backwards and bringing her with me. "I'll make it really quick."

"Oh, will you?"

She sounds disappointed at that prospect, and I laugh out loud, then tug her close, so she falls against me, as I whisper in her ear, "But if you ask me nicely, I'll make it really hard too…"

She gasps, then moans and as I lift her into my arms, she snakes her hands around my neck and snuggles into me while carry her up the stairs.

Leaving Hope at the end of such a perfect weekend was always going to be hard, and we spend ages on Sunday afternoon, just standing in her kitchen, holding each other and kissing, both wanting to prolong the moments before I have to depart. Eventually, I have to leave though, and I pick up my bag and carry it out to the car, holding Hope's hand as she walks beside me.

"Two weeks," I murmur, pulling her in for a last hug.

"I know."

I lean back, brushing my fingertip along her jawline, studying her, imprinting the image of her in my mind to take home with me. "I'm so in love with you."

She gazes up at me and blinks a few times, trying not to cry, I think. "I wish you didn't have to go."

"So do I."

I lean down and kiss her gently. "How am I supposed to sleep without you, when I love you so much?" she whispers in my ear.

Oh God… "I don't know. But if you manage to work it out, can you tell me?"

She shakes her head, her arms tight around my neck and we both hang on, until eventually I have to pull back. "I've got to go." She nods and releases me, stepping back. "I'll call when I get home," I say, opening the car door." She nods again. "Are you okay?" A third nod and I wonder if she can't speak. I'm desperate to pull her into my arms again, but that would only delay the inevitable agony, so instead I take her hand in mine and raise it to my lips, kissing her fingers. "I love you."

"I love you," she manages to say, although there's a crack in her voice, and before I'm tempted to stay, I get into my car, and she closes the door.

As I reverse out of the driveway, I watch her, the fingers of one hand clasped against her lips, while she waves with the other. I wave back, and then pull away, before she can see me fall apart.

Driving home, I manage to restrain myself from pulling over and calling her at least half a dozen times. I know that if I do, I'll want to go back, so I have to get home before I can hear her voice. Who'd have thought I could ever love someone so much that to be apart from them would be like trying to breathe without air. Hope is so much a part of me now that I don't want to think about how I'm going to survive until the next time I see her. I can only console myself that it's just two weeks until Rachel's wedding, and that, yesterday evening, while we lay naked on the love seat, semi-covered with a blanket, entwined in each other, Hope called her parents and made the necessary arrangements so that she can stay with me for an extra day that weekend. We'd decided that, being as the whole of our Saturday is going to be taken up with the wedding, we'd want some time to ourselves, and this seemed like the perfect solution. For now, at least.

I get home at just after eight o'clock, and let myself into the flat, picking up my post and thumbing through it as I throw my keys into the bowl on the table, and shrug off my jacket. There are a couple of bills, and two circulars, and… oddly, a hand-delivered letter, with no stamp, and just my name on the envelope. Sitting at the table, I tear into it, and open the single folded sheet of paper inside, my blood starting to boil as I read…

Logan, baby,

I know you've blocked my numbers – both of them now. And I know you're still angry with me, but I need to explain, and this is the only way.

Sleeping with Zach was the biggest mistake of my life. But you have to understand, I never meant to hurt you, and I'm never giving up on us. We're made for each other. We're a perfect fit, in every way. We always were. We always will be. You know that, just as much as I do.

I've heard from Rachel that you've met someone else, and I suppose I can't blame you for that, but you know, deep down, you're making a mistake. So, I'm asking you – no, I'm begging you – please give me another chance.

Please say you'll meet with me. You can name the time, and the place, and I'll be there.

You know this is the right thing to do. Don't you? In your heart, you know we're meant to be together. Always.

I love you, baby.

Brianna x

I screw up the page, swearing under my breath, and hurl it across the room, my fists clenched so tightly, they hurt. What the hell is she talking about? 'Made for each other'? 'A perfect fit'? Even before I met Hope, I knew that wasn't true… but now?

At the thought of Hope, I unclench my fists and reach into my back pocket for my phone, connecting a call to her, tapping my fingers impatiently on the table, until her image appears on my screen.

"Hello." Her voice grounds me, like it always does, and I feel calmer.

"Hi."

"Something's happened." She frowns.

"You know me too well." I manage to smile at her.

"Tell me what it is," she says, shifting the phone to her other hand and sitting back on the couch.

"I found a note when I got home. A hand-delivered one. From Brianna." Hope's face falls and she closes her eyes. "Hey…. look at me."

She opens her eyes again, but all I can see is fear. "What did the note say?"

"That she regretted sleeping with Zach. That she never meant to hurt me. That we're made for each other. That she wants another chance… do I need to go on?"

"She still wants you back? I thought she must've given up"

"I know. I thought so too. But evidently not. She's asking if we can meet up."

"Are you going to?" Her voice cracks at the end of her question and I reach out and touch the screen with my thumb, tracing the line of her lips.

"No. Of course I'm not. I'm not even going to reply. I love you, Hope."

She takes a breath, then says, "I know. But you must have loved Brianna too, once upon a time."

"God, I hate this." I look up at the ceiling, then back at her image on my phone. "I wish I could be with you, so I could show you that you're all I've ever wanted."

"You did love her though," she persists.

"Yes… in the same way you loved Greg. In the same way you can ever love anyone who's only interested in themselves, knowing that the love you have will eventually destroy itself, and you, if you let it." She blinks rapidly, but I carry on. "My love for you is so much more, Hope, because you give me so much more."

"You give me so much too," she chokes, a tear falling onto her cheek.

"I know. And that's what makes us right for each other. Please… please don't cry. I'm not there… and I hate this."

She swipes her hand across her cheeks. "Sorry."

"Don't be sorry. Just remember, I love you. More than anything. Brianna means nothing to me. And you mean everything."

She nods her head, putting on a brave face. "H—How was your journey?" she asks, and I know she needs to change the subject. I think I do too.

"Not too bad. I nearly called you a few times."

"You did?" She smiles, even though her eyes are still brimming with unshed tears.

"Yes. But I knew that if I did, I'd probably end up turning around and driving straight back to you. So I kept going… but only because I have a job to go to, and a list of appointments tomorrow that defies description."

"Well, it's probably a good thing you didn't call," she murmurs.

"Why's that?"

"Because you'd have caught me crying, and I think I'd have begged you to come back."

"You've been crying?"

She nods her head. "I only stopped about half an hour ago... I miss you."

"I miss you too."

"Two weeks?" she says.

"Yes. Two weeks."

The hardest two weeks of our lives.

3rd May

My Darling Hope,

I know we've only just finished our call, and that I only held you in my arms this afternoon, but I had to write, even if it is just briefly.

I have to tell you how much I love you, although I'm not sure I have the words for that. In fact, I'm not sure the words have been invented yet, to convey the depth of my love for you, but I wanted you to have something written down, something you can look back on and read, at times when we can't speak, or be together, to remind you of how you fill my heart, in case you should ever doubt it.

Let me start by saying that to me, you are everything. You are the sun, the moon, the stars in the sky, and all the heavens that surround us. You are the calm in my storm, and the light in my darkness.

If I achieve nothing else on this earth, other than to love you, and to make you feel loved and safe and happy, then I will have lived a full and well-rewarded life. For what more could a man want, than to bring happiness to the woman who makes his life whole?

This last weekend has been the most perfect yet, but I know there will be more, still better, yet to come. Because I know our love can only grow, binding us together... and that nothing, and no-one will ever part us. Remember that, when you start to feel unsure, or fearful. I am yours, and yours alone, my darling Hope. Always. And there is nothing on this earth that can change that. Because I love you.

Of course, it is one thing to be sure in myself, to know that I love beyond doubt, but to discover that I am loved in return, is a gift beyond words; one of which I'm not sure I am deserving. However, I will strive, every single day, to prove myself worthy of you, of your trust and of your love. I will honour you in everything I do and say. And I promise you to be faithful and true, until the last breath leaves my body.

Logan x

Chapter Twenty

Hope

The weekend of Rachel's wedding has come around way too quickly for my liking.

Obviously, I'm desperate to be with Logan again, but the thought of spending tomorrow with his family has been making me more and more nervous as the supposedly 'happy event' approaches. I'm not going to deny that, as my anxiety has peaked, from time to time – or to be more accurate, on a daily basis – I've re-read that letter... that perfect, magical letter that he wrote to me on the evening of his return to Richmond, just after we'd finished our call, when we talked about Brianna, the note she'd sent him, my insecurities, and the fact that we can't be together, which just makes everything so much harder. When I first received it, I cried my way through it, and so wanted to telephone him and tell him that he is worthy. He's more than worthy. He always was. I wanted to explain that I feel exactly the same way, that I love him too... so, so much. But I didn't. I wrote to him instead, although I know my letter was nowhere near as romantic as his, but then I'm not sure that's possible, which is why I have Logan's letter tucked away in my holdall, in the luggage rack above my head. Just in case this weekend gets too much for me, and I need to refer to it.

The train pulls into Reading station and I grab my bag, alighting onto the platform, and make my way along to the exit. I tried explaining to Logan that, now it's May, and the evenings are lengthening, I could probably manage the journey to Richmond. But he wouldn't hear anything of it, and arranged his appointments to finish by three-thirty, so that he could meet me. The barriers are open, so I don't bother with my ticket, and I spy Logan, standing a few yards away.

He runs straight towards me, lifting me into his arms, as I drop my bag, and he twirls me around, before lowering me, and kissing me deeply.

When he pulls back, he looks down into my eyes. "Do you know, you look about as thrilled about this wedding as I feel," he says, smirking.

"Sorry. Does it show?"

He holds his forefinger and thumb about an inch apart. "Just a little bit."

"It's good to see you." I throw my arms around his waist and hang onto him. I don't want him to think I'm not pleased to be here. I am. I'm just dreading tomorrow.

"It's good to see you too," he says, into my hair. "You'll make tomorrow bearable, and on Sunday, we can forget all about my family and spend the whole day together."

I lean back and look up at him. "In bed?" I ask, teasing.

"If you like." He's deadly serious, and cups my face in his hand, his lips just an inch from mine. "It's up to you what we do, Hope. It's always up to you."

I nestle into him and he twists his fingers into my hair, while I wonder about the idea of spending an entire day in bed with him.

After a moment or two, he pulls back and bends to pick up my bag from the floor, keeping one arm around me as we start our walk out to his car.

Our journey to his flat doesn't take too long and when we get there, we go up the stairs and through the door, before he drops my bag on the floor, and pulls me into his arms. "I bought a slow-cooker," he says, a little randomly.

"Oh?"

"Yes. A chicken stew has been cooking in it all day…" He leaves his sentence hanging.

"And?"

"And that means we can either eat now… or later." He's trying so hard not to smile and I tilt my head from side to side, as though taking my time to decide.

"Later… if that's okay with you?"

He grins, pulling the straps down on my sundress, and undoing the zip at the side, as he walks us back into his bedroom. "I really hoped you'd say that," he mutters, kicking the door closed behind him.

"Do you have neighbours here?" I ask, nearly an hour later, slightly hoarse, and still breathless, lying naked across his chest, my hair fanned out, my face flushed.

"Yes."

My head shoots up and I cover my mouth with my hand. "Oh God."

"Don't worry about the neighbours," he says gently, leaning up and kissing my forehead.

"Really? Are they away then? Or out?"

He shakes his head, grinning. "No… but I think they're the least of our problems. I imagine most of Richmond heard your screams."

I sit up and slap him playfully across the chest. "Stop it. Stop messing around."

"I wasn't."

"God, was I really that loud?"

He nods his head, chuckling, then pulls me back down and over, on top of him, my body along the length of his, and I can feel his arousal, between us. "Ask me if I care?" he says, his hands cupping my behind.

"Do you care?"

"No." He laughs, and then rolls us over, so I'm on my back, and he's raised above me. "I'll prove it, if you like."

"How?" I rest my hands on his biceps.

"I'll make you scream even louder."

I bring one hand down and place it across my mouth, shaking my head. "No," I mutter, moving my fingers just a fraction so I can speak. "I'm going to stay quiet this time."

"Bet you can't."

"Bet I can…"

"Okay… you're on."

He enters me in one swift, hard motion, and I yelp. "That doesn't count," I point out and he nods his head in agreement as he starts to move, and takes precisely twenty minutes to prove me wrong. Twice.

Today, I woke to find him staring down at me, and after a brief good morning kiss, he let his hand wander down my body, his fingertips whispering across my skin, before he twisted onto his back, bringing me with him, straddling him, urging me to take him. It was very deep that way, almost painful, but incredibly intense, and afterwards, he suggested that we should shower separately, because if we didn't, we'd be late for the wedding.

I agreed, and went first, coming out and drying my hair, then applying a little make-up, before getting into my new dress. Looking at myself in the mirror, I have to say, I'm pleased with my choice. I'm even more pleased, that I allowed enough time in ordering this, because the size fourteen that I originally ordered turned out to be too big on the neck and shoulders, so I sent it back and re-ordered the size twelve, which is a little tight on the hips, but is otherwise a perfect fit. The dress itself is knee-length, very fitted, off-white, sleeveless, and has red and blue flowers around the hem and neckline. After a great deal of searching, Amy and I managed to find a cornflower blue scarf to match, and finally, some shoes as well, although we honestly thought we were never going to get the right colour.

I hear the shower switch off and turn, just as Logan enters the room, a towel wrapped low around his hips.

"Jesus," he says, stopping dead in the doorway.

"What?" I suddenly feel afraid that I've got this very wrong indeed.

He walks slowly over to me, his eyes darkening, and I feel my mouth dry, waiting. "You look…" He shakes his head. "You look stunning… just stunning."

"Oh… thank God for that." I heave out my relief. "For a moment, I thought you hated it."

"Hate it? I love it. I love how it clings to your body." He takes my hand and twirls me around. "Obviously you look better naked, but this comes a really close second."

I can't help giggling and he pulls me into his arms. "You're wet." I push against him, but he's too strong.

"It's only water. You'll dry out." He's right, and I let him hug me close. "Of course," he adds, "you naked is something that's for my eyes only."

"Naturally." I rest my hand on his damp, bare chest. "And now, I think you'd better put some clothes on. I doubt Rachel would appreciate you turning up to her wedding like this... after all her planning."

"Don't remind me." He goes over to his wardrobe and pulls out a suit cover, unzipping it. "I've got to get into this monkey suit yet."

I smirk and sit on the bed, watching as he lets the towel drop, and my tongue instinctively grazes across my lips.

"Do that again, and we won't be going anywhere," he warns, gazing at me.

"Get on with it." I chuckle and he bows, theatrically, before getting dressed into his suit, which consists of a white dress shirt, dark grey trousers, and waistcoat, and a grey and blue check jacket.

"Lucas is wearing the reverse of this, lucky bastard," Logan explains, tying his bow tie in the mirror and talking to me over his shoulder.

"So his jacket is grey?"

"Yes, and he's got a check waistcoat."

"And the trousers... please tell me they're not check."

"No. Plain. He looks a lot better than we do."

"Groom's prerogative, I suppose," I muse, leaning back on my elbows and studying him. "Although I'm not sure a bow tie really works."

"I'm absolutely certain a bow tie doesn't work. We all wanted standard ties, but Rachel insisted... bloody woman." He curses under his breath, straightening his tie and collar and then turning to me. "Ta-dah."

I giggle, and get up, walking over to him. "You look lovely."

"I look like a clown."

"A very handsome clown." I rub my fingers along his bristling beard.

"Well, at least I'm accompanied by a beautiful princess, so it's not all bad." He checks his watch and sighs. "I suppose we'd better make a move."

I lean up and kiss him. "Just think, in a few short hours, we'll be back here, and it will all be over."

He nods his head. "Yes, and I can peel you out of that dress and make love to you."

"Yes, you can."

He pats my behind as I turn away and pick up my bag and scarf, before we head out of the door.

After my nerves on our last trip into London, Logan decided he would drive to the wedding. I objected, because it would mean he couldn't drink, but he said that was a small price to pay for my peace of mind… and in any case, he thought it better to keep a clear head with so many members of his family around. Despite my gratitude, his words did nothing for my state of anxiety.

The hotel where the wedding is being held is extremely classy, with a liveried doorman and valet parking, and after I've been helped from the car, and Logan has handed over his keys, he takes my arm, looping it through his so I'll feel safe, and we make our way up the steps and in through the doors, which are held open by two uniformed staff.

"Golly," I mutter under my breath and he laughs.

I can feel the tension pouring off of him though, and I give his arm a squeeze, which he returns. "We're upstairs," he says. "I'll come and introduce you to everyone, but then I'll have to go and find Lucas."

"Okay." I turn to him as we start to climb the stairs. "Actually, shouldn't you be with him anyway, being a groomsman, or whatever it is?"

"Probably, but he and I talked it through, and he agreed I should attend to you first and catch up with him later."

"That was kind of him"

"He's a nice guy. He said he didn't mind in the least, and he can't wait to meet you." He shrugs, and leans into me, whispering, "I've long maintained that Lucas is far too good for my sister," and I look up into his eyes, only then realising that he's not joking for once.

At the top of the stairs, there's a long corridor and we turn to our left, entering through double doors, into a huge room that's so palatial, it takes my breath away for a moment. There are a few other people here, and although I don't really follow fashion, I know enough to realise that most of the women's outfits will have cost more than I make in a really good month. And as for the hats… I didn't think about a hat, and I start to wonder if I'm underdressed. But then spot a couple of other, younger women, who are wearing similar dresses to my own and whose heads are unadorned, like mine, and heave out a sigh of relief, before returning my attention to the decor.

I've never seen so much gilding and velvet in one space, and as Logan guides me further into the room, I take in the rows and rows of gold lacquered chairs, each with a cream sash tied to the back, the deep red carpets, the pots of cream and red flowers dotted around, and the large, ornate table at the front, with an enormous floral arrangement, almost concealing the bespectacled man seated behind it.

"Goodness," I murmur.

"It's all window-dressing," Logan whispers, and then takes a deep, sharp breath. "Come with me."

"Where to?"

"To meet my mother. She's already spotted us, and if we don't go over and say hello straight away, she'll only make a fuss when we do."

My mouth suddenly dries and my palms dampen, but I square my shoulders and prepare for the worst. How bad can it be? She's Logan's mother, not the queen.

We make our way across the room, to a couple standing near one of the tall windows, flanked with deep red velvet curtains, and not for the first time today, I give thanks that the weather has at least done me a good turn and remained cloudy. If it hadn't, with the size of these windows, I'd have been forced to wear my sunglasses, even in here, and that's a sure-fire way to attract attention. As we approach them, I start to pay closer attention to the couple, the man being probably around the same age as Logan, but that doesn't surprise me, as he'd already told me that his step-father is only a couple of years his senior. He's wearing a dark suit and tie, and is very handsome, although his eyes keep darting around the room, as though he's looking for something… or someone. As I turn my gaze to the woman beside him, I revise my opinion. Perhaps she is the queen, after all. Although she bears no physical resemblance to our monarch, she has the bearing of one with royal entitlement, her head held high, her shoulders stiff and back straight… and at the moment, she's looking down her nose, directly at me. Of medium height, and very thin, she's wearing a shocking pink shift dress, with a matching bolero jacket over the top, and a feathered fascinator perched at an angle on her unnaturally dark hair.

"Mother," Logan says, once we reach them, with no affection to his voice. They air kiss, as briefly as possible, and then Logan turns to the man and says, "Jonathan," in a monotone. The man simply nods his head, and it's only then that I become aware of his stare, which is fixed on me. Uncomfortably so. "This is Hope," Logan adds, turning to me and introducing me to his mother, Jonathan seemingly forgotten, despite his insistent, penetrating gaze.

I hold out my hand and for a full ten seconds, Logan's mother simply stares at it, before she remembers her manners and offers her own, in the limpest excuse for a handshake I've ever received, and then quickly pulls away again. It seems she's not about to reveal her first name, but before I can say anything by way of conversation, Jonathan puts his hand forward and I instinctively take it, squirming when I feel his thumb brushing against my skin, in a far too familiar fashion. I pull back from him this time, just as Logan puts his arm around me in a very welcome, protective hug.

"Where's Dad?" he asks and his mother glares at him.

"I have no idea." Her voice is lifeless, with a very slight hint of an Irish accent, but her gaze is intense as she turns it back to me and looks me up and down once more. I'm almost tempted to ask what's wrong with me, but I don't, just in case she decides to elaborate.

"Well, I'm sure we'll find him," Logan says, and without waiting for her response, he turns me around and we step away. "I'm so sorry," he whispers, leaning closer to me as we navigate the rows of chairs.

"It's okay."

He chuckles. "Well, at least you didn't say it was fine," he remarks and I let my head rest on his shoulder.

"What's your mother's name?" I ask.

"Eleanor," he replies. "It was obviously too much to hope that she'd introduce herself… and I didn't want to do it for her. She can be funny about things like that sometimes."

"Eleanor what? Obviously not Quinn. Not anymore."

"No. She's Eleanor Dwyer now, although how long that will last, God knows, given my step-father's wandering eye."

"You noticed then?" I look up at him, smiling.

"Of course. I notice everything about you." He bends, kissing the side of my head, before he straightens and turns back to look around the room, his whole demeanour changing as he stops walking, his eyes fixed on something on the far side of the room. "Oh great," he mutters under his breath.

"What's wrong?" I look up at him, noting the tight line of his mouth, the stiffness of his jaw.

"My father."

I look around the room, turning my head slowly to take everything in and managing to follow his line of sight to a space near the front, not far from the registrar's table, where a tall, middle-aged man is standing beside a large display of cut flowers, his arms around a twenty-something blonde, who's almost wearing a very short mini-dress, cut low at the front and the back, revealing more flesh than is really appropriate for a wedding.

"That's your dad?" I turn back to Logan, who's expression hasn't changed, although he's slowly steering us in the direction of the couple in question.

"Yes. I'm afraid it is."

"And the woman?"

He shakes his head. "Absolutely no idea. I'm guessing she's his latest girlfriend… 'girl' being the optimum word, by the looks of things."

We're a few feet away, when the man turns and I appreciate that he really is Logan's father. The resemblance is there for anyone to see, not just in their shared height and hair colour, but also in the shape of their faces, and the tilt of their heads. There the similarity ends, however, as Logan's father pulls away from his lady friend, and devotes his attention to me instead. His gaze starts at my face, then moves down, pausing for a ludicrously long time at my breasts, and finally wanders lower still, before coming back and settling on my face once more. The expression I see in his eyes isn't the same as the one displayed by Logan's step-father, however. There's no latent desire here, just a cold, hard contempt, which makes me wish I could turn and run.

He nudges his girlfriend forward as we approach and introduces her as Phoebe, to Logan more than to me, and raises an eyebrow towards his son, expectantly.

"This is Hope," Logan says and turns to me. "Hope, this is my dad… Mitch."

I hold out my hand, once again, and he does at least accept it with greater alacrity than his ex-wife.

"It's nice to meet you," I say as we pull our hands apart and he nods his head, as though thinking, and then nudges his elbow into Phoebe again, even though he's looking hard at Logan.

"There's not much more in Hope than expectation, I imagine… eh, son?"

He laughs and Phoebe joins in, although I'm not sure she understands what she's laughing at, and then I feel Logan's arm come around my shoulders, my embarrassment overwhelming me.

"Fuck off, Dad," he mutters and quickly pulls me away to the other side of the room, where he turns us, so my back is to the wall and the gathering guests are hidden from my view, by him.

"I'm so, so sorry," he says, brushing his fingers down my cheek, while I swallow hard, trying not to cry in front of everyone.

I shake my head, because I can't speak, and he leans down and kisses me gently on my lips.

"I love you," he murmurs.

"I love you," I manage to whisper.

"Even now?" He sounds truly doubtful for the first time since I've known him and I rest my hand on his chest.

"Especially now. You're not your family, Logan."

"Thank God."

"Bro! There you are," a voice calls out from behind Logan, and he stiffens, slowly closing his eyes. "Put her down for ten minutes... your presence is required."

Logan sucks in a breath and turns, and then in the tunnel of my vision, I see a man who looks so similar to Logan it's impossible not to believe they're related... and, based on that and Logan's reaction, I know this must be Zach.

He steps forward, resting his hand on Logan's shoulder, who immediately shakes off the unwelcome touch, as Zach looks down at me.

"Hello," he says, lowering his voice. "Who are you?"

"I'm Hope." I hold out my hand, under Logan's dark gaze, and Zach takes it.

"Well, this *is* a pleasure. Where's he been hiding you?"

"In his bed," I reply and Logan huffs out a laugh, putting his arm tightly around my waist, and turning to his brother.

"What do you want?" he says, his tone more gruff than I've ever heard it.

Zach slowly pulls his gaze from me to Logan. "I've been sent to fetch you, bro. I'm afraid you're going to have to leave your beautiful girlfriend, and come and do your duty. Everyone's starting to wonder where you are, and none of us want Rachel to get wind of the fact that you're out here and not where you should be."

"I'll be there in a minute," Logan replies and turns to me, before he realises that Zach is still standing there, his arms folded, waiting. "You still here?" he says.

"I was told not to come back without you."

"Then wait at the door. I'll be two minutes... and don't call me 'bro'."

Zach smirks, then wanders off in the direction of the door, and Logan turns to me again.

"Sorry I said that," I murmur, placing one hand on his shoulder.

"What?"

"That bit about you hiding me in your bed. I probably shouldn't have just blurted that out, but I couldn't help myself."

He smiles. "I didn't mind one bit," he says. "And besides, it's kind of true. At least recently, anyway. And when you're not in my bed, you're in my dreams, which is the next best thing."

I smile back and nod towards the door, where Zach is standing watching us. "You'd better go."

"I wish I didn't have to. After the way my family have been behaving, I feel like I'm leaving you in the lion's den."

I feel like that too, but I don't say anything. "I'll be fine," I murmur and he tilts his head. "I will. I'll find a seat at the back, and keep myself to myself."

"We're sitting together for the meal afterwards, so you only have to get through the ceremony," he says, leaning forward and resting his forehead against mine. "Probably an hour, tops."

"I'll cope."

"Sure?"

"I'm sure."

"I'll come back and find you, so wait here for me."

"Yes, sir… now, go."

I lean up on my tiptoes and kiss him, just briefly, and with one last, fond look, he turns away, crossing the room quickly and exiting the door without even glancing at his brother, who shrugs his shoulders and follows.

By myself, I make a sterling effort not to feel inadequate, or affected by the way Logan's family have treated me thus far, and instead I do exactly what I said I'd do; namely, I find a seat in the back row of the chairs, and start people watching, as best I can. Before my diagnosis, this was always one of my favourite things to do in awkward social situations, and just because I find it harder to see, doesn't mean I can't still enjoy myself…

I'm not sure what the collective noun is for stick-thin, beautiful people, but I've decided to call them a 'forest', because within a few minutes of Logan's departure I already feel like I'm in the middle of a particularly dense, airless woodland, surrounded by elongated twigs, with their heads in the clouds. Even when they're talking to each other, they're glancing around, presumably spotting their next victim… someone they can condemn for having a hair out of place, or for wearing the wrong shade of lipstick, or the wrong style of shoe. Which I suppose makes it no wonder that so many withering glances fall on me. I decide to make the wait more fun by smiling, every time someone walks by and drops a critical eye in my direction. It's amazing, and very amusing, how that seems to confuse them. And thus, I manage to pass the intervening twenty minutes, while everyone finds their seats… baffling the natives.

Gradually, a silence descends on the gathering, and the groom, who looks nervous beyond words, comes through a side door and stands at the front, flanked by another man, who's wearing the same outfit as Logan's, and looks similarly worried. Then a liveried man, wearing a red, tailed coat, announces the bridal party, as the double doors at the rear of the room open and, to the accompaniment of a lone violinist, Zach comes in, with a beautiful woman on his arm. They walk up the centre aisle, and then part at the end, her going to the left and him to the right. They're followed by another couple, who I don't recognise, although they're both similarly attired, him handsome and her elegant and thin. The third couple are identical. And finally, Logan appears. The woman on his arm is a mirror of her three predecessors, and for a moment I wonder if this is the bridesmaid who's been flirting with him. Judging from the way she keeps looking up at him, her eyelids fluttering, I think she might be, and I try not to smile at the thought, and focus on Logan instead. He seems uncomfortable, his eyes darting around the room until they finally settle on mine and he smiles, and then rolls his eyes very slightly, before turning and starting up the aisle. My lips twitch upwards and I follow his progress, watching as he joins the other groomsmen in their neat line behind the best man.

Finally, the violinist stops playing, the room falls silent once again, and the man in the red jacket announces, "Ladies and Gentlemen, please be upstanding for the bride."

There's a shuffling, as everyone gets to their feet, and then, after a momentary pause, the music starts once more and the star of the show appears. I'm surprised, I suppose, that Rachel is as diminutive as she is, bearing in mind the size of both of her brothers. She's a good few inches shorter than me, and there's literally nothing of her, her dress dwarfing her tiny frame, as she slowly makes her way towards the front of the room, on her father's arm, while he grins broadly and nods his head from one side of the room to the other. The diamond and sequin encrusted bodice of Rachel's dress sparkles in the powerful electric lighting, while the full tulle skirt rustles as she passes. The whole thing is a little over the top for my liking, but there's no denying that Rachel looks beautiful. Thin, but beautiful.

As she reaches her destination, the music stops, the registrar says a few words and then we all sit, as instructed, and I finally get a good view of the whole bridal party... the bridesmaids in their bright red, tightly fitted dresses, their long hair piled elegantly onto their heads; the groomsmen in their 'clown' outfits, looking uncomfortable, the groom, less of a joke, but radiating fear, and the bride, the centre of attention, as she should be. Somehow, it feels like a set for a play... a farce, perhaps. Although for Rachel's sake, I hope not.

Logan

Thank God...

They're finally husband and wife. They're kissing, albeit for show, a brief peck, nothing over the top, and definitely no tongues... on Rachel's strict instructions, I recall. And now they're turning back towards the gathered guests, smiles etched on their faces, as they walk back down the aisle.

It's over, and now all I've got to do is walk this girl – Miranda, I think her name is – back down the aisle, dump her outside, and then come back to find Hope.

"It went well, don't you think?"

I turn to the bridesmaid beside me, the one who's been flirting with me ever since I first met her at Rachel's planning meeting, her arm linked through mine as we make our way far too slowly towards the rear of the room. The guests are standing and I'm struggling to make out Hope among the thronging heads.

"Sorry?"

"The ceremony? It went well?"

"Yes."

She gives my arm a squeeze with her hand. "You look lovely in your suit, Logan."

"So you said earlier." She did… three times.

"Well, I must be right then."

I finally manage to make eye contact with Hope, and hold her gaze, smiling.

"What's funny?" Miranda asks, pulling on my arm, in a possessive and really annoying way.

"Nothing's funny."

We're near the back of the room now. "Then why are you smiling?"

"Because I've just spotted my girlfriend. She has that effect on me."

"You… You have a girlfriend?"

"Yes."

"I didn't know that."

"You didn't ask."

"Yes, I did."

I turn and look at her, frowning. "No, you didn't."

"I may not have asked you, but I asked Rachel. I really like you, Logan and believe it or not, I'm not in the habit of flirting with men who are already attached, so I asked her, a few weeks ago, if you were seeing anyone. She said you weren't. Well, to be precise, she said you'd been cheated on by your ex, and that she wanted you back, but you weren't interested."

My frown deepens. What's Rachel playing at? She knows about Hope. At least, she knows more about her than anyone else in my family. "That's only partly true," I point out, feeling sorry for her now. It's not her fault she's been misinformed.

"Which bits?" she asks.

"Well, I was cheated on by my ex-fiancée, who decided to sleep with my brother."

"You mean, Zach?" She's shocked.

"Yes. Zach."

"Wow," she breathes. "And does she want you back?"

"Yes."

"Oh... so the bit that's not true is about you not being interested in her. You're trying again, are you? I have to say, you're a more forgiving person than I—"

"No," I interrupt, before she gets completely carried away with her own version of my life. "That's not how it is at all. I don't want her back. She's history. I'm with someone else..." We exit through the doors and make our way towards the ante-room the hotel has provided for the bridal party, although I keep hold of Miranda's arm and pull her to one side before we get there, and then let her go, standing in front of her. "Look, I'm sorry, but I love my girlfriend, very much. If I'd known Rachel had misled you, I'd have put you right earlier."

She sighs and looks down at the posy of flowers in her hand. "No, I'm the one who's sorry. I hope I haven't embarrassed you."

"Not at all." That's not strictly true, but she doesn't need to know that.

"I hope your girlfriend knows how lucky she is," she adds, her eyes meeting mine, and I smile and shake my head.

"If you met her, you'd realise that's not true at all. I'm the lucky one."

She lets out a long, deep sigh and with a faint smile, turns away and goes into the ante-room.

I'm not really needed now, or if I am, someone will come and find me, and rather than leaving Hope alone in the melée, I make my way back into the main room, and straight to her seat, where she's waiting for me, like we agreed she would.

I pull her to her feet and into my arms, holding her close.

"It's good to see you," I murmur.

"You too." She leans back. "Glad that's over?"

"More than you'll ever know."

I wonder whether I should tell her about Miranda, and Rachel's peculiar part in that episode, but decide against it. Not because I'm keeping things from her, but because it can wait until later, when we're alone and can laugh about it, not at Miranda's expense, but at the absurdity of it all.

"What happens now?" Hope asks as we both sit down again.

"They're having a few photographs taken and then we'll make our way through to the dining hall."

"Don't you need to be there for the photographs?"

"No. These are just of the bride and groom, with my parents and Logan's mother. All the rest are being done later, after the meal. They've had a special area set aside."

"Your parents are going to be in the same room?"

I nod my head. "And that's a good reason for staying as far away as possible."

There's an open bar – which my dad is footing the bill for – and a lot of the guests filter through to there, and while the thought of a stiff drink is appealing, Hope and I decide we've had enough of crowds and stay where we are, holding hands and facing each other, kind of lost in our own world, discussing the assembled guests, the decor and Lucas's undoubted fear, which Hope noticed, along with everyone else, and which is easily explained by the fact that he was terrified all the way through the ceremony, that something would go wrong and Rachel would blame him. We sit like that, holding hands and happy, until a mumble goes around the room that we're expected to start processing through to the dining room.

"That was quick," Hope mutters as we stand and she picks up her bag and scarf.

"Yep. That either means my parents managed to behave for ten minutes, or they've killed each other. Hopefully it's the latter."

She chuckles and leans her head against my shoulder as we join the rather disorderly queue of guests that's filtering its way along the corridor and into the dining room which is further along on the right.

"Look on the bright side," Hope whispers, her voice so low I have to bend to hear her.

"There is one?"

She nods, looking up at me and biting her lip. "There's not long to go now, and we'll be back at your place... and you can peel me out of this dress, just like you promised."

I let out a low groan as I feel my body respond to that thought, and grab hold of her. "Don't say things like that," I growl in her ear and she shudders against me, which only makes things worse from my perspective.

"Why not?"

"Because just being in your presence turns me on... thinking about all the things I want to do to you once I've peeled you out of your dress is... well, let's just say it's having a very difficult effect."

She turns and looks at me as we shuffle along. "Difficult?" She frowns.

"In this suit? It's kind of hard to hide my reactions to you..." I raise my eyebrows and she purses her lips, struggling not to smile.

"Okay... well, look... why don't I walk in front of you?" She moves slightly so she's a pace in front, but keeps her back tight to mine, her perfect behind encased in her skin-tight dress. I shake my head, even though she can't see me, or the smile that's plastered to my lips, and grabbing her waist, I pull her back, hard against me.

"If that was supposed to help, you failed, miserably."

She giggles and leans her head back on my shoulder, her body nestling into mine, in a very public, private embrace.

"I love you," I whisper against her ear.

"Hmm," she murmurs, turning and kissing my neck. "I love you."

I can't stop grinning, but as we approach the mirrored double doors that lead into the dining room, Hope steps back beside me again and I take her hand in mine, sensing her trepidation.

"Is there going to be some kind of formal greeting party?" she asks and I nod my head. "And will your parents be part of that?"

"No. Rachel didn't want to push her luck by getting them to stand together for any great length of time. Not without a brick wall between them, anyway."

"So, it's just Rachel and Lucas?"

"Yes."

"What about his mother?"

"I suppose it was too awkward for her to stand there, if my parents aren't."

"And his father?" she asks.

"He died when Lucas was a child. I'm not sure how."

Hope nods her head. "And does Lucas have brothers or sisters?"

"No," I sigh. "It's just him and his mother."

She turns to me. "You said that with feeling."

I shrug. "I suppose I feel sorry for her."

"His mother?" she asks as we shuffle forward, edging nearer to the door, our conversation whispered between our bent heads, so no-one else will hear. "Why?"

"Because I don't think Rachel is what she'd have been looking for in a daughter-in-law." Hope frowns and gazes at me, waiting for an explanation of that statement. "My sister is fiercely independent. She and Lucas have been together for five years, but they're more like flatmates than lovers. They live entirely separate lives, with different groups of friends, and I'm not aware of them doing anything as a couple. They've never even been on holiday together."

"Never? In five years?" Hope's surprised by that and I shake my head. "Then why have they just got married?" she mutters through gritted teeth.

"Search me." I rest my hand in the small of Hope's back and guide her towards the door, and we pass through and come face to face with my sister, who smiles up at me and kisses me on both cheeks.

"Logan," she says, sounding as though she's surprised to see me.

"You look lovely, Rachel."

"Don't I?" She holds out her skirt and twists from side to side, grinning. "Well worth the ten grand, don't you think?"

I don't reply and instead pull Hope towards me. "This is Hope. My girlfriend... from Cornwall."

"Oh... yes." Rachel's smile fades and she disappoints me by looking Hope up and down, appraising her, and frowning.

"Thank you for letting me come to your wedding," Hope says, but Rachel's already turned away.

"Alistair!" she cries, and Hope glances at me. I shake my head and pull her towards Lucas.

"Hello, Logan," he says, sighing.

"You look like you could use a drink." I shake his hand.

"Only so as you'd notice, but I've been warned to stay off the stuff until this evening, so I'd better not." He nods towards Rachel, who's deep in conversation with Alistair, whoever he is.

"Sorry I've been a bit absent today," I say, pulling Hope a little closer.

He glances at her and smiles. "No need to apologise. It looks like you had a very good excuse." He holds out his hand and Hope takes it. "You're Hope?" he says.

"Yes. It's lovely to meet you."

"You too."

"Come on, Lucas, you're holding up the line." Rachel leans over, intruding into our conversation and I want to be her big brother and tell her to butt out. But it's her wedding day, and she's married now, so I suck down a deep breath, give Lucas a sympathetic look, and take Hope's hand, leading her into the room.

It's filled with a dozen circular tables, that seat ten, each with a large floral display in the centre, sparkling glassware and silver cutlery. The chairs surrounding them are gilded, like the ones in the main room, although the decor in here is dark blue, not red, and to the right, there's a raised stage, where a string quartet are playing something classical, overlooking the small dance area. It's ridiculously over the top and it's all I can do not to turn around and make a quick exit.

"We're over here," I say to Hope, guiding her between the tables.

"How do you know?"

"Because I made sure we'd be seated together, and that our table was as far as possible from Zach's. Apart from striking Brianna's name off the guest list, it was the one thing where Rachel let me have my own way…"

"She did?" Hope seems shocked, but that's not surprising, given Rachel's greeting of her a moment ago.

"Yes. I think she knows how close I still am to completely losing it with him, given his blasé attitude. And no-one wants that at their wedding, do they?"

Hope shakes her head and, once we've found our places, we sit, nodding greetings to our fellow diners, none of whom we know.

"I'm sorry about Rachel." I turn in my seat, to face Hope. "I honestly didn't think she'd be like that."

She places her hand over mine. "Stop worrying about it. At least I've met them all now. It's out of the way, and it can't get any worse, can it?" She manages a smile and I raise her hand to my lips, kissing it.

"I certainly hope not."

The food is excellent, which doesn't make up for my family's behaviour towards Hope, but does at least give us something to talk about, other than their reactions to her, and makes the next couple of hours pass more enjoyably than it might otherwise have done.

After the speeches and toasts, Hope leans into me and gives a deep sigh.

"Tell me that's it," she mutters. "Tell me there's just the rest of the photographs to go, and then we can leave…"

I turn and face her, noticing how tired she looks and the tension behind her eyes, and I let out a breath, because I hate to disappoint her. "I'm sorry."

"Why?"

"Because the evening guests are due to arrive in just over an hour."

Her eyes widen. "There's an evening reception as well?"

I nod my head. "Yes. Personally, I'd rather leave now, go home, have a shower with you and go to bed, but I'm pretty sure Rachel would throw a hissy-fit if I suggested it."

"And if we just sneaked off?"

"I'd never hear the end of it."

She sighs again. "Then I guess we're staying."

I kiss her forehead. "I'm sorry, my darling. I'll make it up to you, I promise."

She nestles into me. "I'll hold you to that."

Chapter Twenty-one

Hope

The disco music has been blaring for over half an hour now, a DJ having replaced the much quieter and more refined string quartet, who packed away their instruments and beat a hasty retreat not long after the meal ended. I wish we had too, but with Logan being not only part of the wedding party, but also a member of the family, leaving early isn't really an option.

My head is thumping, and I'm really struggling to see, probably not helped by the darkness, or the strobe lighting, and as it all starts to get too much, I lean into Logan, my mouth next to his ear, so I can shout above the din, "I'm going to the bathroom."

He turns to look at me and mouths, "Are you okay?"

I shake my head, then lean closer again. "Not really."

"It's the lighting, isn't it?" he says. "I should have realised." He stands and holds out his hand. "We'll go home."

I take his hand and get up. "We can't. It's still early, and…"

He shakes his head. "And nothing. You need to leave, so we're leaving."

I want to hug him, but instead I lean into him again. "I do need the bathroom before we go."

He nods. "I'll take you, and then I'll come back and say our goodbyes. That way, you can get away from these lights, and you'll have the added bonus of not having to face my family again."

I think he's as fed up with being here as I am. His family have behaved quite appallingly, and other than Lucas, none of them have made me welcome, and I know Logan feels that even more than I do, which is why I've got no intention of making a big deal of it. It's not his fault. Even so, the thought of going home is very appealing indeed.

I lean back and smile my gratitude, as he kisses me briefly, then I pick up my bag, while he grabs my scarf and with my arm linked through his, we make our way out of the dining room. The corridor is bright, compared with the darkness of the dining room, and I struggle to see, grateful for Logan's support as we make our way between the other stragglers who've taken refuge out here, presumably keen to escape the noise and heat of the disco, or who wish to have a simple conversation, without having to yell.

We duck between them, until we reach the door to the ladies.

"I'll meet you back here," Logan says. "Wait for me." I nod my head in agreement and head inside, to find the room is deserted, and marvellously cool. There are cubicles along one wall, but out here, it's all plush furnishings and mirrors, although I spy a water dispenser in the corner and make a beeline for it, filling a cup and swallowing down two paracetamol from my bag, which will hopefully help with the headache that's starting to build.

Throwing the empty cup into the waste bin, I go into one of the cubicles, closing the door behind me. I don't take more than a few minutes and am just straightening my dress, when I hear the outer door open, and a rush of noise greets the arrival of someone else into my sanctuary.

"Why?" a voice says, making it clear that whoever it is has come in here half way through a conversation, and that they're not alone. "I mean, why would he?"

"I don't know." The second voice is slightly deeper, a little more refined, perhaps. "God knows what he sees in her."

I hold my breath, not wanting them to realise I'm in here. I don't recognise either of their voices, but then why would I? Apart from Logan's relatives, I don't know any women here. And I barely know them.

The right hand wall of the cubicle shakes slightly and I'm aware of someone entering the stall beside me, just seconds before the same thing happens to my left.

"I know you told me he'd moved on," the first voice says, from my right, "but seriously... how could he? With *that?*"

There's a chuckling from my left. "I can only assume he had some sort of breakdown after we broke up, because I can't see any other reason why he'd be with someone who looks like she does."

"She's so fat," the woman says from my right hand side, and I still, biting my lip.

"Fat? She's gargantuan. And it's not just that. Anyone who knows Logan can see she's not his type..."

My stomach churns, a wave of nausea rushes over me and my hands start to shake, even as I brace myself against the wall of the narrow cubicle. They're talking about me? Fat? No, wait... *gargantuan?* How dare they? I'm a size fourteen... but even if I were a size forty, who do these women think they are?

I wonder for a moment about opening the door and standing outside, waiting for them. Not to confront them, but to embarrass them, and I move my hand away from the wall, towards the door lock, just as it dawns on me that one of them said they 'broke up' with Logan. That means, whoever she is, she went out with him at some point... Oh God... can this day get any worse?

There's a rustling to my right, and the toilet flushes, before the door opens, distracting me.

"I suppose you think you're more his type, do you?" There's a sarcastic note to the woman's voice, as she calls from the outside now, rather than over my head.

"Of course." I can almost hear the smile on the face of the woman who's still beside me.

"It's a shame you messed things up so badly then, isn't it?"

"Well, we all make mistakes," she replies and the toilet on that side flushes now, before the door clashes against the wall of my cubicle, making me jump. "But I'm hoping mine won't prove too disastrous... not in the long run, anyway."

What? What's she saying?

"You mean Logan's still interested?" The first woman seems surprised too. "Even after you slept with Zach?"

Bile rises in my throat and I struggle to swallow it down silently, covering my mouth with my hand as I realise that the woman who's just been in the cubicle beside me, the one who called me gargantuan, must be Brianna. It seems my already appalling day just got so much worse. She's not even supposed to be here…

"What I'm saying," the woman I now know to be Brianna says, sounding like she's stating the obvious, "is that I've been talking to Rachel… a lot."

"And?" the other woman prompts, just as I hear water running.

"And, for some reason, she's taken a real dislike to Logan's latest fling. Rachel reckons she's a millstone around his neck, and that she'll drag him down to Cornwall, and away from his family… and all of us. She's desperate to try and break them up… and so am I. Obviously."

"So you're cooking something up?"

I hold my breath.

"Well, we're trying to. Or at least Rachel is. She says she's got something in mind, but she's waiting until after the wedding to tell me about it. She didn't want to go into too many details about country girl, but I get the impression there's something wrong with her…"

"You mean, apart from the fact that she's got absolutely no dress sense, has the wildest looking hair I've ever seen, and is the size of a fairly average semi-detached house?" They both laugh and I feel tears pricking behind my eyes, not just because of their words – although they're bad enough – but because Logan has obviously told his sister about me, and because – according to her at least – I'm some kind of burden to him. Or did that come from him?

"Yes," Brianna replies, once she's calmed down. "All Rachel would say, was that, if Logan stays with country girl, especially if he moves down there, then there's no way he's ever going to be able to set up his own practice."

"You mean, Rachel thinks this woman would try and stop him from doing the one thing he's always wanted?" The other woman's surprise is obvious, but she's nowhere near as shocked as I am, considering I knew nothing about this ambition of Logan's, even though both of these women seem to know all about it.

"It's what Rachel seems to think," Brianna says.

"And you really think he'll take you back? After what you did."

"Oh, come on, Lucy… you know how persuasive I can be. And with Rachel on my side as well…"

There's a hint of something distasteful in Brianna's voice, but before I can think too hard about that, 'Lucy' replies, "I assume you're not going to tell him about spending the whole of that Paris seminar back in March in Neil Foster's hotel room? Or that you've been seeing him, on and off, ever since? Or that his wife nearly caught the two of you together a couple of weeks ago?"

Brianna chuckles. "Do I look stupid?"

"No, but being as I heard about it from Rachel, don't you think there's a chance she might tell Logan?"

"Rachel's not going to tell," Brianna says, and I can almost hear the smug smile on her face. "Like I said, she's on my side. All she wants is to get country girl out of his life…"

I wish she'd stop calling me that.

"Don't we all." They both chuckle, then Lucy adds, "So, while we're on the subject, you can answer one burning question for me…"

"What's that?"

"Tell me… is Zach as good as Logan?"

There's a moment's silence, then Brianna sighs and says, "No, unfortunately not. But then, I'm not sure anyone is…"

"There's something about Logan, isn't there?" Lucy says, dreamily.

"He just seems to know… everything," Brianna breathes. "It's always so spectacularly varied with him… you never know what you're going to get."

"You just know it'll be good."

"*Hmmm*… Every. Damned. Time. He never gets it wrong. Never disappoints. Not ever."

"Tell me about it. It's been nearly two years since he and I broke up, but I still fantasise about him, all the time."

Okay, I've officially reached an all-time low. Not only does everyone here seem to hate me, even though they've never met me… Not only does Logan's sister seem to think that I'm going to drag him away from his family and hold him back, in dreams of his that I've never even known about, but both of these women have slept with him, one of them wants him back and the other fantasises about him, *and* I'm having to hear about it, trapped in a toilet cubicle in the wedding from hell.

They're both giggling now. "Well, he is perfect fantasy material," Brianna says, eventually. "Although, if I play my cards right, he'll soon be my reality again, so hands off… alright? He's mine."

"I think you'll find he's country girl's now, actually," Lucy says, sounding a bit affronted.

"Well, not for long…"

Their voices start to fade as I hear the outer door open and close and, once I'm sure the coast is clear, I spring from the cubicle, across the room and out of the door, focusing on two tall, thin women who are walking back in the direction of the reception room. Both of their dresses are tight and fitted, showing me that they don't have an ounce of fat on their bones, and while one is brunette with a very neat up-do, the other has dark auburn hair, which falls to her shoulders in a tidy bob. Neither of them is anything like me. In fact, I can't imagine two women who could look more different to myself and as I stand, hugging the wall, observing them, they turn slightly and I do my best not to audibly suck in a breath, as I'm astounded by their sheer beauty. It doesn't surprise me in the least that Logan would go out with, sleep with, and in the case of Brianna at least, become engaged to, women who look like this. What amazes me, is that he'd be with someone like me. They turn away, their heads bent together and I sag against the wall as the reality of my situation hits me.

Logan may have wooed his way into my bed and my heart, but the distance between us is too great, in every sense of the word. I'm a burden to him, and I always vowed I wouldn't be that… to anyone. Not to my parents; not to my friends; and certainly not to the man I love. What's more, I'm damned if I'm going to stay here to be judged by his family and criticised by his exes, none of whom have bothered to even have a conversation with me, let alone get to know me, but who seem to have decided based either on my condition, my appearance, or my 'country girl' accent that we're not suited to each other, and that I'm not worthy of him. And the problem is, they're all a big part of his life, and if they can't or won't accept me, what kind of future do we have?

Panic starts to bubble beneath the surface, but I swallow it down. It's not going to help me now. I need to be somewhere safe, somewhere familiar and comforting... I need to go home.

Without thinking about it, I make my way to the top of the stairs, then run down them and out through the main doors, onto the street.

"Can I help you?" the liveried doorman asks, stepping forward.

"I'd like a taxi, please." I glance around as he holds up his arm and a black cab moves forward.

"Where to?" he asks, opening the door.

I think for a moment about saying 'Richmond', but then I realise that Logan's flat isn't my home, and that it never will be. Then I recall my conversations with him when we first discussed me travelling up to London, all those months ago, and swallowing down my tears, I murmur, "Paddington Station."

Logan

It took me an age to say goodbye to everyone. I'd only intended to tell Rachel that we were leaving, but before I'd even managed to find her, I got caught by a distant cousin, and then my uncle joined us, before I eventually found Lucas and asked him to pass on the message to his bride. He was concerned about Hope, but I reassured him that she'll be fine once I can get her somewhere quiet, with steady lighting, and she can rest for a while.

I was surprised to find that Hope wasn't waiting for me when I returned to the corridor and I've been standing here, outside the ladies' for nearly five minutes now, and I'm starting to get worried. I can hardly go and check on her myself, but what if something's happened to her?

I'm just wondering what to do, when Miranda appears from the reception room. She catches my eye and goes to look away, but I call out to her and she comes over, looking inquisitive.

"Can you help me?" I ask, as she approaches.

"What's wrong?"

"I'm sorry to ask, but it's my girlfriend. She went in to the ladies' about twenty-five minutes ago, and she hasn't come out. She has a problem with her eyes… and I'm worried."

She smiles again. "Do you want me to go and check, to see if she's okay?"

"Would you mind?"

"Not at all."

"She's got long, blonde hair and…" Miranda holds up her hand and I stop talking.

"You don't need to describe her," she says, blushing slightly. "I saw you together earlier."

Before I can comment, she moves towards the ladies' bathroom, passing through the door and I lean against the wall, waiting, and wondering again why Rachel would have told Miranda that I wasn't with anyone, when I was… well, I am. It's not a very kind thing to do, to me, or to Miranda, who seems really nice, now that she's not flirting with me all the time.

The door opens again and Miranda steps out, walking over, as I push myself off the wall.

"Okay?" I ask and she shakes her head.

"There's no-one in there."

"No-one?" I frown, feeling a prickle of fear creeping up my spine.

"No. I called out, and checked all the cubicles. They're all empty."

I stare at her for a minute. "Maybe she went back into the reception room and you didn't see her?" That makes no sense to me. We arranged to meet here, and she didn't like the lighting effects in the other room. I seriously doubt she'd have gone back there, especially without me. "Could she be talking to Rachel, or Zach, perhaps?" Miranda suggests.

That prickling fear suddenly overwhelms me as I remember Zach's reaction when he first saw Hope. I wouldn't put it past my brother to have offered to 'help' her in some way…

"Thanks, Miranda," I mutter and then turn, walking quickly back into the reception room and using my height to look over the tops of the other people in here, until my eyes adjust to the darkness and settle on my brother, who's got his back to me. He's talking to someone, who's obscured from my sight, but I'd know him anywhere, and am just about to take a step forward when he shifts and I see that the woman in front of him isn't Hope. She's younger, skinnier and is gazing up at him, with unbridled admiration… *just his type.*

I move further into the room, searching, and then my heart sinks to my shoes, as I catch sight of a horribly familiar face, attached to a very familiar body, encased in a ludicrously tight red dress that leaves nothing to the imagination, standing to one side and staring straight at me. It's Brianna… who as far as I was aware, wasn't invited, and unless I'm very much mistaken, she's talking to Lucy. *Shit*… did Rachel go out of her way to invite all my exes to this evening reception? And why did she lead me to believe she'd cancelled Brianna's invitation, when she so clearly hadn't? I turn to move away, looking for Rachel… or better still, Hope, but Brianna steps forward, smiling.

"Logan, baby," she purrs, just about audible above the slow number that's currently playing, as she brings her hand up and rests it high on my arm.

I shake free of her. "Don't call me that. And don't touch me. You gave up the right to touch me when you fucked my brother."

A few people are standing around, looking, and Brianna turns to them, smiling, as though we're having a minor tiff, or something.

"Oh… come on… don't be grouchy." She's putting on a fake pout, sidling up against me, but I step away. "You know we were good together. Why don't we have a dance? Or better still, why don't you take me home with you? You can spend the night fucking me senseless. You know you want to."

"Why? You're senseless enough already. And besides, I'm busy."

"Doing what?"

"None of your business… but you're in my way. So would you mind shifting your skinny arse, so I can get on?"

She narrows her eyes, her lips forming into a thin line, as one hand comes to rest on her hip, her audience seemingly forgotten. "I'd heard you prefer your women with more meat on them nowadays." She's showing her claws now.

"What I prefer, or don't prefer is nothing to do with you anymore, Brianna. Get over it. Get over yourself. And stop contacting me. You're just making yourself look desperate, and you really need to get the message…" I raise my voice, just slightly. "I never want to hear from you, or speak to you again. Is that clear? If you were the last woman on earth, I'd still walk away. So do us both a favour and go back to my brother… he's not so choosy."

I turn away from her, noticing a couple of women sniggering behind their hands, Lucy being one of them. I'm not interested though. I only care that I can't find Hope. Anywhere.

Rachel is on the other side of the dance floor, talking to the man I remember as Alistair, so I make my way over to her.

"I saw you talking to Brianna." She grins, knowingly, as I get alongside her. "I knew you couldn't stay away."

"I *can* stay away. The only reason I was just talking to her was to tell her to stay out of my life, although that would have been a lot easier if you hadn't invited her to your reception. I thought we agreed you wouldn't…"

She puts both hands on her hips, turning away from Alistair, and glaring up at me. "In case you've forgotten, this is my wedding. She was meant to be coming as your wife, and just because you don't know what's best for you, doesn't mean we all have to bury our heads in the sand, pretending we can't see the obvious. And besides, she's my friend, and I could hardly just ignore her, could I?"

"Why not? It's been working for me for the last few months. And did you have to invite Lucy too?"

"She's a friend, like Brianna. I've worked with them both for over five years, for heaven's sake. It's not my fault if you've slept with half my friends, is it?"

'Half' might be an exaggeration, considering how wide her circle of friends is, but I suppose in hindsight, there have been a few. "No, I suppose not," I allow. "But you need to stop playing games, Rachel. It's not funny."

"Who's playing games?" she says, letting her hands drop now.

"You are. Stop pretending to be innocent. The way you greeted Hope earlier was downright rude. She may not be one of your friends, but I love her." Rachel's eyes widen in shock.

"You love her?"

"Yes. So stop telling people I'm available, when I'm not."

"W—What are you talking about?" She's a useless liar.

"I'm talking about Miranda. Not only did you embarrass me, you embarrassed her, and considering she's supposed to be your friend too, and that's evidently so important to you, that wasn't a very nice thing to do, was it?" She blushes and even in the dim lighting, it's noticeable. "I don't know what you were trying to achieve, and I don't really care, although somehow I think it's probably connected to some sick game you're playing with Brianna." She blinks rapidly, biting the corner of her bottom lip, and I know I've hit the mark. "You are, aren't you?"

"What?" She shifts from one foot to the other.

"Playing some kind of game with Brianna?"

She takes my hand and pulls me closer to the door, away from the crowd. "Hope isn't right for you, Logan. Maybe you do love her, or at least you think you do, but all she's going to do is hold you back, and probably drag you down to Cornwall, when we all know this is where you belong. I'm just trying to do what's right… what's best… that's all."

I nod my head. "Okay… let's get one thing straight. I don't *think* I love Hope. I *do* love her, and what happens in the future between Hope and me, is for us to decide, and is – quite frankly – none of your damned business. You don't get to say what's right, or what's best for us. You can't mess around with other people's lives, Rachel. And if you try to come between us in any way, ever again, I will walk away from you. Permanently. And I won't look back."

Her face falls. "You'd do that? You'd put her first, before your family?"

"Yes."

"Even though she's going to go blind… and she'll be nothing but a burden…"

"Be very careful, Rachel," I bark and her mouth snaps closed, as I take a deep breath and continue, "I don't understand how you can't get this, considering you've just got married, but let me explain something to you… Hope's problems are my problems, and if the need arises, I will give up *everything* for her, and consider it my privilege, because that's what you do, when you love someone." I turn away, angry and exasperated, but then feel her hand on my shoulder and I look back again to see her staring up at me with tears in her eyes.

"Are… are we okay?" she asks, her voice cracking.

"I don't know," I answer honestly, and her bottom lip starts to tremble.

"I'm sorry," she whispers. "I just didn't want you to move away. I like having you here… with me. I thought if you and Brianna…"

"Don't go there." I shake my head, fuming.

"Please, Logan… don't hate me. Please?"

"I don't hate you, Rachel. But I don't like you very much at the moment either. I can't, when you would knowingly hurt the woman I love." She blinks rapidly and while I don't claim to understand, and I'm a long way from forgiving her, I relent slightly. "You're going to have to give me some time, sis. I'll call you."

I will. But it won't be for a while. Quite a long while.

I turn away again and glance around the room, although there's still no sign of Hope and I feel that prickle of fear creeping up my spine again. *Where is she?*

I make my way back out towards the ladies' in the hope that she might have somehow got confused in the changing light between the rooms, and we might have missed each other, and I come across Miranda, talking to a tall, thin man, wearing a pale grey suit. She looks up and smiles, then frowns and, saying something to the man she's with, comes over to me.

"You still can't find her?" she says, sounding concerned, which is sweet of her.

"No." I keep glancing around.

"Do you think she might have gone outside?" she suggests, and I frown down at her.

"She wouldn't have gone without me…"

She shrugs. "It's quite warm in here. She might have wanted some fresh air… especially if she wasn't feeling well. It's worth a try, isn't it?"

"Yes… I suppose… Thanks." Without waiting to say anything more, I turn and walk quickly to the top of the stairs, and run down to the front door.

Outside, the cool air and traffic noise blasts me in the face as the doorman steps forward.

"Taxi, sir?" he offers.

"Um… no, thanks. I'm looking for someone." I glance around, but there's no sign of Hope anywhere, and my palms start to sweat, my heart thumping hard in my chest, as it dawns on me properly that she's really not here. In which case, where the hell is she?

"Can I help at all?" the man offers.

"I don't suppose you've seen a woman, wearing a white dress with red and blue flowers on it… with long, kind of blonde, wavy hair."

"A very pretty girl?" he smiles. "With a West Country accent?"

"That's her."

"She came out about fifteen or twenty minutes ago," he says.

"And where did she go?"

"She asked for a taxi."

I feel sick. But that can't be right. She'd never have left by herself…

"Where did the cab take her?" I ask.

"Paddington Station."

Paddington Station?

"You're sure she said Paddington?"

He nods his head. "Absolutely, sir."

This makes no sense. She could have just asked the driver to take her back to Richmond. She must have realised that. But even if she didn't, to get back to my place by train, she'd need to get to Waterloo, not Paddington. She knows that from when we came into town to go to the exhibition... unless of course, she's not going to my place. Unless she's going home... to Cornwall. My blood turns cold and everything starts to blur.

"Are you quite well, sir? Is there anything I can do?" The doorman looks up at me.

"No... I mean, yes. Can you get me a cab?"

"Of course." He steps forward, holding up his hand, and a black cab moves into place. "Where to?" the doorman asks.

"Paddington Station."

It's only once I'm seated in the back seat of the taxi that I realise I'm still clutching Hope's scarf, and I bury my face in it, inhaling her sunshine scent, thinking, wondering why on earth she'd have run out on me like this and headed home, rather than going back to my flat. Or, more sensibly, waiting for me, like we arranged. Something must have happened. But what? What can have been so bad – considering how awful the rest of the wedding has been – that she'd rush off by herself, in the middle of London?

I look out of the window at a man standing on the pavement, shouting into his phone, gesticulating wildly with his arms, and almost slap myself around the head. What's wrong with me? Reaching into my inside jacket pocket, I pull out my phone and connect a call to Hope's number. It doesn't even ring, but goes straight to voicemail. No doubt she turned her phone off during the wedding, and she's probably forgotten to turn it back on again... either that, or she doesn't want to talk to me. *Please don't let it be that.*

The taxi pulls up outside the station and I pay the driver, jumping out and running through the concourse, checking the departure screens as I go. Can I be in time?

I grab a uniformed man, who's walking past me. "St. Austell?" I breathe, panting.

"You've just missed it," he replies, then points to the screen. "But there's another one in just over an hour. Get yourself a coffee…"

He wanders off, even as he's talking, and I'm left alone, wondering…

Do I wait and catch that train, or do I go back to hotel, grab my car, and drive down there?

Chapter Twenty-two

Hope

I'm absolutely exhausted. Not just physically, but mentally and emotionally as well. This has been the worst day of my life, not helped by the fact that the train stopped at every single station en route and it's taken me nearly six hours to get home. But finally, the taxi pulls up into the driveway and I pay the driver, thanking him and climbing out, then stopping in my tracks, when I see Logan's car parked in his usual spot.

It's quarter to two in the morning. What on earth is he doing here?

I take a step towards the house, and his car door opens. He climbs out, and stares at me, the outside lights illuminating us. He looks tired. Gorgeous, but tired. He's removed his jacket, and the waistcoat, and the top two buttons of his shirt are undone, with the bow tie loose around his neck. I try to skirt around him to get to the house, but he steps in my way.

"Hope?" He puts his hand on my arm.

"I can't do this now, Logan." I don't look at him, but stare at the ground instead.

"Tell me what's wrong," he says. "Why did you leave?"

"Please… not now. I can't have this conversation with you on my driveway at two o'clock in the morning."

"Then invite me in," he reasons. "We'll talk inside."

"No." I look up at him and see the confusion and hurt in his eyes, but then I wonder how he'd feel if he knew what I'd heard. "You shouldn't have come."

He frowns. "Are you kidding me? The woman I love walks out of my sister's wedding in the middle of central London – a place I know she's scared of – and gets a train back home, in the dark, without telling me, and I'm not supposed to damn well follow to make sure she's okay, let alone find out why?"

He takes a half step closer, but I hold up my hand and he stops. "Please, Logan. Not now. I'm tired. I need to think… and I need you to go."

I can see the shock on his face. "Is that what you really want?" he murmurs.

"Yes. I want to be alone for a while…"

There's a long pause before he says, "Okay," his voice a resigned whisper. "If you're sure that's what you want."

"I am."

He moves closer, and I let him this time. "I'll give you what you're asking for," he says, gazing down at me. "I'll give you time… again. But don't for one second think I'm giving up on us, because I'm not. I'm yours, and you're mine, and nothing is going to change that, no matter how much time you take to think. I might be leaving, but I'm not going anywhere, not really, and when you're ready, you're going to tell me what happened, and why you ran, and then we're going to work this out."

There's a determination in his voice I've never heard before, but before I can reply, he steps away, reaching into his car. When he stands again, he's holding my scarf in his hands and, straightening it, he puts it around my neck and uses it to pull me close to him, then kisses my forehead, before he steps back and gets into his car, the gravel kicking up beneath his wheels as he drives away.

I stand for a minute, wondering if I should run after him, or call him on his phone and ask him to come back, but even if I do, it won't change anything. I have too many thoughts clouding through my head to face him at the moment. And I desperately need to think them through… and to sleep.

I open the front door and let myself in, shutting it behind me and quickly turning on the light.

"Hope?" My father's voice sounds from the top of the stairs. "Is that you?"

"Yes, Dad."

He starts to come down, followed by my mother, both of them clad in their night clothes and slippers. "We heard a commotion outside. Is everything alright?"

"Yes. It was just Logan... leaving."

My mother raises her eyebrows. "We saw him arrive about an hour ago, but didn't go out, because we assumed you'd come back early from the wedding for some reason, and were talking. Why has he gone?"

"Because we weren't talking. Not in the way you mean. We didn't come back together."

My dad frowns, stepping closer. "Sorry?" he says, confused.

"I caught the train back, and Logan drove."

"You caught the train back? Alone? Why?" I can hear fear and anger in his voice. The first is directed towards me, the second towards Logan, and I know I have to say something, no matter how tired I am.

"Because I left the wedding without telling him." I put my bag down on the hall table and kick off my shoes, feeling relieved to be rid of them at last.

"What did he do?" My dad's still angry.

"Nothing. It wasn't his fault." That's what makes this so unfair.

"Then why did you leave?" my mother asks in disbelief.

"Because..." I gather my hair behind my head and then release it, wondering what to tell them and how. In the end, I chicken out. "Because there were some problems with his family."

"What kind of problems?" Dad steps forward, his face like thunder now, his protective instincts going into overdrive.

"His parents treated me like something you'd wipe off your shoe, his step-father kept ogling me, his sister ignored me and his brother acted like he wanted me to be the next notch on his bedpost. Apart from that..."

Their eyes widen, simultaneously. "And what was Logan doing while all of this was going on?" my dad barks, even as Mum places a placatory hand on his arm.

"In between apologising for their behaviour, he was looking after me," I reason. "Honestly, Dad. He didn't do anything wrong."

"Well, it sounds like he has an interesting family," Mum says, smiling a little half-heartedly, making an effort to calm the situation.

I know I haven't told them the real reason I'm back, or why Logan's just driven off into the night, but I can't. Not with them. The idea that anyone might think of me as a burden is a lot for me to take... but for my parents, it's too much.

"I'm tired," I whisper, managing a smile myself. "I'm going to bed."

"Everything is alright between you and Logan, isn't it?" my mother asks, as I start up the stairs.

I turn to look at her, tears filling my eyes. "I don't know," I reply and before the disappointment on her face completely undoes me, I run up to my room, closing the door behind me, then I slide down it to the floor, where I sob silently to myself.

Mum and Dad went home on Sunday afternoon. I'd heard them whispering the night before, while I was crying quietly in my room, and it seems they must have agreed not to mention Logan, or the wedding, because they just chatted about nothing in particular all morning, and over lunch, which Mum cooked to give me a rest. When they left, they both hugged me and Mum made a point of telling me to call her, if I needed to talk. I do need to talk, but I need to talk to Logan. The problem is, I need to think first...

If only I could get my thoughts in order, I might be able to do that. The problem is, it's proving to be impossible, because the words that keep clouding my judgement, that keep echoing around my head, are: 'she's a millstone around his neck'. And that's too much for me to contemplate.

I spent Sunday afternoon and the whole of yesterday expecting him to call, wondering if I'd pushed him too far, whether his silence was a sign that, in spite of everything he said on the driveway, he'd changed his mind, and that he really has given up.

I know I asked for time to myself, and I know I need it, but waking up without him again this morning, is hard. It's harder than ever, and as I walk Archie along the cliff path, my eyes hidden behind my dark glasses to protect them from the bright sunshine, I can't help wondering if the distance between us really is too great now.

The postman has been when we get home, and there's one solitary letter… and it's from Logan. I rip into it, pulling out two sheets of paper, folded separately, then lean against the doorframe, and read…

17th May
My darling Hope,
I'm sorry.

I don't know what I did wrong, or why you ran from me, or why you sent me away when I came to find you, but whatever I did, I'm sorry. I love you, and the idea that I've done something to hurt you is making me ache inside.

When I got back here about an hour ago, I found your bag in my bedroom, and I hope you don't mind, but I went through it, just in case there was anything you might need me to return to you. I decided you'd probably be able to survive without your clothes and toiletries until we next meet… because we will be meeting, believe me. I told you last night, I'm not giving up on you. So when we meet, I'll give you back your things. However, I'm enclosing the letter I found in the side pocket of your holdall. It's the letter I wrote to you after we first made love. I don't know why you brought it with you, but I like the fact that you did. I re-read it just now and wanted to tell you that I mean every word of it still, even more so now than I did then, I think. Can you re-read it too? Now. Please? For me? Just to remind yourself how much you mean to me. In case, for some reason I'm not aware of, there should be any doubt in your mind about that.

I've wanted to call you a hundred times already today, but I'm not going to, even though not hearing your voice is killing me. I'm not going to hassle you. I'm going to wait for you – again – for as long as you need me to. You've said you need time to think, and I'll give you that. But I'm still going to write to you, because that's what I need to do. Because I love you, and I'm not letting you go.

You must know that I would never intentionally hurt you, my darling, so whatever I did, can you please try and forgive me? And believe me when I say that I will always, always love you.

Logan x

His words blur before my eyes, but I open the second sheet of paper and see his previous letter, blinking back my tears, as I re-read it, just as he asked. By the time I reach the final paragraph – his vow to be faithful and true – I'm sobbing, and I make my way to the table, plonking myself down into a chair.

I feel so confused now… so torn. It still hurts to know that I might be holding him back, or that he – or anyone – could perceive me as a burden. It also hurts that he hasn't shared his dreams with me, although he seems to have done so with every other woman in his life. But can I really throw away everything we have? Can I do that, without giving us another chance?

"Oh God…" I mumble, letting my head rest in my hands.

I don't know. I don't know what to do. The only thing I do know is that I can't leave him wondering… or hurting. And while I'm not ready to talk to him yet, because I still haven't worked it all out in my own head, I can at least tell him something. So although I know he'll be in surgery, I pick up my phone, and start typing.

— Don't say sorry. Something happened at the wedding and I need to think it through in my own time. I'm sorry if this is hurting you. I don't want it to. I know I'm being unreasonable and I know all I've ever done is ask you to wait for me, but please can you do so, just one last time? Hope x

I press send without even re-reading it, and get up from the table, tearing off a piece of kitchen towel and wiping my eyes and nose, as my phone beeps. Surely, that can't be Logan…

— Darling, it's so good to hear from you. Obviously, I wish you'd tell me what happened, but I'll wait until you're ready to talk. I hope it's okay if I keep writing. I need the connection to you. I need to know you're still hearing my voice, through my words. Don't worry about asking for more time. You know I'd wait forever for you. Logan x

I suck in a sigh of relief, and tap out my response…

— Thank you x

And then I press send.

He doesn't reply, but then I didn't expect him to. We don't do texting, after all. Not unless we really have to.

I've been avoiding the shop all week. Actually, I've been avoiding everyone all week. Other than walking Archie, I've spent all my time in the house, trying – and failing – to think. The problem is, that when I do, all I can think about is Logan, and how much I miss him. And that's not helping me at all.

Still, today is Friday, and with tomorrow being changeover day, that means I have to go to the shop to get in some supplies, and although I know Amy is bound to say something, I've got no choice. I've put it off until nearly closing time, but I can't wait any longer.

The shop's empty when I let myself in, and Amy looks up, her hand resting on her bump.

"We were going to send out a search party…" she starts to say, and then frowns. "What's happened?" She jumps off of her stool and comes around the counter, putting her arms around me as I burst into tears. "Oh God, Hope," she mutters, then leans back, looking at me. "Tell me… is it your eyes?" I shake my head. "It's not your mum and dad?"

"No."

"Then it must be Logan." She finally hits the nail on the head, and I stare at her. "What did he do?"

"Nothing," I manage to say.

"Then what happened?"

She puts her arm around my shoulder and leads me over to the counter, just as Nick appears through the door at the back, takes one look at me and says, "Bloody hell, Hope… what happened?"

Amy glances at him. "I've already asked that. It's something to do with Logan."

"What did he do?" Nick asks.

"Nothing," I repeat. "It's… complicated."

Nick checks his watch. "Oh sod it, let's close up early and take you upstairs. I'll make us some dinner and you can tell us all about it…"

"How does that sound?" Amy says.

I don't even have to think about it, because I know it's exactly what I need. "It sounds perfect."

They both smile and while Nick locks up the shop, Amy and I make our way upstairs, and sit on their sofa. Nick joins us a few minutes later and pours me and himself a glass of wine, while Amy has an orange juice, and then, as Nick pulls onions, garlic and peppers from the fridge, Amy turns to me.

"Where do you want to start?" she says.

"With the wedding, I suppose…" And so, I tell them everything about that whole weekend, from the excitement of seeing Logan again, to the way his family reacted to me, the sparkling superficiality of the wedding itself, the 'beautiful' people… and finally, that fateful, overheard conversation in the toilets.

"They actually said you'd be a burden to him?" Amy can barely disguise her anger. "And that they didn't want him to move down here?"

"Yes. But to be fair, that's not something Logan and I have even talked about yet. I don't know how he feels about moving here…"

Nick comes over, joining in, "Even so, he's never said or implied that you'd be a burden to him… right?"

"No."

"It sounds like it all comes from his sister, doesn't it?" Amy muses.

"Who seems to me to be a perfect bitch, if you don't mind me saying so," Nick adds and I look up at him.

"I don't mind at all."

He smiles down at me, but then frowns and says, "And were these two women seriously comparing and discussing Logan's sexual… um… prowess?" I nod my head, blushing. "And you heard all of this?"

"Yes."

He shakes his head. "Do women generally talk about things like that?" he asks, looking from me to Amy and back again.

"Some do," Amy replies, before I can. "But that's not really the point, is it?"

"Isn't it?" he says.

"No. The point is, that none of it is Logan's fault."

"Well, except the fact that he's evidently always wanted to own his own practice... and I had no idea," I reply.

"Maybe he decided there are more important things in life?" Nick suggests, and when I stare up at him, he adds, "Like you."

"But I don't want to stop him—"

"Who said anything about stopping him?" he says, interrupting me. "If he didn't bother to tell you about it, maybe there's a reason for that. Like it's not that big a deal to him. Not as big a deal as being with you, anyway."

I take a deep breath, pondering his words and Amy nudges into me. "So... can we agree that none of this is his fault?" she perseveres.

"Maybe," I allow.

"In which case, can I ask why you're not having this conversation with him? Or more to the point, why you didn't have it on Saturday night?"

"Because... because I've never wanted to be a burden to anyone. Ever. And... and I've never felt so unsure about myself in my life as I did after hearing what those women said. Because he'd slept with them both, and been engaged to one of them, and they were... God, they were so beautiful. And I mean, *beautiful*. Because neither of them is going blind... because neither of them has a genetic condition, that makes having children much more complicated than..."

"Blimey, Hope," Nick interrupts. "Slow down. That's a lot to take on board."

"It's a lot to have buzzing around in your head, I know that much."

"But which part is bothering you the most?" Nick asks. "Because we know it's not your RP in itself, or even the fact that having kids isn't going to be as straightforward for you as it is for a lot of other people. You've known about those things for ages now. So, is it the things they said about your appearance, or the fact that they said you'd be a burden to Logan?"

"Well, obviously no-one wants to be called fat, or to hear that people think they resemble a house, but I also really hate the idea Logan would be with me out of obligation, rather than love..." There, I've said it...

"And now that they've sown those seeds of doubt, you're feeling insecure about yourself?" Amy guesses, quite accurately, putting her arm around me. "Oh God… I wish I'd been there with you."

"So do I," I mumble into her and let her hug me for a while.

The smell of onions and garlic wafts across the room and Amy and I separate and look up to see Nick, who's returned to the kitchen and is leaning on the countertop, staring at us. "You do know it's bollocks, don't you?"

"Which bit?" I take the tissue Amy offers me from the box on the table and wipe my eyes.

"Everything they said. You're not a burden, and you're not fat."

I ignore his first comment, because I feel that's something only Logan can comment on and instead I just reply, "I'm not thin either though, not like them. Not like the women he's been with before… and it wasn't all bollocks, was it? The things they said about Logan were true enough, so…"

Nick raises his eyebrows, Amy looks from me to him and then we all burst out laughing.

"I'm sorry… I probably shouldn't have told you that."

Amy shakes her head. "In the grand scheme of things, it really doesn't matter. What does matter is that you shouldn't be worrying about who he's been with before, or what they looked like, because he chose you, Hope. And he chose you, knowing full well about your condition."

"No he didn't," I reason. "I kept it from him at the beginning. Remember?"

"I know. But then when you did tell him, he still chose you," she replies, adamantly.

"And he didn't choose you because he was worried about what your RP might mean for his future, or how it might impact on his career, or where the two of you might end up living, or because he wanted you to be someone you're not," Nick adds, attacking a pepper with his knife. "He chose you because he wanted you. *All* of you." He stops chopping and looks up at us, waving his knife. "You know, that's one of the fundamental differences between men and women," he says. "Women try to complicate things by thinking them through and analysing them to death. Men just see something they like and go for it."

"And there speaks my husband, the philosopher," Amy muses, shaking her head, before she puts her hand over mine. "Phone Logan," she says, seriously. "Talk to him."

"I will."

"When?" she presses, unwilling to let it go.

"Sunday. I'll get through tomorrow's changeover and I'll call him on Sunday afternoon, so we can talk in peace and quiet."

She smiles and I smile back, and for the first time in nearly a week, I actually feel a little better.

Yesterday's changeover was hard work… mainly because I stayed at Nick and Amy's on Friday until gone midnight and consumed a little too much wine. Still, it was a good evening, and I think it helped. I'm definitely going to talk to Logan later today, and I even think I know what I'm going to say, and while I might still be feeling insecure about myself, and struggling a bit with that, because that lack of self confidence just isn't normal for me, I know it's him I need to talk it all through with, and no-one else.

I've just finished emptying the dishwasher, and am thinking about what I can have for my lunch that has a zero calorie content, when the doorbell rings. My guests were talking about going out for a long walk today, so I wonder if they've come to ask for advice as to where to go, and I make my way into the hall, shutting Archie in the kitchen, and pull open the front door, with my best attempt at a smile… and promptly burst into tears.

"Hey… come here."

Logan moves into the house and pulls me into his arms, walking me backwards a couple of steps and kicking the door closed behind him.

"Hush, darling. Don't cry."

I lean back slightly, tears still streaming down my cheeks, and rest my hands on his chest.

"You're here?"

"Yes." He kisses my forehead. "Of course I'm here… this is where I belong."

∽∞∽

Logan

I stroke her hair and let her cry, even though I wish she wouldn't, and feel the warmth of her soft body against mine, knowing beyond any doubt that I've done the right thing.

Eventually, with a couple of sniffles, she leans back again and looks up at me, her cheeks stained with tears, her eyes puffy and swollen and her nose reddened, and manages a beautiful smile.

"I've missed you so much," I whisper, cupping her cheeks with my hands and gazing into her eyes. I'm desperate to kiss her, but there are things to be said first.

"I've missed you too," she says. "I was going to phone you this afternoon."

"You were?" That's a surprise.

"Yes."

"Would it be okay if we sat down? Because I think we both know, we need to talk."

"Of course… sorry."

She pulls away from me and walks into the living room. I follow and it's only now that I notice she's dressed very differently to anything that I've seen her wearing before. Instead of tight jeans and a fitted top, she's got on a baggy pink t-shirt and grey track-suit bottoms, and as she curls up in the corner of the sofa, she pulls down the t-shirt, as though to hide herself. *What the hell is that about?*

I sit beside her and turn in my seat to face her, my arm along the back of the couch. "I know I said I wouldn't hassle you, and I'm really not trying to… and I'm sorry for turning up out of the blue, but I have to know what happened at the wedding. It's been driving me insane all

week. So, do you think you can tell me yet? Obviously, if you can't…"
I let my voice fade as she fiddles with the hem of her t-shirt and bites her
bottom lip.

"It's hard to know where to start," she says eventually, which is a lot
more promising than the negative response I was half expecting..

"Well, you went to the toilet, and I'm guessing something happened
while you were in there? Because when I came to find you, you'd gone."

She looks up at me, uncertainty clouding her eyes. "I—I was in the
cubicle," she says quietly, "and two women came in. They were mid-
way through a conversation, and… and well, it became clear quite
quickly that one of them was Brianna."

"Oh, shit."

She gazes at me for a second. "The other one was someone called
Lucy?" I close my eyes and suck in a breath. "I think you know her?"

"Yes." I open my eyes again and whisper, "Sorry," although Hope
shakes her head, swallowing hard. "What did they say?" I ask.

She shrugs. "To start off with, they were wondering what on earth
you were doing with someone like me. They called me 'country girl',
which really infuriated me, and said I was fat… actually they said I was
'gargantuan', if we're being strictly accurate."

"What?" I shift closer to her.

"It was horrible," she mutters. "But it got worse."

"How?" *How could it get any worse?*

"Brianna said she couldn't understand why you'd want to be with
me when I'm going to be a burden to you. I think 'millstone' was her
exact word." I clench my fists, but quickly unclench them before Hope
notices. "She said I was going to drag you down to Cornwall and stop
you from fulfilling your ambition to own your own practice, and that
Rachel had mentioned something being wrong with me…" She looks
right into my eyes. "Did you tell her about my RP?"

I nod my head slowly. "Yes. I'm sorry. It just kind of slipped out."

"It's okay. I don't mind. Well, I suppose I do. A bit. But only because
you didn't tell me you'd told her… a bit like you didn't bother to tell me
about your plans for the future… your dreams…" Her voice cracks and
I move closer to her, although I still don't hold her. I'm not sure she's

ready for that yet, especially given the look of doubt in her eyes, which is aimed directly at me.

"You're my dream, Hope," I whisper, but that doubt is still there and I let out a long sigh. "I'll admit that I used to want to set up my own practice… before I met you. But none of that matters to me now. It hasn't mattered for a long time. That's why I didn't tell you about it."

"And has the reason it stopped mattering got anything to do with my RP?" she whispers.

"No. It's got everything to do with you." I move even closer to her, so our knees are almost touching. "Setting up a practice takes a lot of time. The hours can be deadly. But in the past, that thought never bothered me, no matter who I was with. Then, when I met you, I realised I wanted to be with you so much more than I wanted anything else… including my own practice." I lean forward, just slightly. "Y— You do understand that, while Brianna might have heard about you from Rachel, and that I was the one to tell Rachel about us, none of her bullshit about your condition… about you being a burden… none of that came from me. You know that? Right?" She pauses for an alarmingly long moment, before she nods her head. "Hope… I've never thought of you like that, although I'll admit, I—I have been less than honest…" She startles and pulls away from me, fear filling her eyes, as I reach out grasping her hand in mine, hoping I'm doing the right thing here.

"When? I mean…" the hurt in her voice almost breaks me.

"Not in the way you think," I explain. "I haven't said or done anything behind your back. What I'm trying to tell you is that, since you told me about your condition, it's been a real struggle not to wrap you up…"

"In cotton wool?" she says, warily.

"No. In my arms. All I've wanted to do, ever since Valentine's day, is to hold you tight and never let you go, to keep you with me, safe and sound. But I know that's not practical and it's not what you want."

"It is," she whispers and I gaze into her eyes, feeling bewildered, as she looks up at me. "Being held by you isn't the same as being smothered by someone else."

"I never want to smother you, you know that. But being so far away from you, not being able to help you and care for you and keep you safe… it hurts." Her eyes widen, and I lean in closer, but she holds up her hand, stopping me.

"I haven't finished," she says, softly.

"Finished what?"

"Telling you about what happened at the wedding."

I lean back again. "You mean there's more?"

She nods her head, settling back, and then says, "Brianna told Lucy that Rachel was helping her…"

"To split us up, so she could get back together with me?" I ask and she nods her head, her eyes widening.

"You knew?"

"Only after a conversation I had with Rachel at the wedding, yes. I didn't realise you knew though." I'd have come back here a damned sight sooner, if I had.

"Well, I wouldn't have done, if I hadn't been trapped in a toilet cubicle, listening to two of your exes comparing notes about you."

"Excuse me?"

"They compared notes about you… about how you are… in bed." She glances downwards, between us, and blushes, then adds, "Lucy explained that she knew Brianna had been seeing a married man for the last couple of months…"

"She has?"

"Yes. Does that bother you?" She looks up, hurt filling her eyes.

"No. I don't care what she does. I'm just a bit surprised, that's all. I didn't think she was like that."

"It's been going on since March, I think Lucy said. Anyway, she asked how Zach compared to you and Brianna said he was disappointing by comparison, and how you'd always been so spectacular, how you'd never disappointed her… and Lucy said you're still the man she fantasises about. All the time. Evidently."

Oh, dear God. "And you heard all this?"

"Yes. Between that and Brianna's supreme confidence that you'd simply fall back into her bed… it was the highlight of my day."

"As if I'd ever fall back into Brianna's bed. Hell, she couldn't even drag me there... although I think she's worked that out for herself now," I remark and Hope frowns.

"What does that mean?" she asks.

"It means that I had a brief chat with her." A look of fear crosses Hope's face and I sit forward. "Don't worry. I just declined her rather unladylike offer to return to her bed, told her to get her skinny arse out of my way, and said that if she was the last woman on earth, I still wouldn't be interested. That's all. There were plenty of witnesses though, so I don't think she'll live that down for a while. Or forgive me for saying it so publicly."

"Oh." Hope does a poor job at hiding her smirk.

"She doesn't mean anything to me, darling. I promise."

She sighs deeply. "Your sister clearly doesn't like me though."

"Well, you won't have to worry about her... not for a long while."

"Oh?"

"I've made it clear that I don't appreciate her attitude to you, or her interfering in my life... whichever of her friends she happens to be using at the time."

Hope sits back a little. "I don't understand..."

"Don't worry about it. It's a long story."

"I've got time," she says, obviously wanting to know.

"Okay, but can we just change position first?"

"How do you mean?"

"Stand up."

She hesitates for a second and then gets to her feet turning around to face me, as I shift into the corner of the sofa and then hold up my hand. She takes it and I give her a slight tug, pulling her down onto my lap. She tenses, just for a moment, but then seems to make up her mind about something – me, presumably – and she turns and puts her feet up on the sofa, before she nestles back into me.

"That's better," I say, trying hard to disguise my relief and kissing the side of her head, as she nods slowly.

"You were going to tell me about Rachel's interference?"

"Yes." I settle back. "Do you remember me telling you about the bridesmaid who wouldn't stop flirting with me?"

"Yes, I do." She twists and looks up at me. "Was she the one you accompanied into the service?"

"Yes."

She smiles. "I thought so. You looked so tortured."

"I felt so tortured. But at the end of the ceremony, it all became clear. She made a definite pass at me, and I pointed out that I was taken. Very taken. She was stunned. Although I think, to start off with, she thought I was lying, because she said she'd asked Rachel – just recently – if I was available, and my beloved little sister had told her that I was."

"She had?"

"Yes. Miranda – she was the bridesmaid – told me that Rachel had explained that I'd had a difficult break up with my previous relationship, but that I wasn't seeing anyone, which is why Miranda had been flirting with me. She was so embarrassed, and very apologetic."

"Oh God... the poor woman."

"I felt sorry for her in the end."

Hope's brow creases into a frown. "That's really not a very nice thing for Rachel to have done. I mean, not only was she interfering with your life, but she was messing with Miranda's feelings too."

"I know. That's what I said to her, when I confronted her. Right before I told her that she won't be hearing from me for a while."

Hope stares at me. "Between your family, and your ex..."

"I can only apologise on both counts."

"It's not your fault."

She sighs and leans into me again, and I hold her close, just for a moment, before I ask the burning question. "I—I understand that overhearing that conversation would have been really upsetting for you, especially coming on top of my family's appalling behaviour, but why did you run, Hope? Why didn't you wait for me, so we could talk?"

She doesn't move, so I can't see her face, but she whispers, "When your two exes left the toilets, I followed them... I saw what they look like, and I started to think they were right." *What's she talking about?*

"They'd said they couldn't understand why you were with me, and they had a very good point. I mean… it doesn't make sense, does it? And… and then I thought about what they'd said about you… about how you are in bed… and about me becoming a burden to you…" Her voice cracks. "I had to get away from there. I needed to feel safe."

"And you didn't feel safe with me?"

"Not at the time, no." That hurts. A lot.

I push her forward on my lap, forcing her to sit up, and hold her face between my hands. "It hurts that you could think like that, Hope."

"I don't. Not any more. It was just… being surrounded by your friends and family, all of whom seemed to despise me… I felt so insecure."

"I understand that. But are you honestly telling me that you didn't think I'd put you first, that you didn't think I'd take care of you, above and beyond everything and everyone else?"

"No. But I was scared."

I take a breath and rest my forehead gently against hers. "And are you saying that you ran because you think I'd rather be with someone like Brianna, or Lucy, than be with you?"

"I don't know. I think so. Partly." She sounds as confused as I feel. "Both of them were beautiful, Logan… they were absolutely stunning. They were nothing like me, anyway…"

I lean back, gazing into her eyes. "Tell me… when you looked at them, what did you see?"

"I—I saw two slim, beautiful, alluring, sophisticated women, who any man would probably give his right arm to be seen with."

"Not this man." She shakes her head. "Shall I tell you what I see when I look at them?" I ask and she shrugs, so I continue, "I see two self-obsessed, preening, egotistical women, who would sell their souls to climb just one rung of the social step ladder on which they've placed themselves, or even just to get their own way." I take a breath, and then reach down, clasping her chin and raising her face to mine. "Shall I tell you what I see when I look at you?"

"I think I'd rather you didn't," she mumbles.

"Well, I'm going to anyway." She blinks a few times and stiffens against me. "I see an angel. I see a gorgeous creature who has bewitched me, body and soul, who fills my heart with love, and who makes me happier than I ever thought possible. I see a beauty beyond words, that's not only skin deep, but comes from right inside you, from your very soul, and which you share so generously, so beguilingly, with everyone who knows you." A couple of tears fall onto her cheeks.

"They made me feel so... ugly... so worthless."

I reach down, playing the fibres of her t-shirt between my fingers. "Is that why you're wearing these clothes?" I ask her. "Is that why you've been hiding down here, away from me?" She nods her head and I pull her closer to me again. "You didn't need to hide... you still don't. Those women – Rachel included – aren't qualified to say who I should or shouldn't be with, because they don't know me. Not like you do. And as far as I'm concerned, you're everything I could ever want." I let my hand drift up the back of her loose t-shirt, both of us gasping as I touch her bare skin for the first time in days. "I wish you'd told me sooner. I wish you'd called me, or written, rather than sitting down here, worrying."

"I'm sorry," she whispers.

"You trust me... right?" I say and she nods. "Okay, then trust me on this... I love you. *Exactly* as you are."

She smiles at me, her eyes glinting with tears as she stutters out a breath. "D—Does this mean I can go back to eating cake?" she asks.

"You mean, you stopped?"

"Yes. I decided to try and lose some weight."

I frown at her. "Why?"

"Isn't it obvious?"

"Well, I'm going to guess that it was because you saw two of my exes, and decided that because they were super-skinny, that must be the kind of woman I went for?"

"Not exactly, but they called me 'gargantuan', Logan."

"Neither of them is very bright. They probably don't even known what it means." She manages a half laugh, but shakes her head, and I continue, "Do you know one of the things I love most about you?"

"What?"

"That you're comfortable and confident with who you are."

"I know. That's one of the reasons this has thrown me so much."

"You can't let the opinion of a couple of airheads get to you, my darling. You normally like the way you look, don't you?" She nods. "Then don't change. You don't need to lose weight to fit into someone else's idea of what's beautiful or what isn't. If you're not doing this for you, then don't do it, because you know just as well as I do that no-one else's opinion matters, other than your own. I certainly don't want you to change. I've never been with anyone who makes me feel as relaxed and happy as you do. I knew the moment I saw you that you were the one for me, and nothing's going to change that."

She smiles up at me. "Funnily enough, Nick said something similar."

"Nick?"

"Yes. I went to see Amy and Nick… that's to say, I went into the shop on Friday, having been hiding away here all week and they talked me into staying with them for dinner, and I blurted everything out to them, under the influence of alcohol… and Nick said something along the lines of men seeing what they want and going for it."

"Then he's not wrong," I tell her. "Did talking to them help?"

"Yes. It helped me to put things into perspective, I think."

"Good… only… did you tell them all about Brianna and Lucy's conversation… in detail?"

She blushes and bites her bottom lip. "I might have done. Sorry."

"It's okay. I get how hard it must have been for you to hear them talking like that. I'm not sure how I'd have reacted to hearing two men discussing how incredible you are in bed."

She twists and looks up at me. "Yes, but there isn't a man on this planet, other than you, who knows about any of that."

"I know… and I'm sorry."

She nods her head. "Contrary to how this might look, I'm really not interested in your past. I don't care who you slept with, or how many women have come and gone before me, or what you've done when you've been with them. I just don't trust Brianna, and I don't like her. But I know that's all in the past."

"Good… that's all that matters. Well, that and getting you out of hiding." I tug on her t-shirt and she giggles. "And maybe finding me a suitable disguise to wear the next time I go into the shop."

"Well," she says, looking sad again, "I'm sure you'll have time. They're not open this afternoon, and I'm guessing you'll have to go home later…" She frowns. "Actually, come to think of it, why are you here on a Sunday? It's a long way to come for a flying visit."

"This isn't a flying visit. I've got the week off."

She grins and then throws her arms around my neck. "Really?"

"Yes… and that's not all." I peel her away from me and hold her hands between us. "I've needed to keep busy during this last week, just to stop myself from going completely mad worrying about you, so I've made some decisions… and I've acted on them."

"What have you done?" She narrows her eyes.

"Well, to start off with, I've sold my flat."

Her eyes widen again in an instant. "You've done what?"

"It hasn't actually gone through yet, but I put it on the market last Tuesday and got a buyer that afternoon. He wants the deal completed by the middle of June and the lawyers say it's possible, so…"

"You've sold your flat?" she whispers.

"Yes. And all its contents – except my personal belongings, obviously. The buyer is looking to rent it out, so it was the best solution for both of us."

"And where are you moving to?"

"Here."

"Here?"

"Yes. I mean, not *here*, here… not if you don't want me to. Not if you're not ready. If you want to slow things down, then I can rent somewhere furnished for a while, but I'm moving Cornwall, no matter what my family, or anyone else says. I'm moving here… to somewhere as close to you as I can possibly get. I told you, being with you, caring for you, keeping you safe… that's what I want to do. It's what I *need* to do. And I can't do it from a couple of hundred miles away."

"And what about your job?" she asks, still taking this in. "Or are you planning on setting up your own practice?"

"No. I already said, doing that would take me away from you too much. But I've got two interviews lined up with practices down here, which is why I needed the week off. One's in St Austell, which is tomorrow lunchtime. It's a small practice, and the pay isn't as much as I've been used to, but the commute is less than ten minutes, and I'll only have to do one weekend on call per month, so I think I'll like it there, if they like me. The other one is in Truro. I'm seeing them on Thursday morning. I don't know quite as much about that practice, other than it's a bit further away, but it's still not too far. It's not Richmond, anyway."

She tilts her head, first left and then right, then shakes it slowly. "You've decided all this, sold your flat and all your furniture, arranged for job interviews…"

"And spoken to my boss, Zoe, to let her know what I'm doing… it was only fair, considering I'll be leaving in two weeks' time and taking my outstanding holiday in lieu of notice…"

"You will?"

"Yes."

"You don't think this is a bit…"

"Impetuous?" I suggest and she smiles.

"Yes. Impetuous."

"It's completely impetuous. Some people might even think it was insane. But I don't care. Zoe was actually really encouraging when I spoke to her about it, which may have had something to do with me having been as miserable as sin for the last week. But I like to think it's also because she agreed with me that when something is right, you shouldn't let anything stand in your way. We belong together, Hope, and while I now know you've been worrying all week about me giving up my supposed ambitions for you, *I've* been thinking that, if I have to move my entire life to be with you, then I will. Living apart makes us both unhappy, and life's too short to be unhappy when there's something you can do about it… so I'm moving here… and then we'll never have to be apart again."

"You really want to move here? With me?"

"Yes."

"But what about the future?" She looks deeply into my eyes, searching for chinks in my armour. "What about when things maybe aren't so easy, when my eyesight fades…" She leaves her sentence hanging, but I think I know what she's trying to say and I cup her face in my hand.

"My future is wherever you are. And when your eyesight starts to fade, then I'll be your eyes."

She shakes her head. "That's too much to ask. You can't give up everything…"

"I can, and I will." I tighten my hold on her. "Why? What did you think would happen when your eyes stopped working?"

She shrugs. "Mum and Dad have always said I could sell this place and go back home to them. But they'll probably be getting on a bit by the time it actually happens, so God knows."

"I'll tell you what you'll do," I say firmly. "You'll let me look after you."

"But your job… I mean, it's bad enough that you're giving up your ambitions, without…"

"I don't care about any of that. Once and for all, I don't have any ambitions, other than to spend my life with you. But if you want us to have some kind of plan for when the time comes, why don't we agree that, as soon as it becomes necessary, I'll give up my job, and we'll run this place together… oh, and I'll take care of you."

She stares at me, tears welling in her eyes. "Oh, Logan," she murmurs, and I lean down, just as she pulls back, her hand firmly on my chest. "Wait," she says. "I… I need to ask you…"

"You need to ask me what?"

She looks up at me, biting her lip, before she whispers, "I know you said you wanted to have children with me at some point… but, what if we can't? What if it doesn't work out for us? What if you're a carrier and we decide against it? Or what if you're not a carrier, and at some time in the future we did have a child? Who'd look after him or her, when I can't?"

I smile down at her. "You want answers to all of that? Right now?" She doesn't reply, so I pull her hard against me, holding her tight.

"Okay… well, if we can't have children for some reason, or we decide against it, because I'm a carrier, then we'll still have each other. And we'll spend our days together, being just as happy as we are now. And if I'm not a carrier and we're lucky enough to have a child, or children, at some point, then you could do whatever you can… whatever you're able to manage. And I'll do the rest. And we'll spend our days together, being just as happy as we are now." I kiss the tip of her nose. "But will you stop worrying about things that haven't happened yet? Again."

"I'm sorry, but I have to know. I have to understand what the future holds. I need some certainty."

"Then understand this… the one certainty in your future is me. Because I'm going to be standing firmly beside you, loving you, helping you every step of the way, doing whatever it takes to make you happy and keep you safe… okay?"

She blinks twice and then bursts into tears. "Please don't rent somewhere…" she murmurs into me. "I want you to live with me. Here."

"If you're absolutely sure that's what you want. Like I said, we can slow it down, if you need to."

"No. The only thing I need is you. Here."

"The *only* thing you need?" I tease, to lighten the moment.

She leans back again, wiping the back of her hand across her cheek. "Well, you could help me out of these awful clothes…"

I clasp the hem of her t-shirt and pull upwards. "I thought you'd never ask…"

My interview in St Austell went really well yesterday and they phoned in the afternoon, about an hour after I got back, and offered me the job. I accepted and then called the surgery in Truro to cancel Thursday's interview. Hope said I was being impetuous again, but I'd rather be somewhere closer to home, so we can spend more time together. This morning, I woke Hope early and we made love, before taking Archie for his walk. She's still a bit shy and she's not quite back to her old self yet, in terms of feeling self-conscious, but we're getting there. She's certainly back to wearing her old clothes again, and that's a great improvement.

"I like that top." She turns to look at me as she clears the breakfast things. She's wearing a fitted, bright pink sleeveless blouse over her tight jeans, and both garments show her figure to its best advantage.

"Thank you," she murmurs, blushing, just as the post drops through the door and she goes to collect it and returns, clasping a solitary letter in her hand and looking up at me, quizzically.

"What's going on?" she says, turning the envelope over. "It's from you… and it's postmarked St Austell."

"I know…"

"Why did you write me a letter and post it to me, when you're here?"

I get up and walk over to her, placing my hands on her waist. "I guess it's become a habit now. It's one I kind of like… so you should probably get used to it."

She leans up and kisses me. "Does this mean I have to write back?"

I shake my head. "Not if you don't want to. But I'm still going to write to you… every single day, to tell you how much I love you."

"Every day?"

"Yes. Every day… for the rest of our lives…"

Epilogue

26th July

My darling Hope,

I decided to leave this note on your pillow, in case you were worried when you woke up and found me gone. I know I normally post my letters to you, and you've become used to reading them after I've left for work, but sometimes the post comes early, and I'm still at home, and I wanted to guarantee that you'd be alone when you read this, so leaving it on your pillow seemed like a good way to ensure that, because this is the most important letter I've ever written – or am ever likely to write.

It's six months to the day, since that first time I drove away from you, having won your promise to let me woo you, and I hope I've used my time wisely. I hope I've proved that I'm honest, and trustworthy and I hope you know that my love for you – which was unspoken then – is completely unconditional and is stronger now than ever, and grows more so every day.

That's not to say that I'm going to stop wooing you, or doing whatever it takes to prove myself worthy of your love, and that includes writing to you, because my letters aren't about to stop. I don't think I'll ever run out of ways to tell you how much I love you, and even when we're old and grey, I'm still going to write you daily love letters, just so you never forget that you are loved... beyond words.

I want to spend the rest of my life making you as happy as you make me, I want to comfort you, to hold you, to keep you safe – without ever smothering you, or wrapping you in anything other than my arms – and to remind you all the time that you are worth so much more than 'fine', my darling. Because you are.

Throughout our relationship, our letters have been a means of keeping us together, even though we've sometimes had to be apart, and while we may no longer be separated, I still cherish the fact that I can tell you my innermost thoughts and feelings in my private messages to you, that only we can share. And that is why I'm writing to you now, in our own special way, to tell you how thrilled I am that my results were negative, and that we can think about having a baby one day very soon. I know this is what you want too, my darling, and I know we have too much love to offer, not to be parents.

Having said all of that, I have one small favour to ask of you. Do you think you could put on as few clothes as possible and join me in the garden? You see, I have a question for you, and I can't wait a moment longer to ask it.

You'll find me, with Archie, under the rose archway. And in case you're wondering, I'll be the one on bended knee, holding the diamond ring, and wearing a pale pink t-shirt and a nervous smile.

In anticipation,

Your dearest Logan xx

Printed in Poland
by Amazon Fulfillment
Poland Sp. z o.o., Wrocław

65977905R00228